**To the unscrup**
**phe for society. . . it**
**personal gain. And**

**that will turn the world's misfortune into his own private bo-**
**nanza.**

The y2k team listened in disbelief as Tim explained the situation.

"The worm has gone wacko. The longer it's in the banking system, the more likely it is to mutate . . . again and again. These mutations may be so changed from the original worm that our deactivation codes won't even work with them." He held up a hand at their groans.

"It gets worse. If the worm, or its mutations, is still in everyone's systems on December 31st, the worms will be archived. Massively archived." Tim spread his hands in a gesture of helplessness.

"Systems will go down. Programmers will use their archives to restore data. What if we have all those worms, still mutating, in all those files, as well as the y2k bugs we haven't yet found? You tell me. What are the odds that we could ever get them all out?"

Annette's voice broke the horrified silence. "That means we have fourteen days to figure out who did it."

# The Chaos Protocol

# The Chaos Protocol

## Nancy J. McKibben

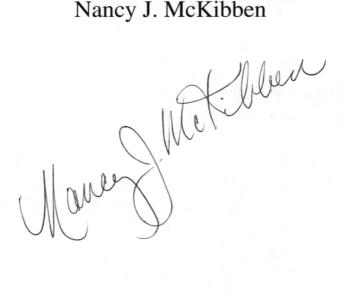

Malmesbury Books

Malmesbury Books

P.O. Box 292609

Columbus, Ohio 43229

First printing, June, 1999

Cover design by Jim Theodore

Published in the United States of America
ISBN 1-893857-90-5

Library of Congress Catalog Card Number: 99-90685

# Acknowledgments

Many thanks to all the doughty readers of my novel in its original and lengthy manuscript form: my sisters Carol Phillips and Patsy Conger, my sister-in-law Jill Hoovler, my mother Dorothy Hoovler, my brother-in-law Pat and my in-laws Jim and Carline McKibben, tireless cheerleaders all.  In addition, my friends Tim Cook, Barbara Bell, Ed Tompkins, and Laurie Clark (and Sylvia Schumacher, Barb Knape, and Catherine Girves, who did not read, but were ever encouraging.) Mystery writer Louise Vetter encouraged me more than she knows by agreeing to read the manuscript of a novice. Len Zawistowski, of the Federal Reserve Bank, retired Major General James Freeze and his wife Dorothy, and  Bank One Senior Vice President Ed Detwiler read and provided expert advice in banking and security; Ed also introduced me to my first mainframe. Finally, thanks to fellow mail-list members Sally Chew (who also answered questions about PC's) and Andrea Becker, and attorney and fellow writer Jim Leo.

My agent and editor Cameron Powell deserves a special mention; he performed a masterful edit in an amazingly short time; suggesting, guiding, and ruthlessly cutting, yet managing to make the process pleasant and instructive for the author. The book is much the better for his touch.

I want to particularly recognize y2k guru Peter de Jager, whose year 2000-discuss e-mail list, ably moderated by Amy Young, provided the foundation of my y2k education.  In addition to reading countless e-mails posted to the general mail list, I also corresponded privately with a number of mail list members who were unfailingly courteous and helpful in providing me with pertinent information, patient explanations of technical matters, and generous encouragement in my writing. I think particularly of Pam Wylie, Leille Sussman, Jim Frazier (who also loaned his name to my fictional reporter), Bryce Ragland, Russ Kelly, Patricia Scotto, Chris Gilbey, Rob Harmer, 'Doc' Don Taylor, Skip Stein, Charles Reuben, Don Fowler, Bob Andrews, Karl Vogel, and Norman Kurland, who moderates the cpsr (computer professionals for social responsibility) mail list..

Many gave graciously of their time and expertise via e-mail and telephone interviews: retired FBI special agent Dave Hanna, Dr. Andrew Thomas and The Ohio State University Medical Center Transplantation Program (liver transplants), Dr. Shirley Fry of Reacts (treatment of radiation victims), Robert Talbert of the International Nuclear Safety Program (nuclear reactor meltdowns), and y2k utilities expert Dick Mills, who has thirty years of experience working with the companies that supply the power industry. The y2k scenarios came from e-mails posted to the mail list, or from my imagination; others were suggested either directly or indirectly by Chris Rohrs, Evan Robatino, Peter Gordon, Bob Andrews, Martyn Emery, and Steve Davis.

Michael Greulich, a former 'federal guy', patiently fielded my innumerable questions about his specialty, legacy systems, was always willing to enlighten me technically, and consulted with other experts to come up with the COBOL 'back door' in the novel. My neighbors Michele (herself a y2k project member) and Jeff Neubauer gave me hours of writing time by making their house my younger children's second home. Thanks to Ben Zacks for his ever prompt answers to my legal queries.

Finally, thanks to my long-suffering family. To my children, Carrie, Max, Susanna, Holly, Rose, and Justin, who all helped in their own ways - by cooking a meal, or setting a table, or picking up the living room, or conspiring to lower the general household volume. My husband Mike was so instrumental in the creation of this book that I can scarcely count the ways. Not only did he free up time and space for me to write, but also collaborated in plotting, came up with the title, and explained and re-explained the workings of PC's, TCP/IP's, viruses and all the other arcane computer lore that I needed to write the book, vetting the manuscript for accuracy as I wrote. Then he pushed me to find a way to publish, although I was convinced it was too late, and supervised and guided the process to completion. For his unfailing support and love, my special thanks.

# Author's Note

Because the year 2000 computer problem is without precedent, its outcome is inherently unknowable. Still, we can prepare ourselves for what we feel will be likely outcomes: we can prepare personally, we can prepare our families, we can prepare our communities, we can prepare our businesses. Please visit my web site www.chaosprotocol.com for a useful list of y2k links on the World Wide Web. If you do not own or use a computer, the year 2000 problem will still affect you; visit your library or bookstore to find out more.

*This book is dedicated with love to my husband Michael. And with admiration to the y2k workers in the trenches, the heroes of this story.*

# PART 1

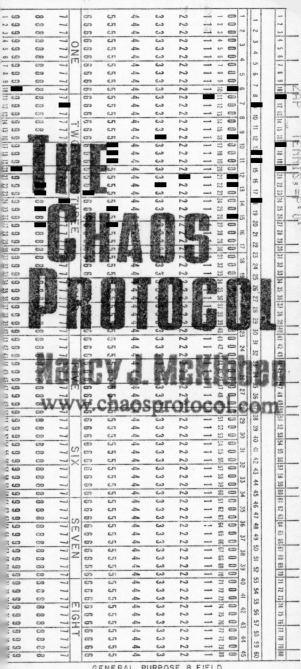

THE CHAOS PROTOCOL

Nancy J. McKibben

www.chaosprotocol.com

GENERAL PURPOSE 8 FIELD

The infamous 80 column HOLLERITH CARD. As they coded, programmers dropped the first two digits of the century because the cards allowed only 80 characters per line. This shortcut also allowed programmers to conserve scarce computer memory – 1965 became 65, and the Year 2000 computer problem, Y2K, was born.

# PROLOGUE

*June 10, 1965, Joliet, Illinois*

"Hey, Harry, come over here for a minute, would you?"

Tim Gallagher, thin, red-headed, and just twenty years old, squinted at the sheet of paper he was coding. It was midnight on the grounds of the former Joliet Army Ammo Plant, now a government installation located ten miles south of town, or, as its employees described it, in the middle of a field in the middle of nowhere. In the building next door, four hulking RCA mainframes flashed the lighted buttons of their master consoles in an array of vivid reds, blues, yellows, and greens, their changing patterns indicating the contents of the various memory registers.

In its heyday during World War I, intrepid workers hand-loaded land mines at JAAP for shipment to the troops in Europe. Now a portion of the complex was Tim's place of work, a small brick building with a corrugated asbestos roof and very thick walls. In the unfortunate event of an explosion, the designers hoped that the blast would blow off the roof, leaving the rest of the building more or less intact.

The Joliet Army Ammunition Plant still used most of its brick buildings to manufacture TNT and load it into various armaments. But three other odd little structures in addition to Tim's were reserved for computer programmers, twelve of whom hunkered in each building.

The programmers were a hardy lot who put in more overtime than a gang of teamsters. By government fiat, Tim Gallagher was added to this select group at the end of his six-month Automated Data Process-

ing Intern Program, becoming one of the youngest programmers at
JAAP. Here, age was immaterial. Programming was still such a young
art that Tim's skills were nearly level with those of the older men, many
of whom had only recently become programmers themselves after not-
ing that it brought a rise in rank and salary.

Tim's pod of four buildings was known as Group 9, and tonight ten
of the gunmetal grey desks in Tim's building were vacant, their occupants having already completed their sixteen hours of mandatory overtime for the week and departed. The linoleum curled under his feet,
and the pall of cigarette smoke aggravated his lungs, but Tim felt lucky
to have the job. Although the training had been less than adequate, he
liked computers and he learned quickly, and the first thing he learned
was to ask questions when he didn't know something.

Harry finished his donut and gave his fingers a final lick, then heaved
himself from his government issue chair and lumbered over to join Tim
in staring at the paper. He was older than Tim by fifteen years, and
paunchy.

"What's the problem?"

"Right here -" Tim tapped a finger beneath a date field that read
09-05-65 "-where it says 65 for 1965."

Harry's broad shoulders rose in a shrug. "That's standard nota-
tion."

"Well, sure, but it just occurred to me — what happens in the year
2000? The date comes up 00. The computer thinks it's 1900, and any
date-linked data is corrupted. Or it thinks it's an error, and shuts down
completely." Tim frowned at the offending data. "And Harry, that
would happen to all the computers in the world, as far as I can make
out. They all use a two-digit date field."

Tim turned in his chair to see Harry chuckling at him and shaking
his head.

"That's a hell of a thing to worry about, Tim," he said, still smiling
broadly. "Number one, it's thirty-five years in the future."

Harry hoisted a beefy hand and began to tick off the points on his
fingers. "Number two, all these mainframes will be on the scrap heap
by then - obsolete. Number three, once we figure out how to expand
the computer memory, we can use four digit years. And number four,"
he wiggled his fourth finger, "number four, whatever happens, it won't
happen on my watch - I'll be retired by then."

He lowered himself into his chair and surveyed Tim with a smile.

"It's okay, Tim," Harry said. "Every COBOL programmer makes that discovery at some point in his career. And we all just ignore it."

"Oh." Tim felt a little foolish. "So you don't see it as a problem?"

"Nah." Harry yawned, stretched, and rubbed a hand meditatively over his burr haircut. "Not our problem, anyway."

The two men returned to their coding. The midnight stillness was broken only by the scratching of pencils, and, from the massive computers in the building next door, the faint staccato click-click-click of the tape drives.

# Chapter 1

*June 10, 1999, Columbus, Ohio: Day 205*

Alex Stauffer squatted on the bank of the Scioto River, using a surgeon's care to impale a nightcrawler on the hook of his new Loomis rod, a Father's Day gift from Karen. A breeze ruffled his hair, and Lowell's famous lines flashed across his mind.

"'And what is so rare as a day in June? Then if ever, come perfect days,'" he quoted aloud, smiling at his eight-year-old son Ethan, who jigged from one foot to the other, anxious to get started. Karen had dressed him with her usual care, and his khaki pants, green boots, and fishing vest echoed his father's attire. Ethan was altogether a handsome little boy, dark-haired and green-eyed, with a mischievous smile, a replica of Alex at that age.

Unable to endure another minute of standing still, Ethan left Alex to his worms and ran the short distance down the bank to look at the water. A moment later Alex heard him come panting back.

"Dad, how are we going to fish in there?" Ethan tugged at Alex's sleeve. "Look at the water!"

Distracted from baiting his hook, Alex stood to look at the river. The Scioto glittered in the sunlight, its color a horrid, fluorescent chartreuse. "My God," he breathed.

"The fish, Dad, look at the fish!" Ethan's voice was tearful, and Alex tore his eyes from the garish water to look at the shore. A dozen dead fish lay there already, and hundreds of others bobbed on the river's surface. What could possibly have happened?

The wind changed then, carrying with it the stench from the water, heavy and putrid. Alex gagged. His eyes raked the shore for his son. It couldn't be good for them to breathe this air; he had to get Ethan home.

"Dad, look!" Alex's head snapped around at the sound of Ethan's voice. The boy had clambered down the bank and was standing on top of a large pipe that was spewing torrents of stinking green liquid into the river. Raw sewage!

Alex ran full tilt down the riverbank, only to see Ethan fighting to keep his balance atop the pipe.

"Ethan!" he screamed, but his son had already fallen and was sliding slowly down the side of the pipe toward the water.

"Dad!" With Ethan's scream echoing in his ears, Alex flung his body up over the pipe, scrabbling for a handhold on the smooth surface. He thrust his arm down to grab the boy's hand, but Ethan slipped, and Alex saw the foul, churning water close over his head. Without a thought, Alex dived after his son, but the fumes blinded him when he resurfaced, and he knew that if he swallowed any of the polluted river it would kill him. He couldn't see Ethan anywhere, and he thrashed helplessly in the water, calling his son's name over and over and over. . .

"Alex!" Karen's voice sliced through the fog. "Alex! Wake up! You're dreaming, sweetheart! Wake up!"

With a huge sense of relief Alex opened his eyes. His t-shirt clung damply to his body, and the covers hung half off the bed. The bedroom was lit by the small table lamp; his wife was sitting up in bed, looking at him with anxious eyes.

"Which one was it this time?" She touched his face with her hand.

"The sewage pipe." Alex's breathing slowed, and he pillowed his head in Karen's lap. Looking at the familiar room relaxed him, and they had learned early in the course of his nightmares to turn the light on at once.

"Do you want to tell me about it?" Karen's hand gently stroked his hair.

"Oh, it was pretty much the same as always. I wonder why Ethan is always a little boy in these dreams." Ethan was now a tall, awkward fifteen-year-old. "He's big enough to pull me out of that river."

"Maybe it's because the kids were little when you first found out about year 2000 problems." Karen's voice was soothing; they had been over this ground before, but the repetition had the calming effect necessary for Alex to sleep again. When the nightmares began several years ago, Alex found himself wide-awake, mind racing, for hours afterward. Sessions with a therapist had alleviated the effect of the nightmares, but hadn't eliminated the nightmares themselves.

The first one had jerked him upright, shaking a startled Karen by the shoulders, shouting, "We've got to get out of here! We've got to get out!" The nightmare had come on the heels of a letter sent to him by an employee of a plant that produced monitors for controlling the manufacturing processes in chemical plants. The employee had claimed that management knew that one of their monitors would fail in the year 2000, but despite the danger to the chemical plants to which they were sold, they would not recall the monitor or even tell their customers it was faulty.

Alex had immediately thought of the disaster at Bhopal, India, where 4000 people died in their sleep when the Indian supervisors ignored an alarm, and forty tons of lethal methyl isocyanate escaped from Union Carbide's storage tank and spread over the city. He did not need a therapist to tell him that his nightmare of trying to escape a building filled with noxious gases was the result of the monitor letter. The sewage pipe dream first occurred after he had read an article describing an Australian coastal city's year 2000 test of its sewage system: the system had malfunctioned. Only the quick thinking of one of the city engineers had prevented the dumping of a day's raw sewage into the harbor.

Alex lay in the now-darkened room and listened to his wife's soft breathing. The real nightmare, he thought, was this: when he opened his eyes in the clear light of day, the nightmare did not dissolve, it became hard-edged reality.

## Moscow

Smiling at his wife Masha, fifty-five year old Sergei Kamenov, professor emeritus of the mathematics department at Moscow State University, propped his slight bulk on the rail in front of the elephant enclosure at the Moscow Zoo. He had suggested the outing to distract his mind from the illness, but the June sunshine that glinted on his balding head did not alleviate the fatigue that plagued him. The thought of the walk back to the metro station made him ache with weariness. I should see a doctor, he thought for the hundredth time. I am too young to feel like this.

Masha smiled back into his eyes, which was easy to do as they were of roughly equal height. She was still pretty, was Masha, even with the graying hair and thickening of body that came with age. When he was younger he had worried that she might tire of his own owlish, good-natured face. Now he was resigned to the way he looked, and he knew that it was his mind that attracted her, not his body. He did not want Masha to worry. Or so he told himself, although he feared she was worried already. Better to go to the doctor and get it over with, perhaps.

For some time now he had suspected that his workload was affecting his health. Not only was he teaching his usual class, and continuing his research; he was also tapped to complete a nasty bit of work for the FSB, the Federalnaya Sluzhba Bezopasnosti or Federal Security Services, the current embodiment of the KGB. Some believed that Russians need not fear the FSB the way people had feared the KGB twenty years ago. But where the KGB and its successors were concerned, Sergei still held to an old adage: calling a turnip a rose will not make it smell like one. Russia in 1999 was far from a constitutional democracy, and with the present continuing unrest, who could say whether the FSB might be not be ascendant again? Sergei felt it wiser not to disappoint their expectations of him.

He was a top - perhaps the top - mathematician in an abstruse field of computer science. He could discuss his specialty with perhaps fifty other people in the world, only six of whom could understand it at his level. His passion was theoretical mathematics, but when the FSB decided to use him, they did not take such niceties as this into consideration. They simply told him what they expected.

And they expected a lot. The man who approached him had asked whether he could produce an algorithm that a programmer could insert into a bank's source code to withdraw money invisibly. He had to ask the man to go away and come back again, because he had to think about it first. But when the man returned, Sergei told him yes, he could do it, and he was careful not to ask why they wanted such an algorithm, although he winced at his own cowardice.

Why had he agreed? He wondered about it still. It was true that Sergei enjoyed a mathematical challenge. He had been certain that if he were given access to the source code of a bank or government agency, he could do exactly what the FSB wanted. And since all the banks and government agencies in the world had laid open their source code to do year 2000 fixes, it was a once-in-a-lifetime opportunity. Not only would it be easier to insert the algorithm in the first place, but once planted, it might easily be mistaken for a y2k bug. He sighed. Masha often accused him of existing in a different world, in an abstraction where he need only think about his numbers, and only incidentally about their real-world effects.

Masha. She was another reason that he did the bidding of the FSB. He had heard too many stories - true ones - from friends whose families had been threatened. And he was not as naïve as Masha thought him, though sometimes he clung to the purity of theoretical mathematics to avoid confronting their applications.

But the longer Sergei worked, the more likely it seemed to him that this algorithm could upset a delicate balance. And if the world was not as wonderful as it could be right now, neither was it as terrible. What would happen when he completed his algorithm and gave it to the FSB? Sergei shivered again in the warm sunshine.

# Chapter 2

*Columbus*

Annette Ashby's small, well-manicured hands thumped an impatient tattoo on her desk. Damn, where was that reporter! It was after ten o'clock already, and although Alex had told her to miss as much of the meeting as she needed to, she chafed at this further delay.

Annette was twenty-eight, intelligent, attractive, good at her job, and in the normal course of things, patient. Where the year 2000 problem was concerned, however, her patience had worn thin.

Over the past four years, most of the press in the country had stonewalled or dithered about reporting the impending world computer crisis. Had the press done its job and warned the public, Annette was convinced, much of the now inevitable calamity might be averted. In early 1998 a few of the larger newspapers began running comprehensive stories about what they termed "the Millennium Bug." Not until July of that year did *The New York Times* run its first belated editorial about the millennium problem, finally making the disaster "official."

Columbus, the state capital of Ohio and a major metropolitan area, boasted a concentration of high-tech concerns: DFAS (the Defense Finance Accounting Services), which issued all government military paychecks, Battelle Memorial Institute, a world-renowned research facility, OCLC (Online Computer Library Center) an immense library computer service and research organization, and Chemical Abstracts, which maintained the world's largest database of articles on chemical research. Nationally known high-tech companies such as CompuServe,

Checkfree, and SYMIX were Columbus-grown, and new high-tech start-ups were almost as common as the Go Bucks! bumper stickers that decorated the cars of ardent Ohio State University football fans.

Nevertheless, Columbus's sole large newspaper, the *Courier,* had for months tried either to ignore the year 2000 question entirely, burying articles about it on the back page of the business section, or to trivialize it by concentrating on articles that talked about survivalists hiding in caves. Columnists wondered about the possibility of their VCRs working after the turn of the century, while neglecting the larger implications of legions of computers that in a few short months either would not run at all, or would not run properly.

Annette was tired of analyzing this willful blindness on the part of the media. Reporters were cynical, they didn't have the necessary technical understanding, they were wary of fringe groups who were making the millennium a rallying cry for their own bizarre agendas.

One problem had long been Jonas Driver, the owner of the *Courier* and a local business magnate. A self-made man, Jonas was as broad and stocky as a bulldog, with the temperament to match. Jonas saw the year 2000 problem as a scam hatched by programmers and consultants to bilk the corporate world. The information technology, or IT, department of the newspaper had realized that their old publishing software would have severe year 2000 problems, but they knew better than to say so to Jonas. Instead they launched an elaborate campaign to convince the boss of the need for the competitive edge which new publishing software - not to mention a new computer - would provide.

To everyone's surprise and relief, the approach worked. The old mainframe was replaced with the latest PC technology. Jonas then offered the old computer with its publishing and accounting systems to his cousin, the family ne'er-do-well, who wanted to publish a mid-size magazine devoted to commercial landscape gardening. Cousin Grant pursued his new career diligently for eighteen months, actually carving out a respectable market niche for his magazine. The family was proud, Cousin Grant was grateful, Jonas self-congratulatory.

What happened next had been repeated so often in Columbus business circles that Annette could imagine it as though she'd been a witness. On February 15 Cousin Grant marched into Jonas' office at the *Courier.* He came unheralded, he came angry, and he came without fully closing the door, to the delight of the listening newsroom.

Grant, in tones of measured scorn: "I always knew you didn't like me, Jonas, but I never expected you to sabotage my career like this. And I never expected you to be subtle."

Jonas, indignant: "What the hell does that mean?"

Grant, incensed: "The computer! The goddamned computer you gave me! It's crashed! It's ruined me!"

Jonas, relieved: "Oh, hell, Grant, computers crash all the time. I'll loan you one of my IT guys to look at it."

Grant, enraged: "Crash? *You* made it crash! You programmed it to delete all my files!"

As Annette heard the story later, the technicians who finally examined the computer came to the same conclusion. The accounting package, a simple, stalwart workhorse that was programmed years ago, was coded to recognize the value 99 as the command to delete a file. When the time came in January of 1999 to bill the magazine's advertisers, the computer read the date 1-99, January 1999, and promptly deleted the files of every advertiser. No bills were sent out that month.

To compound Grant's problems, the computer program that billed subscribers crashed and could not be brought back up again. The IT people surmised that when the computer saw 00 (the year 2000) keyed in as the subscription expiry date, its logic circuits functioned perfectly. Interpreting 00 as 1900, an illogical entry for a subscription term, the computer suffered the digital equivalent of a nervous breakdown and shut down.

The day that Jonas heard this explanation was the day he became year 2000 aware. To restore his good standing in the family, he was forced to purchase an entire, new computer system and software for Cousin Grant. Then he drove, still hyperventilating over the expense, to seek the counsel of a man he had publicly belittled for the past five years - Alex Stauffer.

Annette still smiled to herself at the thought of Jonas coming to Alex, hat in hand. Jonas did change his editorial policy on the spot, for he finally realized that the computer crisis would hurt him where it mattered most - in the wallet.

That week Jonas wrote a Sunday editorial entitled "Beating the Millennium Bug." It paved the way for an important and ongoing series of articles about the year 2000, which was the reason that Annette was now cooling her heels in her office waiting for a *Courier* reporter.

She glanced again at the e-mail that lay on her desk. Alex's wife Karen, the mail list moderator, had forwarded it this morning. *The Report of the Congressional Subcommittee on Government Management, Information, and Technology on the y2k Progress of the Executive Branch of the U.S. Government.*

Disembodied phrases from the report floated through her mind. "Overall Federal y2k progress earned only a C+ this quarter. . ." "Not one of the Agency for International Development's mission-critical computer systems is y2k compliant. . ." "We remain extremely concerned with the performance of six federal agencies who together are responsible for more than fifty percent of all mission-critical computer systems in the Federal government . . . these include the Department of Defense. . ."

The receptionist buzzed to announce the reporter's arrival and Annette smoothed her hair and arranged her face into a pleasant smile. Whatever she thought of his newspaper, Annette would present the facts in so resolute and charming a manner that Jim would emerge from these interviews an enlightened man. Given what she planned to tell him, he really had no choice.

*     *     *

Jim Frazier, who had mightily resisted being assigned to the "year 2000" story when his editor proposed it, entered Annette's office, took a good look at his subject, and began a rapid reassessment. Jim was fifty years old, a stocky, bearded Vietnam veteran who felt he'd seen it all and written about most of it. Women found his hard-bitten manner appealing, and although he was happily married with three children, he allowed himself the occasional dalliance.

"Jim Frazier?" he heard her ask, in a low, pleasant voice as she walked over to shake his hand. "Welcome to Millennium Dynamics."

"You're British," he said in surprise, taking the chair she offered. God, but she was one gorgeous woman, with that coppery hair, those arresting green eyes. And wonderful legs. He had a trained reporter's eye.

"I'm an American citizen," she corrected him, smiling, "but my mother is French and my father is British. He's in the diplomatic service, so I grew up partly in Europe and partly in the U.S. I'm not sure why I wound up with a British accent."

"It's charming." Whatever this story turned out to be, Annette's presence would make it fascinating. He took out a small notebook and pen, and laid a miniature cassette recorder on her desk. She leaned toward him.

"Are you up to speed on this?" she said. "I really don't understand why it was necessary to put a new reporter on the story when the series has been running since February."

Ouch. "I have read all the year 2000 stories in the *Courier.*" Jim succeeded in keeping most of the sarcasm out of his voice. "Jonas decided that it was so important that he needed more staff on it. Anyway, my understanding of the problem is that the early programmers thought their programs and even the hardware would be obsolete long before the turn of the century. I guess that didn't happen."

"Quite the opposite!" Annette said. "And now PC's have lots of y2k issues too, many of them related to the software programs. Hence, our problem. We reach the year 2000. All date-related data becomes corrupt. Or, the computer is unable to process the data at all, and the system crashes." She spread her hands expressively. "In a word, chaos."

"Chaos?" Jim's reporter's cynicism kicked in. "Isn't that a little strong?"

"No, absolutely not." Annette shook her head decisively. "But let's wait a moment before we get into the implications."

Strong woman in charge, thought Jim.

"Y2k," she said, "has become a trillion dollar project -one trillion dollars being the estimated amount to fix this problem globally. The programmers who pointed out to their companies that this date problem wasn't going to go away, and needed to be fixed, were told that the company couldn't afford to spend money on something that wasn't going to improve their bottom line. The business managers who approached the company bigwigs with the problem tended to get fired."

Jim made a face that indicated disbelief.

"Oh, absolutely that happened," she said. "In fact, when Alex Stauffer went to the comptroller of the company where he worked - this was in 1990 - he was given such a cold reception that he left the company."

"And started this company."

"Right, Millenium Dynamics. Alex realized the scope of the problem and decided to become a year 2000 consultant. I'm sure you know that he's acknowledged as one of the top experts in the world. He's a member of the President's National Year 2000 Council."

"Well, he's done all right for himself." Jim waved his hand around to indicate the office building. "This is a for-profit business."

Annette's voice cooled a degree, but she remained polite.

"Yes, he's made a profit," she said. "Good business decisions result in a profit. He was one of the only ones at the time with the acumen to build what he built; he had the first year 2000 web site, the first year 2000 e-mail list, the first year 2000 book. It was his idea to organize conferences of year 2000 experts to share knowledge about the problem and try to solve it. He's helped thousands of people and hundreds of companies."

"You make him sound like a philanthropist."

"You should understand that he began his company with a dual purpose; to tell the world about the year 2000 crisis, and to make a living." Annette was frowning as she spoke. "His firm struggled for the first five years; he became an expert on the subject, but it wasn't until 1995 when companies woke up and began to ask for his advice. He did a lot of traveling and speaking, up to last year, which he hates to do because of his family. You can laugh, but he did it out of altruism. Three days a week," she went on, "Alex oversees the Midwest Bank Consortium Project, at the request of the FDIC."

"I knew that," Jim said, writing it down. "How does this consortium work?"

"Well, the banks, the insurance companies, and the credit card companies were the first to realize that they needed to overhaul their computer systems. So much of their data is dates, and they forecast into the future, too. So the year 2000 was closer for them, in a sense."

"I can see that." Jim stopped writing. The tape player was running, and it was much pleasanter to watch Annette's lovely, animated face.

The consortium problem was not so difficult to understand, Jim found. The small banks, like the large ones, had to find and fix their y2k problems. Unlike the large banks, the small independent rural banks could barely afford the project. The FDIC, a body that strictly regulated the y2k projects of the banks on a monthly basis, had become alarmed when they realized that several of these small banks would not finish their remediation in the allotted time.

Jim knew that Homer Jones, the president of Midwest National Bank, had been inspired to form a consortium of small banks, hoping that their combined efforts would result in a more efficient y2k project. He had proposed to the FDIC that Alex Stauffer, who was about to stop his y2k-related traveling and return to Columbus, use his company, Millennium Dynamics, to ensure that the Midwest Bank Consortium Y2k Project would be done on time. Alex had agreed, and the FDIC had agreed to extend the deadline for finishing.

"Well, okay, that's a nice story," Jim said, scratching his neck. "Human interest, and all. But what difference does it really make if a few little banks go under? The big banks can take up the slack."

Annette raised her eyebrows. "The U.S. banking system relies on the confidence of its customers. What happens if people hear about banks going under because of y2k problems? What if a significant number of people become worried about their own banks? Become afraid that somehow their money will be lost because of y2k problems?"

Although Jim knew that these were rhetorical questions, he answered anyway. "People withdraw their money and cause a run on the bank."

"Exactly." Annette gave a decisive nod. "And it becomes a self-fulfilling prophecy. Even if the banks are ready for y2k, they are forced to close because people lose confidence in them."

"Anyway," she added, "a lot of these little banks are family businesses. Some of them have been around since the 1800's. It would be a shame to close them, or give them away."

"You're a romantic, Annette." It was a gentle accusation. "This whole thing appeals to you as a cause, doesn't it?"

Annette looked into the distance for a moment, considering her response.

"Off the record, then," she said, fixing him with an odd look.

"Shoot."

"I think that the year 2000 computer problem could be the single most cataclysmic event that will happen in my lifetime. I've pledged myself to do everything I can do to ease the catastrophe. I think that businesses will fail by the thousands. I'm afraid that the power grid will go down, and people will die in the cold. I'm afraid that embedded systems will fail and cause disasters we can only guess at - deaths in hospitals from failed equipment, sewage dumped into drinking water. I'm afraid that unscrupulous people will take advantage of the chaos and incite civil disturbances. I'm afraid that hackers and terrorists will plant computer viruses and disable systems. I'm afraid our whole global infrastructure could fail." Her voice was bleak and far away.

Jim stared at her.

"You're not kidding, are you?"

"No," she said. "I wish sometimes I could deny the possibilities, like most people do. But I can't. So, no, Jim, I'm not looking for a romantic cause. This is a passion with me because I feel that every person I convince, every line of code I help to get rewritten, every y2k speech I give - every bit of what I do will make things less bad, however bad they are. Do you see what I mean?" She looked at him with big, earnest eyes.

Jim remembered the question he had forgotten to ask.

"Yeah, so what does Alex do the other two days of the week when he's not making money here?"

"Oh, he devotes those two days to y2k consulting for local charities," she said, rising from her desk. "Gratis," she added, not missing a beat. "If you'd like to come with me now, I'll show you our y2k project in progress."

Jim followed her out the door without saying a word.

*     *     *

Alex lounged in the ergonomically correct leather chair in his company's conference room. He was feeling a little tired perhaps, as a result of last night's nightmare, but fortunately the ill effects of his bad dreams had been confined to losing sleep. None of his colleagues suspected his problem, and Alex did not intend to undermine their confidence in winning the year 2000 battle by sharing it.

At forty-seven years of age he looked like the success he was. His dark custom-tailored suit sat well on his trim body, and the gray in his dark hair only made his frank, handsome face more distinguished. Alex's formidable intellect and single-minded focus were tempered by an altruism that surprised people. After graduating first in his class in the

Harvard School of Business, he and his new wife Karen had gone to Africa for two years to oversee the efforts of Habitat for Humanity, an organization that helped build housing for those who needed it.

The dean of the business school had not been pleased with this choice. "Make your money first," he advised. "Then you can afford gestures like this." Alex nodded and smiled. A gesture that didn't cost anything was not much of a gesture, he thought.

The two years in Africa were followed by a year of travel in Europe. Alex and Karen spent a month floating through the canals of Holland and Germany on a barge. In England's Lake District they hiked and recited Wordsworth to each other. They celebrated Midsummer's Eve in the far north of Sweden, where the sun rose blindingly at two o'clock in the morning and hardly set at midnight. In the winter they skied on Austria's snowy slopes, and on one memorable summer afternoon made love on a Swiss mountainside, nearly rolling down the mountain in the process.

Three years after they had married they returned to the States penniless and optimistic, ready to be serious about family and career. They chose to settle in Columbus, Ohio because Karen had grown up nearby, because the Midwest seemed a good place to raise children, and because Alex had a certain affection for the Ohio State Buckeye football team.

They were naïvely certain that Alex could find a good job at once, and so he did, rising meteorically for a time in the insurance corporation that hired him. Ethan was born, then Elizabeth, and finally baby Katie, and they were able to buy a nice house in the suburbs.

The fancier his corporate office had become, though, the more Alex felt his creativity being stifled. He hated office politics and tried to ignore them, an attitude that eventually cost him promotions. The strain of pretending friendships with those who were eager to stab him in the back was more than he could handle; the whole corporate atmosphere was poisoning him. He was an idea man, he realized, a visionary, but no one in the company wanted his ideas. Alex was struggling with what this might mean to his career when the realization of the coming y2k calamity hit him like a truck. The collision determined the course of his life for the next ten years.

Alex left the corporate world for good and began his own computer consulting firm. He became an expert in the year 2000 problem in all its complexity, knowledge that nobody seemed to want. After five years of financial struggle, some in the business world began listening to him at last. His consulting business took off and he hired more people. When he judged that enough people were ready to listen, he organized year 2000 conferences, gathering experts in mainframes, PC's, embedded systems, business management, legal questions. For three years his life was a commute between conferences and speaking engagements.

Alex glanced idly at the handsome Rolex on his wrist. The meeting of the Y2k Project of the Midwest Bank Consortium would start in ten minutes. Although his wife Karen was not a status-conscious person, she had given him the watch the year his company, Millennium Dynamics, had first turned a profit.

"It's a sign to the world," she said, fastening it on his wrist with a flourish. "You were right and everybody else was wrong."

She had not overstated the case by much, Alex reflected. He smiled at the vagaries of life. For years the name of his former company's comptroller, "Homer Jones", had never crossed his mind unless prefaced by the phrase "that short-sighted idiot". Now Alex would soon be chairing a meeting of his company Millennium Dynamics, and Homer Jones himself would be sitting at the table.

"Hey, boss man!" Tim Gallagher ambled into the room. His hair was grizzled now, rather than red, and his skinny frame was somewhat fleshier, but his earnest demeanor and quick mind were the same as in his days at JAAP. Tim was Alex's mainframe computer expert.

Harry Beuhler trolled along in Tim's wake, rather like the whale his appearance brought to mind. Tim had lured him out of retirement to help them. With his silver hair and rotund figure, Harry reminded people of Santa Claus, albeit a hard-boiled, outspoken version.

"Who're we waiting for?"

"You're early, Harry. Please have a seat." Harry parked his bulk next to Tim, then proceeded to eat a glazed donut that he produced from his battered briefcase.

Alex smiled and pushed the intercom button on the telephone. "Tracy, bring the coffee in now, if you would."

Homer Jones, still bland and unprepossessing, but wearing a better cut of suit, as befitted a bank president, followed Tracy, who entered with the coffee and a tray of pastries.

"Homer," Alex said, "I was just reminiscing about you."

"About what a bastard I was?" Homer sat down to sip his coffee. Tim and Harry smiled; they had heard this story before.

"Pretty much. But I won't get on your case, now that you're a changed man."

"Where's Annette?" said Tim, glancing at the conference room clock. A second clock next to it counted down the time left until the new millennium. 204 days, 14 hours, 5 minutes, 10 seconds, and counting.

"She's with a reporter. The *Courier* is continuing their millennium series, so I told her to take her time."

Alex had known Annette Ashby for seven months. After his last big conference in New York, when he had surprised everyone with his announcement that he would be leaving the conference circuit to go home and work on the Midwest Banks Project, Annette had approached him.

"I've worked in the banking industry for the last five years," she told him. "I think I could help you organize your consortium project." Then she rattled off her qualifications, impressive by any standards. She had graduated from Cornell University, received an advanced degree in business from London University, then worked for a while at Lloyds of London. Moving back to the States, she took a job with BankAmerica in global trade, then became a financial analyst for the Europe department. She was clearly brilliant and on a fast track to a high-powered position. Alex wondered why she was even interested in a project as mundane as the consortium.

"I want to help," Annette said, sensing his thoughts. "I know the year 2000 is a serious problem; I believe what you said in your speech, and I want to do my part. I know that sounds corny," and she actually blushed a bit in embarrassment.

The blush won her the job, and Alex had not been sorry he hired her. She was a model of efficiency and a tireless, uncomplaining worker. The rest of the team admired her competence and worried that she would work herself to death.

"I'm here; you can start." Eddie Goldstein, the company's attorney, shambled in and found a seat. He looked like a rumpled teddy bear; his blond hair was cowlicked in all directions, and his expensive suit was ill at ease on his plump body. Tim leaned over and yanked gently on his tie, which was askew.

"Who puts you together in the morning, Eddie?"

Eddie gestured with his Danish, scattering crumbs across the table. "This is a clever disguise to lull my opponents into a false sense of complacency. Beneath this wrinkled exterior lurks a keen legal mind."

Alex began the meeting. "We won't wait for Annette. Homer, what can you tell us about yesterday's OCC meeting?" The Office of the Comptroller of the Currency was the government body that each month sent a representative to the headquarters of each bank in the country to check on y2k progress.

"Well, the woman commended our efforts." Homer paused. "She did say, however, that she wasn't sure we could finish in time."

Alex blinked. "She said what?"

Tim and Homer exchanged looks.

"She said," Homer paused again, looked at Alex, then continued, "that she didn't see how we could possibly be finished by December. Unless things improve by next month, she'll have to recommend that the FDIC close the bank."

# Chapter 3

The newest branch of Midwest National Bank was only a ten-minute drive away from the Millennium Dynamics office. The y2k project was headquartered here because the building was new and they had office space open, and its proximity made it handy for the consulting company. Annette turned to Jim in the bank lobby.

"Have you ever seen a Central Processing Unit - what most people call a mainframe computer?"

"No," said Jim. His technical curiosity was limited. "Am I missing something?"

"Perhaps not, but they're downstairs, so you may as well have a look. You can talk to some programmers, too."

After checking in with the bank management, Annette led Jim through a set of swinging doors and down a stairwell. She gave him the tour, first key-carding a door into a sterile, chilly room. Here he saw his first CPU's, which looked like nothing more than large refrigerators.

Unimpressive, Jim thought.

Then Annette led him to the y2k programmers' War Room, also in the basement, where he saw assorted geeks sitting before computer monitors whose set-up reminded him of the PC's in the newsroom. The walls were covered with sheets of flip chart paper; Jim saw schedules, priority lists, due dates, and examples of COBOL code. Leo, a dark-haired programmer whose eyes followed Annette, showed Jim how he used software tools to parse (a techno-babble term that seemed to mean seek and find) the bank's ten million lines of computer code in order to locate and change dates like 64 into 1964.

Dull, Jim thought.

Finally, he followed Annette upstairs to see the PC remediation, a process that appeared to be as mind-numbing as what Jim had seen downstairs. Was there even a story here? He was looking for human interest, not technical detail.

In desperation he approached the nearest programmer, a big blond fellow who had spoken to Annette with a heavy accent when they came in - Russian, Jim thought. Volodya was fixing the code that took care of the bank's automatic deposits, the Electronic Data Interchange, or EDI.

"Is this as boring as what they're doing downstairs?"

"Was not boring to create program," Volodya looked amused at the question. "Very boring to remediate program."

"Why are you doing it, then?" Perhaps all these programmers thought of y2k as a cause, and Volodya would say something quotable.

"I am remediating program so I will not be sued." Volodya's eyes glinted with mischief and Jim saw Annette throw him a reproachful glance.

"I think we've seen enough here," she said, ushering Jim out. Volodya's laughter followed them.

"What was that about?" Jim sat down on a bench next to a wide sunlit window in the hall.

Annette sat down next to him, looking vexed, then laughed ruefully. "That was an example of vendor problems. Volodya's company created a system for the bank three years ago that was not year 2000 compliant. Our attorney convinced them that it should have been, so now they're fixing it. Rather reluctantly, as you heard for yourself."

"Well, now I know why the media didn't pick up on y2k earlier," Jim said. He struggled not to yawn. "You're an interesting woman, Annette, but y2k is a bore."

She didn't bother to deny it.

"Yes, I suppose the technical aspects are boring to the average person. Even programmers don't like to fix the code. But the implications are fascinating."

Yeah, right, thought Jim. He moved a little closer to her, and spoke in what he hoped was an earnest, trust-inspiring voice.

"Listen, Annette, I wasn't kidding. The average person hates this geek stuff. I can explain all the technical background in one paragraph.

You're so concerned about raising awareness - give me something people will read."

"You could come to the Lions' Club meeting in Gahanna with Leo and me on Monday," she said. "We'll be talking about y2k preparedness."

The Lion's Club. Shit. She was serious.

"Sure, I can do that, Annette, but what I really want to know about is that stuff you mentioned earlier." She looked blank. "You know, the catastrophic stuff."

Annette regarded him for a moment, her eyes narrowed.

"You just want a story you can sensationalize so you can sell your damn newspaper," she said. Her British accent made the words sound even more disdainful. "I told you that was off the record."

Jim counted to ten, slowly. "If somebody made a statement to you, like you made to me, wouldn't you be curious?" he asked. "Hell, Annette, why wouldn't I want to know?"

He waited while the hostility left her face, and she slumped against the wall.

"I'm sorry," she said with a sigh. "I'm just so torn. I don't know what's going to happen, Jim. Nobody does. I have to be careful about what I say. I don't want to be responsible for panicking anyone into doing something silly, like selling their home to move to some fortress community."

Now they were getting somewhere. He prodded her gently. "But you do think there are dangers?"

"Well, of course there are," she said. "You can start with electricity."

Jim suppressed a snort. "You really think we won't have any after December?"

"I don't know." Annette shook her head. "I've been trying to figure that one out for months. Experts, people I respect, are divided. On one hand, a lot of the controls in electric generation plants that are run by embedded systems - microprocessors, little tiny computers - can also be run manually. So even if the testing is not where we'd like it to be, we may be okay. On the other hand -" Annette's slim shoulders lifted in an expressive shrug -"one of the things that makes our electric grid so successful is that it's so inter-connected. Utilities can sort of borrow electricity from each other on demand, if one has a particularly high load. But that same inter-connectivity can be a weakness. If several parts of the grid go down at once, they can pull the other parts down with them, like dominos. That isn't to say the problems can't be fixed. But do you want to be without electricity for days in January?"

"What else?" Jim was scribbling now.

"Okay." Her expression was intense, inward. "Think about the federal agencies. The latest federal report card was not encouraging. The Department of Transportation comes to mind."

Jim nodded. "And?"

"Last time I checked, they were due to be y2k ready in 2001." She held up a hand at Jim's incredulous look. "Listen, Jim, it gets worse. The State Department and the Department of Defense are two of the federal agencies that are farthest behind. State and the DoD!" She shook her head. "Of course, they're working frantically to catch up. But logic tells me that a number of systems in a number of agencies are not going to be ready. Take the Department of Health and Human Services. Their Payment Management System processes $170 billion a year in federal grants and payments, and that computer system isn't ready yet."

"But the government's always been inefficient," said Jim. "We manage to make do."

"With y2k, it's not just an inefficient system, it's a broken system - and all the systems that aren't fixed in time will break all at once." She became serious again. "Besides that, look at all the sick, poor, and elderly who depend on these government services. And what about human services departments in general, including those on the state and local level?" she continued. "They often have the smallest budgets, and year 2000 problems are expensive to fix. But if these systems aren't fixed? People don't get their checks. Maybe they can't eat, or pay the rent. There's social unrest. Civil disturbances."

"Riots," Jim said.

Annette shook her head again. "I don't know. I just know we have to keep working as hard as we can to fix things, and make concrete plans for emergency measures when things go wrong. It's just sensible."

She sat silent and frowning; Jim wondered if she had told him everything.

"And what about oil?" she asked, taking off again. "Did you ever think about how long that supply chain is? The wells overseas, the pumps, the trucks, the tankers that carry it? Fifty percent of our imported oil comes from Venezuela and Saudi Arabia, and those countries are thought to be twelve to eighteen months behind the U.S. in their y2k remediation. What happens to us if they aren't ready? Not enough oil, not enough gas. Transportation problems. The economy tanks. Heating problems. People suffer or die."

"Wow," said Jim. He was learning more than he wanted to know.

"Did you know," Annette said, in a tone that implied he should have, "that the average grocery store has enough food on its shelves to last just four days to a week? And no warehouses anymore, even if they want to stockpile food. Just-in-time inventory could be a real problem. The food is there, but we can't get it where it needs to go if the trucks can't get gasoline, or if all the railways run very slowly because they need to do their switching manually instead of by computer."

"What else?" Jim asked. The story was getting better, but he was beginning to hope he'd heard the worst already.

"The United States is much further ahead on y2k than the rest of the world," Annette said, standing up. "Maybe Britain and Australia and a few other countries in Western Europe are up with us. But think of all that we import. What will happen if General Motors can't get its little widgets that are produced by some Third World Country? The plants will close. People will be out of work. There may be a recession." She sighed. "The world is so interconnected. We can't hide from it. We depend on each other too much. What happens with y2k anywhere in the world affects all of us."

She watched him writing. "You can't quote me, you know. I already told you this was off the record."

"Not this time." He kept writing.

"Yes, this time." Something in her voice made him raise his head to look at her. "Listen, Jim, I'll get you facts and figures and people to talk to, and you can write a nice rational story - lots of nice, rational stories." He opened his mouth to object, but her look quelled him. "You can get the facts out to people, they need to have them to make decisions. But if you dare quote me without my permission, or sensationalize anything I've said, you'll never get another source from me. Or Alex. And that won't make your boss happy."

"Okay." Jim sighed. He didn't want to fight her. "Throw some more crumbs my way, and I'll decide what I want to follow up on."

*       *       *

Annette flung open the conference room door, and rushed in. "I'm sorry to be so late."

Alex waited for her to take a seat.

"You've come in the nick of time, as it happens." He looked at her. "Maybe you can explain why the OCC is thinking of shutting down the project."

Alex could see that the question distressed her. If the project were closed down, Annette would take it as a personal defeat, as would he. But Annette could regroup more quickly than anyone he knew.

"Well, it's easy enough to explain why," she said. "We identified 20 operating systems and ten point five million lines of code. Only about twenty percent of that is date-sensitive and has to be fixed, but it all had to be checked. We decided, due to time constraints, to use windowing as a fix, instead of actually expanding the year to four digits. Things were chugging along nicely; we were actually beginning to test some of the remediated systems. Tim?"

"We have fifteen of the systems in the testing stage now," Tim said. "This is far better than I expected we'd do. But we've hit a snag."

Alex felt his jaw muscles tighten.

"We can't use windowing for one of the systems. I've looked at it over and over - and Harry has, too - and it just won't work. We've got to expand all the date fields in that system, which is unfortunately a large one - almost one million lines of code."

My God, thought Alex, making certain that his dismay at this unexpected turn of events was not written on his face.

"OK, team we've identified the problem," he said. "What options do we have?" They couldn't give up or make excuses. They had to finish this project, and on time.

"Well, it's a mission critical system, so we can't wait and do it later," Tim said. "I can only see one option, and that's to hire more programmers to do that date expansion. It just takes a certain amount of time to do, and even if we chain our current programmers to their desks, they're not going to get it fixed in time."

"If we have to hire, we have to hire." Alex shrugged.

A small frown puckered Annette's eyebrows. "That's the trouble, Alex. I've got ads in newspapers all over the Midwest, and I'm not getting any responses. Most of the people who were interested in doing a year 2000 project - or who were at least willing to do it for the money involved - have already been hired."

"Harry, what about your old friends?"

Harry leaned back in his chair to consider the matter. "A lot of them have hired themselves out already. I thought I had one guy talked into it - we knew each other way back when, but I hadn't been in touch in years - then his wife got on the phone and said she was sorry, but he was senile." Eddie guffawed and the rest of them joined in. Harry beamed, glad to have broken the tension.

"The President jumped on the y2k bandwagon so late, I don't think they're convinced it's important," Harry added.

Alex sighed. The President's lack of leadership was a sore point with him.

"Well, keep phoning, Harry. Tell them we'll put them up at a hotel during the week, and fly them home on the weekends." Harry nodded.

"Homer," Alex said, "why don't you check with your old cronies at Northwest Mutual Insurance; they started their project relatively early, maybe they're ready to let some people go."

"Right."

"Moving on. Annette, what's the status of that custom software package for EDI?"

EDI was the Electronic Data Interchange software that the Russians headed by Volodya had been working on.

"Oh, they've about finished with it," she said, "despite their original fuss. Volodya's company does quite good work, actually."

"He's a Russian, isn't he?" Harry didn't seem to notice that he had interrupted her.

"I believe he's an American citizen, Harry. He may have been born in Russia." Alex heard a note of exasperation in Annette's voice. He knew she was impatient with Harry's prejudices.

"I can't understand why a bank would want to hire some Russkies who could infiltrate their systems."

"C'mon, Harry, the cold war's over," said Tim. "The rules have changed." Alex knew that Tim had worked in the federal sector himself; perhaps he even shared Harry's feelings. After all, the Soviets had been the designated enemy for years.

Harry harrumphed to himself, but let the subject drop. After two hours, Alex announced the meeting adjourned.

"About time the *Courier* came around," Tim said to him afterward.

"Better late than never." That seemed to be his new motto, Alex reflected. "They'll want to interview me as well, Annette. Check with Tracy to see what my schedule is. Don't be too forthcoming about our present problem, although you might mention casually that we could use another COBOL programmer."

Annette gave his arm a reassuring pat. "Not to worry, Alex. I'll be as charming as ever I can be."

Alex watched his team file out, intent on doing their damnedest to finish the project successfully. He had such a good team, Alex thought. Most of them had struggled for years against the wall of denial that had been erected by an ignorant and frightened public. But as the clock ticked on toward an immovable deadline, he was forced to wonder if his team's good will would be enough.

# Chapter 4

Like the rest of her home, Karen Stauffer's office was large, airy, and comfortably furnished. A brass vase contained gaudy California poppies whose petals trembled in the soft breeze from the open window. One bookshelf-lined wall held a mix of reference materials, technical works, histories, poetry, and novels. *Webster's Unabridged Dictionary.* Shelves of computer tomes. Gibbon's *The Rise and Fall of the Roman Empire.* A. E. Housman's *A Shropshire Lad.* Another wall featured a fireplace built of gray Cotswold stone. As Karen drank her coffee she gazed at the third wall, dominated by her children's framed artwork and punctuated by various family photographs. Her eyes lingered on a photo of their first beach vacation, at a borrowed condo on the New Jersey shore. Ethan had been just four, and so delighted with the whole idea of a beach that he would fling himself down in the sand from time to time and wriggle in it like a puppy. Elizabeth was still a toddler staring solemnly at the camera from her mother's arms while Ethan waved a sand pail.

Their beach photo from last summer was taken in Greece, on the white sands of the Aegean Sea. Ethan, who was now taller than Alex, had struck a strong man's pose while Elizabeth, losing her thirteen-year-old self-consciousness for once, was pretending to feel her brother's biceps. Katie, the little blonde clown, posed like the sister she always tried to emulate, although she was only ten herself. Karen examined the picture anxiously. They still looked happy, didn't they?

The unexpected result of Alex's dedication to the y2k cause was that they had become rich. A relative term, but certainly much richer than they were. When Karen realized that they could afford it, she had insisted that they travel - vacations abroad, accompanying Alex on some of his conferences. She worried about a severe recession in the year 2000. This might be their only chance to travel; take advantage of it. So they had traveled and they had bought this house. The children did not seem changed by their success, Karen thought, although Elizabeth, now fourteen, seemed quieter, and somehow sadder. But perhaps that had more to do with her age than anything else.

New acquaintances were surprised to learn that two of Karen's children were teenagers; Karen's skin was still smooth, and her hair still blonde. Lucky genes, Karen would tell them, but she helped her luck by working out religiously at the health club. With her straight nose, fine brown eyes, and wide mouth, Karen was a strikingly attractive woman.

Karen finished her coffee and brought her mind back to the task at hand. She was the moderator of Alex's y2k e-mail list, and she considered its creation as one of Alex's best success stories.

The idea behind the mail list was simple enough. People who visited the web site were invited, for a reasonable fee, to sign up to receive electronic mail about year 2000 concerns. Y2k project managers, consultants, software vendors, programmers, and interested hangers-on were given a common mail list address that enabled them to post messages to the entire group at one time. Many of the posts were requests for information or advice, others were sightings of y2k articles in newspapers and magazines, others were comments on a particular aspect of the year 2000 problem.

The small world of those who knew about the year 2000 soon became aware that the mail list was the cutting edge of accurate and timely y2k information. Although many people stayed on the list simply to read the posts and absorb the information, posting a question or comment only occasionally, some became frequent contributors. Some of these Karen had met, through her travels to conferences with Alex, others remained only signatures; but signatures whose letters over time gave tantalizing clues to the sort of people they were.

Karen's job as mail list moderator was to download the electronic mail each day, which amounted by now to several thousand messages. She then sorted through it as rapidly as possible, subscribing fifty new members per day, unsubscribing the same number, discarding those with invalid ID's, and reading and posting messages germane to the list, sometimes as many as one hundred a day to the three thousand list members.

After five years of reading other people's mail, Karen felt a part of a strong cyber community. These were people in the y2k trenches, struggling daily to solve the millennium problem. They exchanged vital information with each other, encouraged each other, pondered questions of what it meant to be y2k prepared. They were ruthless when it came to technical information, thrashing it out in endless e-mails until they came to a consensus of opinion. And they were all concerned that the world was now six months from Armageddon and so many were still not ready.

Karen turned back to her screen and began sorting mail. Nobody wanted to hear from the group of survivalists in Arizona who were building a fortressed community, stocking it with food and water, generating electricity from solar panels, and stockpiling guns and ammunition to protect themselves from the expected collapse of civilization. She pushed the delete key. Alex's caveat for the mail list was that it focus on solutions to the y2k dilemma, and running away and hiding was not a solution.

Same treatment for the New Luddites, a fringe group whose solution to the year 2000 problem was to advocate the destruction of all computers. They had been largely ignored as the nutcases they were until last week, when they had somehow gained entrance to the y2k area of the Department of the Treasury. While three of them held workers at bay with bows and arrows (no technology, no guns), several others began spraying acid into computer ports.

When one of the beleaguered DOT programmers realized what was happening to their months of painstaking work, he rushed the nearest archer. In the ensuing scuffle one person was nicked by a flying arrow, and several others received acid burns. The New Luddites were rounded up by security before they could escape the building, and then nearly killed by the irate programmers who pursued them.

Some New Luddite sympathizer evidently wanted their manifesto published on the mail list. Karen could almost smile at this; where was the consistency of publishing an anti-computer diatribe on a forum entirely enabled by computer? Like most people, the New Luddites were finding it difficult to lead lives consistent with their stated beliefs.

As she weeded out the unsuitable material, Karen posted the rest. Here was a message from Leslie Brill, the irascible young PC expert from the Netherlands.

*Dear List Members:*

*I have posted this message over and over again. Just because you have an Apple computer and not an IBM clone, you are not ready for the Year 2000. Your hardware is all right, but as I keep saying, the hardware is only a tiny part of the problem. Look at your software, your operating systems, your data, your data sharing.*

*And please do it pretty damn quickly; we've only got six months left.*

*Regards, Leslie Brill*

Leslie had first brought the PC problem to the attention of the mail list; before Leslie's posts (which produced a flurry of counter-posts until everyone realized he was right), the focus had been entirely on mainframe difficulties.

*Dear All:*

*My father is chronically ill and on medication. I believe that I would be wise to be sure he has a supply of his medication prior to the year 2000. I have contacted the pharmaceutical company which produces it, and they believe that they will still be able to produce it after the year 2000.*

*However, as the company pointed out to me, the drug must still be shipped. If the transportation system is screwed up as a result of Year 2000 problems, then I'm screwed. This medication because it has a shelf life of only six months, it is prohibitively expensive, and some of that shelf life has already expired by the time I get it from my local pharmacy. I'm losing sleep over this.*

*Dennis Murphy*

Karen knew from experience that before two hours passed, she would be receiving thoughtful, concerned posts from mail list members who would have any number of good ideas to help the distraught e-mail poster. She was continually amazed at how freely relative strangers helped each other via the list, drawn together in good will against the implacable computer glitch that threatened them all.

*       *       *

With the muted clattering of computer keyboards as his background music, Leo Hermann nursed his third cup of coffee and tried to remember the entire set of lyrics for the eighties pop song *Video Killed the Radio Star.* He had used this trick for years to distract his mind when he was forced to do some of the repetitious work demanded by certain computer jobs. As a child prodigy at ten he had tried to recall nursery rhymes; in college at sixteen it was the entire texts of lengthy poems that he had memorized from his high school literature book to distract himself from otherwise boring English classes.

In the six months he had worked at Midwest National, he had exhausted Mother Goose, *Evangeline,* and *The Rime of the Ancient Mariner,* and was now reduced to mentally cataloging pop songs. He pushed his coffee cup away; he had to cut back, he thought or he would be too jazzed to sleep at night. He needed his sleep to help him forget about the horrors of his job; a job, he reminded himself, that he had been eager to take.

Leo had been a *wunderkind,* a child who read at four and programmed at five. His father, a mainframe programmer, and his mother, a poet, had shaken their heads at his precociousness and tried to create as normal a life as was possible for a boy who asked endless questions and never forgot an answer. Much of his schooling was done at home to accommodate his insatiable appetite for learning.

Leo's father taught him programming - he was one of the few programmers his age who knew COBOL and FORTRAN. His mother read to him for endless hours, and arranged for him to study piano and violin. As mathematicians often do, Leo excelled in his music studies, and considered a career as a concert violinist. His love of computers won, but his parents' gentle insistence that his studies be wide-ranging had had the intended affect; his world was not bounded by his computer screen, and he was not tempted to live the virtual life of some of his colleagues.

Leo did not look like a computer geek, but neither did he look like a movie star. His thick dark hair was unruly, his pleasant features pronounced and irregular. When women noticed him, they looked at his eyes, which were dark and intense, and his genuinely friendly smile.

Leo gathered up the printouts that the computer had generated and tried to force his mind to the task at hand. The software tool, naïvely named Miracle2000, had just finished parsing a section of source code, which meant that it searched the computer code for key words that indicated date fields. The date fields contained the infamous two-digit century - the source of the whole year 2000 computer problem -and these dates had to be converted to four digit centuries.

The work was intense and tedious in the extreme. "As interesting as watching paint dry," Leo's neighbor at the next terminal had remarked, "only slower," but if Leo let a date slip by, it could introduce a bug which would foul up the data later.

"Look, Leo," the same man had told him in his first week of work when he noticed Leo rubbing his eyes, yawning, and squinting at the computer screen. He pushed a button on his keyboard and the lines of COBOL vanished, to be replaced by a decidedly kinky sexual tableau involving two men and a woman. Leo was startled.

"See, it works, doesn't it?" The programmer's smirk proclaimed his self-satisfaction. "When this y2k crap starts to put me to sleep, I just punch this button. Wakes me up every time. And I've got it programmed so I never know what will come up. Want me to show you how to do it?"

Leo demurred, and the programmer had seemed disappointed. "Let me know if you change your mind. It really doesn't get any more interesting than it is right now."

True enough. Leo now gritted his teeth (and he would need a set of crowns if he kept doing that) and forced his protesting mind to look at the printout on the screen, find the indicated file, insert the required code, go to the next file, do the same thing, over and over. When he rose several hours later to fetch a fourth cup of coffee (which he had sworn earlier that he would not drink) he thought about the job he had left.

In six months Silicon Valley had receded on the horizon like a dim, unreachable Nirvana. Microtech Innovators had hired Leo at the age of twenty, when he left MIT with his Ph.D. in computer science. They gave him a large office, creative people to work with, lots of time to fool around and think. He hadn't disappointed them, either. His brain was behind several of the new applications now running on Windows 98.

"Columbus, Ohio?" Marvin, his pony-tailed boss, had echoed incredulously when Leo broke the news that he was leaving. "Compiling COBOL in a bank? Leo, is this a bad joke or a bad trip?"

Leo assured him it was neither, and remained steadfast in his resolve as Marvin nearly wept, threw an artistic tantrum, and finally promised that Microtech Innovators would always make room for him if he should change his mind. "Just tell me why you're really going," Marvin begged. "Nobody moves to Columbus to work on COBOL. God, I didn't even know you knew COBOL. Nobody under thirty does, unless he's a federal geek."

"Learned it at my father's knee," Leo said, but refused to enlighten anyone at the company as to his real motive. He finally mentioned the need to fix the y2k problem, and the questions stopped; his colleagues decided he was misguided but sincere. In reality, he was a knight-errant on a quest. To prove himself worthy of the woman he loved he would endure a trial; he had chosen to become a low-level mainframe programmer, slaying the y2k dragon.

He had been attending a computer/software trade show at the Cow Palace in San Francisco, flipping through a competitor's literature at a vendor's exhibit, when he noticed a woman deep in conversation with one of the sales reps. Under the lights her reddish hair moved and shone when she gestured. Leo noted that she was dressed simply but elegantly, in a way that was chic, but not exactly American, in a dark, slim dress. He noticed odd details like the buckle on her shiny black shoes and the cranberry lipstick on her full, expressive mouth. While he was perusing the way her bangs tickled her eyebrows, she suddenly turned to him, her green eyes assessing. Her sooty lashes were startling against her pale skin. Leo was smitten. When her lips curved into a smile, he was utterly lost.

"What do you think?" she said to him. "You've obviously been listening for the past few minutes."

Leo stood transfixed. He had not heard a word of her conversation with the sales rep, and his thought processes seemed to have slowed in proportion to the sudden acceleration of his heartbeat. Breathing was difficult under the gaze of her green eyes.

"Let me buy you a cup of coffee and I'll explain why our product is better," he said in desperation, suddenly conscious that he was wearing jeans, tennis shoes, and a t-shirt that proclaimed *Cyberspace: The Final Frontier.*

The sales rep gave her a quizzical, is-this-man-bothering-you look. "Coffee sounds good," she said.

Leo led her to a small coffee bar in the convention center. "I'm Annette Ashby," the woman said.

"Leo Hermann."

They ordered, and he watched Annette stir her coffee. Everything she did had a certain grace.

"Who are you working for now?"

"I'm to start as the senior project manager for a y2k conversion at the Midwest Bank Consortium in Columbus, Ohio."

"That's an interesting career move," Leo said at last. Annette burst into laughter.

"How diplomatic you are! It isn't any kind of career move at all. If I'm lucky I'll get my old job back - or something similar - in a couple of years. If I'm not so lucky, I guess I'll have to start over."

"Then why are you taking the job?"

Annette looked down at her coffee as she stirred it around and around. Leo noted that she had drunk very little of it.

"I'm very concerned about the year 2000 problem," she said at last, raising her eyes to his. "Aren't you?"

Leo didn't know what to say. "I - haven't even thought much about it, I guess. I mean I know it's out there, but it doesn't affect my job much."

"You computer types," Annette said smiling, but with a trace of scorn. "If it's not happening in your own little bailiwick, you just carry on merrily like it isn't happening at all."

Leo felt himself losing ground. "Enlighten me."

"All right," Annette was smiling no longer. "My bank - the one I worked for before - started their y2k conversion efforts pretty early on - in 1994. They're testing now, and should be done by mid-1999. The estimate is that by the end of the project we will have spent 360 million dollars, and countless man-hours on the conversion. They're a big company, and we can afford it, more or less.  But the smaller banks, like those in the consortium where I'll be working, really don't have the money or the resources for it. Most of these banks would have been closed by the FDIC if Alex Stauffer hadn't stepped in and agreed to try and salvage the efforts of all these little banks in the consortium."

"He's the y2k guru."

"Leo, there are so many of these y2k projects that just aren't going to be finished in time! There are so many companies that are just starting now - just starting to assess! They haven't remediated a single line of code.  They start late, they forget things that they should check, they write sloppy code because they're in a hurry, they curtail their testing because they're running out of time.  Then they pass corrupt data to the companies that are year 2000 compliant."

Leo listened.  He absorbed the information effortlessly, as he always had, learning more about the year 2000 problem in an hour than he would have thought possible.  The revelation was fascinating, and disturbing, but in truth he would have given the same attention to a treatise on the African mealworm, as long as Annette was the one speaking about it.

After a while Annette stopped talking and took a drink of water.  "I should apologize for preaching at you," she said.  "But I guess I tend to go on and on if I think someone is actually listening.  Getting the word out has become my mission."

He'd given her a ride to the airport.  In the car he'd smiled at her, wishing she lived in California.  "I feel like I've been converted or something."

It was the next morning he had asked his boss for a recommendation to work for Alex Stauffer, in Columbus, Ohio.

His old friend Brian Williams had him figured out.  "Geeze, Leo, this is kind of drastic," he'd begun, when Leo told him.  "Don't you think?"  Suddenly his face cleared.  "Wait - I bet I've met her.  She was in town this week and she stopped by the office because Alex Stauffer asked her to.  Red hair, beautiful.  Annette, right?"

Leo nodded, mute.

"I took her out to dinner last night."

"Excuse me?"

"Well, I tried to move things beyond the business level, if you know what I mean - don't look at me like that, Leo, you would have done the same. And don't worry, she shot me down very charmingly." Brian sighed. "She told me she wasn't looking to get involved with anyone in any capacity right now, because she was going to totally devote herself to the y2k cause for the next year." Brian had looked directly at Leo. "And I believe her. She's quite a driven individual. So I don't know how much good it's going to do you to move to Columbus."

Leo now frowned at his computer screen. Things were not going as planned. Alex had hired him, on Brian's recommendation, and he had moved to Ohio in January. Although Annette had sent him a brief e-mail of welcome when he arrived, he had worked there for almost a week before he ran into her when they shared the bank elevator. He leaned across her and put his finger firmly over the Door Closed button.

"Remember me?" He smiled down into her green eyes.

"Of course I do! I meant to get in touch with you, Leo, but I've been awfully busy with this project." She sounded sincere. "I hope you're not angry with me."

"Maybe I'd forgive you if you'd go to dinner with me."

Annette shook her head immediately and looked at him with guileless eyes. "Leo, I told you how busy I am -"

Leo cut short her protests.

"Come on, Annette - every night? You're working here every night? Everyone needs a break. We haven't talked since San Francisco; I hoped I would see you sometimes." Leo hoped he sounded persuasive, not desperate.

"Leo." Annette bit her lip and looked away. "I told you I take this job seriously. I'm not free most evenings. I spend most of my evenings, and a lot of my lunch hours speaking about y2k."

"I'm sorry," Leo said softly. "I didn't mean to put you on the spot, I had just hoped -" He stopped, unable to tell her what he had hoped.

"Leo, I'm sorry. I just don't think I have the time to give to a relationship right now. I'm devoting this year to y2k. It's a last ditch effort; I want to do my best. Do you understand?" Her eyes were pleading, her voice sweet and regretful, but Leo felt like he'd been punched in the stomach. Well, he couldn't say he hadn't been warned.

"Okay." He forced a smile. "Just friends. Would you mind if I went with you some time when you're giving a presentation?"

"It would be nice to have some moral support, " Annette had said, smiling back. "Of course you're welcome to come along. Now perhaps you'd better let me out of the elevator before someone calls the repair company."

Leo became dogged and patient. He accompanied Annette to her next speaking engagement, and the next; he hauled y2k literature and carried her laptop computer for the PowerPoint presentation. He arranged podiums and tables and stood next to her after the meeting and answered people's questions. He took her out for a bite to eat afterward (she seemed never to think of food on her own), and helped her critique the presentation. He even bought a couple of shirts after Annette gently asked him whether he really felt that a t-shirt was the appropriate attire for every occasion. He made himself so useful that she not only allowed him to come along, she began to depend on him.

So, six months after leaving Silicon Valley, he had become Annette's trusted friend and colleague. Four or five evenings a week Leo enjoyed their time together, even though it revolved around informing other people of the impending computer crisis. If they were not speaking about y2k, Annette would not see him; she spent her other evenings working at home or at the office. This was not exactly the outcome he had been looking for.

## June 12, 1999: Day 203

Vladimir Vasilovitch Borodin typed the last few symbols of his program into his PC and reached for a floppy disk to back up his work. As he listened to the computer's familiar hum, he glanced at his watch - one-thirty a.m., normal knock-off time for a programmer. Not that he defined himself as a programmer, of course. No, he was a mathematician first, and a manager of programmers second, head of a whole stable of programmers, his own handpicked team, many of them friends from his university days.

A member of the Russian intelligentsia, he had moved easily from private school to university, and then, through *perestroika,* to a computer job in West Germany. When a chance meeting with an American businessman led to the offer of a job in the U.S., Volodya moved quickly. He would miss the superior Russian culture, but the social structure was disintegrating rapidly under Gorbachev, and the rising threat of the Russian mafia made the decision even easier.

New York had featured a great nightlife and lots of fellow Russian émigrés, two of Volodya's prime requirements for happiness. Then his new company abruptly downsized him. American companies had an unreasonable prejudice against hiring Russians, and so he was now forced to take what he could get, often pedestrian programming jobs that were beneath his talents.

Then his luck had turned again — he considered himself a lucky man — and he met Viktor Hopko. Viktor was an immigrant himself, a Ukrainian Jew who had managed to flee Europe after World War II. Viktor had no family beyond an aging cousin in Ohio; his wife was dead, and they had been unable to have children.

Volodya met Viktor at a friend's wedding reception. Circling the room in search of a refill for his champagne glass, he heard hoots of laughter from a crowded, smoky table in the corner. The center of the good-natured commotion was Viktor, who was toasting the newly married couple in a series of bawdy good wishes that would have made the bride blush and flee the room, had she heard them. Amused, Volodya raised his own glass in a toast lewd enough to make Viktor blink; then Viktor snorted with laughter and invited Volodya to join the party.

Although Viktor was, by his own admission, an uncultured peasant far removed from Volodya's former social circles, Voldoya admired Viktor's zest for life as well as his business acumen. The old man ran a wholesale clothing business with a shrewdness that Volodya envied.

Viktor was flattered that a young man of such promise would value his friendship. He became Volodya's sounding board, and after six months he began to regard the talented and personable young man as the son he had never had. When he decided to retire to Ohio to look after his aging relative, he asked Volodya to come with him.

Two years earlier, Volodya could hardly have been persuaded to leave New York. But the series of dismal jobs and a recent failed relationship had disillusioned him and left him eager for a change. He had heard that Columbus was the high tech capital of the Midwest. Maybe his luck would improve there, he'd thought.

Volodya now sighed, and crossed himself, more from superstition than belief. Shortly after settling in Columbus, Viktor had suffered a stroke, lingered for a month, and died. Before he died he had asked Volodya to be his heir, and to stay in Columbus to look after his aged and ailing cousin.

Volodya's American citizenship would be granted soon, and the inheritance enabled Volodya to purchase computers, hire his many friends who had emigrated, and set up a computer consulting business. But he sorely missed Viktor and only tolerated Columbus, which seemed a distant also-ran compared to Moscow's glittering ambience. He was resigned to living there until Viktor's cousin died; then he would relocate his business in a hurry. New York or Boston, or maybe even Los Angeles - they all looked good to Volodya.

If he still had a business to relocate. Volodya's English was superior to that of many Americans, he thought privately, but he couldn't deny that he dropped his articles, and his accent was unmistakably Russian. And although his firm's reputation had begun slowly to grow, the creative programming opportunities that he sought, and he believed deserved, still eluded him.

So now he was American by location, Russian by birth and nature, thirty years old, single, and at this moment, lonely. Volodya was a tall, broad-shouldered man; if he had grown up in America he would have been recruited to play linebacker at some small college. His Slavic good looks - broad face, intent blue eyes, sensuous mouth - combined with an obvious intelligence and easy good humor. He had always been attractive to women.

Volodya pulled a clean, pressed shirt from the large collection in his closet, and culled through a mental list of women who would not be insulted if he phoned at such a late hour. It was a short list, especially for him.

He chose instead to drive to a bar in German Village, a European-looking part of Columbus whose narrow streets and brick houses had been built by German immigrants a hundred years ago. Most of the houses were rehabbed now; German Village was trendy, charming and expensive.

Volodya preferred the new and modern, but German Village also contained more than a few good restaurants and bars. When he walked into Mandy's upscale interior and looked about, he found that his luck held.

"Hello, Julie," he called to a pretty blonde girl who waved to him from the bar.

"Volodya! I haven't seen you for a while," she said, flushing a little when he leaned over to kiss her cheek. American women liked the

European gestures, Volodya had found, and they were unlikely to receive such attentions from American men.

He smiled at her appreciatively. Women also liked that, American or not.

"I am busy man." He pulled his bar stool a little closer to her, sensing opportunity. "How is your job going?" He had met Julie at a consulting job at a small clothing store where she worked.

"Oh," Julie made a face, "my boss is all in a tizzy. Some consultant is there going through all our software and talking about how we have to change the dates in the computer because of the y2k problem. You must know about that."

Volodya nodded and waved a hand. "It is technical problem concerning dates. Is simple to fix, and of little interest to programmers." He looked boyishly at Julie. "What is tizzy?"

Julie giggled. She really was very pretty, with her even white teeth, her dimples, her soft mouth. "You mean tizzy, not teezy. I just love your accent! A tizzy just means he's upset. Having a cow."

Volodya nodded. "Having a cow. I know that one." He met her eyes and smiled at her again. "Would you care to dance?"

She did, and they danced to a slow tune while Volodya held Julie as closely as he dared. She was a nice girl, not brilliant, but nice and pretty. Volodya's longest relationships had been with women who were both brilliant and beautiful. And they had all been Russian. But he thought of the woman at the bank, Annette. She was fascinating; Volodya sensed in her a certain vulnerability that was hidden by her crisp, business-like manner. Still, Julie was pretty, and judging from the way she snuggled against him, available.

# Chapter 5

Leo pushed aside the huge pile of printouts. Despite the glorious June weather (invisible from his subterranean office, of course) he was morose. He had toiled here in obscurity for six months, doing the most boring work of his life, and his only reward so far was the privilege of lugging Annette's lap-top to an endless series of meetings.

Sometimes he felt that his brain cells were evaporating in direct proportion to the amount of code he fixed. God, he hated this job! And he could see that he would soon be asked to start working overtime; the project was falling behind. If Annette had ever had any free time, she certainly didn't have it now.

Leo remembered how worried she'd looked lately. He hated to see her look so harried, but she had good reason. They needed more compilers. It wasn't a skilled job, but you couldn't hire the man off the street, either.

"Hey, Leo!" Volodya stuck his head into Leo's room. "You eat lunch with us." With Volodya, it always sounded more like a statement than a question.

"Sure, Volodya." Leo jumped to his feet, grateful for the diversion. He'd noticed the Russian a few weeks ago when his firm came into the bank to finish remediating their EDI software. Volodya seemed to make friends easily, and he turned up in all parts of the bank. Leo often saw him sailing out on his way to lunch with a coterie of friends, mostly his male programmers, although nearly always accompanied by one or two attractive women bank employees.

Volodya had first stopped next to Leo's workstation when his neighbor was giving himself a wake-up dose of pornography. Although Leo had found the programmer's little penchant pathetic, Volodya seemed to think it funny.

"Do you do such a thing with your computer?" Volodya asked Leo, his face still amused.

"No, I just look for date fields. But if you want to see something funny, look at this." He pointed to a printout covered in lines of code that read: YR 55, YR 78, YR 29, YR 110.

"110? There is no year 110."

"Exactly. That little bit of creative programming had us scratching our heads for some time. You know what I finally figured out?"

"No, tell me," Volodya said, waiting for the joke.

"YR doesn't mean year at all. It means 'wire'. The numbers refer to the wire sizes for some maintenance program. Wire. Y, R. Get it?"

Volodya looked puzzled. "Y, R. Wire," he repeated, comprehension suddenly dawning, and he burst into laughter. Leo grinned.

"You are clever to figure it out," the Russian said, clapping a hand on Leo's shoulder. "Come to lunch with me and we will talk some more."

That first lunch was a revelation of common ground for them both. They were nearly the same age, both were former child prodigies, both were bored silly with their work at the bank. Leo had found it invigorating to talk again to someone in his field who was his intellectual equal. He had realized how much he missed the give and take with his colleagues in Silicon Valley.

Now Leo climbed into Volodya's BMW gratefully, put his head back against the leather seats, and closed his eyes. "You think a job can't get any more boring, and then it does."

Volodya eyed him curiously. "Why do *you* work here? Is it the money?"

"The money?"

"Very good pay now for crummy low-level jobs," Volodya said. "More than we get paid sometimes for regular jobs. Why do you do it?"

Leo hesitated. He was not sure that it was wise to tell anyone that he was in love with the Y2k Project Manager.

"Ah! I know," Volodya said. "It must be woman. You are in love with someone here. I am right, I can see on your face." He then added in a teasing tone, "And who is this lucky woman?"

"I'd rather not say." Leo was not ready to make Volodya his confidante. "She's ignoring my existence, anyway."

"So, you make her see you!" Volodya waved a hand for emphasis. "She works at bank; you do something she notices. Maybe you help her with her work. You are smart guy, you can do something to her computer. She is grateful, she falls in love with you. Problem solved." Volodya was grinning.

Leo smiled back. "Thanks, Volodya, I'll know who to call on when I plan my campaign."

"Really, Leo, I will help you," Volodya insisted.

Their arrival at the restaurant curtailed further comment.

Frankie and Johnny's was a noisy eatery whose decor was distinguished by a mélange of unrelated objects hung from the walls and ceiling. As the two men plunged through the crowd toward their table, they passed a canoe paddle, a wanted poster, a collection of meerschaum pipes, a stuffed owl, and an autographed photo of Will Rogers.

"Volodya! Leo! Sit down!" Voices were raised in friendly greeting, hands gestured for them to sit down. Leo felt relaxed and welcomed, as he seldom did at any other time.

Five other programmers from Volodya's firm, all Russians, sat at the table with two Americans whom Leo recognized as vaguely familiar faces from the bank. The requisite attractive woman, Rita, was from the international banking and human resources department. Volodya greeted Rita with a squeeze around the shoulders and a friendly kiss on the cheek. Leo wondered whether Volodya had slept with every woman who ever appeared at his lunch table. He had never seen a woman object to Volodya's advances.

"Hi, Alyosha," said Leo to the programmer on his left. "How's the project going?"

Alyosha smiled a little and shrugged. He was in his twenties and looked younger, a slight, blonde man with a closed face and pale blue eyes. Usually he worked at home; he had two children and a wife as talkative as he was silent - or so Volodya said.

"We were talking about what we would do if we won lottery," said Fetya, a plump sausage of a young man. His small eyes shone. "I would bring parents to America. Alyosha would send kids to Harvard. Ivan would buy red sports car and sleep with super models." Laughter erupted around the table as Ivan leered. "Andrei needs big house for new American wife and stepkids, Ilya wants to buy many computers - we all want that - and Vasily - what did you want?"

Vasily was long-haired, thin, and uncommunicative, in fact, Leo had never heard him speak a word in English, although he was sure that Vasily understood it. Vasily said nothing now, just smiled and continued his steady French fry consumption.

"Always mystery man," Fetya said. "What do you buy, Volodya?"

"Better statistical probability to be struck by lightning than to win lottery," Volodya said with a smile, refusing to play the game. "Better to have good job."

"Alyosha wants your job, Leo," said Ivan, who was burly and bombastic. His broad Slavic face was creased now by a good-natured grin, although Leo had seen him pound the table with his fist to make a point.

"Why would anyone want my job?" Leo asked. "It's boring. Nothing about it is interesting or creative."

Ivan rubbed his thumb and forefinger together. "Money, silly American. Our lawyer tells us we have to do this y2k job for bank for practically nothing because we fuck it up the first time. Your job looks good to us!" Ivan pounded the table for emphasis and the others nodded their heads.

Leo had a sudden idea. "Could you do it? I mean, none of you knows any of the mainframe languages, do you?"

Volodya snorted. "I think COBOL is not so difficult. And I think a bank teller could do recompiling. Is simple."

One of the American programmers spoke up. "That's probably true, Leo. I've heard that some places are hiring college students and giving them a six weeks' crash course in COBOL, then using them for the grunt work - under supervision."

Leo thought hard. If he could convince Annette to hire the Russians to help with the code compiling, he would accomplish several objectives. The project would move forward more quickly, perhaps saving him from working overtime. Annette would have the manpower she needed, and would be grateful to him. His Russian friends, who evidently needed the work, would have it; perhaps he could even be their supervisor; a promotion of sorts.

The talk moved to politics, then drifted into an esoteric argument about programming logic. Leo talked and laughed with the others, and by the time Volodya drove him back to the bank he had made up his mind; he would speak to Annette about hiring the Russians as soon as possible.

$*$     $*$     $*$

Two hours later Leo stood before the door of Annette's office at the bank, took a deep breath and entered. He had never talked to her in her office before; it made him feel too much the peon, as though "low-level programmer" were written on his forehead, and "project manager" on hers.

"Leo! It's so nice to see you!" she said, and she really did look happy for a moment. Then her smile faded. "I can give you a few minutes," she said, indicating the stack of papers on her desk.

Leo sat down.

"What are you doing?" he asked.

"Oh, an exercise in futility, probably." Annette sounded discouraged. "I've been trying to figure out why our ads haven't attracted anyone else to work on this damned project. I know our salaries are competitive - they're outrageous, frankly - but the market is just so damned tight right now. I should have foreseen this, and hired more people earlier, when they were still available."

Leo smiled. "I don't think I've heard you swear before."

"Well, I'm not a swearing woman, ordinarily, but I feel so frustrated and so responsible for the success of the project - well, I am responsible! Lie to me, Leo, and tell me it will get better."

"Ah, a nice entrée. How's this? We can use that group of Russian programmers to do some COBOL compiling."

"Volodya's group," Annette said. She tapped her pen on the desk while she thought about it. "Of course, they're not mainframe programmers."

"No," Leo said, "but they're all programmers, and they're all smart enough. The compiling task doesn't require any actual programming skill; I'm sure they could do it under supervision with a little training."

"Do you really think so, Leo? My God, that would be so wonderful!" Annette became animated, and Leo looked with silent longing at her full lips, smiling now. "Do you think they'd take the job?"

"In a New York minute!" Leo said, thinking of Ivan at lunch, pounding on the table. "Remember, you haven't been paying them as much for the remediation process."

"True. They got a stipend. But I guess the potential salary would look like a pot of gold - it is a pot of gold. The rates are ridiculous now. But we really need them. I'll talk to Volodya right away." Annette had risen in her excitement, and Leo stood up to leave.

"Leo, this is such a weight off my mind! What would I do without you?"

Leo smiled at her and took his leave; he had no intention of letting her find out.

*      *      *

Annette didn't know what to think about the feeling that Volodya sometimes gave her. He had made his interest in her clear from their very first meeting, and his single-minded focus, despite her gentle rebuffs, was flattering.

"We should get to know each other better," he had said three months ago, after agreeing that his firm would make their software year 2000 compliant. He looked intently into her eyes. "Our backgrounds have much in common."

She adroitly turned the conversation back into more suitable channels, but he appeared not a whit discouraged, nor even affected by her response, and he had continued his campaign at every opportunity, although never in the hearing of others. But truth be told, and she blushed to think of it, she enjoyed his attentions. What woman would not be flattered by the pursuit of a brilliant, handsome man? She found his Russian accent sexy, and his complete self-assurance intrigued her further. In fact, in many ways he reminded her of Mick O'Toole.

She closed her eyes for a moment against the memory. Even after ten years she could hardly think rationally about him. She had been just eighteen at the time, fresh out of her parents' home and living in a flat in London while she studied at the university. One cool October night she was standing on a balcony attached to the tiny bedsit where her friend was having a party. Annette was tired of the heat and clamor inside.

"Is there room for two out here, do you suppose, then?" a male voice said, almost at her ear. The man was definitely Irish, by his accent, but she could not make him out well on the shadowy balcony.

"It's a bit of a squeeze." Annette had meant to discourage him, but the man seemed to take it as an invitation, and the next moment he was crowded close to her, chuckling.

"That's the charm of it. I'm Mick O'Toole." He offered her a large, strong hand.

"Annette Ashby." They shook hands, laughing because shaking hands was a difficult thing to do in those crowded quarters. "Did you come out to escape the heat, too?" she asked.

She felt him smile, although she couldn't see it, exactly. "Ah, no, I followed you," he said, adding in a low voice, "I've been watching you all evening."

"Oh." Even at eighteen, Annette was rarely ill at ease, especially with men; her upbringing on several continents had allowed her to meet any social situation with aplomb. Right now she felt both thrilled and faintly alarmed, so she tightened her grip on the balcony's iron railing and said nothing.

"I was hoping to persuade you to come away with me for a bite to eat," he said. "This balcony is nice and cozy," and indeed his body was pressed so closely next to her that she could feel the heat of it, "but I'd like to be able to see your lovely face."

"You're very forward," Annette said, thinking that she would be a fool to leave her friend's party with a stranger.

"That I am." Mick's gorgeous tenor voice became a shade pleading. "Come with me, sweet Annette? Please?"

A moment later Annette found herself walking down the London street with Mick. Seen in the light of the street lamp, he was devastatingly handsome, his hair black and curly, his blue eyes direct, his movements lithe and cat-like.

"I'm glad you came," Mick said, taking her hand as they walked. Annette, in a state of shock at her own behavior, did not answer. He pulled her into a pub just a few blocks from their starting point. Several men shouted at him, as he came in, and gave him meaningful looks; Mick winked and shouted back.

"What did they say?" Annette asked, still in a daze.

"Never mind, they're a rude lot, Annette." Mick was grinning.

"But they're laying odds on whether I'll seduce you tonight."

Annette gasped and rose to leave, and Mick pulled her gently back down to her seat at the table.

"It's just the way they talk," he said, his voice soothing. "Would I have told you what they said if that was what I intended to do?"

"I don't know." Annette studied his handsome face. "They know you better than I do. How old are you?"

"Twenty-six. A bit older than you are. Do you care?"

"No." They ate pasties and chips and Mick drank a pint of bitters, but Annette didn't seem to need any alcohol; she was getting drunk on Mick.

"Shall I take you home, then?" Mick said at last, toying with her hand as it lay near his on the table. His thumb rubbed lightly back and forth across the inside of her wrist and she shivered a little.

"I have a roommate." Her eyes locked on his, her breath quick and shallow.

He leaned over to kiss her on the mouth. Annette felt her cheeks go hot.

"Isn't it lucky that I've not got a roommate?" he whispered.

They rode the underground together on the way to his flat, the rocking motion of the train throwing them against each other. Annette could feel the heat of Mick's gaze on her body; her feelings flashed between fear and desire.

Mick's flat was little more than a room with a bed. "But that's all we need," he said, "isn't it, darlin'?" He held her face in his hands and tangled his fingers in her long red hair. He did not ask her if she were sure, but proceeded to kiss her in a way that made her know she was.

"Aren't you the eager young virgin?" he said once, amused by her fumbling with his shirt buttons, but his voice was tender. She tumbled into bed with him and discovered that making love - at least with Mick - was just as earth shaking as it was in the novels she had read.

The next six weeks passed like a fevered dream. Annette attended her classes, studied, even did well on her exams. This was possible because Mick was away from town so frequently; when he was home, Annette was with him. She knew little about him, for spending so much time with him. His family lived in Ireland. He was well educated. He was floating around at the moment, he said, visiting here and there and trying to decide what to do with his life. She didn't press him for details; their affair was so intense that she couldn't imagine that it would go on forever.

She was astonished when he suggested one day that he should meet her parents.

"Are you ashamed of me, then?" he said. She knew he was teasing.

"Meeting one's parents just seems rather - well - serious."

"Maybe I'm more serious than you think." He kissed her until she was breathless. "Say yes."

"I always say yes," she murmured as his hands slid under her sweater.

Mick was away for the next several days, so she was in her own flat when she opened the *London Times* and saw his picture looking out at her from the front page, his eyes strangely flat, his expression grim. The accompanying article identified him as a long-suspected IRA member. He had blown himself up trying to plant a bomb near the home of a local MP.

Annette's first reaction was cold fury. He hadn't wanted her at all; he had wanted her father, the important diplomat. She felt for an unfocused moment that if Mick had appeared before her then, by some miracle whole, she would have killed him herself for his betrayal.

She was still sitting in her flat, staring, the *London Times* in her hand, when her roommate came in an hour later. She pried the newspaper from Annette's clenched fingers and rang her parents. They arrived white-faced and appalled to spirit her out of London and into the country for safety's sake.

The police were convinced that Mick had targeted Annette in order to kill her diplomat father, but they were never able to prove it. Annette's parents did not need proof; they yanked Annette from her studies in London, and her father asked for, and received, a diplomatic post in Washington. The Foreign Office was understanding when it came to the IRA.

But no one from the IRA ever came looking for Annette. The uncertainty goaded her; had Mick never loved her? Even IRA members fell in love, presumably. Perhaps he had fallen in love by accident, and managed to keep the affair apart from his life as a terrorist. At times Annette was certain of this, and felt she would never recover from her grief. Then she was furious with herself for grieving over a black-hearted, wicked man who thought it all right to blow people up with bombs. Poetic justice that he should have been blown to a million bits! But the unbidden memory of his smile and his body was enough to kill her own smile, even ten years later.

Annette shook her head. She was all right now; after all, people recovered from all sorts of dreadful experiences. She had even fallen in love again, and lived with the man for a time. They had planned to marry, but Annette had ended the relationship, unable to bear the thought of a commitment.

Her affair with Mick had not only ended her innocence, but also disturbed her equilibrium in some vital way. How could she trust her instincts about men? Up until her involvement with Millennium Dynamics, she had still dated, for there was never a shortage of men who wanted to be with her, but she worked long hours and was not intimate with anyone. She found that few men really interested her.

Volodya would not allow her to ignore him; his single-minded pursuit was what put her in mind of Mick, surely. That and his colossal self-confidence. She would not make the mistake of dismissing Volodya when he hadn't done anything except make it clear that he was attracted to her.

*       *       *

The delight at Annette's suggestion was not universal.

"Hire those Russian fellas?" Harry snorted in derision. "I don't trust them, not a bit. Had lunch with them the other day. One of 'em kept trying to pump me about the mainframe."

"Tried to pump you?" Alex said. "How do you mean?"

"Ah, he kept asking questions about my programming career, and did I ever think about year 2000 way back when, and would I tell him something about how the mainframe works, and did I think he could learn COBOL. I could tell he was up to something." Harry sat back in his chair and crossed his arms as though that settled it.

Alex considered. "Those don't sound like dangerous questions to me, Harry." Harry's face settled into an indignant scowl. "What do you think, Tim? Have you spent any time with them?"

"Not a lot." Tim gazed into space as if trying to remember. "They seem friendly, especially the head guy, Volodya. I see him going to lunch with people from the bank."

"Annette?" Alex asked. "I guess you wouldn't have recommended them if you thought they were untrustworthy."

Annette had expected praise for her resourcefulness, not opposition.

"To be honest, it wasn't my original idea, it was Leo Hermann's." She didn't look at Harry.

"Leo," Alex said. "The golden boy from California."

"Look," Annette said, "aren't we being a little paranoid here? Harry obviously doesn't like Russians. Do you Harry?"

Harry bristled, but Tim intervened before the older man could comment.

"It's natural for us to be suspicious, Annette. We were federal workers for years; the Russians were the enemies."

"But things are different now! Volodya is young; he's an American citizen."

"He isn't that young; I'm sure he remembers the Cold War," Harry said with a dark look.

"Yes, but -"

Alex raised his hand and Annette fell silent.

"I think we don't have any reasonable grounds for suspicion. But, Annette, this is a bank. It's a great place for dirty tricks whether you're a Russian or not."

Annette sighed. "Well, we don't have to hire them, of course. But I really don't have any other alternatives to offer. I think that by now even all of the untrained college students have been sucked out of the market."

"Has their other bank work been satisfactory?" Alex asked. "They did the original EDI job several years ago. Any complaints, Homer? Other than their y2k screw-up?"

"No complaints that I know of." Homer hesitated. "I'd just as soon have them, Alex. We're not going to get the job done, otherwise. Volodya's got what, five or six programmers? That would really help us out."

"Okay." Alex rapped his knuckles lightly on the conference table. "We'll hire them. Harry, you figure out some sort of security system. All work will have to be done on-site, no possibility of taking anything home with them. That sort of thing."

"Right." Harry nodded sourly, displeased with the partial victory.

Annette saw Alex bite back a smile. Still, having someone keep an eye on the Russians was not a bad idea.

# Chapter 6

Volodya was not clear on why Annette had requested a meeting, but he was more than happy to appear. He was sorely disappointed to have seen so little of her since he began putting the remediated software back into the system; was it possible that this meeting was an excuse to see him again? Musing on the possibilities, he knocked on her door and entered at her "Come in."

He was in front of her desk, taking her hand in greeting, then bringing it to his lips, kissing and releasing it, and sitting down, all done so quickly that she had no time to protest.

She bit her lip and remained standing. When she did not speak for a moment, Volodya leaned back more comfortably in his chair and crossed his ankle over his knee. He admired her at leisure; today she was wearing a short linen skirt with a ribbed cotton sweater the color of cream. Its narrow ribs fitted snugly around her slim waist, then widened interestingly as they climbed the contours of her body.

"Mr. Borodin, do not make me change my mind about what I was going to ask you," she said at last, rather severely.

"Okay," he said. His humble reply bore the desired fruit, and she sat down.

"Perhaps you are aware of the programmer shortage, particularly for y2k remediation."

"Of course." Already he saw where this was going.

"Although I realize that this is not work you would normally choose to do, we are in great need of some code compilers for this project, and we'd like to hire your group." Annette folded her small hands before her on the desk and waited for a moment. "The pay is quite good," she added, when Volodya did not immediately reply.

"Is not interesting work," Volodya said, enjoying the game, although he was more than willing to do it for the money.

"We both know that. You do it for the considerable amount of money involved, or not at all. We are not willing to increase our more than generous offer beyond this." And she named an hourly figure that made Volodya smile.

"We would need some small training," he said. Annette nodded, looking relieved. "And you must hire all my team - six programmers and me." Annette nodded again as Volodya considered how far he could push this.

He lowered his voice. "And you must allow me to take you to dinner." His eyes laughed at her, but his face was serious.

"Maybe," she said. Annette smiled at last and pushed her hair behind one ear. *¿Maybe* you may take me to dinner to celebrate the completion of this project."

"But completion of project - that is very long time."

"We'll all be very busy for the next six months, I assure you."

"I will ask again," he said.

"I'm sure you will. Now, when do you expect to complete your current project?"

"Three days. Wednesday."

"All right then," she said, "on Thursday, you can all report to Harry Buehler and he'll explain what you are to do."

"Harry?" He frowned long enough for Annette to notice. "I thought Leo could train us."

"You don't like Harry?"

"Harry does not like me, or any Russian. Old federal programmers are all alike, I think." Volodya tried to smile, to show he forgave Harry (not true), but Harry was the last person here that he wanted to work under. Leo would be pleasanter, and far more malleable. Despite his age and paunch, Harry was as hard as nails.

"Oh, I'm sure you're mistaken." Annette's quick response told him that his fears were well-grounded. "Harry is just a little brusque. But maybe Leo would like a change. Or Tim. I'll see. Someone will get back to you with the details in the next few days."

"Okay. Also, it is all right to work at night? I do my best work then."

Annette ignored any possible double entendres. "We'll be testing day and night, so I don't see what difference it would make." She rose and stuck out her hand. "We're counting on your team to help us meet our deadline. It won't be easy."

"We have dinner after deadline." Volodya smiled meaningfully. "That is my motivation." He went out the door happy, leaving a bemused Annette still standing at her desk. He had no intention of waiting until December for a dinner date.

*       *       *

Leo thought Jim Frazier must now be convinced that y2k was serious. During the two-hour Lions' meeting, he had not scoffed once. He had listened to Annette talk about how to prepare home, business, and family against the millennium problem, had taken copious notes, then left hurriedly to try to finish an article for the morning paper.

Thirty minutes later Leo pulled away from Millennium Dynamics' parking lot, having delivered Annette safely to her car. He thought again about what she had confided to him on the long drive home after last night's meeting; in fact, he could hardly stop thinking about it.

Leo had sensed her discouragement. They'd had a difficult day at work and were running behind schedule; the drive was long, the turnout for the y2k meeting, small.

"Can I tell you something, Leo?" she'd asked.

"Of course."

And she told him about Mick O'Toole.

Listening to her story, Leo found he could hardly keep the car on the road. Her telling was dispassionate, but at the end he heard her voice shaking, and then she began to sniffle. Although he wanted to pull the car over to the side of the road, they were on the freeway and he saw no good stopping place. Instead he took her hand.

"I'm so sorry, Annette."

"I should probably apologize for dumping it on you." She heaved a ragged sigh. "I've hardly told anyone over here - my friends in England know about it, of course. For some reason I think about it on days like today, when everything else is going wrong. It helps to talk about it, but it's hard to find the right person to talk to. It's good of you to listen. I feel silly; I should be over it by now."

"Go ahead and talk, if it helps." She told him more, then, than he really wanted to know about her love affair.

"That bastard!" Leo said when Annette finished.

"Thanks for listening," she said. He still held her hand and she gave it a squeeze. "You're easy to talk to. I think you must be my best friend in Columbus."

Well, he thought, that was something.

Now that he knew about Mick O'Toole, Leo felt inclined to make allowances for Annette. After an experience like that, he thought, she must find it difficult to trust anyone enough to fall in love. His time at Midwest National had convinced him that y2k was a serious problem. Whether or not Annette ever showed an interest in him, he was committed to getting the word out and finishing the job at the bank. And although she didn't seem romantically interested in him yet, neither did she seem interested in anyone else. They were such good friends that she would have told him.

*June 17, 1999:  Day 198*

Alex, feeling vastly annoyed and trying to look vastly patient, watched Tim scoot toward a chair, the last to arrive at the hastily convened meeting. His colleagues were in various states of funk; Harry with arms crossed over his chest and a stubborn look on his face, Annette sitting bolt upright and expressionless in her chair, Homer fidgeting with his pen, trying not to look panic-stricken. All gazes converged on Tim as if he might hold the answer to their dilemma.

"Sorry I couldn't get away more quickly," he apologized, seating himself. "We've just starting testing another system." Normally the testing of another system was cause for celebration. Today his good news was ignored.

"But you read the e-mail?" Alex asked.

"About Volodya's team? Yeah."

Alex handed him a sheet of paper.

"This is a copy of Harry's security restrictions," Alex said, his voice neutral. "What do you think?"

Tim skimmed down the paper.

"Well, they're not such a bad idea." Harry looked smug and Annette opened her mouth to say something, then didn't. "But I think you may have a problem enforcing something that wasn't in place from the beginning."

Several people began speaking at once and Alex held up a hand. "One at a time, please. Would you elaborate, Tim?"

"Our object is to protect the source code," Tim said. "So if nothing goes in or out of the room where the terminals are - no brief cases for smuggling disks, and so forth, then the code is safer. The problem is, Volodya's already had free run of the place to do his integration of the EDI system. Naturally he's insulted at the idea of being confined to two rooms -"

"Insulted?" Harry could not restrain himself. "Why in the hell should he care as long as he gets paid? If he weren't up to something, he wouldn't be so pissed off. He knows he'll lose his opportunity if the room's secure! Hell, let them go! We can hire other programmers."

"Can we, Harry?" Homer was polite, but plaintive. "Annette's been trying for months. We've got to have the programmers or the project goes under; you know that."

Alex again held up a warning hand. "I think we all see the dilemma. We need these programmers because they're all we can get. We need security to protect the source code. Any ideas?"

Annette flashed a look at Harry, then spoke. "Volodya already mentioned to me his reservations about working with Harry." Harry favored her with a fierce scowl. "He thinks Harry doesn't like Russians. Well, it's true, isn't it Harry?"

Harry shrugged. "What's to like?"

"Exactly." Annette sent Alex a look. "It's possible that Volodya would take the job if he didn't have to report directly to Harry."

"Did you have someone in mind?" Alex asked.

"Oh, I don't know. Tim could do it, maybe."

Tim shook his head. "Sorry, Annette. No time."

"Maybe Leo Hermann, then. I know he's bored where he is, and he's very bright."

Alex nodded. "No objections here. Do you think that's all it would take, Annette?"

"Well, no." Annette hesitated. "I think they need to be able to work at night, because that's what they're used to. And they already have friends here, so I don't think their access to people should be restricted."

"Oh, that's just perfect." Harry's face reddened and his voice rose. "Let them *roam* around the building at night, the perfect time for espionage. Let them have friends here so they can recruit people to help them. Hell, Annette, why don't you just give them each a copy of the source code?"

"Harry," she snapped, "you're just feeding your prejudices." Alex had seen her angry like this before, her British sense of fair play brought to the fore. "We're only talking about this at all because you hate Russians. If they were a bunch of Americans you wouldn't be ranting about security restrictions. You'd hire them and be grateful." She glared back at him, her color high.

"I'll be the voice of reason here," Alex said, resigned to making the best of a bad choice. "Harry, I hear what you're saying. The fact remains that we have no concrete reason to suspect Volodya of anything. We can take precautions, yes, and we should. But it's unreasonable to treat them like criminals. Have Tracey get hold of Volodya and set up a meeting. I'll talk to him. He knows we need him, and we don't score any points treating him badly."

"I disagree," Harry said, defiant to the end.

"Disagreement noted." Alex's voice was dry. "Now let's get back to work, everybody. We've wasted enough time on this. Tim, stay here for just a minute, please."

After the others left, Alex sent Tim a quizzical look. "What do you think?"

"Oh, I think you're right. We need them and we've got every reason to hire them." Tim leaned against the doorjamb, his arms crossed. "But you know, I don't trust them either."

*June 21, 1999: Day 194, Moscow*

Sergei removed his glasses and rubbed his aching eyes. It must be very late, and he was bone-cold despite the blanket he'd flung around himself before sitting down at his desk - how many hours earlier? To rest his eyes he gazed for a moment out his window at the pale Moscow sky. Although it was four in the morning, the sky would soon brighten to daylight. Moscow did not share the famous "White Nights" of St. Petersburg, but the hours of darkness in the northern summer were brief.

God, but it seemed cold for June! He suspected that he felt the chill because he had lost so much weight recently. His fingers fumbled with the plug of the electric heater for a moment, then he rubbed his hands together in front of the wire grate. The sudden heat was so welcome and intense that he nearly fell asleep, which was of course why he had not plugged it in earlier.

Well, he mused, for better or worse, the algorithm was finished. For the past two months he had tested it in the testing facilities supplied by the FSB, and he was confident that the algorithm would work on any platform, anywhere. It was an elegant piece of work, but he had to appreciate it by himself, since no one else would know about it, ever.

The FSB would come by tomorrow to pick it up his final copy. And afterward the algorithm would be sent to some Russian émigré or dogged communist or Soviet nationalist sympathizer to insert into the code of some unsuspecting victim. It would then begin to move money out of foreign accounts and eventually, though a tortuous maze of other accounts, into Russia.

Undoubtedly this money, wherever it came from, would be flowing into the coffers of the Russian government. Mother Russia certainly needed the money, but somehow Sergei did not think that the people who really needed it - the pensioners, the unemployed, the sick - would ever see it. No, he imagined that the government had but one aim; to return itself to the kind of world domination it had once known, and to punish the Americans for empowering Gorbachev and ruining the lives of countless Russians who had been toppled from their positions of power.

Sergei wiped a trembling hand across his brow. He had managed to ignore politics for years, but even he could not ignore what he was doing with this algorithm. When the FSB agent had visited him in the testing lab a month ago, Sergei had told him that he would be pushed no further; he would not finish the algorithm. Let them find someone else.

At Sergei's words the agent turned to him, a shadow falling across his face. His next words were friendly, conversational.

"How long has it been," he said, "that you have been married to your wife?"

Sergei had understood. He had apologized - groveled - and that had been the end of his brave defiance. Whatever he felt about the algorithm, he could not sacrifice Masha.

Sergei sighed and unplugged the heater. He had defied the FSB nonetheless, in a way that they would not notice because they were unsophisticated with computers. He had made the algorithm less deadly; the amounts of money that would be siphoned away would be smaller. They would certainly be large enough, but perhaps his caution could keep smaller economies from failing as their ledgers went haywire and people lost confidence in their banks before remedies could be found. Of course, if the algorithm somehow found its way into the hands of a programmer who could decrypt it, it might be altered to be more deadly, and that would be trouble. But the odds were acceptably low. So few programmers had the necessary background.

# Chapter 7

*July 5, 1999: Day 180*

Karen stretched and yawned. The kids were asleep, after a late night of July Fourth fireworks. Two late nights, really, since the Red, White, and Boom fireworks downtown were held on July second to enable people to see fireworks in their own municipalities on July Fourth. Karen had spent most of July second downtown, in a booth donated by Alex's company and run by the city, on Civic Center Drive next to the Scioto River, passing out literature about personal and community preparedness for year 2000. The mayor told her confidentially that he was responsible for denying the same permit to a "doom and gloom" group predicting an apocalypse.

"If people want to read that crap, let them read it on the Internet," said the mayor. "We don't need it on the streets of Columbus. I'm sorry, but this is a war effort, and I'm not interested in their right to free speech at the moment." The same group was, however, permitted to hand out their literature on the street, and many of the questions put to Karen by worried citizens sprang from their reading of pamphlets predicting the imminent collapse of the infrastructure.

New people on the mail list had similar worries. They were worried about the nation's electric grid, and she really couldn't blame them.

The electric grid had been a source of discussion ever since the list began, but concerns over the ability of the electric utilities to generate electricity had climbed when the problem with embedded systems was uncovered. Embedded systems were those built around microprocessors, tiny computers whose software was indelibly burnt into the silicon chip, and this software was prone to the same two-digit date problem as the software of the big computers.

Only a small percentage of the tens of billions of microprocessors in the world were expected to fail due to date sensitivity at the New Year's rollover, but a small percentage still meant millions of embedded systems to test and replace. Nor was it always easy to tell which systems were date sensitive and which were not. The utilities themselves seemed confident that their testing had sufficiently mitigated the embedded systems risk.

Some still feared that the smaller rural electric plants and municipalities would not be ready. A weakness because of the failure of several plants to generate electricity could cause a cascading ripple effect that would bring down the grid across a large region. Enough of these failures could theoretically plunge all of North America into darkness, as catastrophic weather conditions or failed switches had pulled down whole regions in the past.

And that, thought Karen, was the nightmare scenario that haunted the members of the mail list. Electricity not only lit homes and offices and provided heat. Electricity ran the pumps that supplied gas and water to homes, and took sewage to plants that treated it. And ironically, electricity provided power to run the computers on which the world depended. Nobody wanted to learn what it would be like for an entire continent to be without electricity for several weeks.

Enough worry about electricity. Karen skimmed a post about software bugs. The trouble was, she thought, even software that was considered market-ready inevitably contained bugs. Y2k would release a veritable plague of software bugs in the new millennium.

A post from Nevada worried that the nuclear power plant might be forced to close if the 911 system were not ready, since regulations required that the nuclear plant always have access to emergency crews. The local telecom company had decided to withhold information about 911 from the public, at least for now.

Karen could imagine the responses to that note: tell the mayor, tell city council, call a press conference - or tell the 911 people that that's what you plan to do. The silly thing was, the 911 system might well be year 2000 ready, but the telecom attorneys were advising them to say nothing for fear of legal action after January 1st should there be any problems. A ridiculous attitude and one that had fortunately been curbed somewhat by last year's Good Samaritan legislation, which offered protection from liability for those sharing y2k information within an industry.

Still, when she thought ahead to January, she saw the lawyers as vultures, eyeing the dying carcasses of the unlucky businesses that were not y2k ready.

*July 7, 1999: Day 178*

Elizabeth sat shivering in bed, despite the July heat, straining to hear in the darkness. Was it her father again, or something even scarier? She could not think of anything scarier than hearing her father scream in the night, so she finally slid out of bed and opened her bedroom door. Down the hallway, the light from her parents' bedroom fanned out into a puddle on the carpet. With her door open she could hear her parents' voices, a muted murmur that she was not anxious to translate. She closed her door quietly and climbed quickly into bed, her heart still racing.

Two years ago her mom and dad had told the children, a little sheepishly, that her dad was having trouble sleeping, so he was going to a certain kind of doctor. Elizabeth, not quite twelve, had accepted their explanation and thought no more about it. Then a few months ago her parents had finished redecorating the bedroom down the hall for her; she moved out of her old room and into the new one, which was closer to her parents' room. And that was when she realized her father didn't just have trouble sleeping; he was having nightmares. Horrible nightmares, every couple of weeks.

Elizabeth was a heavy sleeper, but she had bounded out of bed the first time she heard the shout, and she immediately recognized it for what it was: total panic. She was in the hall outside her parents' room before she was even fully awake, and she heard her mother's voice, loud at first, to wake her father up, then soft and soothing. Something kept her from opening the door; she did not want to see her father afraid. So she shivered in the hallway and listened while her parents discussed the dream for a minute before finally turning out the light.

Back in bed, she cowered under the covers and tried to make sense of what she heard. Why was her father having nightmares about sewage pipes and chemical spills? Standing outside the door after the second nightmare she heard the words y2k, and that was when she understood. Her dad was having nightmares about bad things that might happen when the year 2000 came.

Looking for evidence for her thesis on the Internet, eventually she linked to a site that she realized was profoundly differently in tone than the others she'd seen. This guy really thought that y2k was going to be the end of the world.

Dr. Robert Bentley - his nickname on the web page was Doctor Bob - thought that after December 31st no one would have electricity, or phones, or much of anything else. The government would collapse. People in the cities would have nothing to eat because the stores would run out of groceries. The people in the cities would go pillaging the countryside looking for food, and a new dark age would descend - except on the fortunate few with the foresight to move to a fortress community guarded by guns and dogs and stocked with provisions.

Elizabeth knew what her parents thought of the survivalists, so she was afraid to ask about what she read on the Internet. She was afraid, period. Maybe her father thought like Dr. Bob, deep down inside; maybe her dad was doing his best but he knew that things were going to be way worse than he had hoped. Maybe he had suspected it all along, and that explained the nightmares.

Elizabeth now huddled in bed, her old teddy bear in her arms. Lately she'd started sleeping with it again. Sometimes, when she was in that half-world between waking and sleeping, the familiar tickle of the bear's soft fur on her face could still evoke the comfort of childhood, when y2k was just an acronym and her father wasn't afraid of anything.

*July 16, 1999: Day 169*

"Double, double, toil and trouble, Fire burn and cauldron bubble." The Three Weird Sisters gestured dramatically as they chanted their magic spell on the stage of Schiller Park. Volodya, sprawled on a hard wooden bench nearby, watched without much interest. He was familiar with the plot of *Macbeth,* but following the Shakespearean English was too much to ask of a Russian. If not for Grigorii's request that they meet at the park, he would probably be sitting somewhere air-conditioned with Julie, not fighting off mosquitoes on a park bench.

Schiller Park was at the hub of German Village; a large, beautifully landscaped oval that contained a playground, tennis courts, library, and free outdoor theatre. On its perimeter sat some of the most expensive homes in the Village. Volodya thought it an odd place to meet; he would have preferred the crowded anonymity of a bar. As he remembered from his training at university, spies preferred to meet in the open air, where they were unlikely to be overheard. Volodya did not think that Grigorii was FSB, but he was furtive, and Volodya had no interest in sharing Grigorii's secrets.

What could Grigorii want with him? He was only an acquaintance. The Russian community in Columbus was growing, but it was still small enough that it was easy to meet most émigrés. Volodya had met Grigorii at several parties; an intense, runty little man, about Volodya's age, handsome in a swarthy way.

"By the pricking of my thumbs, something wicked this way comes!" shrieked one of the Weird Sisters, and Grigorii loomed — if such a small man could be said to loom - out of the dusk and pumped Volodya's hand.

"Hello, Volodya! Let us take a stroll around the park."

Volodya rose with a sigh. After some perfunctory chatter in Russian about mutual acquaintances, Grigorii broached the subject of his meeting.

"I have a proposition for you, Volodya." Grigorii's white teeth shone in the deepening darkness.

"What proposition is that?"

"You are a big computer guy, right?" Volodya did not disagree. "And you are working in a bank, right?" Volodya nodded. Grigorii leaned in closer, and said in a confidential tone, "I have some friends who would pay a lot of money to someone such as yourself. If that someone did my friends a little favor, moved a little code around."

Volodya raised an eyebrow. "What friends?"

Grigorii looked around, suddenly nervous. "Friends at Brighton Beach."

"Brighton Beach!" Volodya's whisper came out a hiss. "The Russian mafia? Grigorii, are you crazy?"

One of Volodya's New York friends had been stupid enough to become involved with that gang of thugs, criminals, and former KGB agents who took their name from Brighton Beach in New York City. After receiving a shipment of enamelware from Russia, via the mafia, Volodya's friend had refused to pay because the goods were of poor quality. A series of threatening phone calls began, which described graphically, and with poor grammar, what would happen to him if payment was not made. The friend had borrowed the money, paid the debt, and fled to Los Angeles, terrified for his life. Volodya had seen enough.

"The money is good, and it's only one small job," Grigorii said.

"Jesus, Grigorii, I don't care what kind of money it is. It's the kind of money people kill you for. I'm not interested." Volodya increased his pace; the shorter man struggled to keep up.

"Volodya, slow down! It is Brighton Beach indirectly, the money comes from official circles in Moscow. That's all I know."

Volodya stopped. "Oh, Moscow officials doing business with the Russian mafia. Big surprise."

"I'm only a messenger," Grigorii said. "I don't know enough programming to take the job myself, but I could get a commission if I find someone else. You're perfect."

"Like I said, you're crazy." Volodya looked closely at Grigorii. "Grigorii, you will have to turn someone. An American is more likely to have the kind of job you're talking about. Some places won't hire Russians."

"Turn someone?"

"Yes. Preferably a woman." Aloud, Volodya considered the possibilities. "Arrange to meet a woman programmer, an American. A smart one. Make her fall in love with you. Convince her to do what you want. She will do it out of love; you would not even have to share the money with her." Grigorii's white teeth flashed in a grin; clearly that idea was appealing.

"You think I could do that?"

"Women like you." That was true, although God knew why. None of Volodya's women would have betrayed her country for the likes of Grigorii, but some women found the little man irresistible. "Grigorii, I am sorry not to be able to help you, but I'm waiting for my citizenship. I don't want to take any chances. You can do this yourself, you'll make more money and you'll have a woman to screw. It's a much better plan."

Grigorii snickered, mollified. "You know any American woman programmers?" he asked.

"I'm sure you won't have any trouble finding the right person," said Volodya. Grigorii was greedy, and he would not hold it against Volodya for refusing, since Volodya's refusal paved the way for more money to be dropped in his own pocket.

"You want to go to a bar?" Grigorii asked, suddenly chummy.

"No, I'm meeting someone. A woman." This was a lie, but Volodya could not afford to spend time with someone like Grigorii. The man was dangerous, if only by association.

"A woman." Grigorii leered at him, then pumped his hand again. "I'll see you around, Volodya."

Volodya said nothing. Dropping his cigarette on the sidewalk, he stubbed it out with his foot. Perhaps he would call Julie; he could meet her somewhere and make true the one lie he had told to Grigorii.


*July 20, 1999: Day 165*

Sixty seconds after emerging into the July sunshine from the sanctuary of 2 Nationwide Plaza, Jim Frazier was sweating like the proverbial pig. Despite his casual khakis and knit shirt - he was covering a human-interest story at the Knox County Fair that evening - the heat was a plague. His visit to KPMG Peat Marwick Accounting at the Nationwide Plaza building had been prompted by a lead about computer fraud and auditing; it had sounded interesting but led nowhere, and now he was looking for lunch at a nearby Wendy's.

Rounding the corner he headed west on Spring Street and traversed the front of the spectacular but prosaically named William Green Building, which housed the offices of Ohio's Workers' Compensation Program. Jim had a nickname for the skyscraper; he called it the Pink Lady.

Constructed entirely of polished pink granite and comprising a city block, the Pink Lady was a definite eye-catcher. Even the Lady's sidewalk was pink granite, set off by glinting brass railings which ran up the stairs of the entrance and drew the eye to the brass door surrounds. Squares of herringbone brick trapped two small locust trees standing guard in front, and fountains spilled over a stair-like arrangement on each side of the impressive entrance.

Today something was amiss. A knot of about fifty people milled about on the granite sidewalk, and as Jim watched, a van pulled up and disgorged ten or twelve more, some of them wielding signs. Hot damn, a demonstration!

Quickly he took out his pen and paper and ran over to the crowd of angry people. The building provided no shade this time of day, and the temperature on the sidewalk was sweltering. Jim picked out a distraught-looking white woman (racially mixed crowd, he noted) and approached her.

"I'm a reporter with the *Courier*," Jim said. All heads swiveled toward him. "Is this a demonstration?"

"Yes." Jim saw that a small boy clung to the woman's hand. "We've been trying all morning to get in to see the Workers' Compensation Agency. Nobody's got their checks this month." She gestured at the other people and they nodded.

An older black woman spoke up indignantly. "I been injured for some weeks and I need that money. They treatin' us like dirt in there. We started out inside, and their security people made us leave. This heat ain't doing my injuries no good!"

A man of about forty caught Jim's eye. He was respectably dressed in a dark suit, and like everyone else, sweating.

"It's true. I've only had benefits for about a month, but I need that money, like the rest of them." He looked at Jim as though sizing him up. "We've all tried to telephone, and we were told - when we could get through at all - that the checks would be a day or two late." Several in the crowd hooted in derision. "It's been almost three weeks now for some people."

"And they won't tell you why?" Jim was scribbling, wondering if he had time to call the newspaper office and get a photographer. The TV people were going to show up any minute, he was sure of it.

The man shook his head. "They're acting real funny about it. Evasive. Like they're scared of something, in my opinion."

Several years ago, Jim remembered, a frustrated client whose workers' comp claim had been denied had entered this building with a gun and taken hostages. The Workers' Comp people were understandably paranoid about unhappy customers.

"How'd you get all these people down here?"

The man glanced around, as if about to share a secret. "This is off the record. One of my friends is a programmer at Workers' Comp. When I told him my check was late, he got a funny look and said there would be a lot more late checks. I told him I was going to go in to their office to complain to somebody, and he said that just one person wasn't going to get anyone's attention." The man hesitated. "This is still off the record, right? I don't want to get my friend in trouble." Jim nodded.

"Well, he got me a printout of the people who didn't have their checks, with their addresses and phone numbers, and I started calling. The plan was that a small group of us would meet with the Workers' Comp people at ten a.m., then by noon we'd report to the larger crowd, which would be peacefully picketing outside."

The man wiped his sweaty face. "They gave us about ten minutes, then almost threw us out. Told the guy at the front desk to keep us out."

While they talked, more protestors were arriving, some on crutches or in wheelchairs. Jim estimated the crowd size at seventy.

He closed his notebook. "Listen, why don't I go in and talk to them? Maybe when they realize that this will be in the papers, they'll be more willing to cooperate."

"Right on!" shouted a young man. The crowd milled restlessly. Across the street curious passers-by were stopping to stare.

Jim raised his voice. "I'll go in and try to find out for you, OK?" Several more shouted their approval, and Jim ran up the steps and through the brass-edged revolving door.

He rode the elevator upstairs to the fiftieth floor. The office was empty except for an obese receptionist who snarled at him. "How did you get in here? We told you all to wait outside!" She pointed imperiously to the elevator.

Jim held up his press pass.

"Oh, shit, that is all we need," she moaned.

"Can I quote you?" This woman was upset about something more than a few protestors. She didn't answer.

"Can I see someone in charge?" Clearly, she was not. The woman beckoned for him to follow her.

"They're all over here, on the front side of the building." The door to every office stood open, their occupants lined up at the windows, peering down as well as they could at the protestors below.

"Mr. Painter, it's a reporter." She abandoned him at the threshold of an open office. A man stood staring out the window at the scene below. When Jim joined him, he saw that the crowd of protestors had grown.

"Mr. Painter?" The man turned quickly toward him; he was about fifty and bald, his forehead furrowed with anxiety. He gestured toward the window.

"Do you see that? What are we going to do?"

"Why don't they have their checks, Mr. Painter?" asked Jim, patient.

"Ask the damn IT department," said Mr. Painter. "I sure as hell don't know." He seemed to remember who Jim was. "Please don't quote me on that." A weak attempt at a smile.

"Maybe you could tell me what's happened," Jim suggested. The man looked hesitant for a moment, then his shoulders drooped.

"I guess it doesn't matter now," he said. "We can't keep it quiet. I don't even know if it's that serious. People just get awfully upset when it's their money."

"If you could explain it to me," Jim said, "I'd be willing to try to explain it to the crowd."

"Would you?" Mr. Painter was pleased and amazed. "Well, it's a y2k problem with the computers. This is July, the beginning of the state fiscal year in Ohio. Well, as soon as July first came around, we started having problems." He rolled his eyes. "Not just with the checks, pretty much with everything that had a date on it. I guess you understand that once we got into the new fiscal year, we had to deal with dates in the year 2000." Jim nodded. "Anyway, as soon as the techies got one bug straightened out, something else would come up. They've been working overtime for the last three weeks trying to straighten our systems out. Our systems have been down more than they've been up."

"It's funny I haven't heard anything about it," Jim said.

Mr. Painter looked uncomfortable. "Well, the policy was supposed to be that we didn't talk about it, not even to the people who weren't getting their checks. We hoped we could get it fixed quickly, and we didn't want people to worry."

A skinny young man rapped on the doorjamb. "Mr. Painter?"

Turning at the summons, Mr. Painter gestured at the young man. "Jim, this is Matt. He's one of our programmers. Ask him about it."

"You mean we're allowed to talk?" asked Matt with more than a trace of sarcasm. Matt leaned toward Jim confidentially. "Don't let them tell you they can fix this in a couple of weeks. In my opinion, it's going to take a couple of months. Minimum."

"Matt, these people can't wait months for their checks! What are we going to do?" Mr. Painter was distraught, Matt, hostile.

"You're paying us all overtime now," said Matt, his face twisted with disgust. "You should have put it in the budget before so we could fix it right! You guys screw up your business plans and we suffer for it!"

"I didn't run the y2k project."

"Right. Nobody's ever responsible."

Jim stepped toward the window again. "Shit. Look at the size of that crowd." The crowd, twice as large as a few minutes ago, filled the sidewalk in both directions and threatened to spill out into the street. Jim saw the Channel 4 van maneuver its way to the sidewalk. News cameras began scanning the crowd.

"What are you going to tell them?" asked Mr. Painter, and Jim remembered that he had promised to talk to the crowd. He had promised to talk to a much smaller crowd.

"Look," said Jim, "I'll talk to them if you agree to let some of them come up and help you figure out what you're going to do about their checks."

"I can't do that!" Mr. Painter was pained. "I don't have the authority. Anyway, how are those people going to help me?"

Jim shrugged. "You don't get it. They won't wait. You've got to figure out some kind of workaround, even if you have to pay them cash, or write the checks by hand. If you involve some of those people in the process, you'll generate good will. They'll believe that you're trying to solve their problem. If you don't, they'll think you're only interested in covering your own ass."

Mr. Painter hesitated, torn between being a decent human being and a bureaucrat. While he hesitated the mounted police arrived on the sidewalk below them.

"Okay. Okay." Mr. Painter gave up. "Bring a couple of them back up with you."

Jim sped back down to the hall and into the elevator. As he sprinted for the front door, he could hear the crowd noise rise. The security guard didn't want to let him out.

"They're getting ugly out there."

At that moment Jim heard the crack of a gunshot. Screams followed, and the crowd surged toward the doors of the building at the same time the officers on horseback began moving their horses toward the crowd. The stairs made it difficult for the horses, and a few people managed to dart past and into the lobby. Someone stumbled and fell, cursing. Jim saw the young woman desperately trying to break from the crowd with her child, just a few feet from the door. He darted out, grabbed her hand, and pushed her and the child through the revolving door. The man in the suit and a younger man followed, but no one else seemed able to get past the police.

"You come upstairs with me." Behind them the disturbance was escalating into a full-blown riot, sirens blaring as reinforcements arrived to quell the crowd. Jim herded his little flock on to the elevator.

"What took you so long?" asked the man in the suit, panting.

"Never mind. Are you all okay?" Jim took a breath mint out of his pocket and asked permission to give it to the small boy, who seemed so far unfazed by his ordeal. "You've been recruited to help the Workers' Comp Office figure out some way to cut your checks. Just give them your ideas. Here's Mr. Painter."

Jim stayed at the office window with the others, watching the rioters group and scatter before the onslaught of riot control. What idiot had sent riot police into a crowd of people on crutches and in wheelchairs? Wait till the national networks got hold of this. He took notes, wincing when the police threw the tear gas canisters that finally dispersed the crowd, then high-tailed it back to his office to write his story. When you were the only newspaper in town, everything was a scoop, but he had the real inside information on this one. It occurred to him to wonder how many state departments the state of Ohio contained, and how many were even now having their first year 2000 problems. Pray God they weren't all as bad as this.

*July 23, 1999: Day 162*

Karen was already sitting at the table with a cup of coffee when Alex came down for breakfast. He liked the way his wife looked in the morning, sort of tousled and sexy. This morning she was dressed in her workout clothes; she must have gone to the health club and come back while he was still asleep. He bent to kiss her.

"You're up early."

"Big trip to the Beach today with the kiddos." The Beach was a water park in Cincinnati. "I wanted to get some work in before we left." She rattled the newspaper at Alex. "Read Jim's column."

"I hope it's something cheerful," he said, seating himself. Columbus' y2k riot was grabbing headlines in a big way; pictures and stories ran in newspapers from Madrid to Hong Kong. Because of his high visibility in the y2k world, Alex had given a number of interviews in the last two days; he continued to stress the importance of looking for solutions instead of panicking. Although it was silly, Alex felt guilty that the first such riot should have happened in his city.

"No, it's good. It's in Jim Frazier's y2k column." The column ran daily, commenting on readers' y2k questions as well as local, national, and global implications. Alex read where his wife pointed.

*Y2K OK by Jim Frazier*

*Where are we in the aftermath of Tuesday's y2k riot? All of us saw what happened; the news coverage was flashed across every major network here and abroad. We saw angry faces, raised fists, people trampled and threatened. A major civil disturbance in the quiet streets of downtown Columbus is disquieting; Columbus is a city where those things don't happen. Aside from the campus riots in the early 70's, our most notorious rioting has occurred after an OSU football victory.*

*The problem began when some people on workers' comp didn't get their checks due to a year 2000 computer malfunction. They didn't assemble in front of the Town Center the next day, demanding action. No, they went through channels, and they were brushed off. Instead of*

*telling them about the computer problem, the officials told
them the checks were in the mail, a patent lie.*

*Two weeks later these people were beginning to get
desperate. They assembled, as is their right, and they went
to the State Workers' Compensation Office to find out where
their checks were. For their trouble they were hassled and
asked to leave the building. Still no answers.*

*That was one of the hotter days in July. People began
to get angry, as people do when they know they're being
manipulated and lied to. The news cameras showed up,
then the police. Then the shot, if that's what it was - police
speculate that it was only a car backfiring in the street -
and all hell broke loose.*

*The riot is well documented. How many of us know
what happened afterward? While the police were throwing tear gas canisters, three of the protestors were sitting
upstairs in the Workers' Comp Office. These three - a young
mother with a four-year-old boy, a businessman in a suit,
and an unkempt young man of twenty-five - were invited to
put their heads together with the employees of that office
to see what could be done to resolve the check problem.*

*Remember when checks were written by people, not is-
sued by computers? That's the way they'll be doing it for a
while at the worker's comp office. It's going to take more
labor this way. But it can be done.*

*That's the message I want to leave with you. Y2k is a
serious problem, one that many of us underestimated for
far too long. But does it mean the collapse of civilization?
Does it mean that our only hope for survival is to crawl
into a cave with a gun and shoot anyone who asks to share
our cache of food?*

*No! But defeating y2k does mean that we'll have to do
something that for many of us will be just as tough — we
have to work together and we have to trust each other. In
recent years many have decried our loss of community, of
connectedness, of neighborliness. Well folks, here's our
chance to get it back.*

"Well said," Alex said as he handed the paper back to his wife. "Maybe I could stop having nightmares if more people thought like that."

"Jim didn't think like that two months ago," Karen reminded him. "We have to keep convincing them, one at a time if need be."

"Let's hope Jim convinced two or three this morning. One at a time is too slow for my timetable."

# Chapter 8

*August 7, 1999: Day 147*

Stepping into the August heat from his air-conditioned car always gave Volodya an unpleasant jolt. He let fall a Russian curse as he navigated the short walk to his apartment, then unlocked the door and stepped inside. He would never get used to Ohio's humidity. Already he was sick of working on Saturdays like this, but his team's progress on the compile was rapid, and the influx of cash welcome.

Upstairs he discarded his jeans and knit shirt. Stripped to his boxers, he savored the touch of the cool air on his skin, and the cool tiles under his bare feet. After finding a beer (a European one, not those shitty American brands) in the nearly empty refrigerator, he collapsed with it in the recesses of his white sofa, put his feet up on the coffee table, and surveyed his domain. The apartment was small but clean because he had it cleaned once a week. Women did not like to be seduced in a dirty apartment.

He wished for more space, a better address, and leather furniture. He had not done too badly, but he intended to do better.

He drank his beer and riffled through the mail, mostly bills and ads. Then he threw them on the coffee table and adjourned with his beer to the spare bedroom upstairs that served as his home office. Most of his personal mail arrived on his computer via e-mail. Opening his e-mail file, he hit the send and receive button, drumming his fingers impatiently on the desk while the modem connected to the mail server. Moments later, six new messages appeared on the screen.

As he prepared to open the first message, he realized that its header was incomplete: no subject and no sender address. Just to the left of the message summary header was a paper clip icon, which in his e-mail system indicated that a separate file was attached to the message. Attached files were handy for e-mailing documents, spreadsheets, graphics, photos, and so on, but they were also a prime source of computer viruses.

Best to check out this message and see where it was coming from. By clicking a certain key, Volodya could examine the e-mail route through the electronic domains, or Internet nodes, and so trace it back to its source. Volodya clicked and read the e-mail's backward route on the displayed screen; Columbus, via Boston, via London, via Paris, via Bonn, via Helsinki, from a domain in Moscow. So the message had come from someone back home. He decided he would open it.

"Vladimir Vasilovitch Borodin," the brief missive began. Volodya straightened in his chair. Certainly, this e-mail was from one of his Russian friends; none of his American friends knew his patronymic, Vasilovitch. "Here is what we promised you. The rest arrives by separate post. We will be interested to see what you can do with it." The letter was signed Quentin.

Quentin. Volodya smiled a little. He hadn't heard that name since KGB spy school (in those days it was still called the KGB), in which case the e-mail was likely from one of his Russian friends playing a joke on him. Spy school was their umbrella name for the mandatory classes required for any student in an advanced state-funded math or science program. Spy school taught them such things as what to do if a Western agent approached and tried to recruit them, and how to use psychological techniques to compromise and recruit foreigners. In spy school the Western agent's name was always Quentin.

Volodya threw back his arms and stretched. The field was narrowing, and he would bet it was Boris, an old schoolmate who now lived in Silicon Valley. He might have sent the e-mail to a friend in Russia to send to Volodya, just to throw him off track. He played these little detective games with several of his programmer friends, but Borya was the most ingenious. Perhaps he should include Leo in the fun sometime.

If it were Borya, the attached file was likely to contain a choice piece of pornography. He still had the last one, in which a naked girl wiggled lasciviously across the screen via some new 3-D algorithms Boris was working on for a Silicon Valley graphics contract. He envied Boris that contract.

Making a copy of the doubtful attachment, he saved it to a floppy disk, then activated the virus scanner and waited.

Aha! As he had thought, the scanner detected a suspicious binary pattern almost at once. Volodya grinned. This was still not hard evidence that the attachment contained a virus, but one took precautions. A small screen popped up and asked: Do you wish to remove the virus? Volodya clicked yes, and in seconds the offending binary pattern was excised from the file. At last he could safely open the message and look at it. Maybe this time it would be two naked girls. Volodya grinned again.

When he finally double-clicked and saw the attachment displayed, Volodya gave a sudden involuntary jerk of surprise, picked up his can of beer, and took a very long drink. The attachment was still unreadable because it was encrypted, and in light of the message that accompanied it, the encryption could mean one thing only — after all these months, the FSB had finally come to call.

*       *       *

Leo had done the impossible; he had convinced Annette to take a night off to go to the symphony with him. It was an outdoor concert; under the stars, with beautiful music to serenade them, who knew what might happen?

Annette protested at first, of course. "Leo, I'm working on some y2k preparedness literature. I want to get it done over the weekend."

For once, Leo was adamant. "How long has it been since you did anything for fun, Annette?"

She didn't answer and he knew she couldn't remember.

"Your mind will work better if you give it a few hours break. You'll be able to finish the same work in less time."

Annette looked pensive. She also looked tired, her eyes slightly shadowed, her smile a little forced. "I love the symphony," she said, her voice wistful.

"OK, then it's settled," Leo had said, pressing his advantage. He had felt fierce and protective. "I'll buy the tickets and the dinner and

I'll pick you up at six o'clock tomorrow night."

Nothing about Saturday could have made Leo unhappy. He welcomed its oppressive heat, gloried in its humidity. He cleaned his apartment in a burst of ridiculous optimism (the odds against her coming there were of course astronomical, but he steadfastly refused to figure the odds) and washed his car. In the afternoon he drove to Michael's Finest Foods and flirted with the girl behind the counter. She helped him choose a dinner for lovers - curried chicken salad, croissants, peach and raspberry tarts, and a wonderful bottle of wine - and said that whoever he was buying for was a lucky woman.

He realized after buying the food that he had no picnic basket, so he went to a kitchen store and purchased their most expensive model, complete with wine glasses. Then he bought a tablecloth and napkins, and lovingly packed it all into the picnic basket at home.

As he packed the car he threw in two lawn chairs, then took them out again, deciding he preferred the intimacy of sitting with Annette on a blanket on the ground. Showered and shaved and completely happy for the first time in months, Leo drove to Annette's apartment.

Annette was dressed in a lime-green sundress that showed a lot of creamy skin in the right places. "You look beautiful," Leo said. He liked the way the sunlight sparked her coppery hair.

"You're spoiling me, Leo." Annette made herself comfortable in the front seat. "But I must admit, I like it."

The symphony pavilion was set on the well-tended green lawns of Chemical Abstracts, the large corporate sponsor. Annette and Leo were early enough to find a choice spot for their picnic, near enough to see as well as hear the musicians. On all sides of them sprouted umbrellas and tables and blankets and lawn chairs planted by picnicking symphony-goers. Children raced about on the unoccupied grassy verges; adults threw Frisbees and blew bubbles. The light-hearted bustle reminded Leo of a tailgate picnic before a college football game.

"This is all very festive, Leo." Annette took in the scene with appreciation. "And how lovely your picnic looks!" She smiled at him and he relaxed. Did she have any idea how he still felt about her?

"Eat hearty!" he said. So many times she didn't; she only poked at a salad with her fork, or forgot to eat at all when she worked late. Tonight she seemed determined to push away her worries at work, and she ate with gusto.

"I'm chock-a-block!" she said when she finished her raspberry tart.

"You Brits," Leo said. He picked up a napkin to wipe a stray bit of raspberry from her lips.

He steadied her face lightly with his left hand, his fingers on her jawbone, his thumb near her mouth, and flicked away the raspberry stain with the napkin in his right hand. Then because her face was so close to his already, and her eyes were so wide and solemn, and because she was altogether desirable, he began to bend his head to kiss her.

"Annette, hi!" A voice came booming at them. "Not interrupting anything, am I?"

Leo stifled his urge to kill the intruder and reluctantly leaned away from Annette. Their lips had barely brushed.

"Oh, hello, Rod." Annette jumped up to shake the hand of a thin, bearded young man. "Rod lives in my apartment complex."

"Pleasure to meet you," Leo lied.

"Annette's the one who put me on to the year 2000 problem." Rod was plainly enthralled. He gazed at Annette with adoration.

"Rod's organized the whole complex, haven't you Rod?" said Annette. "He's really taken it upon himself to let all our neighbors know about it, talking to them and passing out literature. We're having a preparedness meeting in September."

Rod finally left them as the music began.

Annette sat with her legs drawn up beneath the skirt of her green sundress, her arms clasped around her legs, her chin resting on her knees. Maestro Siciliani began with a Hungarian peasant dance by Bartok, and although a breeze had sprung up, he was soon sweating profusely with the ardor of his conducting.

"The poor man's working so hard up there," Annette said when the piece was finished. "I feel guilty, Leo, but it's wonderful to have a break like this. What else do you do in your time off?"

"Oh, not much." Leo was a little embarrassed by the question. "I lead a dull life, I'm afraid. I read a lot. I play the violin. There's a nursing home across the street. I go over there once a week and play for them."

"Do you really? Tell me what it's like." Annette's look was so admiring that Leo was embarrassed anew.

"It's not a big thing. I like to play and they're a captive audience. Some of them sleep through it. I play a couple of classical pieces, usually, then I take requests. I'm becoming an expert on old hymns and pop songs of the thirties and forties. And of course we talk afterwards. A few of them even have computers, and I can help them. I think it's great that a person over seventy would try to learn to use a computer."

"I think it's great that you would do what you do. Promise me you'll play the violin for me sometime."

Leo smiled. "Any time. Tonight if you like."

She made no reply and they both fell silent, entranced by the music. The sky gradually emptied of light, deepening to indigo, then black. The oppressive heat eased. Stars perforated the darkness overhead, and the small white lights wrapped around the trunks of the trees near-by added their twinkle. Annette and Leo stretched out next to each other on the blanket. The finale of Tchaikovsky's *Symphony No. 5* rolled over them, and Leo ached with love and longing.

Annette rolled over on her back at the end of the piece and looked up at the stars. "Do you ever wonder, Leo, if there will be concerts like this again next summer?"

"What?"

"Suppose the year 2000 comes and the symphony isn't ready? A lot of non-profits aren't, you know. Or maybe if the recession is severe enough, people won't be able to afford tickets, or corporate sponsors will go out of business..."

"You're very gloomy suddenly."

"I think about it all the time." Her face was a pale, unsmiling oval in the dim light. "Sometimes it really frightens me."

Leo scrambled to a sitting position. "Sit up."

Annette sat up. He took her shoulders in his hands and looked into her eyes as well as the darkness would permit.

"Annette, everything will be all right," he said softly but firmly. He shook her very gently. "You must believe that."

"I suppose I must." Her voice was small. She sounded very unlike her decisive corporate self.

Leo couldn't bear it; he pulled Annette to him and held her against his chest, whispering into her hair. "It will be all right. Please don't worry."

Annette did not move from the circle of his arms; her face snuggled

against the beating of his heart. They sat in the dark together and tried
to let the reassuring warmth of their bodies and the music of Gershwin's
*Summertime* inoculate them against their fears.

*   *   *

The concert ended with fireworks, and they began the trek back to
the car. Leo did not want to fall back into the year 2000 rut. He
changed the subject.

"I could play the violin for you tonight," he said, his voice light, his
heart thumping nevertheless. "I cleaned the apartment today," he added,
ingenuous, when Annette was silent. "It's still early." Without much
hope.

They were in the car, waiting amid the throngs, and Annette still
had not answered.

"Leo, thank you so much for this evening," she said at last, not
looking at him. "You're such a dear friend. I'd be ever so lonely
without you."

"I think you're lonely anyway." Leo felt stretched tight with disappointment, and a little reckless. Dear friend was better than no status
at all, but it was so much less than he wanted.

"I've hurt your feelings," she said, contrite. "Leo, I've told you,
this just isn't a time when-"

"When you can clutter up your life with anything except year 2000,"
he finished for her. "Yeah, I know. You've told me."

"Well, I *have* told you. You already know. What do you expect me
to do?" Annette's voice was plaintive, but Leo was unmoved. He
stomped on the accelerator, nearly propelling them into the next car in
the slow-moving line.

"I keep hoping you'll realize what an idiot you're being for putting
your life on hold like this," Leo said at last.

"That was rude, Leo."

"It's the way I feel." Leo sat in angry silence as they drove down
Olentangy River Road toward Annette's place. She did not invite him
in, and he offered only a curt goodnight at her door. By the time he
reached home, he was cursing himself. What good did it do him to treat
her badly? He had no choice but to go at her pace or forget the whole

thing and move back to Silicon Valley. He tried to be happy that she had let him hold her, but the memory was an exercise in frustration.

\*       \*       \*

Later that evening Volodya eased himself into the swivel chair at his computer desk to begin his examination of the attached file. First he deleted his earlier copy; it was no good once the virus scanner had removed part of the code. Then he used the encryption key, which arrived in a separate post as promised in the message, and opened the original file. After his initial shock, he no longer felt threatened. The KGB — well, actually the FSB now, but much the same organization — had come to him years ago, after he had put in his letter for permission to emigrate. He could still recall Igor Slatkin, the weasely little agent who came to his office at Moscow State University to ask for his cooperation.

"We are not asking you to be a spy, of course," and Igor had given a self-conscious little giggle as he adjusted his glasses and patted his greasy hair. "But you work with computers, and it may be that you could be of service to us some time while you are living abroad. If that is the case, we will be in touch with you, and I trust that you will be able to help us, yes?"

Igor's voice trailed off and Volodya was quick to assure him that yes, yes, he would be happy to help him in any way he could. After the obligatory handshake he had ushered him out of the office and then quickly had gone to wash his hands.

Now Volodya studied the code on the computer screen. Although the compiled code was of course unreadable, it was accompanied by brief, relatively simple instructions that told him that he was expected to find a way to insert these algorithms into the bank's source code.

How had they known he was working at a bank? He was pretty certain that he was not under surveillance, and who in Russia knew about his job except his family? Ah, of course: he had e-mailed the news to his family, who told Ilya, and then Ilya told his parents. Ilya's mother was a doctor, but his father was a retired KGB chief.

Although the FSB wanted him to place the code, he was not meant to know what it did. Perhaps the same algorithm had been sent to a number of expatriate Russian programmers, on the chance that at least one of them would succeed in actually planting it. None of them had to understand it to plant it.

But Volodya wanted to know more. He was not the stooge of the FSB; he wanted to know what the code did. To figure that out, he would have to decompile the code. With the use of a special decompiler this step took about five minutes. Now he had before him on the screen the raw assembler code. If he studied it for clues, carefully analyzing it to determine what the algorithms were instructing the computer to do, he could eventually build a kind of flow chart that would reveal the code's purpose.

Now came the challenge. Concentrating the whole force of his considerable intelligence on the cryptic symbols of the assembler code, Volodya began the painstaking process - part intuition, part skill, part sheer determination - that would eventually conquer the algorithm. He did not notice when the light wore away from the sky and the stars appeared in his window, and he was still pounding the keyboard when the sky began to lighten again.

Sunday's church bells were pealing when Volodya finally realized how ravenous and exhausted he was. He ate two bowls of corn flakes, took a shower, and went to bed, where he wrestled with the elusive equations in his sleep. By five o'clock that evening he was back at his desk.

A pattern had begun to emerge, and the more he looked at it, the surer he was that it was the work of someone he knew. A non-mathematician could never understand how an equation could bear its creator's signature as surely as a great master could be identified by his brushstrokes. But Volodya was certain, given the spare elegance of its expression, and given that the particular field of mathematics was so thinly populated, that he could narrow the algorithm's author down to three men, two Russians and a Chinese. One of the two Russians was Sergei Krzyzanowski, his former professor, and Volodya was confident that it was in fact he who had created the algorithm. One puzzle was solved; he was on the hunt, certain that he could solve the other.

Volodya's mathematical brilliance was both methodical and intuitive, and his persistence was ferocious. By ten o'clock he could tell that the equations were finally beginning to yield to the force of his mind, and at midnight he triumphed.

"Yes!" He slapped his hands on the desk. He felt a flush of pleasure that was almost sexual, as if he had just seduced and conquered a beautiful but willful woman. Then he looked more closely at the algorithm.

*¡Bozhe moy, î* he whispered. My God.

# Chapter 9

On Monday morning Leo went straight to Annette's office door and knocked.

"Come in." Her accent made him smile; it was part of all he found endearing about her. Wrongheaded as he thought her, he had come to apologize.

"Hi." He sidled in. "Did you get my message?"

"I got in so late last night I didn't even listen to them." Annette looked tired and anxious; impulsively Leo reached across the desk, took her hand, and squeezed it.

"Hey, I'm sorry," he began, then realized that she was echoing his words. Both of them grinned with relief.

"I'm glad we're friends again, Leo. I did have a very good time."

"Me, too. Except for the end."

"Well, we'll forget about that bit, shall we?" She was smiling, svelte and proper in her dark business suit, and he thought of the way her skin had looked in the lime sundress.

"Whatever you say." Sometimes he hated himself for his wimpiness. Maybe if he had the nerve to vault across the desk and kiss her, everything would resolve itself into the ending he wanted. Or maybe not. He couldn't risk it, so he said good-bye and returned to the programmer's room.

\*　　\*　　\*

Volodya did not come to work until noon, for once he had solved the algorithm, he had sat staring at it in fascination until almost three a.m. Even at work, he continued to think about the code.

The algorithm was sophisticated and ingenious, and Volodya admired it tremendously. Its function was to transfer money — a lot of money — from the bank whose source code it entered, into an account which it then created. Even better was its randomness; the money was withdrawn from a different bank each time, randomly selected, with random amounts of time between withdrawals. This left no pattern to follow in tracing the disappearing money.

The algorithm was self-limiting; it would withdraw only a certain amount and then cease its activity. Otherwise it could siphon out money until the financial system collapsed altogether. Volodya was sure that the worm had been tested rigorously in the FSB lab; even so, such testing could not assure its behavior in a banking environment. No doubt the professor had designed deactivation codes in case the worm did not behave as expected. But it could mutate. Any self-replicating code presented that danger.

The algorithm activated itself in an ingenious manner. If activation commands were put directly into source code, they would be obvious to one and all. So, rather than being called in a recognizable sequence, the algorithm's commands were dispersed throughout the program and therefore hidden. The final command collected the dispersed commands and called the module. The whole thing was extremely difficult to trace.

When the TCP/IP signal left the bank, the professor's code in effect rode on its back, making the code's progress invisible and untraceable. This signal jumping was called wormholing, and it was strictly illegal, because such 128-bit encryption was not permitted to cross the national borders of the U.S. Volodya had in fact never seen wormholing used before; both its illegality and the extreme difficulty of coding it made its use rare indeed. Volodya admired his professor's canniness and wished that he had thought of it first.

But as much as he admired the code, Volodya wished he had never seen it. He detested the FSB, and he hated their assumption that he would tamely do as they told him. They expected him to risk all that he had built in America to commit a crime for them. The risk was all on his side, the gain was all on theirs.

Further, even if he chose to cooperate, what the FSB expected of him would not be that easy to do, he thought, as he began the day's remediation task.

First, he would need access to the bank's source code. He had access through his compiling job, but sitting in this little room with only a dumb terminal and no hard drives meant that he could not bring the code in on a floppy disk and slip it into the computer. Second, he would need enough time to decompile the bank's source code, insert Sergei's source code, and recompile the combined code. Unfortunately this could not be done from his computer at home; he would have to do it while in the bank, and given his present status, this was risky. If anyone became aware of what he was doing, he would be suspected immediately.

Whether he planted the code or not, Volodya had no intention of getting himself screwed for the FSB. He wished he knew exactly how soon the code would activate. Already the year 2000 disruptions were beginning, but the nearer to December it was, the more likely that the code's effects would be misinterpreted as the result of year 2000 computer disruptions. This was only mid-August. If he cooperated, he would have more than adequate time to plan and execute. If he did not, he would need the time to create a valid alibi.

"Hey, Volodya."

Volodya looked up from his terminal at Midwest to see Ivan standing next to him.

"I need to talk to you," Ivan said. He rattled the change in his pockets, shifted from one foot to another.

"Sit down," said Volodya, indicating a chair. Ivan removed his hands from his pockets and sat. The others had gone to lunch, so the room was private. "Is something wrong?"

"I got e-mail from FSB this weekend," Ivan said at once.

"Ivan!" Volodya said in a hiss, looking quickly at the door. Fortunately it was closed. "Are you crazy? That is not a thing to talk about here. Even in Russian."

A stubborn look settled over Ivan's blunt features. "I have to talk, I am worried," he said, lowering his voice. "The room is not bugged. Who else speaks Russian?"

Volodya swore to himself. "Hurry up, then. And keep your voice down."

"I got e-mail, Alyosha got e-mail, Andrei got e-mail, Fetya, Ilya, -" he named each person on the programming team - "all of us, I think, even Vasily, but he will not talk about it."

"Vasily is smart," Volodya said.

"So you will not admit it either," Ivan said. "Never mind. We know anyway."

"Well, why tell me?" Volodya asked. "I can't help you."

"Because we don't want anything to do with whole damned idea!"

"None of you?"

"Well, if someone wants to do what they say, he will not admit it to others," Ivan said, looking less certain.

Volodya shrugged. "Then don't do it."

Ivan's face darkened. "You know it is never that simple. We all have family at home." In Russia, he meant.

"Then follow orders from Russia," Volodya said impatiently. He did not enjoy hearing his own reservations discussed.

"Even if I wanted to plant the stupid fucking bug, I do not think I could," Ivan muttered, his forehead sweaty. "I am not a magician! I said I would think about it, I admit, just to keep them off my back. Then I looked at it again. If I try to put it in here at the bank, I will get caught."

"Then my advice is not to try it," Volodya said. Those idiots at the FSB. Had they sent the algorithm to every Russian in America? He didn't want his programmers arrested trying to place the code; nor did he want to be implicated himself because of someone else's connection to him. Nor did he want to talk to anyone about it, including Ivan.

"If one of you tries it, and is caught, what happens to the others, eh?" he asked Ivan. "You never should have discussed it."

All the lines of Ivan's face drooped. Volodya felt a little sympathy, but not much. Ivan should have known better than to involve other people.

Ivan raised his hands, palms up, raised his shoulders, raised his eyebrows. "But what are we going to do?"

"Follow your conscience," Volodya said dryly.

*August 18, 1999: Day 136*

Jim stretched the kinks from his back and took out his notebook, ready to begin today's y2k story. He'd driven to St. Paul's Church in the local suburb of Worthington to interview a woman who was directing a food canning effort against the possibility of a y2k-caused food shortage. Not only were the people there canning food for themselves, they were also sharing it with neighborhood pantries to distribute to the needy.

It was an upbeat story, and he was glad to be able to write it; some days the millennium problem scared him more than he liked to admit. A nice woman, a homeschooler, she'd said, and she'd given him a great quote - where was it? Ah, yes.

> *Prepare for the worst, hope for the best. If y2k is a hiccup on the computer screen, what have I lost? I have a bunch of food stored, that I can eat any time. I have relationships with my neighbors, some of whom I had never even met before. I've seen the better side of a lot of people; I have more of a sense of community than I've ever had in the twenty years I've lived here. My kids are seeing people work together for a cause. People are sharing and caring, as corny as that may sound.*

Then she had become more serious. "I don't want to see things crumble. I pray that they don't. But if there are some disruptions, and people have to depend on each other again - well, maybe the hardship could be a good thing. I don't want to sound like Pollyanna, but maybe what we lose in ease of living would be worth the gain in community."

More power to her, thought Jim. She'd even handed him fliers about y2k preparedness and urged him to pass them around in his neighborhood. Well, maybe he would. People like Holly gave him hope.

Jim felt heartened by the contact. His wife accused him of being schizophrenic on the y2k question, and she was right. Some evenings he came home so depressed by what he found out at work that he felt hardly able to function. Being in contact with the Millennium Dynamics people and people like Holly was the antidote; fix what you can, prepare, educate, share. His articles were his war effort, and he no longer doubted that it was a war. Now he only wondered whether it was a war they could win.


*September 3, Friday of Labor Day Weekend, 1999: Day 120*

"Hey, Volodya," Leo yelled from the tiny kitchen. "Don't you have a bottle opener in here?"

The small apartment was hot and smoky, and Leo felt the need of another beer.

Volodya had invited some of his friends, mostly Russians, to his apartment for a party. The party plan seemed to involve mostly talking, eating, and drinking; when the crowd forgot about the Americans present they lapsed into Russian, and Leo escaped into the kitchen.

Leo was enjoying himself; conversation was not the forgotten art form in Russia that it was here, evidently. It was nice to be among people who felt no compelling need to turn on the TV.

Volodya appeared in the kitchen and rifled noisily through a drawer.

"I know I have opener - ah, it is here on counter. Come back and sit down, Leo. We promise to speak English." Volodya grinned at him and Leo followed him into the living room.

Volodya sat down next to a girl whom Leo knew only as Julie. She did not join in the conversation too much at first, when they talked about politics and art and religion, but as the volume rose and the drink consumption increased, she seemed more at ease. Volodya's arm was draped around her shoulder, and Leo felt he could taste his envy.

"Volodya, how do you like Homer's e-mail?" Ivan, one of Volodya's programmers, all but shouted the question; he had plainly drunk more than was prudent.

"Homer is very dull man," Volodya said to general laughter. "I may have to give it up."

It dawned on Leo that Volodya was talking about Homer Jones, the president of Midwest National.

"Homer Jones sends you e-mail?" he asked Volodya. The beer was making him a little slow tonight, he thought.

Volodya looked surprised at the question, then burst out laughing, along with the other programmers. They laughed for some time, and Leo waited patiently, the brunt of the jest, to be enlightened.

"You are funny, Leo," said Volodya at last, wiping his eyes. "I read Homer's e-mail, yes. He does not send any to me. It is puzzle, no?"

"You read his mail," Leo repeated. "You read his - Volodya, you read his e-mail without his permission? You mean you hack into his computer?"

Volodya nodded, unperturbed. "Sometimes is useful, for information."

Leo was speechless. Volodya slapped him on the back.

"You Americans are easily shocked," he said, amused. "Don't worry, I don't do it for blackmail. Homer is too dull to blackmail anyway." More laughter.

It was a clear invasion of privacy. Some of it was surely confidential business communications, the rest perhaps terribly personal. Leo was now duty-bound to tell Homer, and probably Alex, too. And what would happen then? Volodya and his programmers would be fired at once, and they were absolutely irreplaceable. The Midwest Bank y2k project would never be finished without them, and the bank would go under, exactly what they had tried so hard for eight months to prevent.

"Well." Leo paused, feeling his way carefully. "Why do you do it, then?"

Volodya lounged on the sofa, with Julie leaning on his chest while he fiddled with her hair the way one might absent-mindedly pet a dog. His gaze met Leo's. His other guests pricked their ears to hear what he would say. Then he winked.

"I do it because I can."

Volodya's programmers made Russian noises of agreement at their leader's wit, and Leo felt a little tired of their adulation of Volodya.

"Well, I can, and I don't," Leo said.

Volodya looked at Leo with the amused arrogance that he usually saved for Midwest's lesser programmers, and his eyes glinted.

"Maybe you can't," Volodya said. He sat easily on the sofa, his arm around Julie, that smile on his lips. For an instant Leo felt he was back in high school, the tolerated but not-quite-popular nerd.

"Of course I can," Leo said.

A minute later he was seated at Volodya's computer, being urged to put his money where his mouth was. The programmers ranged themselves behind him, taking bets on whether he could hack into Homer's computer or not, and if so, how quickly.

"Five to one," he heard Ivan say, betting against him.

Leo's hands descended on the keys with a vengeance. He had never done this before, but that didn't mean he couldn't. They all grew quiet, watching. Leo's fingers flew over the keyboard.

"I have never seen it done that way before," said Volodya. "You are very quick for hacker virgin," he said, laughing.

"Look!" said Fetya. "He's already in!"

*"Bozhe moy!"* Volodya said. The screen displayed an e-mail to Homer from his wife. The Russians began to applaud and exchange money. Volodya clapped him on the back, laughing, and handed him a beer. "You are real person, Leo. You are one of us." He raised his own beer to Leo's. *"Na zdarovye."* To your health.

Leo smiled, basking in the glory reflected by his friends' sincere admiration. Since leaving Silicon Valley, he had missed such attention. Most people in Columbus had no comprehension of his talents, and if they suspected his singular abilities at all, Leo found they still didn't much care. Except perhaps for Annette. Thinking of her gave him a twinge of conscience.

As the party went on, Volodya's guests showed no signs of tiring, but by two a.m. Leo had had enough of the smoke and the noise. He told Volodya he was going. This brought a pout from Gallina, a Russian medical student who had shadowed him all evening, making it clear in several languages that she would like to sleep with him. Leo looked at her lively, attractive face and was tempted for a moment, but he told her goodnight. Volodya walked him to the door and they stood outside in the clear air.

"Gallina is nice girl; you are making mistake."

Leo shook his head with a smile.

"I'm sure she's nice, Volodya," he said. "I'm just not interested right now."

"You don't have to be *monk* while you wait for other woman."

"I'm sure Gallina can find someone else."

"She likes Americans," said Volodya with a shrug. "Well, okay, you go."

"I'll see you on Labor Day at Alex's party." Leo felt the fresh night air beginning to sober him up. "Are you bringing Julie?"

"No, why would I?"

"I thought you two were sleeping together."

"Yes, we do that sometimes. Tonight, probably." Volodya laughed. "But I will come by myself to Alex's party." He waved good-bye and closed the door.

Leo slid into his car's front seat, rested his forehead against the coolness of the steering wheel, and swore. Why did Volodya have to admit that he was reading Homer's e-mail?

If Leo told, he compromised the project and he made himself look like a hacker to Annette and the rest of the team. His newfound Russian soulmates would also disown him. They would think him not only the worst kind of humorless nerd, but a betrayer of their trust.

# PART 2

# Chapter 10

*Labor Day, September 6, 1999: Day 117*

From the spacious upper deck of their three-story home, Karen surveyed the party in progress with the discerning eye of a hostess. The pool, life-guarded by Ethan and his buddies from the pool where he worked, was still full of the shrieking offspring of the employees of Midwest Bank and Millennium Dynamics. The all-weather basketball court was empty of sweaty teenage boys; the last heat of the summer had finally driven them into the pool, too. The adults were scattered across the wooded grounds; some in the pool, some playing croquet, many just sprawled on the lawn furniture, or enjoying the air conditioning of the vast house.

This get-together was billed as "Summer's Last Hurrah" on the invitations that Karen had sent. She hosted one or two such parties each year for Alex's company; fortunately the size of their house had grown with the success of the company. This year everyone seemed to need these breaks more than ever, and this was party number three. Overtime was becoming more frequent as the bank project ran down to the wire; people seemed more on edge, and all appreciated an official chance to relax.

Annette, for example, whom Karen could see talking to Leo, would certainly have been in her office today without the obligation of a party to attend. She was one of the most single-minded people Karen had ever known, and Karen felt fond and protective toward her

"Hey," said her husband, wandering onto the deck behind Karen and putting his arms around her. He kissed her neck. "Great party."

"Hey yourself." Karen leaned back, enjoying the feel of her husband's body. "It's really too hot for that, you know."

"Later, baby." He was teasing now; he never called her baby. "In the air-conditioned comfort of our bedroom."

"Later I'll be scraping you up off the floor with a spatula." Karen laughed. "You know how these things go. You and your little war council won't be able to resist having a meeting after everyone else leaves, and by the time we get to bed, we'll both be too tired."

Alex made a rueful face. "Maybe not. So who are you watching from up here?"

"Oh, I'm just checking things out. Don't Annette and Leo make a nice couple?"

"Annette and Leo?" Alex sounded surprised. "Where?"

"Over there in the hammock." Karen pointed to where Leo was paying court to Annette while she lounged in their hammock.

"Leo goes with Annette when she does her awareness presentations. I don't think they're interested in each other."

Karen stared at him. "You must be joking. Just look at him. Obviously head over heels, poor thing. And Annette is oblivious to anything but her job."

"She's an intense young woman." His gaze wandered. "What do you think of the Russians?"

"They seem nice enough," Karen said. "A bit shy, perhaps. Except for Volodya, he seems to know everyone. The life of the party type."

"I think he's the one who likes Annette," Alex said. They watched Volodya's confident progress across the back yard.

"Oh, well," Karen said, "all the young men like Annette, when it comes to that."

"No, look." Volodya had joined Annette and Leo at the hammock.

"Volodya is more assertive than Leo is," Karen said. "He'll make sure she notices him. And he is quite handsome and European."

The telephone's urgent shrill interrupted them. Karen dashed into the house to answer it, then returned with it in her hand. Her face wore an odd expression.

"Alex, it's the President."

Karen giggled suddenly, then clapped her hand to her mouth.

"I can't help it, Alex, it just sounds so melodramatic." Alex and the President had been roommates for one year in college, although it was not a connection that Alex ever cared to cultivate. When the President had finally begun to understand that the year 2000 problem existed, he had formed a National Year 2000 Advisory Council and asked Alex to be a member. Since his appointment, the President had been a frequent caller, especially of late, and Karen's original awe had evaporated. Privately, she thought the President was becoming a pest. He had implemented only a few of Alex's awareness ideas; more than any- thing now, he seemed to need Alex's reassurances that everything would be all right come January 1st. These were assurances that Alex was reluctant to give.

"Hello, Mr. President." Despite his reservations about the Presi- dent, Alex could not help but be thrilled that the commander-in-chief chose to telephone him for advice.

"Alex, good to hear your voice. And what are you doing on this fine Labor Day weekend?" The President's voice was hearty; press- ing flesh over the telephone.

"We're having a little party out here for my company. We find it keeps morale up." Alex waited for the President to cut to the chase.

"I was just wondering what sort of reaction you'd seen from your mail list since that last y2k initiative," said the President, sounding un- characteristically hesitant.

Alex sighed to himself. "The e-mails I've gotten have been posi- tive, sir. Everyone seems to be pleased with the global perspective, although some of them point out that it may be too late to be anything more than a token gesture."

Maybe the president phoned so often because he so rarely heard an honest opinion.

"Now you're scolding me, Alex," said the President, but his voice was dispirited. "You notice I talked about Year 2000 in my Labor Day speech."

"I'm afraid I didn't catch it, Mr. President, because of the party, but I certainly give you credit for that." The President had in fact been talking about Year 2000 concerns in every speech he had made since March, and that alone had finally caught the world's attention. If the President of the United States talked about it incessantly, it must be important. That had been Alex's argument for months, and when the

President finally implemented it, and saw that people were listening, Alex suddenly became one of his most trusted y2k advisors.

"I'm going to release that federal funding for state and city y2k efforts," said the President suddenly. "I'll do it by executive order; we don't have time to do the dance on Capitol Hill. And I'll cut the bureaucratic red tape for getting it."

"That's a good move," Alex said. He had suggested just this more than a year ago.

"I should have listened to you sooner," said the President. "But Alex, you should be in my position. Everybody wants my attention, everybody thinks his bailiwick is the most important. And a lot of them are important! Between the folks predicting the end of civilization and the folks who said the whole thing was a blip on the computer screen, it was pretty hard to decide what to do!"

"I know, Mr. President." Alex was sympathetic. "But you can still be a leader, even now. You can mobilize people, make it a war effort, encourage them to make preparations. People can do amazing things, even in a short time, for a common cause."

The President sighed. "Sometimes I think that as a country, we don't have too many common causes any more. But you're right. We need a slogan, maybe, a rallying cry." His voice strengthened, picked up enthusiasm. "I'll work on it, Alex. We'll keep in touch. Enjoy your party. Alex — tell them to keep up the good work, we're counting on them."

"I'll be happy to tell them. Good-bye, Mr. President." Alex cradled the phone as Karen waited for a report.

"He's taking it seriously, now," Alex said at her questioning look. "I get the feeling it's keeping him awake at night."

"Good! I hope it's giving him nightmares." Karen had despaired of any help from politicians some months ago, and now concentrated her own efforts on grass roots preparedness. "When I think of all the good he could have done, months ago, and then think of the little good he'll do now that he finally gets it . . ." She shook her head, angry.

"Better late than never." One of Alex's maxims was that they could not give in to despair, or the cause was already lost.

"Well, I guess we'll find out in a few months, won't we?" She took the phone from him. "On with the party, sweetheart, the troops are waiting."

\*      \*      \*

Hardly aware of the noise of the party Annette sat sideways in the hammock, her eyes closed against the glare of the sun, and pushed with her sandaled foot to make the hammock swing. Leo sprawled nearby in a lawn chair, occasionally reaching over to push the hammock when she forgot, or when the effort seemed too great.

Doing nothing felt wonderful. Unoccupied by y2k concerns, her mind drifted to Leo, as it frequently had since the night of the symphony. When she had become aware of his feelings for her, she was ashamed of herself, because she should have seen it sooner. All that time Leo spent helping her - that was for her, not for the Year 2000 effort.

She opened her eyes for a moment, shading them with her hand, and looked at Leo. Although most people would not consider him handsome in the conventional way, his face, relaxed now in the sun's warmth, had character.

Leo smiled at her; he had such a genuinely nice smile. "Do you need anything?"

She shook her head and smiled back. It was on the tip of her tongue to ask him to sit in the hammock with her, but she closed her eyes again.

The mesh of the hammock rose suddenly and tightened under her; there was a bounce as it swung wildly, and Annette slid into the center of the hammock and thumped into another warm body. After a confused impression of tangled limbs and the ground rising to meet her, Annette found herself yanked to safety.

Volodya was under her in the hammock, his arms locked around her to keep her from falling, his face just inches away, blue eyes mocking. The unexpected intimacy of his embrace was unsettling. He was close enough to kiss her, and she wondered what it would be like. He was not just good-looking, he was dashing in the way that only European men were. When he grinned at her suddenly, she had the uncomfortable feeling that he had just read her mind, and she wriggled to free herself. He held on tightly.

"That was nice example of law of physics," he said. "I shifted center of gravity. I saved you."

"Volodya, you idiot, let me up," she said, laughing. He obliged, and

Annette scrambled to her feet, flushed and still laughing. By this time Leo was standing. He caught Annette's arm to steady her .

"I saved her." Volodya looked pleased with himself.

"You nearly threw her out of the hammock," Leo pointed out. Volodya grinned wolfishly at her, and Annette blushed, thinking of their enforced embrace in the hammock, a move that Volodya had doubtless planned.

"Let's go eat something, shall we?" she asked. They turned toward the house, where the barbecue smoked on the deck, and Annette found herself flanked on each side by a personable and brilliant man who wanted her. After months of self-imposed romantic exile, it was a nice feeling.

\*       \*       \*

Alex's y2k team was meeting in the living room, a term that inadequately described it. Glassed in at the end that overlooked the pool, the rest of the room was beautifully paneled in oak that reached to the cathedral ceiling. Overstuffed tapestry and leather seating beckoned to the room's occupants and vases of fresh flowers stood on the end tables. Evening had brought an unseasonable chill, and a small fire glowed in the enormous fireplace.

When Volodya saw the fireplace he parked himself in a leather chair nearby and refused to budge, even when Leo told him that they needed the room for a meeting. Annette watched the Russian as he sprawled there in his khakis and white linen shirt. He looked right at home in the Stauffers' well-appointed living room.

"I come to meeting," he said. After Leo and Annette eventually persuaded him that he would have to leave, he tried to persuade Annette to come with him.

"But I'm the project manager!"

"You should not have meeting on holiday. Come with me, we will find something more fun to do. You too, Leo," he added, but he was looking at Annette.

"Volodya, you're such a tease. Let's walk Volodya to his car, shall we, Leo?"

After Volodya's BMW had finally zoomed away, they hurried back to the house. "Volodya really hates being left out of things, doesn't he?"

said Leo.

"Oh, I think he just likes being in charge," said Annette with a laugh. "I think he wishes he were Alex. He told me several times today that he intends to buy a house like this. His family was quite well-off in Russia, I think, and he has every intention of living like that over here."

"Well, it's the American way," Leo said. They hurried to the living room to find Homer, Tim, Karen, and Eddie already there. Alex came in a few moments later, and closed the tall sliding doors at the end of the room.

"I should start the meeting by apologizing for having it, according to my wife," Alex began, with a teasing glance at Karen. Some laughter, but no resentful faces.

"As I told everyone at the party earlier, the President encourages us to keep up the good work." This brought a snort from Harry, whose kindest comments on the President began with the epithet "liberal, commie-loving wimp."

"Regardless of political leanings," Alex said. "I think we owe the President our thanks for talking about y2k the way he has for the past few months. Way late, I know, but I think he provides some damage control."

Annette nodded. "People have heard of the year 2000 problem, and are willing to listen," she said, "much more so than before he started speaking. Leo and I see it in our awareness meetings."

Harry was never shy about sharing his opinions. "Locally, I think that series of y2k articles by Jim Frazier had as much as anything to do with waking people up." Heads nodded. "And they're going to run a series on preparedness this month."

"We're making progress," Alex agreed. "Can we speculate on our progress at Midwest? Tim?"

Tim stood up, then decided that this was a casual meeting and sat down again. "Our remediation efforts have picked up tremendously since we were able to hire Volodya's team." Everyone waited for Harry's snort of derision, but he disappointed them. "And of course we've been testing, too, for a couple of months. We actually have two programs ready to put back in production."

There was some scattered applause.

"The testing is taking too long, which comes as no surprise." Tim scratched the back of his neck. "I'd say we need to start asking people to work more overtime."

A faint, collective sigh ran around the room.

"With overtime, and the extra bodies we have," Tim continued, "we should have the remediation done in another month - by the beginning of October. Then if we're lucky, we may be able to get enough of our systems testing done to do some end to end testing with the banks that Midwest exchanges data with."

Alex was silent for a moment. "Well, it isn't ideal, is it?" The testing period was far too short. "But I certainly can't fault anyone's efforts. Let's keep on it and see where we are in another month."

"What about the PC testing?" asked Eddie, the lawyer. Eddie, whose idea of dressing down was to wear a loud tie with his dark suit, had astonished everyone at Millennium Dynamics by appearing in a yellow knit shirt and navy Bermudas that showed off his pale legs to no great advantage. "Where's Susan?" Susan was the largest pregnant woman any of them had ever seen, and her girth was the subject of many fascinated conversations around the office coffee machines.

"Ah, I was getting to that," Alex said. "Susan, as you may know, is expecting." The room erupted with laughter at his understatement. Alex went on, "Susan has done a great job, and we are indebted to her. Unfortunately she phoned today to say that her doctor told her last week that he feels her blood pressure is too high, and he's recommending complete bed rest for the rest of her pregnancy." Exclamations of dismay.

"Susan was really upset that she won't be able to finish the job, but she gave me several pages of notes" - Alex held them up - " over the phone and said she'll be available to talk if we need to call her. Fortunately - miraculously! - she managed to check all the commercial off-the-shelf programs, all the operating systems, all the hardware before she left. All the y2k upgrades are patched in, and all the impossibly old systems replaced. The testing is done, except that we need to test PC's and mainframes together, something we can't do until the mainframes are done. Annette and I discussed it earlier today, and we'd like to give Susan's job to Leo."

Leo looked momentarily surprised at the announcement, but he took the papers that Alex offered him.

"What do you say, Leo?" Alex asked. "There's a raise with it, and it's more in your field."

"Thanks, sure, I'd be happy to," Leo replied, already reading the papers. "But what about the legacy systems work I've been doing? And Volodya's team?"

"Well, for the next month," Alex said, "you'll be doing Susan's job in addition to what you're doing now. After the legacy systems are remediated, we won't need Volodya's entire team any more; we'll probably just want Volodya on site and on call for debugging his part of the program. At that stage you'll drop the mainframe stuff and concentrate on coordinating mainframe/PC testing. Are you okay with that?"

Leo nodded, looking unconcerned that his workload had just doubled.

"Alex, can we ask Karen what's going on with the mail list?" Annette asked. None of the y2k team had time to read the hundred or so messages a day which Karen posted to the list, although she forwarded messages to them which she found appropriate.

Karen smiled at everyone. "Well, there's good news and bad news, as you might expect. The good news is, after all this time, we do have people posting to us to say that they've finished their y2k projects. Lots of companies are done, actually, and most of the project managers offer help on the side to those who still need it." She paused. "The bad news is, a lot of companies still need help, and are unlikely to even come close to getting done."

Homer broke in. "Are you talking about the US, or world-wide?"

"The U.S. seems to be in better shape than the rest of the world, but we won't have it all done either. Australia, the U.K., Sweden, Canada, Holland, and New Zealand are in better shape, too. Asia seems to be zipping along at a faster clip than they were at first, based on other countries' help and experience, but they started so late that they can't possibly finish, except for Singapore."

"Singapore?" Tim asked.

Karen made a face. "Evidently the government is so restrictive about so many things that they never had the problem of software diversity that we have. All their software programs had to be alike. And of course they have fewer mainframes to begin with. I don't know what the moral is there. We've gotten lots of e-mail from South America in the past month." Karen continued her survey. "They're scrambling, but I don't see many of them making it. We already know that Russia is a mess, but I don't know that we get any e-mail from them. We get some from Hungary, some from Poland. "

"So you're saying that most of the world won't be ready?" Leo said.

"I would say that based on our e-mail list," Karen corrected him. "I suppose it's a fair sample, I don't know. Bear in mind that the people who write to the list are the ones asking for help, or providing it. How many people don't know enough to ask for help, or don't speak English and so can't use the list? I hate to think!"

Everyone looked gloomy, considering the implications.

*        *        *

After the meeting, Alex and Karen collapsed on the leather sofa.

"Whew!" Karen exclaimed. "I wish I had their energy." She closed her eyes and put her head back against a cushion. Alex admired her profile, still smooth and serene despite her forty-five years.

"You still look pretty good," he said, kissing her on the mouth.

Karen opened her eyes and smiled at him. "Aren't you sweet?" she murmured.

"What were you and Annette talking about in the kitchen?"

Karen laughed. "Oh, men! Annette's eyes were finally opened today. She realized that the boys are in love with her. Well, she wouldn't admit it was love, but she'd certainly already noticed Volodya."

"So she was asking your advice?"

Karen pursed her lips and was thoughtful. "I think she wanted to talk about it with someone. And she wondered what I thought of them both."

"And?"

"I said that Leo was sweet and reliable and Volodya was romantic and mysterious."

"Sweet and reliable?" Alex made a face. "I think you've doomed Leo. Women always go for romantic and mysterious."

Karen punched him in the arm. "So you think! But I don't think Annette wants to make any choices right now. She said she's going to concentrate on her job and let the chips fall where they may." She regarded Alex thoughtfully.

"Are you all right, darling?" she asked.

"Just tired." They walked up the stairs together, Alex hoping fervently that tonight would be nightmare-free. He needed a night of oblivion before he faced the stepped-up pace tomorrow in the year 2000 struggle.

*September 7, 1999: Day 116*

Sergei lounged on a rickety bench in the park near his apartment. Everyone seemed to be there on this beautiful autumn day that arrived disguised as summer. Two young boys were sailing wooden boats on the pond, standing in the water with their pants rolled up above their knees. Giggling, they pushed their boats this way and that, getting each other wetter and wetter, until a stern babushka shook her finger at them and herded them back to dry land.

A gaggle of little girls ran down the path in front of Sergei, each of them sporting the inevitable gigantic white bow in her hair, as if a flock of migrant butterflies had flown through the park and alighted, mistaking the girls for flowers.

Sergei watched the familiar scene with affection while he pondered the death sentence he had just received. Two weeks ago he had run into Dr. Svetlana Onegin, an old friend, and mentioned to her that he intended to come in for a check-up some time. She had given him one discerning glance, then insisted that he come to the clinic that afternoon. She had written down his symptoms, run some tests, and asked him to return in a week. He had seen her again today.

"You have hepatitis C," she told him bluntly as he sat across from her desk in the shabby room that passed as her office. "It is a viral disease usually caused by infected blood. Have you ever had a blood transfusion?"

Sergei nodded. "I was shot by accident during a training maneuver in the army. I needed a transfusion." He paused. "But Svetya, that was more than thirty years ago!"

Svetlana was not surprised. "Hepatitis C may not show up for years after the initial transmission. Only recently have we even had a name for it, hepatitis C. Before that we called it non-A, non-B."

"But hepatitis is not so serious, is it?" She was looking rather grim, he thought, for something as mild as hepatitis.

"Other forms of hepatitis are more treatable." She seemed to be weighing her words, which was unusual for Svetlana. She was infamous for her brutal bedside manner. After a lengthy pause, she became decisive once again.

"Hepatitis C has no treatment," she told him. "I am afraid, Sergei, that you have cirrhosis of the liver. This means that your liver is scarred, and will be progressively unable to function properly. You already exhibit some of the symptoms - jaundice, distended abdomen, weight loss. Have you vomited blood?"

"No!" said Sergei, frightened.

"Your blood tests show the elevated liver enzymes and you test positive for for HCV - the hepatitis C virus. A liver biopsy would show us the extent of damage to your liver, but judging from your symptoms, the damage is extensive already. Given the deplorable condition of our hospital, I would not recommend the biopsy."

"You say there is no treatment. What will happen to me?" Sergei tried to speak calmly. Svetlana looked distressed, but she would not mince words.

"My dear Sergei Ivanovitch, your liver is dying. It is covered with scar tissue and is increasingly unable to filter the toxins from your body. Eventually these toxins will affect your mind, you will lapse into a coma, and you will die." Sergei shivered. "The only thing that can save you is a liver transplant."

Reeling from the impact of her words, Sergei immediately grasped this straw. "A transplant? I can get a transplant?"

Svetlana dropped her professional stance. "Seryozha, if you have friends in high places, perhaps it can be arranged. You would have to go abroad; we do not do liver transplants here, only heart transplants. Our hospitals are in such terrible shape, we can hardly provide normal care." She looked fierce for a moment. "I would like to personally cut out the liver of our fearless leader and give it to you!" She smiled wryly. "Of course, his liver is probably in far worse shape than yours."

Sergei had tried to laugh at her grim joke, but his hands were shaking when he left the clinic. Now, he was struck by the beauty of the day, the brightness of the sunshine, the way the leaves danced on the trees when the wind blew. Since he'd arrived in the park, he had been watching the children. Youth and age. Life and death. He could not go home to tell Masha, not yet. He was not ready to die, and a desperate man might yet find a way to live.

# Chapter 11

*September 8, 1999: Day 115*

Annette was working at the Stauffers' tonight, a plot hatched by Alex and Karen to slow her down a little, she suspected, but she didn't mind. Working here was less efficient. The children wandered in to say hi, Karen brought hot chocolate and plopped herself down for a chat - even Alex was much less formal than in the office, teasing her and making sure she went home early enough to get some rest. But it was homey, and she always felt more relaxed when she left.

Tonight Ethan and Elizabeth were all abuzz over a project they were to do for school.

"Teen Bug Busters!" said Ethan, striking a superhero pose. "It's a service project. Kids who know about computers are going to be trained to help charities look at their y2k problems. The first class is tonight."

"What a good idea!" said Annette, who had always worried about the charities. Alex had his pro bono work, but he could only do so much.

Elizabeth hurtled off to answer the doorbell and returned with Leo in tow. "We'll be ready in just a minute," she said. "I want to change my jeans. Wait!" She dashed upstairs.

"Well, Leo, hello," Annette said. He was dressed in corduroys and a sweatshirt, and when he smiled, Annette thought again how nice he was.

"Hi, Annette."

"Ethan and Elizabeth were telling me about their service project," she said. "Another of Alex's good ideas."

An odd look flickered across Leo's face, but he didn't say anything.

"But it was Leo's idea, Annette," said Ethan. "Wasn't it Leo?"

Leo shrugged. "I'm helping out with it."

"But Leo," said Ethan, insistent. "Don't you remember? You told me how you were watching some twelve-year-old kid at Radio Shack help a customer figure out a computer problem, and then you thought, you know, 'Awesome, those kids could help with y2k.' You talked to the principals at the high schools. And you're going to train us, right?"

Leo spread his hands, smiling a little. Annette, staring at him open-mouthed, thought he looked embarrassed.

"What can I say?" he said at last. "Yeah."

"Leo, that's a wonderful idea!" said Annette. "Why didn't you say anything to me?"

Elizabeth came thundering down the stairs and saved Leo from having to answer. "Let's go!"

Annette waved them off.

Two hours later she logged off her laptop and was gathering her papers together when Ethan and Elizabeth burst into the house with Leo. She could hear them laughing and talking with Karen and Alex in the kitchen, and was about to join them when Leo appeared bearing a tray with two cups of cocoa.

"Compliments of Karen. Have you finished?"

She took the mug he offered and sipped the warm chocolate. "For now. How did your meeting go?"

"Great!" He threw himself on the loveseat next to her. "Some of those kids are so into computers, it's about the only thing they're comfortable talking about. But they're excited about helping the charities, it'll do them some good and keep them out of trouble. Smart kids are always tempted to make mischief with computers. The concentration of information and power in the hands of an elite."

"And you're part of that elite?" Annette said.

"Well, sure, but I got over the power trip long ago," Leo said. "Anyway," he continued, "a lot of those kids think of themselves as nerds in the derogatory sense of the word, and I'm sure it'll do them good to be heroes."

"Were you ever a nerd, Leo?" she asked, grinning.

"I was a lot younger than most of my friends - in fact, I had mostly adult friends, people who were intellectually curious about the same things. When I got to grad school - I was nineteen then - that's when things started to even out. I looked older than I was. I finally started dating." He shook his head. "It's funny, Volodya and I have a lot in common - the whole child prodigy thing. But when it comes to women -" He broke off suddenly. "Never mind. Seeing the kids tonight made me remember how out of place I felt sometimes when I was growing up."

"But, Leo, you turned out very well." Annette was suddenly anxious that he should know this. "No one who meets you would ever think of you as socially inept. Any woman would be happy to go out with you."

"Any woman except you." Leo was grinning, and Annette realized she had been caught out. "You look pretty when you're blushing." He leaned toward her to touch her cheek with his fingertips, then removed the cocoa mug from her hands and set it on the table. She realized with a start that he intended to kiss her, and, what's more, that she wanted him to.

His lips were gentle, moving softly against hers, exploring, but she could feel the passion restrained beneath. Then his hands were on her shoulders, pulling her to her feet, although he hadn't really stopped kissing her, and then he pulled her close and she couldn't tell whether it was his heart she could feel pounding or hers.

The kiss went on and on, and Annette began to feel light-headed. Dizzy with desire, she thought. She had never been kissed so thoroughly in her life, and she pressed her body against his. When Leo abruptly released her, she staggered, dazed.

"Goodness!" Her knees were so weak she had to sit down on the loveseat. Leo sat next to her, looking lustful and sheepish at once.

"I'm sorry, Annette, I kind of forgot where we were." Leo's finger traced the line of her jaw, ran lightly down her nose, then outlined her lips. "Would you like to go somewhere else - your place, my place?"

"No," she said. She leaned her head against the back of the loveseat and closed her eyes, mustering the scraps of her self-control. Next to her, Leo sighed and moved away.

"Annette?" She opened her eyes to look into his. "What am I

116

supposed to think? Are you angry?"

"Hardly!" Annette could still feel the imprint of his mouth on hers. "I don't know what to think myself. I wanted you to kiss me. I didn't expect to be swept away like that." She put her hands to her cheeks; they were still flushed. "This wasn't on my schedule."

"Maybe your schedule isn't flexible enough." Leo regarded her steadily, and Annette felt a little tug of desire. "Maybe you should try to work me in."

"Maybe we should take it very slowly."

"Ha! One kiss in eight months? That's your idea of moving quickly?"

"I think that kiss covered a lot of ground," she said. She realized that she was staring at Leo's mouth and she wrenched her eyes away, but not before he noticed. If he started kissing her again, she thought, she would follow him mindlessly, to his place, to hers, wherever. But if her body was ready, her mind wasn't.

Leo stood up. "Have it your way. I won't push you."

"You're such a sweetie." She would have liked to kiss him, but she didn't trust herself. By mutual consent they joined the Stauffers in the kitchen for a few minutes, then drove home in their separate cars.

As she drove, Annette found herself reliving Leo's kiss. Her impassioned response had caught her by surprise; perhaps her body was trying to tell her something that her mind was too stubborn to hear. Four more months of y2k preparations. That seemed a good long time to wait, if she was serious about keeping to her original commitment. Maybe it was time to loosen up the schedule.


*September 24,1999: Day 99*

The cameras that registered the activities of Midwest National Bank's patrons and employees were computerized, the films automatically archived by date on a weekly basis. The security supervisor reviewed them at random, unless occasion warranted.

Today the camera was recording a crime, but even upon closer viewing the security supervisor would be unlikely to recognize it as a crime. The programmer caught on film was simply doing a job and doing it efficiently.

The programmer first checked his e-mail on the computer terminal. The angle of the camera did not allow a view of the computer screen, so no visual record would exist of the e-mail that the programmer received - an e-mail sent from a home computer that very morning. The e-mail contained a macro and an algorithm, both mailed in uu-encoded, or non-binary form, to avoid the bank's virus checker.

The film continued to roll. The programmer hit the single key that was designed to trigger the macro. The macro inserted the code, recompiled it, changed the code back to binary form, then entered the library where the code would be stored, deleting the programmer's name from the log.

The camera could not comment on the brilliance of the macro that handled the compile, converting the attachment into a neat package of code to store in the mainframe's source code. Nor could it document the programmer's choice of a hiding place for the algorithm, a normally unreferenced object library. This was a storage area for subroutines, the sets of computer instuctions that performed certain small tasks over and over again. Because this library no longer performed a useful function, but had been overlooked and left in the program, the algorithm would rest there safely.

The camera faithfully filmed the actions happening before it, but today's record would be tossed away as useless, if it were ever viewed at all. The only cell of film that carried anything approaching evidence of a crime was the one that contained an image of the programmer's smile.

*September 27, 1999: Day 96, Moscow*

Sergei huddled in the uncomfortable chair in his friend Konstantin's anteroom. His heart pounded unsteadily and his body was bathed in a clammy sweat from climbing the stairs. Cursing his country's inability to do a simple thing like keep the elevators running, Sergei waited to be shown into Konstantin's office. As his sickness subsided Sergei noted with approval the plush carpet and expensive furniture in the office. Konstantin was a high-ranking bureaucrat in a country of bureaucrats; he had done well, and was therefore all the more likely to be able to help him.

"Sergei Ivanovitch Krzyzanowski," the young receptionist said, nodding at him. He rose with rubbery legs and made his way across the carpet and through his friend's door.

"Kostya," he said as he entered.

"Seryozha!" Konstantin rose, his arms outstretched in welcome. The smile on his broad face quickly changed to a look of concern.

"My friend! Sit down! You are not looking well at all, Sergei, here, let me help you." Konstantin solicitously moved a chair near his desk and helped him ease down into it. He shook his friend's hand and looked into his face.

"The disease progresses," he said, returning to his own leather chair. "I am sorry to see you looking so ill, Sergei."

"With a new liver, they tell me, I will feel like a young man again. What news do you have for me, old friend?"

Konstantin's face became even more somber.

"Speaking frankly, Sergei, it is not possible to obtain a liver transplant here. You knew this yourself already." Konstantin was agitated; he hated to give his friend bad news. "I wish I could tell you something else."

"As you said, I knew this already. I wish you to find a clinic for me abroad."

Konstantin looked away from him, his eyes focusing on some point outside the office window.

"I am so sorry, my friend," he said at last. He walked around the desk and took Sergei's hand. "You will not be permitted to leave the country."

"What! There must be some mistake." Sergei removed his hand in protest. "I am a private citizen; I have some funds. We have the freedom to leave the country; I can emigrate if I want to."

Konstantin sighed. "Some of us have that freedom. Sergei, they do not tell me everything, and I do not want to know, but evidently you have had some dealings with the FSB lately."

Sergei stared. "At their request! I did what they asked! Why would they question me?"

"It seems that now you have some knowledge that they do not want to leave the country."

*September 28, 1999: Day 95*

Janet Brock key-carded the door of the mainframe room, entered, and approached the bank's year 2000 test box. She carefully lowered the hinged panel on the front that contained a laptop computer used for monitoring the output of the mainframe itself. After typing a few instructions into the keyboard of the laptop, Janet waited for the spate of reports that it was her job to check.

Janet was the Subject Matter Expert, or SME, trained to look at test results and interpret them. She was a large, pleasant woman who normally headed Midwest National's information technology testing. Ostensibly she was still the IT testing head, but while the y2k conversion project was in place, the Millennium Dynamics people were running the show. Janet was a team player, and she had no problem with this; she was even feeling rather optimistic this morning. The testing was going surprisingly well, with fewer bugs to fix than she would have expected. God must be answering her prayers.

As the test results, in the form of an on-screen report, began to appear on the screen of the laptop, Janet compared it to another set of outputs that should match it. She knew the bank's system thoroughly; she had worked here for fifteen years, and this was a good job for her.

Right now she was checking the computer reports against her personal reports. For years now she had maintained this routine, and instructions for it were customized into any new software that the bank purchased or upgraded for her. Because - face it - there were always going to be times when the computer was down, and the times were never convenient.

So even throughout the y2k testing, Janet maintained her private workaround and received a replicated copy of the compile log each time the mainframe compiled, routed right on to her desktop PC.

Oops. Janet stopped scrolling down the screen and looked at the output in puzzlement. According to the computer, this library was rarely used and had not been called in eighteen months. According to her replicated copy, this library had been called just a few days ago.

Janet instructed the computer to call up the library records. Nothing. But according to her data, this library had been called all right, and only a few days earlier. And who had called it? She looked at her compile log and noted the name of the programmer on her pad.

Well, the computer had nothing else to tell her. She would have to pay the culprit a visit and ask him why on earth he had found a need to call that library. After scribbling the information in her notebook, Janet continued to peruse the test log for abnormalities.

That afternoon she interviewed the programmer, listening carefully to his esoteric, but highly plausible explanation. He was rather sweet, really, and the anomaly was explained to Janet's satisfaction. She put a careful checkmark next to his name in her notebook.

# Chapter 12

*September 30, 1999: Day 93*

Norman Krebbs sometimes wondered if his life would have been different if his mother had named him Matt or Bill or even Joe - a more regular sort of name. The other kids had teased him about his name - "Norman isn't normal!" was the usual chant - and although that had faded with time, Norman thought perhaps that he had chosen an accounting career just because it seemed so suited to his name. With a different name, he could have been a test pilot or an archaeologist.

In more lucid moments, he realized that he chose accounting because it suited him. He was obsessively neat. Double entry bookkeeping represented his idea of an orderly universe, with God entering a debit in the ledger for each sin, and a credit for each act of kindness. Although his pastor had pointed out the theological inadequacies of this view, Norman still kept the image in the back of his mind.

All in all, Norman was proud of being a bean counter, and he even liked the derisive term, capitalizing it in his mind. Captain Bean Counter, he thought in his playful moods, whose mission is to seek out and destroy any imbalances in the accounting system! Not that he looked like a super hero, with chiseled features and well-defined muscles. No, his features were not chiseled, but rounded, and his muscles were less defined than hinted at. Norman was disappointed in his looks, but Iris, his wife of three months, told him that his blue eyes were beautiful in his rather round face, and even if his mouth didn't look sensuous, she knew for a fact it was.

With that in mind, Norman sat down to wrestle again with the month's end balancing cycle for the Department of Defense. Norman worked at Defense Finance Accounting Services, DFAS, one of five centers that was created in 1990 by merging seven other agencies to handle payments to all branches of the military. Almost one-third of the Department of Defense budget was disbursed by the Columbus center. Because Norman did his job well and had worked there for eight years, he was assigned to balance the "special fund," which other accountants referred to disrespectfully as the slush fund. In fact, most employees were not supposed to know that such a fund existed, but such secrets tended to leak out over time.

The special fund was by definition a slippery creature to balance, but Norman was so conscientious that he had always managed it, up to now. And now he could see that a huge - really huge - amount of money was missing and unaccounted for.

Norman stared out his window for inspiration. DFAS, which they all pronounced "Dee-fass", accenting the first syllable, was housed in the former Rockwell aircraft construction plant, on the south border of Port Columbus International Airport, parallel to the runway. Although the immense, sprawling complex contained about a million square feet of floor space, and Building 6 itself once housed the simultaneous construction of several large military aircraft, Norman's allotment was only nine by twelve, four humble walls and a door. The interior offices were windowless and the other offices overlooked the parking lot, so he appreciated his window and his view of the runway, but today the sight of the commercial jets lifting off did not thrill him as it usually did. What was wrong with his books?

Hours of poring over the reconciliation process log had yielded no explanations, and Norman was growing frustrated. Balancing the special fund was a point of honor with him; he had to find the error. He sighed, and prepared to review all the logs again.

Four hours later Norman was no closer to the truth. He knew that it was possible that a transaction could have taken place, the money been withdrawn, and the paperwork still be in transit - and in that case, he would have the explanation next month. Although this had happened to him once or twice, it had never involved such a mammoth amount of money. Maybe some bright boy in the State Department had authorized the purchase of a load of borax from Russia - although that would be a shitload of borax.  Maybe it was two or three simultaneous purchases, which would explain the large amount of money.  Officials were sometimes skittish when it came to acknowledging the Russian transactions, and certainly no one felt any compunction to let him in on the secret.

Well, Captain Bean Counter was out of ideas and out of time.  He would make a note to check on it next month - not that he would forget! - and he would make sure it balanced.  His honor as an accountant was at stake.

*    *    *

Volodya, Leo, and the Russian programming team sat in the shiny vinyl booths at Dalt's Restaurant, arguing noisily about Russian politics. Tim and Harry and another programmer were seated on the other side of the restaurant; Volodya would have invited Tim to join them, but not if it meant eating with Harry, too.

A lull came in the argument, and the programmers realized they could hear Harry's voice.

"The wife's trying to lower my cholesterol again," Harry was saying in a resigned tone.  "Better give me a stinking salad."

Tim laughed, and then could be clearly heard to order a steak sandwich and a Manhattan on the rocks with a twist of lime.

"Harry is on a diet," Ivan said, smiling broadly.  Everyone laughed; since Harry's unsuccessful altercation with Volodya weeks ago, he had been the butt of many jokes.  "Hey, Vasily, why are you staring at Harry?"

Vasily whipped his head around.  "I am trying to see how many pounds Harry needs to lose," he said.  Ivan laughed.  Volodya looked at his team and took a bite of his own hamburger.

After a few minutes of amused eavesdropping, they had lost interest in Harry's commentary on his grandchildren, but now his laughter drew stares from all over the restaurant.

". . . and I said, hell no, you don't have to do that.  I can fix that code right now, and you won't have to touch your source code.  So then I used the back door, and they just scratched their heads like it was magic.  Never did catch on."

"I still don't understand what you did," said the third person in Tim's party. "What's a back door?"

"Oh, you PC guys missed out on the fun, didn't they, Tim?" Harry asked. "See, a back door is when you write a line or two of your code like this." He scribbled something on a napkin. "It's null, see, doesn't perform any function in the program."

"Okay," said the third man.

"Now, suppose you decide you want to change the source code for some reason. That's just a pain in the butt - compiling and recompiling it, testing it over and over. But, when you've made yourself a back door, it's simple. You just write your new code, and then call it from another program. For example," Harry scribbled some more. Leo saw Ivan and Vasily exchange glances, then Alyosha actually looked in Harry's direction.

"Oh, I see! That's really clever," said the programmer in Harry's party. "Excuse me, guys, I need to use the john." The third guy took off.

Tim spoke. "You didn't tell him that we put those back doors in the bank's source code, did you Harry?"

Harry snorted. "Not likely! Only a few people know about that. If we need the back doors, we'll use them; it'll be a real time-saver and God knows we need to save time. But I'm not going to tempt anyone to do something improper by telling them about the back doors." Harry picked up the napkin he had written on and crumpled it, shoving it into his trouser pocket. The two men made ready to leave.

"I'll get the tip, Tim," said Harry. "I've got some change in here someplace." He rummaged around in his pockets for a moment, and then the napkin fell on the floor as Harry pulled out a handful of change. Harry didn't notice. He probably couldn't even see his feet over that paunch.

*     *     *

"Here is CD you like. Miles Davis." Reaching across Annette's desk, Volodya extended the plastic case.

"Why, thank you, Volodya." Annette took his offering. They'd had a cup of coffee together yesterday at the bank. Chatting about jazz, which they both liked, she had mentioned that her favorite recording of Davis was missing. And now this.

He was lingering in her office. She really couldn't ask him to stay; this wasn't business. But it was sweet of him to give her the CD. She rose and walked with him to the door. When he turned to say good-bye, she noticed again how very blue his eyes were.

"I have nice stereo system; you should hear it," he said.

Annette laughed. "Oh, Volodya, how many women have you lured into your apartment with that old line?"

Unfazed, he smiled at her, his eyes assessing and approving. "For you, I will think of better way."

*       *       *

The programmer spread the napkin on his knee and studied it avidly.

DATA DIVISION (Ref. PMAP of a 'CALL')

Define Values (hex) to create machine language of a CALL..

01 XXXX  PIC 9(X) COMP VALUE IS "14,733,842"

(X 'E0D244')

LAST DATA DIV. ENTRY:

01 XXXXXXXX PIC 9(4)

01  TAG-ABCD  OCCURS  2  TIMES  INDEXED  BY XXXXXXXX.

05 Define to Reflect Object Code

05 Structure of a Call.

05  Use as many as you need.


05 FILLER PIC X(NNNN)

Note: NNNN must be 1/9 (one ninth) of space between beginning of this 01 Level (minus # Characters defined in 05 levels) and location of dummy parameters.


PROCEDURE DIVISION.

Note: Scatter moves throughout the PROC. DIV. But Execute SET XXXXXXXX to 9 first..

MOVE FIRST-XXXX TO FIRST-XXXXXX.

MOVE SECOND-XXXX to SECOND-XXXXXXXX

(Note: After all moves are accomplished, perform the call.)

PERFORM CALL-DUMMY-PARAMETERS THRU CALL-

DUMMY-EXIT..
(Note: Dummy Parameters may be located anywhere)
CALL-DUMMY-PARAMETERS.
IF "this or that", IF "these or these" (Enough for 48 BYTES of
Actual CALL.)
CALL-DUMMY-EXIT.

A smile of triumph spread across his face. It was a way in! He had suspected it from Harry's explanation, but seeing the written code clinched it.

Harry and Tim had carefully programmed back doors into the bank's source code, a trick from their days as federal programmers. They simply programmed null code - code that was essentially useless and served no function - into the program. However, this null code could be made to function later. If they wanted to insert a new piece of source code into the program without doing a recompile - and nobody wanted to do that, it was too slow - then they could design the new code so that it could be called by the null code. The null code now had a purpose and was no longer null. This was a back door, a kind of programmer insurance against having to do lengthy recompiles when the source code needed a change.

Once the code was inserted, it was invisible. It left no trail, and no one would have any idea how it got there. Tim might suspect, eventually, but they would still have no idea who could have inserted the code, and by the time they found it, it would already have done its damage.

The programmer folded the napkin carefully. He could sit at home, at his own PC, and insert the code from there. No one to see him, no one to suspect, no chance of getting caught.


*October 5, 1999: Day 88*


Leo collapsed gratefully into his bed, resigned to a hangover. Two a.m. He wondered if Volodya always kept such late hours. He had phoned Leo in a jovial mood, taken him out to dinner at a local rib house, and offered him a job in the event Volodya's company ever started doing really well,

"We would make good team," Volodya had said. Leo was flattered.

Leo mostly avoided thinking about what he would do after December, since he still hoped that Annette would be involved in his future. He knew that she was attracted to him; her passionate response to his kiss was proof of that.

But he wanted more from her than acquiescence; he wanted wholehearted commitment. Because he had been the initiator of their entire relationship, he was waiting for her now to give him a signal that it was something she wanted, too, not something that he was pushing her into.

Well, he might like working for Volodya, he decided. And Volodya was right on one count; he needed to think about the future. He remembered Annette's sad little story about Mick O'Toole.


*October 29, 1999: Day 64*

Norman Krebbs was ready. For a month he had planned his attack on the DoD special fund with the precision of a four-star general; it would yield up its secrets and balance or else. Captain Bean Counter to the rescue! He began with the standard account reconciliation process, divide and conquer. When it yielded no results, he moved on to more obscure inquiries.

By lunchtime Norman was beginning to feel slightly nauseated. Nothing was working. In fact, something seemed to be terribly wrong. He forced himself to eat the sack lunch his wife had packed. If he ate, he could concentrate better and find the silly mistake that was eluding him.

At three o'clock Norman abruptly pushed back his chair. His face was chalky, his hands were sweaty, and his heart pounded in his ears. He was sure, one hundred percent, undeniably, beyond a shadow of a doubt sure that he had not made a single error. And if he hadn't made any errors, then he had an abomination on his ledgers, and only one way to account for it. Fraud. Massive, unthinkable fraud.

Pull yourself together, Captain Bean Counter. There's a master criminal out there, and it's up to you to capture him. Norman scolded himself until he was able to release his white-knuckled grip of the desk chair. He had to think clearly.

One thing he knew. This was the kind of information that was deep-sixed the moment it was found. He was certain that the fewer the people who knew, the better. His immediate supervisor was retiring in two weeks; he wouldn't want to know. His supervisor's supervisor was at a meeting in Washington, D. C. That meant that he, Norman, would have to jump the chain of command and get this information into the right hands.

Norman considered. Then he logged off his computer, left his desk and trotted down the hall as if he were going to the bathroom. Instead, he headed toward the catwalk. It overhung the former construction space that sat like a vast, empty hangar between the two sets of offices in Building 6, the runway side offices and the parking lot side offices. His destination was at the opposite corner from his own office; he figured on a fifteen-minute walk; ten if he hurried. Never mind, he would have some time to think.

As he trotted past the dozens of offices that lined the corridor, Norman wondered which of the occupants was behind the embezzlement he had just discovered. Surely the perpetrator was someone on the inside. Could it be someone he knew, another payment clerk who smiled blandly at him each morning while secretly socking away mammoth amounts of cash? Indignant at the thought, Norman marched along faster, now past the bullpen, where lower-ranking payment clerks were denied proper offices. They had instead to work in partitioned cubicles in an otherwise open area. Norman hated the bullpen, congested, noisy, and public as it was; maybe a disenchanted bullpen occupant had taken the money.

Reaching the catwalk, Norman bounded up the ten stairs. He often fantasized about the catwalk. Eight feet wide and fifty feet long, it would make a terrific set for an action film. He could picture the good and bad guys clambering up and down the catwalk while getaway cars, or maybe even tanks, careened around in the cavernous construction space below, the echoing silence shattered by the sound of automatic gunfire. Now he had discovered the high-tech equivalent of that sort of action scene - computer fraud. The results were less bloody, perhaps, but just as destructive.

Norman clattered down the catwalk steps and zoomed left into the corridor, nearly flattening a colleague. Better slow down, he was beginning to pant. On his right loomed a set of the enormous tub files which dotted Building 6. Four feet high and fifteen feet long, they contained file after rotating file of the hard copy defense contracts whose payments DFAS processed. Norman wondered whether all the contracts still had to be kept on paper, or whether some were computerized now, and whether that raised problems for the y2k project team, who, last he'd heard, were still working feverishly to meet their deadline. At least that was not his problem.

"Hey, Norman." Norman swiveled around guiltily to see Sylvia Gardener, a member of the programming team with whom he'd been working on a special project. It had ended just a few weeks ago. The IT department was in a different building, and he hadn't seen her since.

Norman stopped walking; he didn't want Sylvia to know where he was going. "Haven't seen you in a while, Sylvia, how's your life?"

He always tried to be nice to Sylvia, since she seemed to be such an unhappy person, but she embodied most of the qualities he disliked in a woman. She was loud and graceless and her attempts at humor were mostly insulting. She was smart, though; of all the IT people on the team, she was the one who seemed to understand best how the accounting system should work. He could imagine the notes scribbled in the margin of her personnel file: hard-working and intelligent, low social skills.

Today, though, she actually smiled at him, making her thin face with its tangle of dishwater blond hair almost attractive. "My life's great!" Her pale blue eyes looked deeply into his; she always made him nervous that way.

"I'm glad to hear it." Norman didn't want to stand there and exchange pleasantries, but she seemed in no hurry to go anywhere. "Any particular reason your life is great?"

"My boyfriend," she told him conspiratorially, yanking something on a chain from the neck of her sweater. He examined the small enameled egg.

"Nice. Wrong season, aren't you?" Sylvia could be counted on to wear a flag pin on the Fourth of July and a Santa Claus sweater for Christmas. Today, in fact, two little jack-o-lanterns swung grinning from her ears, not really a match for the Easter egg on the chain.

"My boyfriend gave it to me, silly. It doesn't show under my sweater anyway." She tucked it back, leaving a faint bulge on her chest. "He's a really nice guy, Norm."

"I'm glad for you, Sylvia." The boyfriend had made a definite change for the better in Sylvia's personality. He glanced at his watch, wishing Sylvia would take the hint.

"Important meeting?" Sylvia asked with a sneer, as if she doubted his presence would be required for an important meeting. Maybe she hadn't changed so much.

"No, I just left something in my car. How about you?"

"Just doing some follow-up on our project." Sylvia took a step toward the nearest office. "So long." She disappeared inside and Norman hurried down the corridor.

Glancing at his watch again, Norman put Sylvia out of his mind and tried to outline a strategy. The office of the Accounting and Finance Officer, usually shortened to the A & FO for convenience, seemed even further away than usual, given the burden of his knowledge. The phrase "shooting the messenger" kept coming into his mind. Each person who passed him seemed to stare suspiciously, knowing that he was outside his usual bailiwick. Norman finally had to slip into a bathroom to fortify his resolve. He washed his hands and face nervously. What on earth was he going to say?

At last, the windowed door with the sign Accounting and Finance Officer. Norman took a deep breath (up, up and away, Captain Bean Counter!) and opened the door.

"Do you have an appointment?" the A &FO's secretary asked, in a tone that implied that she thought it highly unlikely.

"No. Is he in?"

"He's with someone else right now."

"Is he with someone important?"

"He's with the Administrator," the secretary said. "Not that it's any of your business."

The Administrator must be the Administrator of DFAS itself, and doubtless the first person the A & FO would tell, once Norman enlightened him. Norman decided to save the A & FO some time.

"I'll wait," he told the secretary, and seated himself near the door to the interior office. As soon as she looked down again at her desk, he sprang up, opened the door, and was in the inner sanctum before the secretary could reach him. The A & FO, a large, bearded man, looked askance at the secretary.

"I'm terribly sorry, sir," she began, but the A & FO waved her away.

"Never mind," he said in a voice that reminded Norman of the locusts that rasped outside his window in August. The man bent a lowering gaze on Norman.

"You mind telling me what's so damned important?" The other man, the Administrator, looked at Norman with detached interest, as if he were a biology experiment gone awry.

"It's the DoD Special Fund, sir." Norman saw the two men exchange glances.

"What about it?" The A & FO didn't ask, he demanded. Norman hadn't quite worked out the best way to tell them, and under the combined gaze of the two important men, diplomatic explanations failed him.

"Some money is missing," he said, finally. "I'm the one who balances the account every month. I've done it for a long time, and I've never come up short like this before. I thought you should know."

"You came clear up here to tell us about an accounting error?" the A & FO snapped.

"No! It's not an error!" Norman all but shouted. "You can look at the ledgers yourselves. The money is gone."

"Well, now, son, it's good that you're so conscientious. Why don't you just show the problem to your supervisor and let him help you figure out where you went wrong."

"I did not make a mistake, sir," said Norman slowly and distinctly, as if to a dim child. "I'm telling you because I didn't think you'd want my supervisor to know, given the amount of money involved."

The Administrator spoke at last. "How much is it, then?"

Norman took a deep breath before he spoke. "The Special Fund is missing eleven million, seven hundred and fifty-eight thousand, six hundred and twenty-seven dollars and thirty-five cents."

# Chapter 13

In the midst of his y2k worries, Homer Jones took time to celebrate. Today was the signing of Frank Morgan's loan, the result of nearly a year of negotiations. The loan was a coup for both of them.

Homer had grown up a farm boy in southern Ohio, and the rapid loss of Ohio's farmland to commercial development had always alarmed him. He hated to see the rich black topsoil disappear under the asphalt of countless parking lots, but Midwest's location in the small town of Powell, on the northern edge of Columbus, meant that he was privy to deal after depressing deal, farmers selling their land to developers for big bucks.

Frank Morgan was a childhood friend who'd lived on a nearby farm. His brother had long been slated to take over the family farm, so Frank had borrowed money and bought a small farm outside northern Columbus, where he prospered as much as a small farmer could. He really needed more acreage, and when he learned that the farmers on either side of him wanted to sell, he contacted Homer at once to see if his bank could secure the loan.

Buying two farms was an expensive proposition, but Homer went after the loan with zeal, even persuading the loan officers to loan Frank the deposit money on the properties. An East coast developer had his eye on the land for his long-term portfolio. Homer felt a quiet satisfaction in knowing that he was helping the land stay green and stay local.

So although he did not usually attend loan signings, Homer was hosting this one in his own office. He wanted to shake his friend's hand, and take him out to lunch afterwards to celebrate.

"Frank, Charlotte, it's great to see you here." Homer shook their hands and steered them to the table where they would sign the papers with the bank's loan officer. Frank and his wife were beaming, their dream about to come true at last. Salt of the earth, thought Homer, a phrase his father used to describe honest, hard-working people. Homer meant it as a high compliment.

Homer took a seat and listened to Charlotte's southern Ohio twang with pleasure. She and Frank had been high school sweethearts, and seeing them always made Homer feel nostalgic. The loan officer was explaining the lengthy process of paper-signing when Homer's phone buzzed. Annoyed, he picked it up.

"I gave strict orders that I was not to be disturbed."

The voice at the other end was that of Mark Pilcher, Midwest's senior loan officer.

"I'm sorry, Mr. Jones, I need to talk to you right away."

"It can wait until after this loan is completed, surely."

"It concerns this loan, Mr. Jones, and I don't think you want the Morgans to hear you discussing it on the phone. Can you meet me in the conference room? We need to talk somewhere private."

"I'll be right there." Homer put the phone down. Couldn't his employees do anything right? "Sorry, Frank and Charlotte, somebody's messed up something and I have to run out and check on it. I'll be right back."

"Shall I start them with the signing, Mr. Jones?" the loan officer asked.

Remembering what Mark had said, Homer shook his head. "No, I'd like to check this out, first. Some minor glitch. Sorry to inconvenience you." He gave Frank and Charlotte a reassuring smile, then trotted in the direction of the conference room. This had better be good, he thought.

He strode into the paneled conference room where his senior loan officer was sitting at the table with a sheaf of computer printouts. He sprang up as soon as he saw Homer.

"Mr. Jones, we can't do the loan," Mark said.

"Can't do the loan? Of course we can do the loan. We're signing the papers right now. Everything's checked out. Frank and Charlotte are approved."

"It's not the Morgans, sir - it's us."

*¿Us?¡*

"Us. The bank. Midwest. We're not solvent, sir, that's what I wanted to tell you. If we make that loan, our capital will fall below the minimum required by the bank's charter."

"That's not possible." He took the stack of computer printouts and perused them.

"I was running the transaction ledger this morning and the computer flagged the Morgans' loan and a whole list of other pending loans. Look at this withdrawal." Homer's eyes followed Mark's finger. "It put our reserves too low."

*¡Nine million, five hundred and twenty thousand dollars!¡* Homer was briefly stunned. "Mark, that's ridiculous. I don't remember a transaction this size, and believe me, I'd remember."

"I know." Mark's eyes were dark with worry. "I looked to see whether we might have made some separate recent transactions that added up to the amount in question. I drew a blank."

"Exactly," said Homer, relieved. "So this is a mistake. Some computer error."

"There's no computer record, either."

"What!"

"See for yourself. The withdrawal is recorded, all right, but the money wasn't taken from one account, or even several - it came from the bank's general deposits. And there's no record of who withdrew it."

Homer tried to compose himself. "Mark, get Tim Gallagher in here. This has got to be some stupid computer error, and we need to get it taken care of now. Show him what you found. I'm going to go talk to the Morgans." Homer strode down the hall to his office, then halted for a moment outside to catch his breath. He didn't want to alarm his friends.

"I'm sorry, Frank and Charlotte, we're having some computer problems, and we can't sign the papers until we get them resolved. I'm meeting with our head computer guru in just a minute to work something out."

Frank's eyebrows rose in anxiety. "You know we have to sign those papers today, Homer. Under the terms of the purchase, we only have a hundred twenty days or we lose the deposit. The farms go to that developer. Today's the last day." Frank took Charlotte's hand and they looked at Homer.

"C'mon Frank, I'm not going to let that happen, am I? You just sit tight while I get this straightened out. I'll ask my receptionist to bring you some coffee while you wait." He saw them relax, trusting him.

Tim was already in the conference room, hunched over the print-outs, when Homer returned.

"Can you tell what's wrong?" Homer asked.

"From a quick perusal, nothing. Why did you call me, anyway, and not your own IT guy?"

"I thought it might be a year 2000 problem."

Tim shook his head. "That's not likely yet, Homer, because we haven't put any of the remediated systems back online. We're still testing."

"Well, something's wrong!" Homer could not keep the impatience from his voice. "Do you think someone can make a nine point five million dollar withdrawal without our having some record of it? The amount must have been entered incorrectly or something - there can't be that much money missing from the bank!"

"I'll look at it, Homer - I need someone to explain the bank's pro-cedures to me." Tim's voice was soothing, but his brows were drawn together.

"Mark can help you. How long is it going to take? I've got some-body sitting in my office waiting to sign loan papers."

"Give me an hour - but it may take longer." Homer nearly groaned aloud. He was tempted to hide in here while Tim struggled to make sense of the printouts, but he couldn't leave his friends in his office, growing more and more nervous about the delay.

"I'll be in my office" Homer said. "Call me as soon as you find out something."

Homer approached the office with dragging feet, and spent the next hour and a half making small talk and bad jokes about computer problems to Frank and Charlotte. When Tim finally rang the office, Frank's face lit up. "They must have found the problem."

"I'll be right back," Homer promised. "Maybe the bank should throw in a couple hundred thousand dollars extra for keeping you wait-ing so long." They all laughed and Homer made what he hoped was his last trip to the conference room. Tim's summons hadn't mentioned how long the problem would take to fix.

Tim was standing when Homer entered, and Homer could tell by the look on his face that the news was not good.

"What's wrong? Is it going to take all day to fix the computer?"

Tim led him to a chair. "Sit down, Homer." Tim sat in the chair opposite and was silent for a moment, as if he wanted to choose his words carefully. "There's nothing wrong with the computer. All the printouts indicate that the computer is working just fine."

"What then?"

"Well," Tim said, "in a sense you were right when you asked me if this was a y2k problem. It looks like the money has been embezzled, maybe by somebody with access to the source code, somebody on the y2k project. Your auditors need to look at the other possibilities. At this point, I don't have a clue how it was done. But the money is gone, all right."

Homer jerked to his feet. He heard a sudden buzzing in his ears and the room tilted crazily and went dark. An hour later, after the Morgans had left, Homer drank a stiff shot of whisky, then sat down at his desk to phone the FBI.

\*     \*     \*

"The money's gone," Homer repeated. "Just gone." His suit was rumpled and his tie askew, as if his distress had somehow transferred itself to his clothing.

"What do you mean, gone?" Annette asked.

The y2k team waited anxiously for his story. The meeting was clandestine, convened at Alex's house late that afternoon, and Harry and Leo had not been invited. Homer drew a shaky breath and explained the morning's events, including the denial of Frank's loan.

"Oh, that poor man!" exclaimed Karen. "How did he take it?"

"I don't think he'll ever speak to me again," said Homer. "And I don't blame him."

Tim sat frowning; he had spent all day combing the records with Homer. Alex leaned against the leather sofa and rubbed his eyes with his fingers.

"Okay, Tim, whom do you suspect?" The words fell like stones into the room.

"Well, I sure don't suspect Harry!" Tim said. "I've known Harry for years, Alex. He's an honest man, I'd swear to it."

Alex waved his hand tiredly. "Let's do this right. It's nothing personal, Tim. Leo isn't here either."

"Why ever not?" Annette was indignant. Alex cut her off with less than his usual patience.

"Because I want as few people as possible to know about this. No one is to say anything to anyone yet. Including family. Do I make myself clear?" A meek silence answered his words.

"Tim, again, I'd like to hear what you have to say about it." Alex sat down, lips compressed, eyes grim.

"I'd say that someone sabotaged the source code." Tim dragged the words out with reluctance. "As much as I don't want to think that. I went through all kinds of possibilities with Homer, and that's what I narrowed it down to. The bank auditors can check out the other possibilities, but let's face it, the source code was there for all to see, and we had all kinds of people handling it."

"You're saying anyone who worked with the source code is a suspect?" This came from Eddie.

"Yes, our personnel, the bank personnel, and Volodya's group."

"But if it's some sort of virus, couldn't it have come in from outside the bank?" Annette asked.

Tim frowned, working it out. "That would be more difficult," he said at last. "The possibility exists, but I think we should probably look at the more obvious ways first. Most embezzlement is an inside job."

Eddie had more questions ready; he had already considered the legal implications of disappearing money, and he didn't like the liability.

"We had security in place, right? And we've been checking and testing the source code like crazy, right? So how easy could it be to change the source code without anybody noticing?"

"Nobody said it was easy to do," Tim said. "It wouldn't be easy. In fact, I think it would be pretty difficult, which narrows our field of suspects considerably."

"To whom?" Annette's voice was sharp. She already knew who the brilliant programmers were.

"To Leo. And the Russians. And Harry. And John Carr from the bank. Those are the obvious ones."

"Tim, this list doesn't make sense." Annette's accent became more clipped; Alex had noticed that she was always at her most British when she was upset. "What about the other banks in the consortium? Don't they have access to each other - including us - through their own IT departments?"

"That's another remote possibility. The best possible people from each bank were brought in here to work the y2k project. Our best suspects are right here at this bank. I don't like it either, Annette." Tim's shoulders were slumped and Annette took pity on him.

"What do we need to do, then?" she asked.

"Think back. We're looking for suspicious behavior. I don't think the person who took the money would be stupid enough to deposit it in an account in his own name here in town, but we may have to look into that possibility, if only to rule it out."

Homer nodded. "A few words in the right ears, and I can find out how much money is in all those accounts. I'll do it tomorrow."

"But that can't be legal!" Annette protested.

"Of course it is. A bank has every right to know how much money their customers have in their accounts." Homer was unapologetic. "Don't worry, Annette, it's perfectly legal." Another brief, miserable silence.

"But why do you suspect Leo?" Annette said in a small voice. Karen looked at her sympathetically.

"Because he's smart and he had opportunity," Alex said. "Just like the Russians and the others. I can't say I really suspect Harry, although he's smart enough. I just couldn't stand the thought of having him here ranting about the Russians. Especially now that it looks like he could be right. Still, Harry had the opportunity."

"Well, Volodya is the most obvious suspect," said Eddie. "He has no real stake in this project, like Leo does."

"It seems unfair to suspect him just because he's a Russian," Annette muttered. "He hasn't done anything either."

Alex was thoughtful. "Well, as Harry pointed out to us at the time, he was quite upset over the security restrictions. And we did compromise on several of them, so he may have had more opportunity than we originally intended to give him."

"This is dreadful." Annette's voice was high and tense. "I'm the one who said we should hire Volodya and ease the security restrictions.

Does that make me an accomplice?"

Karen left the room hurriedly and returned with a large plate of brownies. "Have one," she commanded, passing them around. "Alex, I don't think that encouraging this paranoia is accomplishing anything."

"All right," said Alex. "Apologies to all I've offended. We all hate this situation, but we have to deal with it. I'm afraid Leo and Harry will have to be left in the dark for a while yet. Volodya and his programmers and the others have no reason to know anyway. Homer's going to check on the bank accounts. Eddie, any other suggestions?"

Eddie shook his head.

"Right. Let's just all—" Alex threw up his hands suddenly. "Let's just sleep on it. We have to beat this, or all our y2k work all year is for nothing. The bank goes under anyway, which is going to have the bad effect on the rest of the banking system that we were trying to avoid."

Tim stood up. "I guess I should point out one other problem," he said.

Alex sighed. "Sure, why not. What's the problem?"

"Well," Tim said, "I don't claim to know everything there is to know about viruses, but I have a lot of experience, and I've never seen anything like this before. It may take a while to figure out how it was put in, and how to get it back out again. And the virus may not take any more money out of Midwest National. It may be programmed to go from one bank to another."

"You mean it would leave Midwest? But that's good, surely," said Annette. "Then Midwest will be all right."

"It might be better to contain the damage to one bank," Tim said. "My real worry is the roll-over. After the millennium, computer systems will become unpredictable. No one may ever get the virus out."

\*      \*      \*

Karen had never seen Alex plunged into such gloom. At dinner he listened to the children's stories and made appropriate responses, but afterward he bolted immediately into her office where he remained incommunicado for several hours.

"Dad had a bad day at work, didn't he," Ethan remarked as he polished off a huge snack just an hour after dinner.

"I'm afraid he did."

"That's too bad." Ethan gave his mother a peck on the cheek and bounded upstairs to do his homework. Elizabeth was in her room already; lately she seemed to come out only for meals. Katie was practicing pliés and pirouettes in the living room. She pouted for a while over her daddy's absence, but she was never unhappy for long. After Katie went to bed at nine-thirty, Karen ventured to knock on the office door.

"Come in." Alex found a smile for her. "It's your office. Come in."

She found him sitting at her computer reading the posts from the mail list. When she leaned over and put her arms around him, he reciprocated with a kiss.

"I'm trying to cheer myself up," he told her, clicking on another e-mail. "The troops are still working out there, aren't they?"

"As hard as ever. The posts about the electric grid have been more optimistic lately. Perhaps it won't go down after all."

"I hope they're right." He swiveled out of the chair and sat down on the love seat, making room for Karen next to him. She cuddled against his chest, and they sat in silence for a while.

"Something will happen to put things right at the bank," Karen said at last. "Don't be discouraged."

"Discouraged?" His arms tightened around her. "That doesn't come close to the way I feel right now. Homer came to my office this afternoon to tell me about the money, and when he told me that he had to turn down the Morgans' loan, he broke down and cried. I didn't know what to say to him. Then I had to voice suspicions about my own staff - did you see the looks on their faces? I hated making those groundless accusations about Leo - even about Volodya. And having to check their bank accounts!" His voice trailed off.

"You did what you had to do. Everyone will feel better tomorrow. It was just such a shock."

She could see Alex's jaw tighten. "I hope I find the bastard who did this."

"You really have no idea?"

"Just suspicions."

"Well, stay angry, darling. That will serve you better than guilt and depression."

The phone shrilled and Alex leaned over and picked it up.

"Mr. President!"

Karen listened to one side of the conversation with growing curiosity as Alex became more and more animated. When he finally hung up the receiver, she was avid.

"Well?"

"The weirdest thing," he said slowly. "The President wants me to talk to someone at DFAS. The Department of Defense just discovered that someone is siphoning money out of one of their accounts, and they can't figure out how it's being done. Isn't that bizarre?"

"But why are they telling you?" Karen wondered, then dimpled. "Not that you aren't brilliant and all."

"They're telling me because they suspect their source code has been tampered with in the course of their y2k remediation, and they thought maybe I'd run into something similar because of my y2k involvement."

"Do you think it's the same virus as the one in the bank?"

"Anything is possible at this point. I think I'll call Tim before I talk to DFAS."

Alex was on the phone for the next two hours. When he finally emerged from her office complaining of a sore ear, Karen leapt on him.

"Alex, I have a great idea!" Her eyes danced as she explained it. "What if we were to put out a question on the mail list from you — we could describe the virus problem and ask everyone if they've ever experienced anything like it. Maybe their responses could give us some clues. What do you think?"

"We couldn't say it was the bank or the Department of Defense. But I suppose we could just call it an organization - something generic - and say funds were being snatched."

"Alex, I'm sure you'd get lots of responses if you made it a personal appeal. So many people are grateful to you; they'd want to help. Let's write it right now!" She tugged him toward the office again.

The next morning the following post appeared on the screens of thirty-five hundred y2k warriors:

*Dear Fellow Fighter in the y2k Effort,*

*This is an appeal for your help, which you've been more than generous with in the past. An organization that*

*shall remain nameless has appealed to us. They believe
that their source code was tampered with during y2k
remediation, and now their funds are being siphoned away.
They found no indication of tampering when they checked
their source code; however the incontrovertible proof is
that the money is disappearing without a trace.*

*Needless to say this organization may face bankruptcy
without our help. The situation is all the more unfair because an unscrupulous person took advantage of a
company's honest effort to resolve its y2k issues.*

*Many of you have been exposed to such computer mal-
feasance before. If you can give us any ideas from your
own experience as to how such a thing might be happening, please share your knowledge. I don't want to turn our
mail list into a recitation of 101 Illegal Computer Strate-
gies, so please e-mail me privately if you have any ideas or
experience.*

*Many thanks for your help, past and future.*
*Warm regards,*
*Alex Stauffer*

*November 1, 1999: Day 61*

The response to Alex's letter was immediate and overwhelming.
When Alex found fifty e-mails on his screen by noon, he quickly assigned the job of reading them to Tim. By three o'clock he had another
fifty to read.

"It looks to me like every programmer on the mail list was once a
hacker," Alex remarked, floored by the volume of mail.

"Now boss," said Tim, "you should know that the only sure way to
keep people out of a system is to figure out how they can get in before
they figure it out for themselves. The good guys use the bad guys'
methods against them." Tim's spirits seemed to be much improved by
the e-mails he now had to read.

"But how are you ever going to sort it all out?"

"We have our ways," Tim said, jovial. "Some of them are duplications; some won't apply to our situation."

"Listen to this," he said, reading from an e-mail on the computer screen. "'I'm in the Air Force, and the systems on our base were hacked recently. Subsequent investigation revealed that the word 'password' was often used as a password, making access to the systems ridiculously easy.'"

"But this is a bank," Alex said. "Surely the security here is better than that!"

Tim shrugged. "Well, that was the Air Force. Protecting our national security, right? A small bank like this is an easier target because their security is probably more lax than one of the behemoth banks."

"Here's a new one on me," he added, frowning in concentration as he squinted at the screen. "It's called a Spartan horse. When an Internet user is online, it pops a JavaScript dialog box on the screen. It looks like a legitimate Windows box, requesting information, and most users are fooled into entering their usernames and passwords. Then that information goes to the hacker."

"I've heard of that one," Alex said. He pursed his lips thoughtfully. "This stuff is good for us to know about, for Millennium Dynamics, but for this situation - I don't know. Most embezzling is still done from the inside. If our user already has source code access, I'm not sure he needs these other techniques."

Tim punched up another e-mail. "Social engineering. Now doesn't that sound just like our boy Volodya? Listen. 'When hackers talk people out of their information rather than using technical means, the term is social engineering. Often technical support workers can be convinced to reveal their own or others' passwords and similar information over the phone or via e-mail. In my company, a brokerage, we had such a case.'"

Alex laughed wryly. "I knew you wouldn't be able to resist using Volodya's name for long, Tim. You're as bad as Harry. And you're right, that does sound like him." He shook his head. "I'm continually astonished that so many people have so little integrity."

*       *       *

Later, at Midwest, Alex slouched in one of Homer's armchairs, enjoying the rich, smell of leather and wondering whether one of the people on his mail list could possibly help them figure out the bank's problem. He sat up as Homer hurried in.

"The board of directors for Midwest agreed to call in the FBI," Homer said without preamble.

"I'd hope so."

Homer raised his eyebrows. "You're naïve, Alex. The board would rather lose money than admit the bank has a problem. Everything for them is public perception. The only reason they agreed to call the FBI was because Frank agreed to keep quiet - but only if the bank agreed not to try to collect on his deposit loan and only if the bank agreed to call the FBI. You know, Alex, if Frank went to the papers with this story, our customers would withdraw their money so fast your head would spin. In half a day we'd have no bank."

"Have you talked to the FBI yet?" Alex was intrigued; he knew the FBI had a computer crime division now. Maybe they were familiar with the bank's problem.

"I talked to them before I got the Board's approval - not my usual business protocol, but I figured Frank deserved the courtesy. George Mumford is the agent; we've worked together before. He was assigned to a fraud case here about a year ago. George is also assigned to the DoD case. They've been scrubbing their systems for the last couple of days, but haven't come up with anything yet. I think the President annoyed the federal guys when he asked for your help."

Alex shrugged. "I hate politics. The important thing is to find the damned virus and get it out of there."

"Oh, I agree. George is going to come in and look at the files with Tim. He doesn't want to be identified as FBI, though."

Alex thought for a moment. "Okay, he can be our IV and V guy." At Homer's puzzled look he explained. "That's Independent Verification and Validation. Those are the people who look at the system after it's been remediated and tested, trying to find problems that the original remediators and testers have overlooked. If we had enough time to do this project properly, we'd actually be using some IV and V people. That gives George a job description and access to the mainframes. And it would be normal for him to ask questions of the bank personnel in the course of doing his job if he were IV and V."

"Before you leave, Alex, take a look at this." Homer handed Alex an e-mail printout. "I'm not sure if this is a good laugh, or another reason to cry."

From:       y2kRay@aol.com
To:         Homer Jones, President, Midwest National
            Bank
Subject:    Banks at Risk

Hey, Bank!

# The Hackers are coming!

Hurray, hurray!
I hope that your code is
Locked up okay.
When will they come?
Is today the day?
Remember, I warned you

From y2kRay

"Y2k Ray?" Alex cocked an eyebrow. "This worries you, Homer?"

"Well, no, not initially," Homer said. "But I got another one, a different poem, a few weeks ago, before anything ever happened to the money. I thought it was just some crank, and I deleted it. Now I'm thinking I should have saved it."

"Save this one," Alex advised him. "Show it to the FBI. If you get another, then we can worry."

Homer rose and accompanied Alex to the door. "It's good to have the FBI on our side, at least, don't you think, Alex?" His voice was edged with worry.

"Absolutely." Alex knew that the FBI computer system was enormous; surely they'd had lots of experience with this kind of problem. "Sometimes these things just take a couple of days to figure out." Homer nodded, but Alex wasn't sure whom he was trying to convince - Homer or himself.

*November 16, 1999: Day 46*

"So, how are hacking skills developing, Leo?" Volodya asked, setting his glass of beer on the counter of the bar where he and the other
Russians had met Leo after work.

"Oh, c'mon Volodya," Leo said.

Vasily wandered over. His long hair contained in an unkempt pony-
tail, his fingernails unclipped, his t-shirt tucked half-in and half-out of his
pants, he was the stereotypical computer nerd.

"Darts, Leo?" he asked.

Amazed, Leo took the darts and followed Vasily to the dartboard.
He had become accustomed to the Russian's never speaking to him; it
was like keeping company with a mute. To have Vasily approach and
address him was akin to seeing a paralytic rise from his wheelchair and
walk.

Vasily tossed the first dart. Bull's eye. "There is rumor at bank,"
he said.

Leo tossed his dart, which stuck at the outer limits of the board.
"Rumor?"

"About embezzlement. Lots of money gone." Another bull's eye.

Leo felt his skin crawl. Why was Vasily telling him this? His dart
hit the metal edge of the board and clattered to the floor.


*Moscow*

Sergei had planned to make contact with the Americans weeks
ago; but he had been so ill and weak he could scarcely get out of bed,
let alone compose the difficult algorithms necessary for what he had in
mind. He was better now, able to use a laptop in bed. When he was
unable to concentrate, he switched to reading the y2k mail list he had
been following. He was concerned about Russia's readiness for the
year 2000, and he had found this list on the Internet. Although he had
been reading it for months now, he did so anonymously and illegally. He
did not wish to identify himself by joining. For one who possessed the
right skills, it was an easy system to hack into. Perhaps such precautions were unnecessary, but when one grew up in a police state, one
took such measures as a matter of course.

When he read Alex's post appealing for help, he realized at once what must have happened. His own algorithm must have been inserted and activated already, and they needed help against it. He hacked into the user profile logs on Alex's domain, obtained his e-mail password, then pulled up Alex's mail on Telnet, musing that most people who used e-mail thought the system was secure. A passworded system like Alex's was much more difficult to hack than a standard e-mail user's system, but for someone who knew what he was doing, not a problem. Sergei skimmed through the posts Alex had received in response to his appeal for help. Would anyone mention the wormhole? So far, they had not even hinted at it.

But reading the post gave him another idea; he would appeal to Alex for help. Sergei had been wondering whom to contact. Alex had the ear of the President; Sergei had read this in a magazine article on the Internet. Reading Alex's letters to the mail list over the months had convinced him that Alex was a man of integrity. He could trust Alex as a middleman between him and the U.S. government, which he did not trust any more than he trusted the Russian government. Once convinced of the enormous damage the worm could do, the U.S. government would be eager to learn how to deactivate it. Sergei would contact Alex and offer to make a trade.

Of course, if he were to contact Alex via computer, Alex must not know where the message came from. He could not send his message via the normal e-mail route, but he knew other, undetectable ways. After all, that's what wormholes were for.

# Chapter 14

*November 17, 1999: Day 45*

The monitor glowed and Leo read its contents hurriedly. He'd never seen anyone using this PC at the bank; it was stuck in a little side room used mostly for storage. He was taking a chance, looking at Homer's mail while inside the bank itself, but he was too worried to wait, and he knew he could hack quickly.

What did Homer know about the rumored bank virus? He scrolled through the e-mails. Didn't Homer ever write about anything important? Then a subject header caught his eye and he clicked the e-mail open, concentrating so intently that he failed to hear the door open and the footsteps approach. By the time he heard Tim's voice it was too late to clear the screen.

"Is that Homer's e-mail you're reading, Leo?"

\*     \*     \*

Alex sat behind his desk. Leo sat, too, his face flushed. He ran a hand through his already-rumpled hair. Tim sat down next to him.

"Are you going to fire me?" Leo said, raising his eyes then dropping them again at the fury on his boss's face.

"You mean it's true?" Alex asked. "You were hacking into Homer's computer?"

"I can explain," Leo said, a tinge of defiance in his tone.

"There is no explanation that I would accept for that." Alex's face was tight, and a muscle jumped next to his mouth. He stood up and paced to his window, stared out sightlessly, then sat down again at his desk, his movements precise and controlled. "Tell me what you have to tell me."

Alex listened to the halting explanation with his eyes on Leo's face.

"I was at a party at Volodya's in September." Leo spoke slowly. Alex raised an eyebrow at this, but said nothing. Leo looked beyond Alex as he spoke.

"We were drinking. I hacked Homer's computer."

"I see."

Leo stared out the window. "And then last night one of the Russians told me there was a rumor about a big embezzlement at Midwest. They all seemed to know about it." Here Leo stopped so long that Alex was about to prompt him. He went on at last. "And it made me wonder, since I knew that at least Volodya was hacking - maybe more of them - maybe all of them - it made me wonder whether any of them might be involved."

Alex frowned. "You said you were the one who was hacking Homer's computer."

"Well, yes, but -"

"Were you?"

Leo stared at him. "The Russians did it, too," he said, finally.

"That night? While you were there?" Alex asked.

"Well, no, I didn't actually see them." Leo's voice trailed off. "They told me."

"Then why didn't you tell me about the Russians before?" Alex asked.

Leo continued to look out the window.

"Well?"

"I didn't want them to get in trouble," Leo muttered at last. "It didn't seem malicious."

Alex's mouth tightened.

"And I hacked into Homer's computer just now to find out about the money," Leo said, his voice low and angry. "I couldn't figure out why nobody had told me. I mean, I'm a part of the y2k team."

"Or maybe you already knew," Alex said, "and you wanted to find out for sure if the rest of us knew yet."

"How would I know?" Leo asked. Then his face darkened. "You

consider me a suspect, don't you?"

"Let's just say that your actions today do not inspire trust," Alex said. He drummed his fingers on the desk. "And your explanations don't inspire trust, either, frankly. Please wait across the hall, Leo. I want to talk to Tim."

Leo nodded and rose. "I'm sorry, Alex," he said without looking at either Alex or Tim. Then he left.

"Shit," Alex said after the door closed, the monosyllable vibrating with frustration. "This on top of everything."

"I really like Leo." Tim leaned back in his chair with a sigh. "He may be telling the truth."

"He didn't look me in the eye, he made excuses, he mumbled, he was defiant - I don't know whether I believe him," Alex said. "And he should have told us about the Russians."

"I'm not excusing him," Tim said.

Alex templed his fingers, brooded, swiveled the chair.

"Listen, I know you're mad at him, but he's young," Tim said at last. "Keep him on, and I'll watch him. He doesn't need to come to the meetings for a while. I can tell him what he needs to know."

Alex considered this solution. "And the Russians?"

"We need them, Alex." Tim's mouth twisted. "At least this way, they're here where we can keep an eye on them."

Alex sighed. "They've been here all along, and nobody caught on to them, if they're the guilty ones. Okay, Tim, Leo's yours."

"What about Harry then?" Tim said.

"What about him?"

"C'mon, Alex, you can't think he's really a suspect."

Alex threw up his hands. "Hell, Tim, I didn't think Leo was really a suspect. I guess I'd better suspect 'em all."

"But Harry came out of retirement to help us-"

"And I happen to know that one of Harry's grandkids is chronically ill, has no insurance money left, and is being financed mostly by Harry." Alex stared Tim down. "Harry could use some extra money, too."

"Couldn't we all." Tim walked to the door. "Maybe you should put my name on your blacklist, too, Alex."

\*       \*       \*

An early fire burned in the fireplace and Karen and Alex read and napped in its warmth while Brahms played on the stereo. Katie was asleep, Ethan listening to CD's in his room, and Elizabeth was reading e-mail on Karen's computer. A muffled shriek from Elizabeth brought her parents rushing into the office where they found their daughter standing behind her chair, as if for cover, while she pointed a finger at the computer screen.

"Look!" she cried. "That's the weirdest thing I've ever seen! How did it do that?"

In the center of the e-mail screen a HyperTerminal screen had planted itself and was displaying a message.

"I was just reading a message, Daddy, I didn't do anything, and all of a sudden this screen just came in on top of everything! It can't do that, can it?" Elizabeth knew enough about computers to know that e-mail wouldn't appear on screen unless you downloaded it first.

"Look what it says, Alex," whispered Karen. They had been so puzzled at the method of the screen's appearance that they hadn't noticed the message.

> *I can help you with your virus if you can help me. Can I trust you? Please respond with a message on the DoD homepage.*

"That's too weird," breathed Elizabeth. "It's like the voice of God or something."

No one disagreed with her.

\*      \*      \*

Annette replaced the telephone receiver. Leo had agreed to pick her up at her apartment and bring her home again. Tonight's summons to the Stauffers' was a surprise, and her car was in the garage overnight for repairs.

Annette flung herself in the shower, dressed quickly in black leggings and a fuzzy angora sweater, then looked critically at herself in the mirror. She looked soft and approachable, she thought. She just had time to add perfume and silver earrings before the doorbell rang.

Leo. Annette felt a shiver of excitement. He didn't know it yet, but tonight after the meeting she was going to ask him in. Ever since his kiss - nearly two months ago now, how could she be so slow? - she had debated what to do.

Tonight's meeting was the push she needed. She didn't have her car, so Leo could drive her home. Then she would just ask him in. And then - well, she certainly hoped he would kiss her. She might even kiss him first.

She threw the door open to Leo and stood on the threshold, eyes sparkling.

"Hi. Are you ready?" Leo wore a battered leather jacket and jeans; he eyed Annette appreciatively. "You look great."

"So do you," Annette said recklessly. Now that she'd made her decision, she couldn't wait for that meeting to be over.

                    *       *       *

An hour after the Hyper-Terminal message appeared, Annette, Leo, and Tim joined the Stauffers in staring at the computer screen. Although he was still furious with Leo, Alex thought that his PC expertise could help them, so he'd asked him to come over.

"I think the signal must have come in through a wormhole," Leo said.

Elizabeth stared at him. Alex had allowed her to stay in the room for a while to hear the explanation; it seemed only fair. "A wormhole! What's that?" she asked, her face wrinkling.

Alex had a different question. "How do you do it?"

"Well, I can only tell you theoretically, of course; I've never done it. It's illegal," Leo said, his face flushing. "I mean, it's illegal to send this kind of code outside the U.S. It's a special kind of 128-bit encryption sent via the TCP/IP signal. I don't know that anyone has ever been prosecuted for it. But you can see that it would be an invasion of privacy. Also, it's very difficult to pull off, from what I hear. I don't know whether I could do it myself. You need to know a lot of obscure mathematics."

"I don't really understand it," Annette admitted, "but I guess that doesn't matter. Who do you suppose sent it?"

"Sorry, Elizabeth, this is where we have to send you out," Karen said. Elizabeth consented to a kiss and a hug and left docilely enough.

Leo and Annette sat on the loveseat, Alex pushed the office chair back from the desk and perched on it, Karen took the armchair and Tim the ottoman.

"Let's think," said Alex. "What do we know about this guy?"

"He's brilliant," Tim said at once.

"Or he has a brilliant friend who created the message for him." This was Leo.

"He knows who Alex is." Karen spoke slowly. "He may think Alex has high-up friends." She was frowning. "Why would he think that?"

"That's in the public domain, Karen — Alex is on the National Year 2000 National Council," Annette said.

"I have a question — what's the virus he's talking about?" Leo asked. Guilty glances were exchanged around the room.

"I just heard from the Department of Defense that they're losing money from an account and they can't figure out where it's going. They asked me to help because they thought I might have heard of other y2k espionage cases." This explanation was adequate for the moment, Alex decided.

Leo digested this information in silence.

"He needs our help," said Tim.

"He created the virus," Leo added. They all looked at him. "Well, how else can he help us with a virus unless he can disable it? And how can he disable it unless he created it — or knows the person who did, which is the same thing for our purposes."

"So what do we tell him?" asked Annette. "What kind of help do you suppose he wants? It couldn't be money; the virus gets him that."

"Unless the money goes to somebody else and he just knows about the virus," Tim said.

"Any other thoughts?" Alex looked around the room at the serious faces.

"I think we'd better contact him right away!" Annette exclaimed. "He's our only hope of saving the bank; let's find out what he wants."

Annette clapped a guilty hand over her mouth.

"Alex, I am sorry."

"Leo knows," Alex said shortly. "And since we don't have a clue how the money was removed, I agree with Annette; we'd better post a message to this guy right away, or we may never figure out where the money went. Tim, is there any reason you can think of that the DoD wouldn't want us to answer this message on their home page?"

"Can't think why not. I'm sure they want their money back, and this could be the same virus. Best chance anybody has, at this point."

"Alex," Leo said slowly, "I'm wondering whether this virus might also use wormhole technology."

"Why do you say that?"

"Well, if we assume that the person who sent the message and the person who devised the virus are the same, then the possibility exists. And you have to wonder how the money was withdrawn invisibly — wormholes are invisible."

"How do you happen to be such an expert?" Tim said.

Leo flinched visibly at the question. "I told you, I've never done it myself. But you have to understand, at the level at which I work — was working, at least, in Silicon Valley — at that level there's a lot of talk about how to do this or that. High-level programmers like things like wormholes, because they can show how smart they are. So a lot of guys dabble with things that are on the edge of illegal — or things that flat *are* illegal — more for prestige than for gain, if you see what I mean. They think they're above the law." He seemed to be having trouble meeting Tim's eye, and Annette sent him a curious glance.

"Are you going to phone the DFAS guy?" Tim asked.

"You guys compose the message," Alex instructed. "I'll be back in a minute."

The message they came up with was brief and to the point:

*We want to help. Tell us how.*

"Shouldn't we make our help conditional?" asked Annette. "He might ask for something horrendous."

"The condition is that he tells us how to find and deactivate the virus code," Tim said shortly. "Anyway, we need to find out what he wants."

Alex returned with the okay to display the message on the Department of Defense home page.

"I think that's it for tonight, everybody," Alex said, yawning. "Now we just need to wait."

As team members pulled on winter hats and gloves, Leo materialized at Alex's side.

"Could I see you privately for a moment?"

Alex nodded and closed the office door.

"Have you told Annette?" Leo asked.

"I thought I'd leave that for you."

"Oh." He was silent a moment. "What happens to Volodya?"

"I talked about it with Tim, but I think for now I'd rather have him here where we can keep our eyes on him, along with the others."

"He may be innocent."

"Of taking the money? Oh, I'm aware of that. And you'd better stay friendly with the Russians anyway, because if they are fooling around, we don't want them to suspect that we know. And Leo." Leo looked up.

"I want you to know that you're still a suspect," Alex said. "For all we know, you could be inventing the Russians' hacking to cover yourself. As far as we can know, you may be the only hacker there is."

\*     \*     \*

"Would you like to come in, Leo?" Annette asked with a smile, when they reached her apartment. She'd been anticipating this moment all evening, wondering what he'd say.

But he didn't react, didn't even turn his head in her direction.

"I need to tell you something," he said.

Annette hid her disappointment. Maybe he was just tired, or upset about the money vanishing. It was a pity that he should be out of sorts on this night, of all nights, but she knew how she could cheer him up. The thought made her smile again.

"Do come in, then," she said, with mock gravity, drawing out her British accent for fullest effect, "where we'll be more comfortable."

She took his hand as they walked to her door, ignoring his abstracted air.

"Leo," she sang, "why, you're a million miles away." The next moment his arms were around her, and he was kissing her hungrily. His kiss was just as she remembered it, and she returned it with passion, for once unafraid of her feelings.

He released her and stepped back.

"I have to tell you something," he repeated.

He was so silly, she thought. Like a little boy. He was going to tell her about his last girlfriend or something. He sat down on the sofa, and she sighed and snuggled next to him.

"Leo, what's wrong?" Her voice was tender, cajoling. Of course he was still worried for her, thought she was still full of fear and doubt. He had no idea of the decision she'd made. As if to confirm her resolve, to send him the message in the clearest possible way, she laid her head on his chest and nestled closer.

"Today Tim caught me hacking into Homer's e-mail at the bank," Leo said, "and he told Alex." His gaze was fixed on the wall opposite him. "And I told Alex that Volodya, and maybe the other Russians too, have been doing the same thing. I didn't tell anyone before, because I was afraid the Russians would be fired and I knew we couldn't complete the compile without them."

Annette sat up.

Her heart seemed to be trying to bump its way out of her chest. So this was what would always happen when she allowed herself to be vulnerable. This was her reward for opening herself up. She had never felt so strong a sense of rejection, at least not since Mick. To think that Leo would sabotage this moment! Never again, she thought, her disappointment flaring into anger.

"You must have known it could harm the project," she snapped.

Leo looked at her. "I told you, I was trying to save the project." His eyes begged her to understand, and he reached for her hand. She snatched it away.

Annette took a deep breath; there wasn't enough air in the room.

"I'm really sorry, Annette," Leo said softly. "Can't you forgive me?"

Her throat ached, she could feel the tears underneath. "Tonight was supposed to be special," she said to him, then dropped her eyes. "I don't want you to be here, Leo. You'd better go."

Leo sat for a long, silent moment, hoping perhaps that she would relent.

"Annette, couldn't we talk about it?" She felt his eyes on her and shook her head, her self-control too fragile to risk speaking. Finally she heard him rise and fumble with his jacket.

"We'll talk later," he said. She sat with her face averted until at last she heard him close the door and go out.

"I trusted you," she whispered to the empty room.

*November 18, 1999: Day 44, Moscow*

The little message box on the Department of Defense home page seemed to dance and wiggle on his screen. Sergei rubbed his eyes; his eyesight appeared to be getting worse with the passing days. Still, the Americans had responded. "How can we help you?" they asked.

Sergei made ready to use the wormhole to reply. Without warning a huge wave of nausea struck him and the room swung on its axis. He nearly fell from his chair, and it required all Masha's strength to help him regain the sanctuary of his bed.

Damn! thought Sergei fiercely. His mind was no match right now for the disease that wore on his body; he could not send a message until the effects of the current attack subsided. Suppose the disease had progressed too far? Suppose it were already too late? Unconsciousness came as a relief from the despair that engulfed him.

*Columbus*

"George Mumford." The FBI agent at Alex's door stuck out his hand with a smile. Last night's phone call to the Bureau about the e-mail hacking and the computer worm had been enough to bring an agent to his doorstep by nine o'clock this morning.

"Of course. Please come in." George was African-American, about thirty and more trendily dressed than he would have expected an FBI agent to be. Alex admired his tie, a dark burgundy silk dotted with tiny buckeyes. "Are you an Ohio State fan?"

George smoothed the tie. "Living in Columbus, I sure am. But I actually graduated from Princeton. My family was surprised at my career choice - Dad is a surgeon, Mom's a pediatrician, my sister's an attorney. But I like computer fraud." He grinned. "Everybody's weird, right?" He followed Alex into Karen's office and paused before her PC. "Is this the computer?"

"Help yourself."

George sat down at the keyboard and poised his long fingers over it for an instant, and Alex understood why George's father might have harbored hopes that George would become a surgeon. "You said the message came in on HyperTerminal, right?" Alex nodded and George pulled up HyperTerminal, which Alex had left open since the incident, and studied it. "No clues here." His fingers moved busily over the keyboard, ferreting out secrets. "Nothing in the HyperTerminal log, either."

George reached for the commodious briefcase he had brought with him. "I have some special utilities with me," he said, unbuckling the case and indicating the disks inside. "I'm going to run them on your machine - with your permission, of course - and see if we can find anything. I promise it won't damage your machine." Alex nodded and the first disk went in with a whirr.

Two and a half hours later Karen came in with soup and sandwiches. George was sitting in his shirt sleeves, his tie loosened. Alex sprawled on the love seat.

"No luck?" she asked, handing the soup around.

"We had a nice long talk about the Russians - and Leo and Harry. But George hasn't found anything yet on the computer."

Stretching, George peeled himself out of the chair and sat down with his soup. "Thanks. Looks delicious. Wild goose chases always make me hungry." They ate for a moment in silence.

"He's probably going to contact you again, the same way."

Karen was dismayed. "You won't take my computer, I hope! I really need it."

George laughed. "I've never heard anybody say they didn't need their computer. No, what I'd like to do is install a sniffer. Then when our friend comes back, we'll be able to track him. You can still do all your normal work on the machine, I promise."

"What's a sniffer?" asked Karen.

"It's a program that I'll load onto the hard drive. The sniffer runs in the background and watches for suspicious acitivity in mail, files, whatever it's been programmed to check. This little sniffer - we call it the Bloodhound - is quite an advanced tool." George inserted a CD, punched a few keys, waited fifteen seconds for it to load, and removed it. "That's all there is to that. You call me the minute you get another message. We'll be able to check it now and figure out where it came from."

"That's handy," Karen said. "I don't suppose these are available at MicroCenter."

George picked up the disk and put it in its sleeve. "No, this is a pretty hot property. You keep an eye on your machine; I'll start checking out the Russians."

"Can't you question them now?"

"We don't know enough. No hard evidence. Nothing that connects them to this worm that isn't coincidental. In fact, beyond the fact that Mr. Borodin, and maybe the others, are suspected of hacking, they're no more suspicious than any other employee. Did you know that the majority of hackers are insiders? Company employees are always the leading suspects."

George stowed the rest of his disks in his case, rebuttoned his shirtsleeves, and reknotted his tie. "Have to look like a respectable special agent," he said, slipping his jacket on. "You can use your computer now, ma'am. Just give me a call when the next message comes and we'll see what we've got. And your husband told me on the phone that your daughter saw the first message?"

"Yes."

"I'm afraid you're going to have to make this computer off-limits to your kids. And your daughter is not to tell anyone about it. That goes for the rest of your y2k team, too. And I'll ask you both not to discuss it with anyone, please."

They said good-bye to George, then Karen kissed Alex, who was on his way to the office.

"He seemed quite confident about his sniffer," she said. "Do you think it will work?"

"Hey, he's the FBI. I hope it works."

*       *       *

Annette awoke with a headache, and when she remembered what Leo had told her the night before, it immediately grew worse. Last night she had been numb, unable to think. Today she wanted to cry, but she was angry, too. Leo had ruined the evening she had so anticipated, he had threatened the project, and he had been less than honest with all of them.

Considered in the cold light of day, his actions were perhaps less reprehensible than they had seemed last night. Still, what reason could he have had for hacking into Homer's e-mail? How could there be a good reason for something like that? He'd said he was trying to save the project - did she believe him? Perhaps she should call him and ask him about it, but she really wasn't ready to talk to him yet.

Hacking. From the sound of it, all the programmers were hackers. She had expected better of Leo.

Thinking about it made her head hurt. She would go to work and try to forget about it for a while. She worked like an automaton all day, holing up in her office and avoiding any possibility of running into Leo. At three o'clock Alex came in to consult with her about a project question; she took one look at his concerned face and burst into tears.

Alex left her office and returned in a moment with a box of Kleenex, which he portioned out until she was in control of herself again.

"You're going to have to work with him, Annette," Alex told her firmly. "Get a grip."

At these words Annette stopped sniffling and glared, which, she realized, was the effect he'd hoped for.

"Leo's staying. And we're going to keep Volodya at his job for the moment. But we'll be watching him."

"Volodya?" Annette repeated. "I hadn't given Volodya a thought!"

"You don't think he's the one pulling the money out?"

"We don't have a bit more proof than we had before. I'm not so convinced that it couldn't have been someone from outside the bank. But no, Alex, it's not Volodya I'm upset about."

Alex smiled kindly at her. "I'm sure Karen would be happy to lend an ear if you need to talk to someone. From the male point of view, I'll just say that Leo appears to be really sorry for what he did. You have to decide whether that's enough."

*       *       *

Norman was surprised and pleased when the FBI, in the form of George Mumford, came to see him for a second time. If asked, Norman would have described his first interview, on the day after he talked to the A & FO, as fun. He had never expected to talk to the FBI in his lifetime, and he enjoyed this tiny bit of notoriety - it was very tiny, since both the Director and the A & FO told him pointedly that he was not permitted to discuss his discovery with anyone inside or outside DFAS. Knowing classified information was turning out to be a burden; he was constantly guarding against a slip of the tongue, and he couldn't speculate with any of his colleagues about who might be pulling the money out.

Now George was here, so Norman fetched coffee and settled himself comfortably while they chatted about this and that, covering much of the same ground they'd covered the first time George came. George confided that they had no new suspects, and Norman commiserated. Then George set his coffee mug down on the desk in a slow, deliberate fashion and his face, as he spoke to Norman, was concerned and earnest.

"You know, Norman, you've been extremely cooperative."

"What I want you to know is this: we are very good to the people who cooperate with us. It's like this: there's a boat, and the people in the FBI who are conducting the investigation are in the boat, and when people cooperate, we pull them into the boat with us. But the others, the ones who don't help us, or actually try to hinder us - they drown."

George picked up his coffee mug again and sat back in his chair, his eyes still on Norman. What a strange thing to say, Norman thought, almost as if I -

His jaw dropped when he realized why George had returned. "I'm a suspect!"

"Let's just say we haven't ruled anyone out yet. You do have a very good understanding of how the Special Fund works. That would be to the advantage of anyone trying to defraud the DoD."

Norman rubbed his neck, a nervous gesture. "But I would never do anything like that! Ask anyone." Sweeping his arms wide, he appealed to the honor of his profession. "I'm an *accountant!*"

George actually chuckled. "I hate to break it to you, Norman, but most embezzling is done by accountants, or at least by people who have a knowledge of accounting."

"But I'm the one who discovered the money was missing! I'm the one who told the A & FO!"

"You could have planned it that way," George said. "You wouldn't look like much of an accountant if you didn't notice that eleven million dollars was missing."

"I'm not a programmer. I wouldn't know how to steal eleven million dollars that way."

"You could have a partner here at DFAS in the IT department. In fact, I happen to know that you worked with the IT department recently to design an accounting package for your division."

Norman stood up and looked out the window. A 727 rose into the air on the nearby runway, and he wished he were on it, winging his way to Tahiti. He turned back to George.

"George, after you've been an agent for a while, and interviewed hundreds of people, don't you get a feeling for who's telling the truth and who isn't?"

"Sure."

"Well, then." Norman rubbed the back of his neck again. "You should know that I'm telling you the truth!"

George smiled at him with a touch of sympathy. "I wouldn't be doing my job if I dropped a likely suspect because I liked him, or felt intuitively that he didn't do it. And the truth is, Norman, a few people out there are such convincing liars that they fool even us. So what I'm looking for is cooperation and evidence."

"Well, I can cooperate," said Norman with a sigh, dropping back into his chair. "But I sure can't offer you any evidence."

George handed him a business card. "You just call me if you think of anything." Norman saw him to the door, then returned to the window and stared out again, dispirited. Never had he dreamed that he could be considered a suspect. Captain Bean Counter under suspicion.

Well - his shoulders went back - if he could find out who did take the money, then he would no longer be a suspect. He jutted his chin defiantly; he hated being falsely accused. Maybe it was somebody on that project George had mentioned; his eyes narrowed and he began mentally reviewing the list of programmers he knew. As he concentrated he designed a new headline for his next exciting adventure: Captain Bean Counter Clears His Name.

\*     \*     \*

At midnight Leo put down his violin. For the last two hours he had been playing a Bach violin partita, over and over. The mathematical regularity of the notes was soothing, and it took all his concentration; he needed the mental escape. As he wiped the rosin from his bow and loosened the strings, he reflected on his day, the second worst in his life.

The worst had doubtless been yesterday, when he had admitted his hacking to Alex and Annette.

Today he had talked to everyone else. Harry was characteristically blunt.

"What the hell did you think you were doing, boy?" he asked. Tim was tougher, and Leo winced at the memory of his well-deserved rebuke Surprisingly, it was Homer, the one most directly affected by Leo's actions, who was the most kind.

After Leo's abject apology, Homer invited him to sit down. Homer's office was impressive; dark paneling, book-lined walls, fine paintings. Leo perched on the edge of the burgundy leather armchair and waited with resignation to be lambasted. Instead, Homer told him about his own lapse of integrity.

"Alex and I used to work for the same insurance company, did you know that?"

"No."

"And one day in 1990 Alex came to my office and gave this impassioned plea about the need to do something about the year 2000 computer crisis. I'd never heard of it before, but what he said did make a certain sense. So you know what I did?"

"Started the company y2k remediation?"

Homer surprised Leo with his snort of laughter. "Nope. I told Alex that I'd only be with that company a few more years, and I wasn't going to jeopardize my career by going to bat for him and his y2k suggestions."

"Oh." Leo wasn't sure what he should say. Homer looked at him shrewdly.

"Pretty short-sighted, eh? Well, Alex wouldn't stay with the company when he realized that nothing was going to get done in the y2k arena. Before he left, though, he went to the CEO and gave him the same pitch he'd given me. The CEO was an old guy, never touched a computer, wasn't interested. But, the CEO did think about what Alex had said. And he started asking questions of people in different departments. How did this computer system affect the company? What would happen if it went down? Would it work in the year 2000? The CEO asked questions like that for a year. Then he told his board of directors that the company was going to do a y2k project. And he asked me to head it up."

Homer grimaced. "Talk about poetic justice! What a nightmare
that project was! The company had mainframes so old you couldn't
believe they could still be running, sitting right next to brand new ones.
Computer languages nobody had ever heard of, let alone programmed
in. More than five thousand PC's in a network managed by both UNIX
and Windows NT — and those were sharing the work with more than
a thousand dumb terminals from the seventies. It was a miracle that
system ever worked!" He paused.

"It took us forever to inventory everything; we ended up with 30,000
computer programs, 80 operating system variants, and almost 50 loca-
tions. But in the end we got it done." His story finished, Homer smiled
at Leo. "So I know how it feels to make the wrong choice."

Leo felt his throat constrict with emotion. He cleared it several
times, looking for control. "Thanks, Homer."

"Hey, Alex forgave me, I can forgive you." Homer had stood up
and stuck his hand out. "You're a good man, Leo. Just keep an eye on
your Russian friends."

So. Leo finished wiping the neck of his violin, then flicked the cloth
over the shiny brown body before stowing it in the case with the bow.
They might forgive him, but none of them trusted him now. Except the
Russians. Alex should have listened to his story, Leo thought, with a
trace of stubborness. He couldn't admit to himself how bad it must
look to everyone. They would all forgive him, at least eventually, once
they decided again that they could trust him. He would have to live
with his actions.

But Annette had not come near him. She hadn't returned his calls,
either at work or at home. He didn't have the nerve to approach her in
person.

Maybe she had decided that he just wasn't worth her time. Leo
recalled how trustingly she had come into his arms, how ardently she
had returned his kisses, finally, after all his months of waiting. And then
her hurt, dazed look when he told her, as if he'd struck her when she
expected a caress. His admission of guilt had changed everything, perhaps irrevocably. Dear God, he thought. It was as close as he had
come to a prayer for some time.

*November 19, 1999: Day 43*

The tension at Millennium Dynamics was palpable. The members of the y2k team carried on with their duties; all mission critical systems were now remediated, and were being tested day and night. With the end in sight, everyone redoubled their efforts; the goal was within reach, they might actually be finished on time.

But beneath their daily efforts were two questions that passed wordlessly among them at every contact: when would the money disappear again? And why hadn't they received the message they were waiting for?

*         *         *

After several unsuccessful efforts to focus her mind on the report she needed to write, Annette gave up. She had spent the past two days avoiding Leo, and the effort was wearing on her, particularly since she suspected that her reaction was not entirely justified.

The tension of having to work with Leo, when all she wanted to do was put as much distance between them as possible, coupled with the tension of waiting to hear from the wormhole user, had already resulted in headaches twice this week. Annette could feel one starting now, and she rubbed her neck gingerly.

There was a double rap at the door, then it was flung so wide that it rebounded against the wall.

"Annette!" cried Volodya, grinning at her surprise.

"Volodya." Annette blinked. He was laden with sacks of food; at the delicious smells, Annette realized how hungry she was.

"I bring you lunch." Without further preamble, he dumped the sacks on a table near her desk, then pulled two chairs to the table. "You will join me?" Intended as a question, it came out much more like a command. Annette smiled a little.

"You're very kind," she said, trying to retain a certain formality. Volodya was all too easy to encourage.

Volodya began pulling food from the sacks, and the pungent smells of sweet and sour chicken and moo shoo pork filled the office. In his black turtleneck and tweed jacket, he cut a dashing figure, especially among programmers whose wardrobe choices seemed to alternate between flannel shirts and t-shirts.

"Here, you have rice," he said, shoving a plateful at her. "And here is egg roll. Do you like chicken or pork?"

"Perhaps we could share them," Annette suggested. The warm spicy food filled some unmet need; she was touched that Volodya had brought it to her.

"You will not go out to lunch with me," Volodya said, reading her thoughts. "So I bring lunch here." He watched her eat. "You turn me down three times this week."

"I'm sorry." Annette said. "I rarely go out for lunch, really. I have so much work to do here."

Volodya shrugged. "Is nice to eat with you here. More private." Again he grinned his unsettling grin. Annette chose to ignore that remark, concentrating instead on the delicious food.

Fifteen minutes later she felt replete and relaxed, sipping green tea from a styrofoam cup while Volodya told her a ridiculous story about a drunken friend who had urinated on an eternal flame burning at a Lenin memorial. Somehow he had shortcircuited a gas valve control, extinguishing the flame and landing himself in jail. Volodya was a good storyteller, and Annette found herself laughing for the first time in a week.

"It is good to see you laugh." Unexpectedly Volodya covered her small hand with his large one, leaning toward her across the table. "You have looked unhappy this week."

The concern in his voice nearly undid her. She blinked fiercely and willed herself not to cry. "I'm all right," she managed in a reasonably steady voice. "It's just a personal matter. I'll be fine." She forced the rest of her tea past the lump in her throat.

Volodya looked at her shrewdly, but did not press the matter. His hand rested atop hers until she gently withdrew it. Gathering up the remains of their lunch, he stuffed it all into the sacks and chucked it in the wastebasket.

"Maybe I bring you lunch again." He snatched her hand quickly and kissed it.

"I am too fast for you," he said when she blushed and jerked her hand away. "See you later." He closed the door behind him, and Annette felt as though a hurricane had just blown in and out of her office.

Volodya's behavior made it difficult for her to believe that he could have planted that virus or whatever it was. Despite what Tim said, she tended to believe that someone from outside the bank had done it. Given Volodya's antics with the e-mail, she wasn't wise to encourage him, she supposed — still, he was a difficult man to discourage. That thought made her smile again as she began writing the report she had abandoned before lunch.

*        *        *

Volodya was very pleased with himself as he sauntered back to his room at the bank. Annette was grateful for the lunch and for his company, and gratitude could have interesting results.

Volodya had realized at the Labor Day party that Annette was Leo's reason for moving to Columbus, but this did not stop him from making his own advances to her. Leo would not confide in him about Annette, so why should he not pursue her too?

If he won, Leo lost. If he lost, Leo won. That made it a zero-sum game, in terms of game theory, a branch of mathematics which Volodya embraced philosophically as well as mathematically. Volodya's job at the bank seemed duller than ever. Annette's conquest offered a welcome diversion.

# CHAPTER 15

*November 20, 1999: Day 42, Columbus*

Karen drank a third cup of coffee and wondered whether she would ever catch up with the mail list. In the past two months the mail list had exploded to more than four thousand members; she seemed to stay consistently two days behind on her posts. Elizabeth and Ethan both helped her now; she had explained the sorting process, and they knew what to dump.

And there was so much to dump! Every crackpot millennial group in the world seemed to be picking on their mail list. Some of them were waiting for aliens, others for the Second Coming of Christ. Still others were predicting apocalyptic natural events, tidal waves, volcanic eruptions, earthquakes. Groups of New Luddites still sprang up here and there trying to hack computers — only their hacking was done with axes.

The combined idiocy was almost enough to make Karen laugh, except that the ravings of these groups threatened to bump the real mail list members off the list. So she and her children frantically sorted and deleted each day, making room for people with legitimate questions.

Only six weeks left! Alex was hardly to be seen around the house these days, and when he was, he wore a hunted look. The bank money was still untraceable, and the strange messenger seemed to have vanished.

Alex had spent the summer with Karen working on their own preparations, installing a diesel generator and an underground diesel fuel tank.

A second tank held drinking water, and an unused guestroom was well-stocked with canned and dried food. An enormous woodpile loomed near the back door. They were probably over-prepared, but Karen and Alex both expected that they would be sharing with those who had neglected to prepare at all.

Since the family was taken care of, Alex apologized to them and spent most of his time at his offices or the bank.

It was all very apocalyptic, thought Karen. She couldn't even wish the crazy time to end, because that would mean the year 2000 was at hand, and even the current craziness was preferable to an unknown and possibly malign future.

Karen turned back to her mail list. Another recent development was the spate of e-mails from the less-developed part of the world. Earnest and woefully uninformed, their senders composed missives of exquisite politeness and doubtful grammar. Today a manager from Nigeria inquired about the y2k compliance of his old 386 and 486 PC's.

At least his problem was solvable, if inconvenient. Some systems were so old that they were unusable after 1999, a common problem in countries which could not afford constant upgrades to more current equipment.

She sighed as she posted his e-mail. Some businesses would be unable to afford new equipment, and if they did nothing, they would just go under. Even a small business would be hard-pressed to do anything useful in the remaining six weeks. Some held the opposite view, of course; that only the small businesses were flexible enough to go back to manual operations if that became necessary.

Most of the postings now were about preparedness and contingency planning. Endless discussion threads about brands of generators or the best place to hide cash squirreled away over the past months. Still, at the same time the bulk of the consultants soldiered on. No one was sitting on his hands, waiting for January 1st to overwhelm them while time yet remained for systems to be fixed and tested and put back into production.

This e-mail was from Ben Neal, a y2k computer consultant, reminding the list at large to be sure that unremediated systems were left off line after December 31st. No doubt there would be a number of these systems that could not be run after the rollover. Companies that were unable to do the whole y2k job in time had to triage. Only the systems deemed mission-critical, vital to the existence of the company and the health and safety of the employees, were fixed before the rollover. The others would have to wait.

To Karen's annoyance, the computer screen flickered for a moment, then went black. She frowned; this was not the time for computer problems. As she clicked the mouse impatiently, a new HyperTerminal screen suddenly appeared, complete with a message. So the mysterious correspondent was back. And what did he want? Holding her breath, Karen read the message:

> *I created virus at my government's request. I will exchange virus deactivation code for liver transplant, which I am unable to obtain in my country. You must also help me and another person to exit my country, because I am not permitted to leave. I will give you my name and location when you agree to my terms. This time leave your message on White House home page.*

So that was it! Well, no one could ever have guessed that they'd be asked to provide a liver in exchange for a computer code. She didn't know how reasonable a request it was, but they'd better put the wheels in motion; still staring at the message on the screen, she dialed Alex's pager number.

*     *     *

"Mr. President," said Alex formally. He had never phoned the President before.

"Alex! Have you got something for us?"

"I'm happy to say we have." Alex heard the President exhale in relief. "He says he'll tell us how to deactivate the code if we bring him to the States and give him a new liver."

Silence on the other end. "Bring him from where?"

"He said he'd provide his name and location when we agree to his terms."

"Where do *you* think he is?" the President asked.

"Theoretically, I guess he could be anywhere an oppressive regime is in operation, which could include a country like Iran or China. But practically, I'd think he has to be in an oppressed country which has the kind of support for him to have learned some pretty high-level programming." Alex paused. "This is only speculation, Mr. President. I'm sure you have advisors who know more about this than I do."

"So you think it's Russia?"

Alex suppressed a grin. "That's my guess. We won't know for sure until we contact him."

"Through the DoD home page again?"

"No," said Alex, "this time he wants to be on the White House home page."

The President sighed. "What next? Does he want the liver air freighted to him, too?"

"I was wondering about that. Can you just promise somebody a liver?"

"It's not a subject I'm familiar with," the President said. "But lately the House Speaker has been talking about sacrificing for your country. If there's a problem finding a liver, perhaps the Speaker would be willing to step up to the plate."

\*     \*     \*

George had come out as soon as Karen phoned, and now he sat at the computer assessing the sniffer results. As far as she could tell, and she was no expert, he was running through the same checks over and over, a frown furrowing his face. After half an hour of this, George smacked his hand on the desk and swore.

*¡Damn!î* He turned to Karen immediately. "I am really sorry, ma'am, I forgot you were in the room for a minute. Please forgive my outburst." He turned back to the keyboard and rattled his fingers over the keys for a second. "Nothing showed up, nothing at all. I can't understand it."

George rifled through his case, found a disk, and loaded it. "This is a similar sniffer program written by a different crypto team." He put the disk away and stood up. "Try again."

"You think it will work this time?"

George frowned. "It should have worked before. Call me the minute you get something."

*Nov. 21, 1999: Day 41, Columbus*

With the posting of the third response to Sergei, the pace quickened. The wormhole flashed across the screen once or twice a day now. Knowing that one could come any time made Karen nervous; she found herself flinching when she sat down to moderate the mail list.

George was nervous, too. He came faithfully after each message was received, examined the hard drive, muttered under his breath, and installed a different sniffer. On each occasion he brought several other FBI agents with him, introducing them as agents from the FBI's computer fraud center in Washington - the National Infrastructure Protection Center, or NIPC. They called it Nipsy. These agents, who were also working on the case at DoD, were no more successful than George. On his fifth trip he threw up his surgeon's hands and declared defeat; he still monitored the messages, but he no longer installed anything on the computer.

"That is not a good sign," said Alex to his wife. "It means that the FBI threw their best technology at this worm and it didn't make a dent. You'd better believe that they're anxious to get this mysterious sender over here so they can find out how it works."

It wasn't until Saturday the 21st that Sergei indicated to them that they had all the clues. After some arranging and rearranging of words, the message read:

> *I am Sergei Krzyzanowski, professor of mathematics at Moscow State University. I will give deactivation key to Alex Stauffer only. I do not trust your government or mine. My wife Masha must come too. My other conditions stand.*

George, who had been summoned, read it with them.

"Sergei Kriz - what kind of a name is that?" Alex asked of no one in particular. "It's all consonants."

George read the message several times, then dropped it into his briefcase. "This appears to be the whole message. Let me know if he sends anything else. I imagine that from here on in, we'll be contacting him directly and he won't be bothering you any more. I'm sure I don't need to remind you not to say anything about this."

"But George," Karen said, "what is that supposed to mean, he'll give the deactivation key only to Alex?"

"I don't think it's anything to worry about." He clicked the brief-case shut. "The CIA will probably handle that end of it, so unless Alex is a CIA agent, and you haven't told me, I don't think he would be involved. Thanks for your cooperation. We'll be in touch."

*November 22, 1999: Day 40, Columbus*

"You are sure you do not want to come?" After walking her to her car, Volodya was still smiling, but Annette sensed that he was growing tired of her evasions. His attentions to her had grown steadily since the first time he brought her lunch, and she had welcomed them as a diver-sion. She was unable to bring herself to speak to Leo, but miserable without his friendship. Volodya made her laugh, though, and she was grateful.

"I told you I can't, Volodya," she reminded him again. "I'm going to the Stauffers' house for dinner tonight."

"You will not go to dinner with me." Volodya bore her no ill will for this; indeed, his strategy seemed to be simply to continue to ask her until she said yes at last - out of embarrassment, out of weariness, out of a simple desire to stop his asking.

"I can't turn down a dinner with my boss." The Stauffers were her friends, but it was an easy answer.

Volodya sighed. "Probably there is a Russian proverb describing this situation," he said with comic resignation. "I will go home and read my e-mail - alone."

They were standing next to her car by now; Annette reached for the door handle, but he reached across her and opened it first, forcing her to back against him to avoid the door. If she turned around now, he would kiss her; she knew the hungry look in his eye. For a moment she considered it, but instead she slipped deftly around him and slid into the seat. Waving good-bye, she pulled out of the parking lot. She could see in the rearview mirror that he watched her.

Annette sighed. She could not humor him. Keeping Volodya at arm's length was a full-time job, and lately she wondered why it was so im-portant anyway. Leo had stopped leaving messages for her, although he still looked at her in that imploring way. If only she could get past her feeling of betrayal. Her reaction was probably as much to the timing of Leo's confession - on the night when she had finally signaled her trust by inviting him in - as it was to what he had done wrong. Annette realized this, at some level, but right now she couldn't distance herself enough to examine the situation rationally.

And she was tired, really really tired. The work at the bank was never-ending; she worked every night and could no longer remember her last day off. Volodya and his carry-in lunches and sometimes even dinners were her only distraction. He was good-natured and charming and kind to her. What harm would it do to kiss him?

As she followed the winding driveway that led to the Stauffers', the house rose before her, its lights warm and welcoming. Elizabeth greeted her with a squeal of pleasure, unlike her usual dignified fifteen-year old self, and Ethan blushed, as he usually did in her presence. Katie pirouetted and pliéd and arabesqued across the living room, and Karen came out of the kitchen to hug her.

"I have to invite you to get Alex to come home," she said, smiling. "So you're doubly welcome." They filed into the dining room, a formal but inviting room with an Oriental rug and chandelier. Annette loved this house and its inhabitants; it was one of the happiest places she knew to spend an evening. Dessert and coffee before the fire followed the homey dinner of meat loaf and mashed potatoes. Alex excused himself to put Katie to bed, the two teens went off to finish homework, and Karen and Annette were left alone before the hearth.

"I could go to sleep," Annette murmured, her feet propped on a tapestry footstool.

"Alex told me you needed a break; that's part of the reason I asked you." Karen looked at Annette over the rim of her coffee cup.

"And the other part?" Annette was too warm and sleepy to be suspicious.

"I thought we could talk about you and Leo."

Annette's eyes flew open.

"Annette, I know it's none of my business, but I hate to see you both so unhappy when I'm so fond of you both." Karen spoke sympathetically. "You should talk to Leo, really."

Alex came in then, and Karen changed the subject.

Driving home later, Annette felt sure that Karen was right. She should talk to Leo; she would do so at the first opportunity. But when she saw him at the bank the next day, she was overcome by an unwonted shyness. She longed to talk to him, but she was afraid and awkward; talking to Leo now was difficult, fraught with danger. Suppose he was angry with her?

Ashamed of her waffling, at last she set a date for herself. She would talk to him on Thanksgiving. Both of them had been invited to the Stauffers'. The house was large; they could easily find a place to be alone. Just a few days more, and they would definitely talk. In the meantime, she had her work. Sometimes she wondered where she would hide from herself once the year 2000 deadline was over.

*November 24, 1999: Day 38, Columbus*

"Leo, you are avoiding me." Volodya stared hard at his friend. "I don't see you much any more."

"Sorry, Volodya, I'm just busy," Leo said, wondering if the accusation were true. He'd gotten over being angry at Volodya for causing his rift with Annette; Volodya and his e-mail reading habits were only the indirect cause, after all. "Maybe we could go out and get something to eat tonight. I've got some stuff to finish up for Alex, but I could do it later, I guess."

"Okay, good, I ask Annette, too."

Leo was startled, but he was not in a position to confide in Volodya about his present troubles. "Sure," he said, but his heart was beating faster already. Maybe if he worked things right, he could take her home and somehow persuade her to talk things over. Did she really hate him? Was she going to be angry forever?

"Five-thirty, then." Volodya gave a wave and walked off, but Leo hardly noticed.

\*       \*       \*

"Dinner tonight?" Annette sounded doubtful. "Oh, Volodya, I just heard from Alex there's a meeting tonight at seven-thirty."

"Leo is coming, too," Volodya said.

"Oh." He heard the change in her voice. "Well, perhaps if we hurry, then."

"I will come by your office at five-thirty." Volodya hung up the phone and considered for a moment. Ah. He rang Leo's number.

"Leo, this is Volodya. Annette says you have surprise meeting tonight."

"Oh." Leo sounded disappointed. "Well, do you still want to grab something to eat?"

"Okay - unless you have to finish report for Alex."

"Oh, yeah." Leo's hesitation was brief. "Well, I suppose I'd better since we've got a meeting now. We'll make it another time, Volodya, okay? Maybe this weekend."

"Okay, sure." Volodya listened to the click of the phone as Leo hung up. Then he smiled.

*     *     *

Annette was surprised and annoyed to find herself going out alone with Volodya; if Leo had come it would have been a business conference. Now it had all the appearance of a dinner date, and she knew that Volodya would take full advantage of it.

She had said yes because she didn't want Volodya to think that she and Leo were angry at each other. She now felt hurt that Leo wasn't coming, although she knew she was being illogical. After all, Leo couldn't help it that Alex had called the meeting and he had to finish a report. But she wanted to see Leo. After accepting Volodya's invitation, knowing that Leo would be there, she had felt both exhilarated and nervous. She needn't have waited until tomorrow to talk to Leo. The dinner might have been a good excuse.

She tried to smile at Volodya as he explained Leo's absence.

"Where do you like to eat?" Volodya asked as they hurried through the chilly November wind to his BMW.

"Somewhere nearby." Annette climbed into the car, huddling into the seat. "This nasty damp weather reminds me of England."

"Is warm compared to Moscow," Volodya said with great good humor. He was not wearing an overcoat.

He backed the car expertly and sped from the parking lot. He was a fast, aggressive driver. The lights of the Powell antique stores flicked by, then they headed south into Columbus on Route 23.

"We make one stop before dinner," said Volodya apologetically.

"Where?" Annette was immediately suspicious.

"To see old lady," Volodya said with a laugh. "Very old, with cats. She does not speak English; only Ukrainian and a little Russian."

Annette was mystified. "Is she a relative of yours?"

"No, I take care of her for my friend Viktor."

Fifteen minutes later they stood on the second floor of an apartment building while Volodya pounded on the door.

"She is a little deaf," he explained.

After a minute of persistent loud knocking, they heard someone fumbling with the locks inside. The door opened and a very short old woman peered around it.

"Volya!" she cried, flinging the door open and embracing him. Volodya patted her gently on the head, like a small child, and said something in Russian. The old woman replied and held out her hand to Annette.

"This is Gospodina Baranova," said Volodya. "*Gospodina* means 'Mrs'." Annette took the wrinkled hand, which gripped hers with surprising firmness, and smiled.

Gospodina Baranova smiled back, then began chattering away in Russian, or perhaps Ukrainian, herding Volodya and Annette into the apartment before her like chickens. The woman was hunched and shapeless, her waist only hinted at by the apron tied over her dark dress. Brushing several protesting cats from the sofa, she invited them to sit down, still chattering away. Then she bustled off into another room.

"She wants to give us tea," said Volodya, spreading his hands helplessly. "It won't take too long. She doesn't see too many people, just these damn cats." He pushed away a large, black cat with his foot and began brushing cat hair from his trouser leg, frowning at the offending feline.

"How often do you visit?" Annette asked, fascinated by this new side of Volodya.

"I call her every week. I visit every month." Volodya beat an encroaching cat off the sofa with a magazine and brushed his pant leg again.

Annette surveyed the apartment, which, although small, was furnished with massive dark pieces of furniture, probably antique. One, the sofa on which they sat, was new - incongruously sleek and modern. Tables crowded with African violets stood at each window. Everything looked dusty.

"Is strange place, yes?" said Volodya. "I buy her sofa because there is nowhere comfortable to sit in whole room."

Gospodina Baranova came bustling back in bearing a black lacquered tray painted with flowers and occupied by a sugar bowl and tea cups and several plates of foreign-looking cookies. She offered Annette a cookie and said something to Volodya.

"Is my job to pour tea," said Volodya, rising from the sofa and nearly stumbling over a cat. He took two of the teacups to a sideboard dominated by a brightly painted samovar. Lifting the small pot from the top of the samovar, he poured a dark liquid into the cups, then added hot water from the spout at the bottom of the samovar.

Gospodina Baranova took the cup of tea which Volodya proffered, put a lump of sugar daintily between her lips, and began drinking her tea through it.

"Is peasant way of drinking tea," said Volodya with some distaste. "But she is peasant, like Viktor was." He took a swallow of his own tea. "Shitty tea."

The old woman regarded them with her dark button-bright eyes, then leaned forward and patted Volodya's cheek and Annette's hand and said something to Volodya.

He grinned wickedly at Annette. "She says you will make good wife for me."

Annette nearly choked on her tea, which did taste like tepid dishwater. "You made that up," she accused him, her cheeks hot.

Volodya continued to grin, ogling her in a lover-like way as Gospodina Baranova took in the scene with evident pleasure.

"Did you explain to her that we're not. . .?"

"I don't bother to; she doesn't always believe me. She's very old, and sometimes a little crazy. She has her own ideas." They choked down the tea and munched cookies while Mrs. Baranova watched them closely. Annette tried not to think about the stray cat hairs on her plate.

"We should go now," Volodya said, looking at his watch. He took a swat at the black cat, which clearly considered him an interloper.

"We haven't been here long, though. She's probably lonely."

"I explained that we have schedule to keep. Anyway, she has stupid cats to keep her company."

They made their way to the door, avoiding cats, and Volodya bent and kissed Gospodina Baranova on both cheeks. She smiled fondly at him, then took both Annette's hands in hers and shook them fervently.

*¡Dos vy danya!î* cried Annette, remembering the Russian phrase for good-bye.

Back in the car, Annette reflected on the visit.

"It's kind of you to take care of her."

"Is obligation," said Volodya with a shrug, refusing the compliment. Then he turned to her with a twinkle. "She wants to come to our wedding."

Annette felt herself blushing again. "Oh, stop teasing, Volodya." But she couldn't help smiling.

Annette rode back to the office after dinner in a dreamy state, sated by the meal and the warmth of the car, only to be buffeted awake again by the wind when they reached the parking lot. She did not object when Volodya tagged along with her to her office; he was going to work tonight, too. She rubbed her arms after he took her coat off, still feeling the chill in her thin blouse.

"You are cold?" Volodya asked, looking as if he wanted to warm her up.

"I'm fine," she said quickly. He continued to look at her.

"I would like to kiss you."

"What makes you think I want to be kissed?" Annette raised her chin. Her heart unaccountably began to pound.

"I think you are curious." Still holding her gaze with his blue eyes, he closed the gap between them, and put his arms around her. Annette lifted her mouth to his; she was curious, after all.

There was nothing tentative about the Russian's kiss. He tasted like tobacco and the wine they had drunk at dinner, and his hands were firm and hot against the silk of her blouse. Ignoring the censorious little voice carping in her brain, Annette kissed back. She did not often play this game, but tonight her will power had deserted her.

She was leaning against the office wall with Volodya's body pressed against her as they continued to kiss. His hands strayed to her waist, then to her hips, pulling her closer. Annette sighed and loosened her hands from around his neck, then put them on his chest and pushed.

She wasn't going to make promises that she didn't intend to keep.

She had to push pretty hard.

"Annette?" Volodya asked at last, easing himself away from her. Not waiting for an answer, he smiled at her, then kissed her again, lazily, sure of himself.

"Volodya, that's enough, I have a meeting to go to," Annette said when she could draw breath. He was standing very close indeed.

"I am curious, too." He bent his head to kiss her again.

A sudden rap at the door. "Annette?" Leo stuck his head into the office.

Annette tried to move away from Volodya, but his body was still blocking hers, deliberately, she thought. He turned slowly toward Leo, and Annette moved away, flustered. "Oh, hello, Leo," Volodya said, smiling.

Leo's expression froze for a moment, then wavered, then hardened. He ignored Volodya.

"We're about ready to start, Annette. Alex wanted me to see if you'd been held up. But I can see I should have phoned."

Annette swooped to her desk and grabbed her file. "See you later, Volodya. Thanks for dinner." He grinned at her, but took the hint and left.

Leo was still waiting, silent, in the hall. His silence continued as they walked together. Annette could stand it no longer.

"Leo, I'm sorry, that was a mistake -"

"Yeah, I'm sure I wasn't meant to see it."

"No, I meant the kiss was a mistake-"

Leo stopped suddenly, and Annette ran out of words at the look on his face.

"Annette, you don't have to make excuses to me. You're free to kiss whomever you like. But don't pretend it was a mistake. I didn't see any struggle going on in there." He looked steadily at her.

"I meant -" She wasn't sure what she meant. Why had she let Volodya kiss her like that? Just because the Russian wouldn't take no for an answer? How admirable was that?

"Leo, I'm sorry. Don't take it to heart so. It's just a game to Volodya. Pursuit and capture. It doesn't mean so much to him."

"Well, it means a lot to me. And I didn't think you wanted to play that kind of game." He took a step down the hall. "We'd better go."

He flung the words over his shoulder. "And you'd better fix your hair and your clothes first."

Face burning, Annette slipped into the nearby ladies' room. She looked at her mirrored self in embarrassment — flushed cheeks, swollen lips, rumpled blouse - what had come over her? Vowing to have nothing further to do with Volodya, she smoothed her hair, applied lipstick, and splashed cold water on her face. Leo was still waiting when she emerged looking respectable again, but he didn't speak, and she could find nothing to say to him.

# Chapter 16

*November 25, Thanksgiving, 1999: Day 37, Columbus*

Alex was sprawled in his chair before the fire, half-asleep, breathing the ambrosia of the baking pumpkin pies and anticipating the feast to come, when the phone rang.

"Mr. President." Alex was more than a little surprised when Karen shoved the phone at him; he hadn't heard anything from the President since Sergei had identified himself. "What can I do for you?"

"Alex." The President sounded uncharacteristically hesitant. "Funny you should ask. The CIA tells me that they'd like you to fly to Helsinki today so you can be around when our friend shows up."

"You're joking." He saw Karen's head jerk up at his tone of voice.

"I wish I were. The consensus is, Sergei may refuse to leave Russia if you're not around. So we'd better have you around, just in case."

"But Sergei doesn't know what I look like. Couldn't someone impersonate me?"

"Your photo is at your web site. We have to assume he's seen it. So it's best that you be available."

Why did Alex suspect he was being conned? "But I wouldn't actually have to do anything, right? I mean, I'm not trained to do anything."

"Oh, of course not. Not at all. We just want your warm body." Was he imagining things, or was the President's voice just a trace too hearty?

"Today is Thanksgiving." Alex felt like a selfish child as he said it.

"I know it, and I can't tell you how sorry I am, Alex. I'm asking you to be a patriot, and fly to Helsinki and probably sit around a hotel room for a few days. Will you do it?"

"Well, of course I'll do what I can." Alex looked at his wife. "I'll have to check with Karen, but I'm sure she feels the same way."

"I knew we could count on you, Alex." The President sounded relieved. "Someone will call you later to give you your flight details. Thanks again. I thank you, your country thanks you." The phone clicked.

"My country thanks me," Alex said, turning to his wife. She gazed at him suspiciously.

"Did you just agree to do something dangerous?" Karen asked.

\* \* \*

The Stauffer household was abuzz with the news of Alex's sudden trip to Europe. The various relatives assembled for an early Thanksgiving dinner seemed to think the trip was a y2k effort, and Alex did not disabuse them.

When Leo arrived he was subjected to a dizzying round of introductions. Someone handed him a glass of wine and steered him into the living room where he sank gratefully into an unoccupied chair.

"Hello, Leo."

Annette's voice raised conflicting emotions, and he turned to look at her. She was wearing a soft, coppery dress and her hair was clipped back from her face with shiny barrettes. She looked more approachable and friendly than in all the previous week since she had sent him out of her apartment. Leo felt an unreasonable anger.

"Hi."

Annette's expression faltered at the hostile monosyllable, but she soldiered on.

"Leo, you're still angry," she began, and Leo could not help himself; he pictured her in Volodya's arms, and was at once embroiled in the same seething tide of frustration and jealousy he had experienced the night before.

"Yes, I'm still angry." He stood up and walked out of the room, not trusting himself to speak. When he looked back and saw Annette sitting disconsolately by the fireplace, he felt both satisfaction and shame.

He wandered onto the deck and gazed out at the leafless trees. Ethan and some male relatives were playing basketball, and Leo joined them, trying to purge his roiling emotions with physical exertion.

Because the plane to New York did not leave until three, they managed an early Thanksgiving dinner, toasting Alex and the success of his trip; then Alex grabbed his bags and Leo hustled him to the airport.

"What's eating you, Leo?" his boss asked. Alex's anger toward him seemed to have cooled, but Leo felt he was still being watched and assessed. "I'm the one who's being snatched from the bosom of my family on a holiday weekend."

Glad of the opportunity to tell someone, Leo unburdened himself to Alex as they drove.

"She was kissing Volodya?" Alex said in surprise. "Maybe he caught her off guard."

"No." Leo's face was grim. "I can tell the difference. And she didn't deny it, either."

"Well, Volodya is causing you all kinds of trouble, isn't he, Leo?" Leo swallowed his anger; he deserved the gibe.

"You'd better talk to her, " Alex said, frowning. "Volodya is a suspect, whether Annette wants to believe that or not. I don't want her mixed up with him; she's the project manager and it's a conflict of interests. Of course," he added, "you're a suspect, too. But we can at least try to limit our liability."

"Well," Leo said, "she won't return my calls, and she avoids me at work. And I'm so mad at her now I don't think I want to talk to her."

He stopped the car at the curb and they handed the luggage to an eager porter.

"Best of luck with your trip."

Alex looked fresh and ready for action. "I would never tell Karen or the kids this," he said, "but I'm kind of looking forward to it. I've never been in a Tom Clancy novel before." He grinned, and Leo grinned back. "I won't be able to telephone, probably, until I get back to the States, so you and Tim and Harry keep Karen happy, okay? I know she's worried, even though what I'm going to do seems pretty innocuous. Keep the y2k fires burning."

"Of course." The two men shook hands, and Alex settled the strap of the laptop computer case more comfortably over his shoulder. He turned to go, then called back to Leo.

"Leo -" Leo turned - "talk to Annette!" Leo waved and nodded and Alex strode into the terminal.

Leo turned his collar up against the November wind, which had begun to bite, and climbed back into his car. Talk to Annette? His fingers tightened on the steering wheel. What he really wanted to do was throttle Volodya.


*Moscow*


Sergei crossed himself rhythmically, with the great sweeping arm motions of the Russian Orthodox, and bowed solemnly with the rest of the supplicants as the priest swung his censor toward them. As the pungent smoke drifted into his nostrils he chanted with the others: *Gospodi Pomiluj*. Lord have mercy.

Masha had thought him too ill to come to the church, but these services eased his restless mind and gave him some peace from the disease in his body. Tonight's vespers service was even more crowded than usual, and the prayers more fervent, for everyone held in their minds a vision of the dark, poisonous smoke over Sosnoviy Bor, and they prayed for the safety of their brothers and sisters in St. Petersburg.

How many had just died there, Sergei wondered, and could the dead now hear the prayers that ascended to them in Heaven along with the clouds of incense? He closed his eyes and for a moment felt more a part of the invisible Church that had gone before, than of the Church he inhabited now. The feeling was so strong that when he opened his eyes, he felt that he must be in the wrong place, and for a moment he was dizzy. He was frequently disoriented now, a symptom that the doctor had warned him of; he could scarcely focus his mind on his work. In the face of his impending death, his work no longer seemed important.

The voices of the choir rebounded and echoed in the vast dome above him. The Znammeny chant was comforting and otherworldly. In two more days the Nativity fast would begin, and the words of the chant called the faithful to repent in preparation for the coming of the Christ Child, God becoming man and dwelling among men.

Sergei crossed himself again and bowed, wondering if he would still be alive at Christmas. The last few weeks, mostly confined to his apartment and too ill to work, had changed him. He was beginning to believe that it was too late for him, that even if the CIA were to contact him, the disease would kill him before he reached safety. In the face of his own death, he examined his life, and did not like much of what he saw; the arrogant humanist, the rationalist, who wondered sometimes about God, but had no time to honestly examine his beliefs.

The scent of the incense burned in Sergei's nostrils; how clearly it brought back to him the services of his childhood. His old babushka had dragged him to the cathedral and thumped him smartly on the head when he became fidgety at the hours of standing. Baptized secretly, as so many were, he had forsworn God for years afterward.

Returning after many years away, Sergei had felt welcomed and sustained. With the meticulous attention of a mathematician, he had catalogued his sins and asked for forgiveness; he even reconciled with a colleague. How minor that dispute appeared in the face of eternity!

One more transgression weighed on his soul, and to repair that fault he could only pray to God that he not die until the deactivation code was securely in Alex's hands. He no longer asked himself why he had ever agreed to create the algorithm, knowing its destructive capacity; he knew now that he had been greedy for new intellectual challenges, even at the price of hurting other human beings. Blithely ignoring the consequences of his actions, he had chosen to obey the FSB, exercising his intellect instead of his conscience.

Again the priest censed them, and Sergei prayed for strength and patience. He listened to the Gospel reading, then shuffled forward with the others to kiss the cross that the priest held. The church was always crowded, often hot, and several times he was jostled and pushed as he approached. Sergei genuflected, and the priest thrust the cross at him; he brushed his lips briefly against the cold metal.

As he made his way out of the nave, a woman bumped him. When he tried to make eye contact she looked away, but Sergei felt a thin, hard square of plastic being pushed firmly into his hand. A diskette! He slipped it quickly into his coat pocket and tried to spot the CIA agent who must have given it to him, but he could not tell who it might have been. Before he left he stopped to venerate one of the many icons of the Mother of God with Christ; the solemn faces seemed to look compassionately at him.

Masha was waiting for him in the cold street outside; she was too angry with God right now to take comfort from the services. A miracle, Masha, he wanted to tell her, thinking of the disk in his pocket, but he was too weary to talk, and as she took his arm he just smiled and shuffled down the street with the gait of an old man.

Back at their apartment an hour later, Sergei leaned back in his chair and sighed.

"You have decoded the disk?" Masha's voice was sharp with worry. "What does it say, Seryozha?" Sergei looked fondly at his wife. When they had met in university she was a physics student, large-boned and healthy with an infectious laugh. Callow youth that he was, her body was the initial attraction, but her soft heart and sharp mind were what finally won him. She was stouter now, but still beautiful to him, and he was distressed to see how worried she was.

"We are taking a little holiday, Masha," he said as a joke. "We are going to St. Petersburg to a mathematics conference. You must telephone Igor Petrovich and tell him to expect us tomorrow." They would not really attend the conference, of course; this was just a sop to the FSB, who could be expected to keep them under surveillence once they reached their destination. Igor was a mathematics professor who lived in St. Petersburg; the FSB would hear the conversation, one must assume the phone was bugged.

"St. Petersburg!" Masha breathed. "We will have radiation poisoning!"

Sergei recounted the plan recorded on the diskette.

"You will have to drive, Masha: I don't think that I can."

"You know I would do anything for you, Seryozha." Masha kissed his forehead and gazed at him with her large, kind eyes. "Now you must rest until we leave tomorrow. I can take care of the details. At least there will not be much to pack." She rolled her eyes in the droll way he loved.

Sergei closed his eyes. Brave Masha, leaving her life behind her to escape with him to the West. Then he slept.

*November 26, 1999: Day 36, Helsinki*

*NUCLEAR ACCIDENT IN ST. PETERSBURG*, the headline of the *London Times* screamed at Alex from the news kiosk in the Helsinki International Airport.

What the hell, he thought, stopping to stare at the paper. Before he could read the accompanying story, two men in the lobby rose to their feet and approached him, laughing and hearty, as though they had been waiting for him to emerge.

"Alex!" cried the older one, who looked about fifty, square of face and fit - his handshake was so firm it hurt - but otherwise unremarkable in appearance. "You remember Ray."

Ray stuck out his hand, beaming. He was in his early thirties, tall, blonde, and strikingly handsome in a Nordic way. Alex pumped their hands and, as he suspected he should, pretended to know them.

"Our car is right this way," said the older one, adding in an undertone, "I'm Terry, by the way."

These were the CIA agents, then; the man from the State Department, who had met with Alex before he boarded his plane at JFK Airport, had shown him photos and described what the agents would do when they greeted him.

They stepped outside into Helsinki's early morning darkness, and Alex felt the cold skitter of snowflakes against his cheek as he watched Ray swing his luggage into the black Volvo that waited at the curb. How dark it was, he thought, as he climbed into the back seat. He'd forgotten how short the daylight hours were this far north.

"Nice flight?" asked Terry as they pulled out into the Helsinki traffic. Then without waiting for an answer, he half turned in his seat and handed Alex a sheaf of papers and a passport. French, Alex saw.

"Open it."

Alex flipped it open and stared at the recent photo of himself. "Pierre Cormier" read the name beneath.

"I don't understand," he said, continuing to stare blankly at the photo.

"Well, since it's an international medical team, we didn't want too many Americans. When we found out you're fluent in French, it seemed like a natural fit." Terry's explanation made no sense to Alex. "And this paper here is some information on radiation sickness, just so you know what to expect when we pick up the radiation victims. You can't take it in with you though, we're supposed to be experts and it would look funny."

Alex found his voice again. "There must be some mistake," he began.

"We'll stop at a safe house outside Helsinki," Terry said, "to pick up the medical gear and change vehicles. Ray here is going to drive the ambulance to Lomonosov. That's halfway between St. Petersburg and Sosnoviy Bor, where the nuclear reactor is, they might not have told you that." Terry sounded apologetic, in case he was repeating some detail that Alex already knew.

The Volvo was beginning to feel stuffy. "Something's wrong," Alex said, his voice sounding a little too loud. "I'm supposed to wait in a hotel room in Helsinki until Sergei comes. I don't need a phony passport to do that." He saw Ray and Terry exchange glances.

"What are you talking about, Alex?" Terry was frowning at him. "We were told that you'd agreed to come with us to get Sergei out."

"Christ Almighty." Alex finally grasped what was going on, and his bewilderment morphed into fury. "That lying bastard."

"Which lying bastard would that be?"

"The President." Alex had remembered the cryptic phone conversation. "He told me that I needed to come to Helsinki to meet Sergei here. He didn't say a word about Russia. Neither did the guy from the State Department."

"Right. So it's not, technically, a lie." Terry watched Alex, taking his measure, then spoke. "The powers that be are afraid that Sergei won't give up the deactivation code unless you're there."

"Shit." Alex sat bemused while Terry filled him in. The Americans had learned of the nuclear accident on Wednesday evening, through an intercepted e-mail from St. Petersburg, but the public announcement came the next evening on Thanksgiving, while Alex was in the air. The Russians claimed that the radiation was contained after the initial accident, an announcement that few were willing to take at face value after Chernobyl.

The beleaguered Russian government, frightened of civil unrest at home, squeezed by Western diplomats, too broke to remedy the situation anyway, had agreed to allow an international committee to inspect the nuclear reactor at Sosnoviy Bor. In addition, they had asked an international disaster relief agency to assume responsibility for treating the victims of the accident, and they were even now setting up staging operations in St. Petersburg and Helsinki.

"So the President knew about all this when he called me yesterday." Alex hardly needed Terry's confirming nod.

"At that point it was confidential."

Alex felt another surge of anger. "Go on."

"After the Russian government announced the accident," Terry said, "and announced the international inspection team, they announced that Medicine Without Politics would be coming in to aid the victims. You've probably heard of MWP; they do a lot of work in St. Petersburg and Helsinki is one of their European bases. Their big project this year has been raising money for ambulances to replace some of the Russian ones. They were going to drive the ambulances into St. Petersburg in a couple of weeks, loaded with medical supplies, and present them to the city in a special ceremony. Instead, the Russian government has given them permission to drive in today, unload the supplies in Lomonosov, and transport the radiation victims to the airport in St. Pete."

"The airport?" Alex asked.

"Yeah, that's why this accident is such a godsend for us." Terry glanced out the car window, something he had been doing ever since they left the airport. "Alex, we've been watching Sergei, and he's pretty sick. One of our problems in getting him out is that he's in no condition to do anything that requires exertion. We've arranged to meet him outside Lomonosov; we'll disguise him and his wife as radiation victims and fly them out of the country with the rest. That way he'll have medical monitoring. The FSB is unlikely to be checking this flight very closely, and my guess is that the airport will be a mob scene anyway - a lot of St. Petersburg citizens are leaving the city until they get confirmation that it's really safe from radiation. I can't blame them."

*Columbus*

Karen looked at the Friday morning *Courier* in disbelief, then quickly skimmed the article describing the nuclear accident near St. Petersburg. That's where Alex was - or close enough. Radiation could be windborne across the Gulf of Helsinki, couldn't it? She felt a little sick.

The phone rang and she picked it up automatically.

"Karen Stauffer?"

The voice sounded official; had something happened to Alex? Karen gripped the phone until her fingers hurt. "Yes, this is she."

"Mrs. Stauffer, this is Bill Martin from the State Department." Karen waited in rigid suspense. "The President asked me to phone and let you know that your husband is in no danger in Helsinki as far as we know. We believe that the accident really was a small one, at least in terms of radiation leakage, and the chances of your husband being exposed to any significant amounts of radiation are low. Are you all right, Mrs. Stauffer?" Karen had not spoken.

"Oh, yes, sorry. I'm all right. Thank you so much for calling. It was kind of the President to think of us. Can I talk to my husband?"

"I'm afraid not." Martin sounded sympathetic. "In a few days, perhaps. I don't know whether we'll be in touch with him or not, but I can pass on a message if we are."

"Tell him that we love him." Karen heard Martin make a sympathetic noise.

"I'll surely do that, ma'am. You sit tight and try not to worry now."

"I'll try," said Karen, clicking the phone's off button. She leaned her head against the smooth wood of the kitchen cabinets. At least he was only in Helsinki, she thought.

*Helsinki*

"I didn't sign on for this," Alex said after Terry had given him the pertinent information. "I'm not a doctor, and I'm not an agent."

"The medical personnel, including our doctor, will fly in separately from Europe and the U.S. and meet in Lomonosov," Terry said. "We're not expecting you to act as a medic."

"Well, what are you expecting then?"

"You just have to be there, so our friend can see you and hand you the deactivation code." Terry's voice was persuasive. "This operation has the highest priority. The President and the DCI - Director of Central Intelligence - endorse it. The State Department non-concurs - I love that phrase - but they have to support it."

"Why do they - *non-concur?*"

"State?" Terry rolled his eyes. "Because of the diplomatic repercussions if something goes wrong. Bad publicity for Russia. They're supposed to be a free country now; they don't want the West to know that their policies still make it necessary sometimes for citizens to defect. Bad publicity for us, too, of course. The Cold War is supposed to be over." Again he scanned the street outside.

"Force of habit," Terry said, when he saw Alex watching him. "And, case in point about the Cold War not being over. Helsinki is crawling with agents, being so close to Russia. Especially now. The more unstable their government looks, the more the FSB steps up their activity, and the more we step up ours." He shook his head. "Some things never change."

Alex turned his gaze to the clean streets of Helsinki while he pondered the dirty politics of his former roommate, the President. He hated subterfuge, and was tempted to tell Terry to hail him a cab back to the airport; but as his anger cooled from boil to simmer, he acknowledged that more was at stake in getting him over here. He couldn't forget about the worm.

"What do you know about the radiation levels?" he said in a low voice.

"I asked the same thing," Terry said. "Right now the jury is still out. Unfortunately we can't wait until they decide whether it's safe or not. Our exposure will be relatively short, and we'll be wearing some protective gear."

Alex thought of Karen and the kids. The thought of driving into a possibly radioactive zone was terrifying, and he was weighed down with guilt over what it might mean to his family. The risks appeared enormous. But what choice did he have, really? If they couldn't fly back to the States with Sergei and his deactivation code, the deadly algorithm would continue to mutate, burrowing from bank account to bank account, sucking money from the world's banks and causing a collapse of confidence. The stakes were too high; the die was cast.

"Okay," he said at last, and he could feel the tension in the car relax. "I'm your man."

# Chapter 17

By Friday the media were hinting that the accident at Sosnoviy Bor was the result of a year 2000 test gone awry. Was that possible? Karen wondered. Many countries, the U.S. and Sweden among them, had announced in the course of the last eighteen months that if they could not be certain of the safety of their nuclear plants during the year 2000 rollover, then the plants would be closed then and reopened later. Last year Finland had begun demanding year 2000 readiness information from the Russian sites of Sosnoviy Bor and the Kola Peninsula, because both were close enough to threaten Finland with radioactive fallout in the case of a nuclear disaster.

To keep herself from worrying about Alex, Karen was working on the mail list. Ordinarily a holiday weekend would have slowed the volume of e-mail, but the bad news at St. Petersburg resulted in a spate of posts about nuclear reactors.

Karen posted the last message to the list and sighed, leaning back in her chair. She would feel so much better if she could just talk to Alex, although he had warned her that he would probably be incommunicado for a few days, until Sergei and his wife were actually in the United States. The bustle of visiting relatives kept Katie from worrying about her daddy, and Elizabeth and Ethan were very good about not talking about Alex's safety in front of their little sister.

Ethan and Elizabeth were wired, constantly speculating about where their father was now, and what he might be doing. Their scenarios featured Alex as a master spy, a thought that made Karen shudder. Sitting in a hotel room in Helsinki might not be glamorous, but at least it confined her worry to radioactive fallout, without factoring in espionage as well.

## En route to St. Petersburg

Masha was too nervous, and Sergei too ill, to think that they were saying good-bye to Moscow as they left the city in the early Friday morning dark. The Lada, a cheap and dirty Russian version of the Italian Fiat, blended invisibly with the hundreds of other Ladas on the road.

"Are you all right, Seryozha?" Masha was anxious about her husband. It was difficult to adjust the temperature in the Lada; when she turned on the heater, which was certainly needed, the heat blasted out so fiercely that she had to turn it completely off fifteen minutes later. Then she had to remember to turn it back on again before Sergei began to shiver with the cold. His pallor beneath his fur hat was marked, and he had scarcely spoken a word since they left.

"I am saving my strength," Sergei murmured, laying a gloved hand on her leg by way of comfort. Poor Masha, he thought, bearing the tension of this journey alone. Despite his nervousness, he could hardly stay awake; could he be slipping into a coma? Sergei turned his face toward the steamy window and soon drifted off again as the Lada made its way closer to St. Petersburg.

*       *       *

"What?" Alex awoke to the sound of Ray's impatient voice. He felt stiff from his perch in the jump seat of the ambulance, and groggy from jet lag. And jumpy. Undeniably jumpy.

"We'll be in St. Petersburg soon. You should wake up." Alex was fully awake at once. They had made only a few stops on the trip, the first outside Helsinki to don their MWP medical scrubs, the second at the Russian border. Ominous as it looked, with its two sets of parallel barbed wire fences and guard towers, the crossing was uneventful. The Finnish border patrol saluted and waved them through. The Russian soldiers, painfully young and obviously under orders, glanced cursorily at the passport of each driver and passenger, then let them pass without further comment. When Alex released the breath he had been holding, Terry laughed.

His first glimpse of Russia had been like his last glimpse of Finland; miles of pine forests with few signs of habitation. Overcome by jet lag and the monotonous landscape, Alex had slept for a good part of the trip. He suspected it was a defense mechanism; as long as he was asleep, he couldn't think about the crazy and dangerous thing he was doing.

"Have you traveled in Russia much?"

Ray gave him a sideways look. "Some."

The terse reply was not lost on Alex, and he fell silent. Dusk was deepening; he felt as if he had spent most of the time since his arrival in the dark.

On the outskirts of St. Petersburg, Terry pulled out the radiation gear they had been given. The protective head covering looked like a gas mask.

"Are you going to wear yours, Ray?" he asked.

Ray snorted. "Not a chance. The people here drive like lunatics, and I can't see with that thing on. And if something goes wrong later, I want to be able to see what I'm doing."

Terry let the masks drop back on the floor. "When we go into the hospital, we'll wear surgical masks. They told me that those will give us some protection." Ray and Alex nodded, and Alex again turned his attention back to the city.

St. Petersburg, built on the Neva River, was dazzling, but Alex was hardly in a position to appreciate it. His stomach was getting jumpier and jumpier; he knew they had to be close to their destination. Night had fallen, but he caught confused glimpses of elaborate, domed churches, vast squares, memorials, fountains.

They turned due west and hurtled toward Lomonosov. Somewhere beyond Lomonosov lay Sosnoviy Bor, its radiation leak nicely contained as the Russians claimed. Or not.

\*       \*       \*

Sergei floated above the car and watched himself, dreamily. He appeared to be awake and occasionally dozing, but he realized he must be delirious. He watched Masha, too; she was driving faster and faster, glancing fearfully at his useless shivering hulk.

Sergei noted that although the traffic into St. Petersburg was light, the traffic going the other direction was heavy; and the people in those cars looked tense and angry, blasting their horns, edging out of the crowded lanes and weaving up the berm. The evacuees, thought Sergei, woozily unconcerned. Evidently they didn't believe what the government said about the radiation being contained.

Radiation. It occurred to Sergei for the first time that they were driving right into a hot zone, and if his liver disease didn't kill him first, the radiation poisoning might. The irony of the situation was vastly amusing, and Sergei began to laugh softly and happily, while his terrified wife clung white-knuckled to the steering wheel and pushed the protesting Lada to the limits of its speed.

*        *        *

Late afternoon, St. Petersburg. Professor Krzyzanowski failed to appear at a mathematics conference meeting. A conference in Moscow, then a directive.

*Kill the professor.*

*        *        *

The road to Lomonosov was empty of all traffic save the ambulances; Alex wondered whether the government had closed it, or whether people were avoiding it for fear of radiation. With lights flashing and sirens wailing, the squadron of ambulances arrived at the Lomonosov hospital, at what looked like an emergency room exit. The hospital was brightly lit, its uneven concrete work and peeling paint a mute testimony to the country's economic woes. While the hospital personnel unloaded boxes from the back of the ambulance, Ray and Terry jumped from the ambulance and ran inside. Alex followed, feeling like a phony, hoping that their patient was not really too sick.

The MWP medical personnel were waiting in the lobby with their patients already on stretchers. Following Terry's gaze, Alex spotted a burly man of medium height with brown skin and handsome, even features. His nametag proclaimed him to be Dr. Eduardo Echevarrio, and his black eyes studied Alex intently.

"Dr. Echevarrio, how was your flight?" Terry asked, striding over to the man and taking his hand.

"Thank you, I was quite comfortable. And were you pleased with the ambulance?"

"I think our patient should be very pleased with his transportation." After this odd exchange the two of them put their heads together, and Alex could no longer hear their whispered words. Ah. It had been a password exchange to verify identities and make sure that Dr. Echevarrio ended up in the right ambulance. Alex looked around surreptiously to see if anyone in the lobby had noticed. The patients, some bandaged, some not, waited impassively on their stretchers for the busy medical personnel to shuttle them out to the waiting ambulances.

"Pierre!" Ray had to call his name twice before Alex remembered who he was supposed to be. Ray motioned him to accompany Dr. Echevarrio; the stretcher-bearers slid the patient carefully into the back of the ambulance, and the doctor immediately set to work on him, Alex looking on helplessly. Eduardo's patient was a young man in his twenties; he didn't have any noticeable burns, but his face was an unhealthy color. Alex saw him open his eyes once, look around in an unfocused way, and then close them again.

As Ray pulled away from the hospital, Alex realized that Terry was not in the front cab. Had something happened?

A block from the hospital the ambulance slowed for a moment near a corner, and the passenger door opened. "Drive!" said Terry as he hopped in, and they sped off.

"Okay, Pierre, I'll take over. You sit up front. We realized it might look funny if we had more people in this ambulance than in the others, so I lost myself for a minute and let Ray pick me up where they wouldn't notice. Pierre, this is Eduardo." Eduardo raised a hand in greeting.

"How is he?" Alex asked, nodding at the victim.

"He seems not so bad to me," Eduardo said. "He wasn't hooked up to an IV when they gave him to me. I'll just watch his vitals until we rendezvous." Alex thought he saw the boy's eyelids flicker, but then he was still again.

"In ten minutes," Ray called back to them. "Let's pray our folks are there."

Alex did pray, fervently. The nearer they came to success, the more nervous he was.

*       *       *

By the time Masha had reached the appointed filling station, she was shaking with nerves. Sergei thanked God that he had recovered somewhat; maybe it was just an adrenaline rush at the knowledge that they could soon put themselves in someone else's hands.

The gas station was typical. Two pumps sprang up starkly from a ground black with diesel oil and pollution from the city, the payment kiosk was bare of goods and filthy, and the toilets proclaimed their presence from twenty feet away. It was a dismal meeting point; Sergei wondered if the Americans were making some ironical allusion in choosing it.

They sat silently in the car, turning the ignition on and off as they needed the heat. The man in the kiosk seemed to have no interest in life beyond the girlie magazine he was perusing; he entirely ignored them.

"Are you all right, Masha?" Sergei asked. She whirled on him.

"Am *I* all right? Are you joking, Seryozha? I thought you were going to die in the car!" She snatched up his mittened hand and held it to her lips. Sergei could only sit and watch; tears rolled weakly from beneath his eyelids.

"I am so sorry, dear Masha. You married a coward. Yes," he said when she shook her head and tried to shush him. "I could have said no to them and I didn't. Now see what we have come to. Fleeing our own home. Becoming exiles. Because of me."

"What is done, is done." Masha was fatalistic. "Just give the Americans the code and get well again. For me." She continued to clasp his hand in hers as they waited for the ambulances.

# Chapter 18

*St. Petersburg*

"We're having a little mechanical trouble," Ray was saying, radioing the agreed-upon alibi to the lead ambulance. "I just want to pull into that gas station and check it out. I've already radioed the ambulance following me; if the trouble is severe, we'll all transfer to that ambulance. Roger . Out." Ray turned off the siren and pulled into the gas station, the second CIA ambulance trailing him.

Alex peered out the small side window of the ambulance, his breath quickening. There! He saw the Lada. A window rolled down and an arm reached out and waved three times, evidently a signal. The ambulances drew alongside the Lada, their rear ends away from the man in the kiosk, who looked up with only mild interest when they pulled in. Terry jumped out and opened the hood, then ran to the kiosk and explained in Russian that he needed to check something in the engine. The man nodded, and dropped his eyes once more to his magazine.

"C'mon, Pierre, help me with the stretchers." The other two agents had climbed out of their ambulance and were opening the back doors. Carefully Alex and Ray picked up the stretcher with the young man on it and eased it from the ambulance. The gravel crunched under their feet in the still night air. Out of the corner of his eye Alex could see the door of the Lada open.

As they were maneuvering the stretcher into the second ambulance, Alex heard a Russian voice call his name.

"Alex! Glory to God! I bring you what I promised," and the man -

it must be Sergei - held something out in his hand. A diskette. The worm deactivation code. Alex smiled, but he couldn't reach for it until the stretcher was stowed in the ambulance.

Without warning Alex's patient sprang off the stretcher, snatched the disk and went rocketing away from them. The code! In simple reflex action, Alex followed, fueled by a surge of adrenaline, ignoring the shouts behind him, bent only on recovering what they had come so far to find.

Footsteps pounded behind him, then a man sprinted past; the other CIA agent from the other ambulance, Alex thought. Then ahead, more shouts, and the sound of bodies thudding against the tarmack. In the dimness an arm rose and descended, Alex heard an odd, sharp cry, and one of the men scrambled to his feet and took off; it had to be the man with the disk. In two steps Alex had him; with a flying tackle he launched himself at the shadowy man, felt the jar of flesh and then the harsh scrape of asphalt under his hands. An impression of thrashing limbs and the thud of a fist against his temple, then hands were pulling them both up off the ground.

"What the hell do you think you're doing!" Terry's disembodied voice was furious as he hauled Alex to his feet. "He's got a knife, are you trying to get yourself killed?"

Ray and one of the CIA agents from the second ambulance were holding the young man from the ambulance, who still struggled to escape while they pried his fingers open. "The diskette, get the goddamned diskette!" More running feet. This time it was Eduardo.

"Where is he?" In the ill-lit parking area, Alex caught the glint of a hypodermic needle before Eduardo plunged it into the faux radiation patient's neck. The young man collapsed at once.

"Go get the stretcher." Terry's voice was a hiss of fury that Alex did not think of disobeying. As they ran panting back to the ambulance, a sudden sweep of headlights lit up the tarmac and a car pulled in. Alex froze. Had the man at the kiosk called the police?

"Come on!" Alex recognized Ray's voice and followed. Ray grabbed the stretcher and the two of them ran back to Terry. Unceremoniously they dumped the drugged man on the stretcher and ran it back to the second ambulance, where the two MWP doctors waited, silent and wide-eyed.

When Alex turned around to go back to Terry, Ray grabbed his arm. "Don't." His instruction was terse.

"The other man?" Alex asked. "The one who ran past me. Wasn't he a CIA agent?"

"Yes. Dead. Knifed. Never mind that now, we haven't got time." Alex saw the headlights again, saw the car pull away. A moment later Terry was tugging on his arm. "Let's go. Get in the ambulance with me. Ray can drive the other one."

Alex climbed in, then pulled the ambulance curtain aside. Eduardo had hooked an IV to Sergei's arm, and his wife lay on the stretcher next to him.

"Shit." Terry turned around in his seat. "You're going to have to drive for a minute, Alex. I've still got to put their make-up on so they look like radiation burn victims. We can't wait here any longer."

"What about the guy at the kiosk?" Alex asked.

"He's one of ours," Terry said. "And he's now the proud owner of Sergei's Lada. He won't be calling anyone. Now drive."

Alex did as he was told.

"Just follow the road." Terry's voice sounded strained. "And for God's sake, don't have an accident." Fifteen minutes later he instructed Alex to pull over, and he climbed back in the driver's seat.

"God," Terry said as he pulled back out into the road. "What else could go wrong?"

"What happened?" Alex dreaded the answer.

Terry shook his head. "I don't know for sure. The patient in our ambulance was no patient. He must have been an FSB agent. The knife looked like one of theirs. Maybe one of us said something while he was in the ambulance - in English - that was suspicious. Then when we pulled him out of the ambulance and Sergei tried to give you the disk, he figured it was something important and grabbed it."

"Did he know we were waiting for Sergei?" Alex said.

"I don't think so." Terry checked his rear view mirror again, adjusting it nervously. "If they knew where Sergei was, there would've have been a bunch of FSB agents here to greet us, and they would have taken Sergei before now. No, I think he was just a plant who happened to get lucky. They probably just stuck him in with the patients and told him to keep his eyes open, because you never know what might happen with foreigners around." Terry's shoulders slumped. "And they were right."

"Now what?"

"Now we do exactly as we planned." Terry's voice was calmer now. "Their agent goes through the airport on a stretcher; he'll be knocked out for hours, and he won't remember what happened when he wakes up. Sergei and Masha have got their make-up on and they're heavily bandaged. For further credibility, they both have vomit bags, like the kind you can get in a joke store, only more convincing."

"And the agent who died?"

Terry's sigh was short and sharp. "He's dead, that's all. The back-up car took his body. Just be thankful it wasn't you, you idiot. What would we tell your wife if something happened to you?"

What will you tell *his* wife, Alex thought. He remembered the man's cry and felt sick.

"We're paid to do this, Alex. You're not." Terry seemed to read his mind. "I appreciate what you did, but please don't do it again. There were plenty of us there to handle it."

Terry was silent for a few moments. "Listen, Alex, we don't have time to mourn. We've still got to get the code out of here. We're coming into St. Petersburg now; you just do your job, which is to take Masha's stretcher in. They'll have gurneys there waiting for us, and a few Russian medical personnel if we need them. Just run her in as fast as you can, speak French, and pray to God they don't look too closely."

Alex nodded. The sound of the sirens wound down as they pulled to a stop before the airport. Terry grabbed Alex's hand and shook it. "Good luck!" He jumped out of the ambulance and ran to the back to open the doors. Alex followed suit, running to the first ambulance.

"Okay, Masha, be brave," he whispered, holding her hand as the stretchers were loaded on gurneys and rushed inside. Terry and the woman doctor were ahead of him with their patients; Eduardo, and Sergei behind.

Everyone in the airport seemed to know who was being transported, and why. Many people jumped back and crossed themselves, shaking their heads. Alex ran through the concourse, focused on Masha, scarcely looking around. Unfortunately the rendezvous and the FSB incident had separated them from the other ambulances, and they would have to pass through customs without the cushion of all the other radiation victims. Please God, let the plane still be there, Alex prayed as he sprinted down yet another corridor.

\*     \*     \*

The airport agent seemed conscientious, bent on doing his job. He looked at the first radiation patient, checked records, and waved him through. When he got to Terry's patient, the FSB agent, Alex could feel himself begin to sweat, although Terry appeared unruffled. He asked a question in Russian, which Terry answered in Russian. When he finally nodded at Terry to proceed to the plane, Alex felt sick with relief. Now it was only he and Ray, with Sergei and Masha.

The FSB agent walked back to their stretchers. He stared at Sergei and Masha hard, as if he were trying to look past the bandages and identify them. Alex's prayers accelerated. So did his pulse. He watched the agent step closer to Masha's stretcher and he prayed that her nerve would hold. She had the look of a rabbit aware that the fox is about to spring.

Alex watched as the agent actually lifted up the corner of a bandage on her face, then quickly lowered it again, a look of disgust on his face. He must be suspicious. Alex could feel the sweat soak his shirt and he thought frantically, then had a sudden inspiration.

"*Que faites-vous?*" he asked the agent belligerently. What are you doing? Alex swore in French and gesticulated, hoping to distract him from Masha. The agent looked up, annoyed.

Suddenly Masha sat bolt upright, practically in the agent's face, gave a tremendous moan, and appeared to vomit profusely on the front of his shirt. At almost the same moment Sergei leaned over his stretcher and began weakly gagging.

The agent sprang backwards, swearing, looking sick himself at the putrid odor rising from his shirt. He began stripping it off hastily, and Alex leaned over to him.

"*Pouvons-nous aller maintenant, s'il vous plait?*" Please can we go now? he asked, pulling his face into a mask of indignation.

"Yes! Go! Please!" The agent waved them through in disgust, and Alex pushed the gurney toward the plane, his knees so weak that walking was difficult.

# PART 3

# Chapter 19

*November 29, 1999: Day 33, Columbus*

Halfway through her Monday morning workload, Annette opened her office door to a cheerful deliveryman bearing an enormous bouquet of flaming gold and scarlet chrysanthemums and dahlias. Leo! she thought, snatching the card.

"I am still curious" read the message inside. The flowers were from Volodya, then. Typical that he should send them to her office and not to her home. Not only was he a show-off, but the flowers sent a signal to any other interested males that he was establishing his claim.

Annette shook her head; she was being unfair. Volodya was pursuing her and the flowers were a lovely way to get her attention. Leo's signals were just as clear; he was angry with her and didn't want to be around her. Even though she had worked at home all the long weekend, he never called, not even to argue with her. Annette felt worse and worse about her own behavior; for how many days had she not returned his calls?

She should call him and try to straighten things out; she would call him, she decided. After work today, or tomorrow, perhaps, although she was working at such a pace now that the only thing she did after work was go to bed. In the meantime, she would do what she usually did to keep her mind off her problems; she downloaded a report on her computer screen and soon lost herself in it.

\*     \*     \*

Columbus looked small and cramped this morning, as it always did when Volodya returned from a weekend in New York, but the comparison did not depress him this time. He checked his clock radio as he dressed; nearly noon already, but he hadn't returned to Columbus until early this morning.

And of course the thought of Annette made him actually eager to be home again. He smiled with satisfaction whenever he thought of last Wednesday's encounter, and he thought of it often; he was extremely anxious to have Annette in his bed. Sex for its own sake was a worthwhile goal, of course, but he also believed that a sexual encounter subtly altered the balance of power in the relationship. In his experience, women always gave more than men; once one made love to a woman, she ceded some of her power. And Volodya preferred to be the one in control.

That Leo had seen them together was serendipitous; he could hardly have planned it better had he tried. Probably Leo was mad at him, which was unfortunate, but probably Leo was furious with Annette, which was perfect.

It was a pity that the news of the meltdown (if that's what it was) at Sosnoviy Bor came at a time when the rest of his life was humming along smoothly. The news was disquieting, and he wondered whether the accident really could have been caused by a year 2000 fault. For months now he had discounted everything he heard about y2k as hysteria, assuming that it would all be fixed in time. How unpleasant for everyone if that were not true.

He had friends in St. Petersburg, whom he had e-mailed when he heard the news, but they had had little to tell him except that many people were evacuating themselves until the international committee declared that the accident was contained, and no one was happy with the government. But how long had it been since a Russian was happy with the government?

He moved briskly, checking the crispness of his laundered shirt, knotting his tie, taking more care than usual as he brushed his hair, admiring the way it flicked at his collar, just long enough, he thought, to be sexy, but not so long as to look unkempt. He hoped that Annette liked her flowers; they had cost him a small fortune, but the colors reminded him of her hair, and the New York florist assured him that they would arrive at her office first thing Monday morning.

He smiled into the mirror. He would be working late tonight, since he was late getting to work, but Annette was probably working late, too. He would stop in to see her in her office; perhaps they would have lunch together, or dinner, or, who could say, perhaps even breakfast. Right now there were too many variables to predict the outcome, but the game was going his way.

*       *       *

November's pale sun hardly lit the sky this morning, thought Karen. She sat at the kitchen table with a mug of coffee, not even dressed yet, her feet freezing on the ceramic tile of the floor. Again she told herself to stop worrying about Alex. A delay was just that, a delay. Even if the operation went wrong, Alex was still okay, because he wasn't directly involved. Again she read the AP news bulletin on the Courier's front page.

The headline read: *Nuclear Inspection Team Sounds All-Clear at St. Petersburg.*

> *This morning an international inspection team from the International Atomic Energy Agency, the International Nuclear Safety Program, and Asea Atom in Sweden, announced that radiation levels at the Sosnoviy Bor nuclear reactor plant in St. Petersburg, Russia were sufficiently contained not to pose a threat, either to St. Petersburg or to the rest of the world.*
>
> *World concern peaked when the Kremlin announced Thursday, November 25, that a small accident at the Sosnoviy Bor plant, only 45 kilometers from St. Petersburg, had resulted in the release of radiation, and as many as five deaths. Due in part to favorable atmospheric conditions, and in part to the design of the plant, the inspection team found that radiation dispersion was confined to within ten kilometers of the site.*
>
> *The team also reported the accident's likely origin was a series of flow channel ruptures. The released radiation was dissipated when it passed through the plant's 'con-*

*finement rooms', which are designed to slow the escape of the radiation into the atmosphere. The accident may have been caused by human error, but because the operators in the immediate area of the accident received severe burns and high doses of radiation, they have not yet been interviewed.*

*Although first reports linked the accident to a y2k test, the inspection team believes that scenario is unlikely, given what they have seen so far. "Fortunately, nuclear reactors are in general resistant to the kinds of y2k accidents which threaten other facilties," said inspection team head Sven Ivarsson. "Critical operations are analog rather than digital, and therefore not susceptible."*

*In his closing remarks at the press conference, Ivarsson stressed the generally excellent safety record of the nuclear power industry as a whole, and said that he believes that nuclear power plants in Russia and Eastern Europe are safer now than they have ever been.*

The phone rang. Probably Tim with his morning check-in call; or maybe Leo. They all worried about her, if not Alex, and called frequently. Even Harry had called once, a thought that made her smile.

"Hello?"

"Karen?"

Her grip on the phone tightened; she could scarcely breathe for a moment. "Alex?" she managed finally. She tried to keep the tears out of her voice. "Alex, I've been so worried."

"Don't cry." His voice was tender. "I'm fine, really. I'm in the States, but I can't say where yet. Everything went okay."

"When will you be home?"

"I wish I could come straight home." He paused for a moment. "I have to be debriefed."

"Debriefed? That sounds very cloak-and-dagger."

"Yeah." He sounded dispirited suddenly, and Karen was concerned anew.

"Are you sure you're all right? You sound odd."

"It was a long flight and a short night. You don't know how good it is to hear your voice again!" His voice was fervent, and Karen wondered what he wasn't telling her. "I really missed you and the kids. Tell me what happened while I was gone."

Karen filled him in with their activities, keeping her stories light and amusing. She didn't understand what was going on; she thought he'd be jubilant, now that the code was recovered and could be fixed. Instead he sounded melancholy.

"I have to go now," he told her after they had talked for fifteen minutes. "I'll call you later today, maybe when the kids are home. Call the office for me, will you?"

"Of course," she promised. "I love you, sweetheart."

"I love you." He rang off. Karen held on to the phone for a moment. He was back, he was fine, Sergei was back - perhaps that was the trouble. Sergei might be really ill, sicker than they thought. Maybe too sick for a transplant. Well, Karen couldn't help being happy that her husband was back, whatever else was wrong. She dialed Tim's number to share the good news.

\* \* \*

When Leo saw Annette and Volodya waiting together for the bank's elevator, he nearly turned and walked the other way. Too late; Annette had seen him already

"Leo!" She waved and he turned toward her reluctantly. Her eyes were dancing and her smile contagious; she looked alive and vital and gorgeous. Laying her hand on his arm, she said, "Leo, Alex is back! I just heard!"

Leo had to smile back, genuinely relieved. "That's great! Do you mean he's in town?"

"Not yet, but soon." She hesitated. "Leo, can't we talk?" Her eyes pleaded with him.

At such close quarters she was difficult to resist.

"Elevator," Volodya sang out, and they stepped toward it automatically, Annette still looking at Leo with a question in her eyes. When the door opened, Volodya put a proprietary hand at the small of Annette's back and steered her gently into the waiting elevator. Then he bent his head toward her and Leo heard him say in his heavily accented English:

"I am glad you liked flowers. Where do you want to have lunch?"

Leo's gut clenched. He stepped backward out of the elevator and stood next to the stairs as the elevator went up. What kind of game was Annette playing? Why was she having lunch with Volodya now? Was Leo utterly deluding himself in thinking that he was the one she cared for?

He remembered, in horrid detail, the scene in Annette's office.

He was still seething. She was the one who had cut him off, would not forgive him, would not return his calls, or listen to his apologies. And she was the one who had chosen to go out with the one man most calculated to infuriate him. Volodya was more of a hacker than he would ever be. How could she refuse to forgive him for hacking, and then go out with Volodya? And not only once, it seemed - anyone could make a mistake once - but still? His head hurt with the illogic of it.

Leo went over it all again in detail, stoking up the coals of his anger. She could look at him with her beautiful green eyes, but he would harden his heart. As long as she was seeing Volodya, he wanted nothing at all to do with her.

He did not feel a bit better after making this decision.

*November 30, 1999: Day 32*

Annette and the other team members listened as Homer stood up in the y2k meeting and read solemnly.

*From:*       *y2kRay@aol.com*
*To:*         *Homer Jones, President, Midwest National Bank*
*Subject:*    *Banks, Beware!*

*Hey Bank!*

*There once was a hacker named Fred*
*Who took the bank's money and fled*
*Rob a bank with a gun?*

*That would not be much fun -*
*So he tampered with source code instead!*

*Warning you,*

  *y2kRay*

Eddie stifled a chuckle as Homer finished his declamation. "Hey, Homer, it's not illegal to be crazy, last I heard," he said.

"Well, Alex told me to save them," Homer said. "Here's the other one I got." He launched into a solemn rendition of 'The hackers are coming, hurray, hurray.'"

Eddie was laughing and wiping his eyes by the time Homer finished. "C'mon, Homer, you can't be serious. The guy's obviously loopy. Anyway, the worm's out today, so the messages can't be serious."

"Don't be sure," Tim said. "It's stupid, but it does have the facts. It talks about source code. It talks about the money being gone."

"Was the other one a poem, too? Was it a limerick?" Annette asked.

"It was a different kind of poem, but it was a poem," Homer said. "There were three different kinds of poems. I'm glad someone is taking this seriously. There could be a clue here that will help us find who put the bug into the bank."

"Well, anyone using those poems to find the culprit is definitely clue-less," Eddie said, dissolving into laughter again at his own joke. "Anybody here know any computer hacker poet nerds? I thought not."

Annette sat quietly. Leo's mother was a poet.


*December 1, 1999: Day 31*

By Tuesday morning Sergei had deactivated the code, and notice was sent to the world's banking community. Several other banks that had lost funds and realized that the now-deactivated algorithm was the cause contacted the FBI. At the y2k team meeting, Homer speculated that banks in other parts of the world had also been affected.

"We just haven't heard about it because no bank is going to advertise the fact that they've lost money - and especially not right now, less than a month before the rollover."

Tim agreed. "It could be tens of millions and even hundreds of millions of dollars, according to the FBI. Banks are still reporting their losses." He brightened. "But now the damn thing's gone. We can all sleep again *and -*"he paused dramatically "- we can finish up our project. Folks, I think we're going to make it!"

Cheers erupted. Someone threw a report into the air and its pages floated down and settled around the room.

"Alex should be here," Annette said. She'd hardly spoken at this meeting; she felt a glacial chill emanating from the end of the table where Leo sat. He had been given security clearance for this meeting, because they needed to hear his reports. How humiliated he must feel to be here under those conditions.

"He'll be in tomorrow, I think," Tim said. "He told me he needs some time to decompress - sounds like it was a pretty hairy trip. I don't know any details."

Annette gathered her straying thoughts. She was supposed to be in charge, after all, when Alex was away.

"All right. Is testing complete in all departments? Tim?"

"We could test for the next six months and not catch everything," Tim said. "We've tested the mission critical systems more heavily than those that aren't. But we could have done a lot more. Figuring one error per thousand lines of code - that's an industry standard - we've probably introduced fifteen thousand new bugs into the system."

They sat silent for a moment, stunned.

"Then how does anything work?" Eddie demanded.

"Well, that's why we tested the mission-critical systems more thoroughly. I'm pretty comfortable with their risk level. Risk levels on the other systems are higher. Not every bug is harmful, but systems will break down. We just have to be aware that we're going to be finding bugs for at least six months into the year 2000. We'll fix them as we find them. But we pretty much knew that it would shake down that way, given the limited time we had to prepare the banking consortium to be y2k ready."

"Okay, that's the legacy systems. What about the PC's, Leo?" Annette managed to sound business-like. Leo managed, too, although he would not look directly at her.

"PC's are under control. All BIOS-checked. All custom software checked, and a lot of it eliminated. One of the goals was to standardize the software used in different departments so we could control the interfaces better when we were windowing."

"Ah, c'mon, Leo, put it in English," Eddie whined. "Take pity on the poor non-techie." They laughed; this was Eddie's constant lament.

"Okay, Eddie. The hardware - the actual machine itself, no grimacing, you asked for it - of each PC has been checked and made compliant. That's what I meant when I said BIOS - that stands for basic input-output system. Custom software - software designed for a particular person to do a particular task - has been either made compliant or eliminated. COTS - commercial off-the-shelf software - what we buy from MicroCenter and load into our machines - has been standardized. All departments are using the same standard accounting package, for example. That means that when departments pass information back and forth on their PC's, the interfaces - the way they connect to each other - won't be screwed up. Data can go from one department to another with no foul-ups. And, most importantly, all users have been trained in how to enter dates so that the software will continue to work. Is that clear enough for you, Eddie?"

"My heartfelt thanks."

Annette looked at her agenda. "Embedded systems were finished a month ago. Did anyone come up with anything we missed?"

Heads shook.

"All right. Contingency plans. As far as we're concerned, Thursday, December 30th is New Year's Eve. Any celebrating should be done that night, but let's not carouse too much, because a big weekend of work awaits us.

"The bank will close on Friday at noon, and will not re-open until Monday, January 3rd. I think most of the banks in the area are following that schedule, aren't they, Homer?"

"I've certainly been pushing for it. I'd like a whole week." Homer was regretful.

"We'd all like a whole week, but the big boys thought that might be too long, so we'll open when everyone else does."

"What about TV's?" asked Harry. He too was at the meeting on sufferance.

"TV's?" Annette did not understand the question at first.

"Well, sure. New Zealand goes to midnight first on the globe, six a.m. our time on December 31st. That's an eighteen-hour difference. We need TV's to watch what's going on in the rest of the world. Seeing what happens in the rest of the world will give us a few hours more of preparation if things are gonna get really bad."

"Of course. Harry, you're in charge of it, then. Delegate if you like. Be sure we have enough here at Millennium, and in the bank. A couple for each floor, clearly visible. Rent them if you need to." She wagged a school-marmish finger. "Be sure they're year 2000 compliant." Everyone moaned at this poor joke.

"I'd really like to save the rest of this meeting for sometime in the next couple of days after Alex comes in. That's all." Annette shuffled her agenda pages nervously. "Leo, could you stay for a moment, please?"

After the rest filed out, Leo looked up from his papers.

"Is this business or personal?"

"I thought we could talk," she said. "I wanted to talk to you before - I was going to try to talk to you on Thanksgiving, but then -" She floundered and stopped. This was going badly.

"You want to talk? Okay, fine." Leo's mouth was a thin, tight line. "I thought maybe, after all the months we've been seeing each other as business colleagues only - at your request - I thought that over the past couple of months you were finally realizing that I love you. That maybe you were seeing me as something more than a warm body to carry your laptop to y2k meetings."

Annette's face colored.

"Then, I made a major mistake. I did a wrong thing. I got caught. I apologized to everybody, and they all forgave me. Except you." His eyes accused her and Annette's blush deepened. "You cut me off. Wouldn't even speak to me. I was praying that you'd forgive me, that we could move on." He paused for a moment as if unsure how to continue. "Then I see you with *Volodya*, for God's sake! You shun me because I hacked twice in my entire life. Then you go out with the e-mail hacker king himself? I don't see the logic, Annette."

"Maybe the real story is that you're in love with Volodya, and I've been kidding myself about the way you feel about me."

That statement took her breath away for a moment. Leo was jumping to all the wrong conclusions, and underneath the anger she could see how hurt he was. She didn't know what to say to him.

Leo misunderstood her silence. "So it's true, then. And we still have to work pretty closely together for the next four weeks. We're going to have to call some kind of truce." His voice was steady, but his eyes looked past her.

Annette found her voice at last. "It's not true, Leo! Stop imagining how you think I feel."

Leo brought his gaze back to her face. "Then tell me - how do you feel about me?"

Perhaps if he had taken her in his arms and kissed her first she would have found the right words. But he didn't, and she looked away.

"I'm very fond of you," she said at last, her voice barely audible.

"Fond of me." The echoed words sounded small and mean. "As a friend? As a lover? Are you fond of Volodya, too?"

"Volodya has nothing to do with this!" Her anger felt good, better than the guilt he was heaping on her.

He turned his back on her and began stuffing his papers haphazardly into their file as if he could not bear to be there an instant longer. Annette watched as he walked to the door, her brain empty of words that might stop him.

# Chapter 20

*December 2, 1999: Day 30*

Thirty days more, thought Alex, back in his office. Karen had wanted him to stay home another day, but he wanted the distraction of work. Time later to digest what had happened in St. Petersburg.

Thirty days. It wasn't long compared to the ten years of his life that he'd dedicated to fighting the millennium bug. Despite all his efforts to warn, to educate, to raise awareness, Alex wondered how many systems would fail thirty days from now.

Reading the paper that morning, Alex was struck by the unintended consequences of year 2000 preparations. The price of gold was up, for example; some were convinced that banks would fail, others that it would be the failure of the electric grid or the telecommunications network that would bring the banks down with them. In either case, people were buying gold. Some were putting their cash into gold and silver coins, because of their portability; some of the wealthy were actually reported to be loading up on bullion. The gold-buying had been increasing for the past two years, but had reached a crescendo in November.

Wall Street was described as "volatile," a euphemism for unpredictable. Yesterday stocks had dropped precipitously, but earlier in the week they had climbed. Every positive announcement about year 2000 readiness, especially in the electrical utilities, was greeting by a buying spree. A joint announcement yesterday by the federal Department of Transportation and Department of Energy that their inability to be year 2000 ready would result in budget cutbacks and job losses had caused another stock market drop.

The *Courier* described fraud risk from federal employees as being "at an all-time high" due to cutbacks in federal fraud investigators. Federal high-tech workers were finding it easier and easier to defraud the government of millions of dollars, especially, Alex was interested to note, in the Department of Defense. And if those people were hard to track now, he thought, just wait until the year 2000, when hundreds of y2k computer glitches would muddy the waters even more.

Further from home, the paper reported a serious build-up of Iraqi troops near the Kuwaiti border. The U.S. had responded by sending the carriers U.S.S. Nimitz and U.S.S. Eisenhower into the Gulf for "training maneuvers." That was direct year 2000 fallout. The Iraqis were hoping that the high-tech capabilities of the U.S. military would be crippled in the year 2000 rollover, leaving them free to seize the Kuwaiti oil fields without American interference. Alex hoped that it was just Iraqi optimism and not foreknowledge. He could not exclude the possibility that the Iraqis had managed to plant some sort of year 2000 computer virus that would cripple American military efforts. The Iraqis or anyone else with a vendetta against the U.S. government.

Pessimism was not a luxury he allowed himself, however, and he gave himself a mental shake. As long as time remained, he could find ways to help, and afterward, if need be, he would help pick up the pieces.

\*       \*       \*

Glumly, Norman said good-bye to George Mumford. The FBI still had not found its man, and George still seemed to regard him as a suspect, stopping by every few weeks in case Norman had decided to unburden his conscience. Suppose they never figured out who planted the worm. Would Norman remain forever a suspect to the FBI, to the government that employed him? Would there always be a smirch on his file?

After sifting through the names of every IT person he knew at DFAS, he could come up with no one who might have a motive for stealing this enormous amount of money. The truth was, Norman didn't know most of them well enough to have any idea about their motives or their opportunities. And the IT department here at DFAS was enormous, and Norman knew only about five of them, and how likely was it that the person who did it was also a person he knew?

Norman was glum, but he was not a quitter. He kept the names of those five IT people uppermost in his mind; he could keep his eye on them, in the interest of clearing his own name. It was the least, and it seemed, the most he could do.

*December 3, 1999: Day 29*

Alex hadn't meant to sleep late, but he'd had another nightmare. This one included dead FSB officers and bloody CIA corpses and the appearance of a demented Sergei, laughing horribly and declaring that he had tricked them all. Then Karen appeared to tell him that all the money had disappeared from their account, and Homer arrived to repossess the house and turn them out into the street.

So he was still in bed at ten o'clock when Karen told him that Homer was on the line and handed him the cordless phone. Still groggy, he put it to his ear.

"Hi, Homer. What can I do for you?"

Homer's voice was tight and strained. "Alex, the money is missing again."

"What!" The news woke him up quickly, one name in his mind. Sergei!

*December 4, 1999: Day 28*

Alex looked around the conference room at the faces of his y2k team. They all looked tired, and discouraged beyond measure by the knowledge that the money was again disappearing from the bank.

"I heard from the people with Sergei today," he said at length. "He had the liver transplant yesterday, and unfortunately he can't talk yet, he's still hooked up to a breathing tube. And he's pretty weak. But when they asked him about the algorithm, he became violently upset, and shook his head to say that he had not done anything further to the code. I'm afraid he had kind of a relapse, and the doctors won't let him be questioned again until he's regained his strength."

"Do they believe him?" Tim asked.

Alex sighed. "I don't know if they have an opinion. I think they can figure it out, once they talk to him at length, but he's too sick now. But given that he denies it, I think we should proceed as if he didn't do it. That means we have to figure out who did, and how."

"You mean Volodya?" This was Harry. Alex heard Annette's sharp intake of breath.

"Harry," Alex said, " as painful as this is for you to accept, you and Leo are still as much suspects as Volodya. We have nothing on Volodya except his hacking, and that seems to be an activity that was not confined just to him."

Harry's face reddened at the rebuke. "I didn't hack anybody's e-mail," he muttered.

"No," Alex repeated, " I don't mean just Volodya. All the Russians. And until I find out otherwise, some of the Americans, too." A long, uncomfortable silence followed Alex's words. Leo's eyes were on the conference table; Harry looked stubbornly ahead.

"But I thought we had established that Sergei planted the code," Annette said. "I don't understand why you still suspect Volodya anyway." Her tones were more clipped and British than usual; Alex saw Leo shoot her a quick glance and then look away again.

"Annette, Sergei couldn't have planted the algorithm himself." Tim explained again. "He - or more likely the KGB or whatever it's called now -would have sent it to someone else to plant. They had to have source code. Volodya had access to our source code, and he's Russian. Maybe he knows Sergei."

"They're all Russians," said Annette, "if that's your criterion. Any of them could have planted it."

Homer spoke up suddenly. "We need to find something that will bring the FBI back in."

"I've had them here before. You'd be surprised at how effective their interrogations are, and George said that almost no one refuses to talk to them, even though they're not legally obligated. When Leo told me about Volodya reading my e-mail, the bank had to file an SAR - a Suspicious Activity Report - with the Treasury Department, and both the FBI and the INS have access to those files. If we could give them a little bit more evidence of wrong-doing, they'd be willing to talk to him."

Leo spoke up. "Maybe I should check the EDI code that Volodya's company originally remediated. We've been assuming that the bad code was planted after they started working on the compile, but they could have tampered with the EDI as well."

"Leo, you can't check the code," Alex said. Leo didn't seem to get it. "You or Harry. You still work here, you can come to the occasional meeting, like today. But you can't work on the code while you're suspects."

Scowling, Leo pushed his chair away from the conference table as if he were leaving, then thought better of it and sat taking notes, or perhaps just doodling, on the pad in his lap.

Alex assigned duties, then adjourned the meeting.

"Annette, can I speak to you, please?"

Alex watched the team leave; Annette remained seated. He noticed again how tired she looked, her eyes smudged underneath and her face pale.

"I suppose you want to ask me about Volodya," she said, folding her hands.

"Well, I don't want to interfere in your private life, Annette, but this puts me in an awkward position. We're investigating him."

"You want me to stop seeing him."

"Well, actually, one of the FBI agents suggested that you go out with Volodya."

"You *want* me to go out with him?" Annette said slowly.

*        *        *

Leo entered Annette's office feeling belligerent but curious. She had never summoned him like this before, and he would bet it wasn't business.

She smiled briefly at him and he took a seat. She looked very tired, he thought.

"Leo, I owe you an apology."

He watched her knot her fingers together.

"The office is not the best place for this sort of discussion, but you've been avoiding personal encounters; I hope you're not angry that I've taken advantage of my position to bring you in here." She looked away for a moment; Leo could almost feel sorry for her.

"Leo," she said softly, "I'm sorry that you saw me in the office with Volodya. I was - indiscreet, and I'm sorry you felt hurt. But Volodya can be quite charming, and I was feeling a little angry at you because you had cancelled out on the dinner plans knowing that I would be there."

Leo jumped from his chair and stood glaring, his anger diverted from Annette to Volodya. "He told me you weren't coming to dinner after all, because of the meeting." Annette's eyes widened for a moment, then she shook her head.

"Oh, Leo - never mind Volodya," Annette said.

"It was just such bad timing that night. The worst possible timing. Finally I had made up my mind, I was beginning to feel I could trust you, and after I asked you to come in that night, you told me about the hacking. I overreacted. Like I probably always do ever since Mick O'Toole. I'm sorry."

Leo felt the last bitter dregs of his anger drain away, and he sat down.

"I'm sorry, too," he said. "Maybe we could go somewhere for dinner tonight."

"You'd better hear the next part before you decide what you want to do." Annette bit her lip. "The FBI wants me to continue to go out with Volodya."

"I see," Leo said. "Well. And so is that what you want?"

"I didn't say no."

Leo felt the color leave his face. What perfect cover she now had: her patriotic duty required her to date Volodya.

"Leo," she said. "Don't look that way. This is something I have to do for the project."

"Of course," Leo said. "The project. Right." He stood up. "I'll talk to you later, Annette."

Leo left her, not at all pleased with the implications. He swore to himself. Volodya was sauntering towards him, perfectly dressed, perfectly charming. Perfectly treacherous.

"Leo!" Volodya looked delighted to see him, but Leo felt that the smile stretching his own lips was patently false. "Leo, I was just going to ask Annette to go to lunch with me. You come, too."

"I can't, Volodya, not today. Sorry." He was a coward; he didn't want to watch Volodya with Annette.

"You are mad at me, Leo?"

Leo choked down all the answers that sprang to his lips and made a heroic effort. "I'm fine, Volodya. Just busy today."

"Good." The Russian looked relieved. "I still want you to work for me. It is not good for friends to fight over woman."

Leo fled down the hall at that remark, his fist itching to pound Volodya. "See you later," he called over his shoulder. "You bastard," he added under his breath.

Leo found himself in Alex's office.

"I want to work on the code," he said. "I want to clear my name. I want to get Volodya if there's any way I can do it."

Alex regarded him narrowly. "Clear your name?" he repeated. "How do I know you wouldn't be putting another worm in the code? Or preventing the present one from being discovered?"

Leo throttled an impulse to plead; he knew that Alex would be resistant to an appeal based on emotion.

"It's not logical to put another bug into the system," he said. "One is sufficient. Why would anyone risk getting caught putting a second one in?"

"You might keep the bug from being found," Alex said. "You might take it out so you won't get caught."

They faced each other across the desk.

"Alex," he said finally, with emphasis, " if I'm the one who put the worm in, and you let me work on the code, and I secretly deactivate it - wouldn't you be ahead of the game even if you never caught me?"

Alex looked at him sharply, then nodded his assent.

"All right. I'll okay Harry on the same basis, and you'll both have to work under Tim's supervision."


*December 6, 1999: Day 26*

Alex stretched in his chair - ergonomic or not, it kinked his back up after fifteen hours of sitting in it - then massaged his neck with one hand while he read the report that Leo had e-mailed him earlier. Although it was nearly eleven at night, Alex wanted to know what, if anything, Leo had found in the EDI. Leo's behavior bothered him more than he liked to admit. He would much prefer that the culprit turn out to be one of the Russians rather than Leo or Harry, and the way things looked now, Leo's guilt was a distinct possibility.

Leo reported that he had worked from eight a.m. until ten p.m. The EDI program had already been debugged with Sergei's code, so, Leo reported, he was searching for anecdotal evidence of tampering. Leo had looked at phone records and compile logs, searching for any sort of anomaly that might indicate that an unauthorized user had engaged in an unauthorized activity. Of course, the Russians were authorized users of the EDI system, and an authorized person making unauthorized use of the system was much more difficult to flush out.

Leo also said he'd looked at source code variables in routines and libraries of the EDI program, searching for any little hint that something was awry. He found nothing. According to Leo, if the Russians had accessed the bank using this program, they'd left no discernible evidence that Leo could find.

Alex sat back in his chair with a sigh. Of course, using this method Leo could search the code for months before coming up with anything, if indeed anything was there. Talking at lunch today with Tim and Harry, who were using the same methods to check the mainframe code that the Russians helped compile, Alex had found that they were no more successful than Leo. But until someone had a better idea, this was their best option.

And unless they got lucky, it was a lousy option. Time was too short. Alex watched the stock reports, and they didn't look good. The U.K. had already seen a run on its banks; Barclays Bank was forced to close for several days, and reopen with limits on how much its customers could withdraw. Thanks to an extremely expensive and thorough advertising campaign, American citizens still seemed to feel a certain confidence in the banking systems. They were withdrawing more money than usual, but the Fed had had the foresight to print part of the year 2000 currency early, so that more cash than usual was available. They were also said to be stockpiling old bills, normally shredded, in case of extra demand. So far, things were okay.

But it was a house of cards as far as Alex was concerned. What if word got out that a new bug was siphoning money away from banks around the world? Who could blame people if their confidence was shaken and they wanted their own money out of the bank fast? And how much money was being taken out by the worm, and how fast? Did the creator of the current algorithm intend to topple the world's monetary system?

Alex re-read the last sentence of Leo's report. "I will continue to search the EDI code until I break it." If Leo were guilty, then the whole report was just a sham to cover himself. If he were innocent, Alex could imagine what Leo was really thinking - that he was determined to break the code and with it, perhaps, Volodya.

# Chapter 21

*December 7, 1999: Day 25*

Alex ushered the FBI agent into Annette's office.

"This is Special Agent Jerry Stemkoski. He's working with George."

Jerry appeared to be in his mid-fifties, tall and thin; thin hands, thin face, thin, hawkish nose. When he smiled courteously and shook hands with Annette, she was struck by his watchful air.

"Alex tells me you haven't turned up anything yet," he said. His voice was deep and pleasant, a radio announcer's voice.

"No, not yet. Please have a seat." Alex sat down too.

"I just have a couple of questions to ask you, Miss Ashby. We'd like to know a little bit about your relationship with Mr. Borodin. Has he ever threatened you in any way?"

Annette barely suppressed a smile. "No, of course not. I'm sure I'm very safe with Volodya."

"I'm glad to hear that. The Bureau appreciates your help, Miss Ashby."

Annette waved a hand. "Annette, please."

"We realize, Annette, that this sort of situation is quite unpleasant for most people. In fact, we're a little leery of people who are enthusiastic about the opportunity to deceive someone."

Annette said nothing.

"When Alex told me that you'd agreed," he went on, "I wanted to talk to you first. When our agents work undercover, we make sure that they're aware of the dangers." He was watching her like the hawk he resembled.

"Dangers?" she said.  She was hard put not to giggle.

"Not *physical* dangers, in this case," he said, "but psychological ones.  I hope we'll be able to break the case soon, so you won't have to do this for long, but even if you do it for only a few days, you'll naturally feel guilty about lying, especially if you're lying to someone with whom you have emotional ties."

"I think emotional ties is a little strong," she said.

Jerry's expression didn't alter.  "Do you like Mr. Borodin?"

Annette chose her words carefully.  "I suppose I do."

"You'll have to be careful then.  Our undercover people find it almost unavoidable - they develop emotional ties to the people they're watching.  Even the worst criminal usually has a few good points, and the agents naturally respond to those —"

"My understanding," Annette said crisply, "was that I would be making myself available to Volodya to hear anything he might have to say that could lead us to the saboteur."  She paused.  "I wasn't aware that we'd decided the saboteur was Volodya."

"Ah, yes," Jerry said.  "Er, sure.  Fair enough.  But I just wanted to explain that when we have people in deep cover that goes on for months or years at a time, we have to do a thorough psychological analysis when they come out.  And occasionally we lose one."

"What do you mean?"

"Very occasionally, an agent will turn.  Go over.  Become a double agent; we think he's working for us, but he's gone over to the dark side. Doesn't happen often, but it happens."

\*      \*      \*

"The Russians?"  Janet Brock smoothed her frizzy hair with nervous fingers and frowned in concentration.  "I never noticed that they made more mistakes than anyone else.  Fewer, maybe.  Any time I had to check their work, they always had an explanation."

"Well, Janet" Alex said, " I don't expect you to come up with anything right off the top of your head.  But we have reason to suspect at least one of them of fraud - I can't tell you exactly what - and I need you to go over your notes and think back and see if you can recall anything that seemed odd to you at the time."  Alex did not know how hopeful he could be; Janet was eager to help, but she seemed to be drawing a blank.

"But Alex, it's been six months," Janet said, her forehead creased in frustration. "I wish I could remember better, but I've worked a lot of overtime, and it's all a big blur to me right now."

"Janet, you're a conscientious worker." His voice was reassuring. "No one is questioning that. Please look over your notes and keep thinking about it. Sometimes things come to mind that don't occur to us at first." He leaned toward her. "Janet, this is really important. It's a big scam and it involves a lot of money and no bank can afford it right now. And I must ask you to keep what I've told you confidential; we don't want them to know that we suspect anything."

"I've never been one to gossip."

"I appreciate your cooperation. Keep us posted, and call me if anything comes to mind - even over the weekend, even if I'm at home." Alex shook her hand and watched her walk out. Maybe she would come up with something, maybe not. The few discreet interviews he had conducted led him to think that the culprit might have covered his tracks so well that he would never be found out, and that meant disaster for the bank.


*December 10, 1999: Day 22, Washington, D.C.*


Sergei was up early, not that anyone in the hospital ever gave him the option of sleeping late. Nurses came in at all hours to check his vital signs, draw his blood, and generally bother him. He had no complaints. This hospital was like a health spa compared to the conditions in his own beleaguered country. Because of his security status, only a few nurses with special clearance were working with him. In his gratitude for the new liver he was a model patient, and his nurses seemed to have grown fond of him.

He felt wonderful, better by the day. The doctors told him that his recovery was good, faster than they had hoped for. Over and over again Sergei thanked God for the miracle that brought him to the U.S.

"Sergei, my man."

The door was open already, and Terry strolled in with a laptop computer under his arm.

"Good morning. You are early today. Do you come to interrogate me?" Sergei still felt somewhat offended by their questions; of course his code had de-activated the algorithm! That's what he had designed it to do.

"The time has come to show us your gratitude for that fine new liver." Terry swiveled the tray table across Sergei's lap, deposited the laptop, and bent to plug it in. The CIA had reconfigured the room's electronics in anticipation of Sergei's arrival; the networking port was connected to a special FBI network that gave its users access to a number of special, powerful features. Sergei's eyes gleamed at the sight of the computer; he was finally feeling well enough to use one again.

"Okay, Sergei, you can help us here." Terry was deadly serious. "Alex tells me they're not having much success with the virus at their end. They suggested that you work on it." Sergei nodded; this made sense. "We want you to figure out which banks the algorithm accessed, when, and how much money was removed. Analyze your data. You created the thing; maybe it went awry somehow and part of the algorithm is still sitting at Midwest." Sergei opened his mouth to protest that this was impossible, but Terry forestalled him. "Hey, we don't know, do we? This is the first time you used it - the beta test. Maybe there were some bugs you didn't foresee."

"I will do my best, of course," Sergei said, drawing himself up in his bed.

"Not that we don't trust you, Sergei, but we've got two Company geeks coming in to sit beside you and watch every move you make. We want to learn as much as we can about this algorithm, and we don't want you to try anything stupid." Terry motioned to two young men to come in.

"Sergei, this is Vu. He's Vietnamese-American." Vu smiled at Sergei and shook his hand. "Vu is dying to see how this works, so you be sure to answer all his questions."

Sergei smiled kindly at the young man.

"And this is Chad." Chad looked like a body-builder. Sergei could not believe that his thick, stubby fingers would fit on the keyboard, and he smiled to himself at the contrast in the two young men. No doubt this would be his job for the next few months, instructing the CIA in the workings of his algorithm. This was the price of his new liver and his new chance at life. He began demonstrating the algorithm to Vu and Chad, but at the back of his mind he was praying that the CIA could use his creation more wisely than the FSB.

*December 13, 1999: Day 19, Columbus*

On Monday Homer received another missive from y2k Ray, this one more cryptic than the others.

*The source lies open.*
*Silently the virus comes -*
*Empty is the vault.*

"Do you really think that y2k Ray did it?" Annette asked Leo after the meeting. She could hardly say the name without giggling. "Tim said he's beginning to think that putting the worm in was an outside job. So it could be y2k Ray." Her voice was light. "I'd be so happy if it would turn out to be someone from outside the bank."

Making Volodya innocent, Leo thought. He made himself smile at her; they hadn't talked in a few days. "Anything is possible, I guess. We're not finding anything on our end. But it won't do any good to give those e-mails to the FBI."

"Why not?" Annette asked. "Can't they trace them by the e-mail address?"

"Theoretically, yes. But a hacker who doesn't want to be traced can alter the message header so it shows a bogus route. Then nobody can trace it. That's what spammers do."

"Oh," Annette said. "I guess you would know." She was silent a moment, then changed the subject. "I was impressed that you recognized that last poem as a haiku."

"Yeah, I learned all about that stuff from my mom," Leo said absently, his mind fixated on Annette's previous words.

"I didn't tell anyone," Annette said, lowering her voice.

"Tell anyone?"

"That your mom is a poet," Annette said. "I didn't want to add fuel to the fire, have someone thinking you were y2k Ray because the messages are in poetry."

"It's not even good poetry," Leo said, pained. She seemed oblivious to his reaction.

"I know you didn't do it, Leo," she said, laying a hand on his arm. "Despite the hacking. I believe in you."

"Thanks." Leo thought the words would choke him. "Listen, I've got to go, Annette. I'll talk to you later."

*       *       *

"Leo, you are coming?" Volodya stuck his head in Leo's office door. They had struck an uneasy truce over the past few weeks, and Leo had agreed to play pool tonight with Volodya and the others if he were free.

Leo shrugged and pulled on his coat. Andrei and Ilya walked with them through the building, then raced ahead to the car when they reached the parking lot. The wind was bitter.

"I'm not going, Volodya," Leo said.

"We play another night, then." The Russian stood with his legs braced, his overcoat unbuttoned and flapping in the wind and watched Leo walk away.

"No," Leo said, halfway to his car already. The wind was blowing so hard that he had to turn around and shout to make himself heard. "I don't want to play your game any more."

*December 14, 1999: Day 18*

Annette stumbled up the two steps to her apartment door, so tired she could hardly summon the strength to turn the key in the lock. Volodya had walked her to her car and then tried to insist that she come with him instead, or at least let him drive her home. She knew how that was supposed to end.

"You are too tired," he argued, taking her briefcase and her arm to escort her to his car. "You will have accident. Let me take you home. I will pick you up in morning."

"No," she said, marching resolutely back to her own car. "Please don't push me, Volodya."

"Push you?" He set the briefcase on the ground and put his arms around her. "Annette, I am worried about you. You are too tense." He kissed her cold cheek. "You need to relax."

"And I suppose you are just the man to relax me?"

He smiled and kissed her again, this time on the mouth. "I think you would like it."

For the past two weeks he had pressed her to sleep with him, charming but relentless, and no arguments that she made touched his resolve. "We are adults. It is natural thing. You worry too much about it."

She hadn't learned anything that convinced her that he was guilty of planting the algorithm. He was far from reticent with her, and he certainly didn't mind talking about himself, but if he'd done something illegal (besides the hacking, she reminded herself), he'd given no indication.

She jerked open the kitchen cupboard and fumbled for the bottle of aspirin, nearly emptied since her first talk with Jerry Stemkoski. Life as a spy did not agree with her. She was sure Volodya had no idea that she was leading him on, and every minute that she spent with him was a lie whose consequences she paid in headaches.

How could anyone be a double agent, she wondered, or even a single one? She had been lying to Volodya for only days; people who worked undercover had to keep up the pretense for months, even years. How could a life centered around deception be good for anyone?

As she waited for the aspirin to take effect, Annette considered phoning Leo. Sometimes she felt better if she talked to Leo. Other times, she felt worse, because she knew that Leo hated the whole situation.

With dragging steps she undressed and fell into bed, knowing that she might spend several restless hours before she slept.

*December 16, 1999: Day 16*

Leo had arrived early for the y2k meeting, hoping to spend a few minutes alone with Annette. Two evenings ago he had been headed to the bank parking lot when he had seen Volodya gather Annette into his arms and kiss her as though she had given him the right. And of course, she had. He asked himself again whether his little excursion into hacking had been worth the cost.

As he watched his colleagues fill the chairs, he speculated on the subject of the meeting, which had been hastily called, and wondered why they had decided to let him come.

These meetings were becoming increasingly gloomy, thought Leo. On one hand, they had their y2k concerns with Midwest. The project might be finished by December 31st, in a manner of speaking, but nobody guaranteed that the systems would be fixed. They wouldn't really know until the rollover. Nor had anyone found the algorithm yet, although not for want of searching. And from the look on Alex's face, they were about to hear yet another piece of bad news.

"I heard from Sergei today," he began, as soon as they were seated. "That is, I talked to Terry, who passed on what Sergei had to say. And it's not good. He said that Sergei has been analyzing the algorithm, looking at the way it worked when it was going from bank to bank, setting up accounts and withdrawing money and so on. His data is incomplete, of course; not all banks have reported their losses yet."

Alex, who was rarely at a loss for words, was silent now. "Well, there's no easy way to say it. The algorithm was designed to change itself under certain conditions. Somehow, one of the changes, the replications, speeded things up. From that point, the money started disappearing at a much faster rate than Sergei designed it to. Much too fast a rate. I don't need to tell you how bad this could be."

Leo watched the shocked faces of his colleagues.

Alex continued. "Regardless of what happens on December 31st with the rollover, that algorithm is going to wreak havoc."

"You mean it's going to foul up the banking system," Leo said.

"The whole banking system?" Eddie asked.

"Well, possibly," Leo said, following the logical train of thought. "Probably, in fact. We know Sergei designed the worm to move and to be random. Suppose this new, more malevolent worm moves to a bank in some small, under-capitalized third world country."

They sat silent for a moment, digesting the possibility.

"Then," Annette said, "that worm could bankrupt a whole country, couldn't it?"

Leo nodded. "And in a pretty short time, too."

"Houston," Harry said, "We have a problem."

"Of course, it could do the same thing to a big bank in a more prosperous country," Leo said, "but it would take longer, and the effect on the world's economy would be more direct."

"But even the collapse of a small, poor country can have a depressing effect on the global economy," Annette said, "and once word gets out about the worm, I can't imagine what would happen in the banking world. Maybe worldwide bank closures while they make some concerted effort to find the worm and eradicate it."

Alex frowned. "Don't forget about the effect of the rollover. That's already a destabilizing factor if the rollover causes people to lose faith in the banking system. So far I don't think they have, at least not here in the U.S. But -" he paused for effect. "If we don't get the worm out before the rollover, we may never get it out."

This statement brought forth some noises of disbelief, but Tim and Harry were silent.

"That's right," Tim said, finally. "At the rollover, we'll see lots of systems crashes. Programmers will use their back-ups to recover data, then try to figure out how to debug the system. Even if we believe that the worm has been eradicated in current programs, it will have been archived in the back-up data. Every time the back-up data is used to recover a system, the worm has the potential to be resurrected in one of its mutated forms. It could become like the AIDS virus, hibernating then erupting."

"But that could happen now!" Annette protested.

"I'm afraid you're right," Tim said. "But the worm has gone wacko. The longer it's in the banking system, the more likely it is to mutate. . . again and again. These mutations may be so changed from the original worm that the deactivation codes that Sergei has developed won't even work with them." He held up a hand at their groans.

"Those bastards!" Eddie was red-faced. "Why would they ever take a chance like that?

Leo had the answer. "Because they can," he said, looking at Annette.

Tim waited for quiet, then went on. "It gets worse. Everyone is archiving their systems for y2k. They archive anyway, but you can bet there will be extra archiving, special archiving on December 31st in case of y2k systems crashes. Now, if the worm, or its mutations, is still in everyone's systems on December 31st, the worms will be archived. Massively archived. Hundreds of thousands of times over." Tim spread his hands in a gesture of helplessness.

"We've got to get the worm out before December 31st," he said.

"By December 29th, in fact, to give us time to put out the deactivation codes to other banks. After the millennium arrives, systems will go down. Programmers will use their archives to restore data and applications that become corrupted by the rollover. What if we have all those worms, still mutating, in all those files, as well as the y2k bugs we haven't yet found? You tell me. What are the odds that we could ever get them all out?"

Annette was the first to break the horrified silence. "That means we have fourteen days to figure out who did it."

*       *       *

The programmer sat down in front of his computer terminal at home, his decision made. He would protect himself by wiping his computer. It might take him a good part of the night, but self-protection could hardly carry too high a price.

The worms with their macros were still in his computer files, and even though they were encrypted, they were not safe. Another programmer could decrypt them, given time. He should have saved them to a floppy disk and hidden them long ago.

He saved the incriminating files to disk, then deleted them, but deletion alone was not enough. Most people did not realize that a deleted file remained on the hard drive, re-named so that the operating system did not recognize it, until it was eventually written over. Only after the file was written over was it actually deleted. Until then, a good programmer could easily find the deleted files, so he would have to wipe them from the hard drive. He installed the wiping utility, another item with which few computer-users were familiar, and wiped the files containing the worms and macros from the hard drive. Now they were truly gone, except for the copy he had saved on the floppy disk. He would have to hide it somewhere.

Methodically he worked his way through his computer files, saving, deleting, and wiping anything that might look suspicious. He deleted and wiped much of his e-mail from his friends, even though it was for the most part innocuous. He had saved a few e-mails hacked from other people's computers just in case they might come in handy some time; these, too, were wiped from memory.

The process was time-consuming, and when he was finished he

had to decide where to hide the two disks. One disk contained only the worms and their macros. The other contained the worms and their macros as well as other legally questionable information, and most importantly, the numbers of his bank accounts in Switzerland and the Cayman Islands, where he had transferred the worm money. In the event that he was ever found out, he would use the first disk to deactivate the worm; then no doubt the FBI would confiscate the disk. But he would still have the second disk, which gave him access to the workings of the worm (which he could re-clone to his liking) as well as to a comfortable amount of money in the foreign accounts.

He pushed his chair away from the computer, trying to stretch the exhaustion from his body. His mind was on hyper-drive; this might be his survival. He prowled the apartment for an hour, sticking the disk into various crevices and cracks, trying to determine the best hiding place. Finally he stood in front of his CD collection, which numbered about five hundred. He selected a CD from the center of a shelf, opened the jewel case, and tried inserting the disk between the two pages of the paper cover in the front of the case. If he taped the disk down, it would be invisible, and it was unlikely that an agent would think to look between the pages of the cover, especially if they had already looked at several hundred other CDs. He snapped the case shut and frowned; it would not snap securely because of the thickness of the disk, and the weight of the disk's plastic case made it suspiciously heavy.

Ah! He retreated to the kitchen and used a sharp knife to bend the disk's metal clip until it flipped off. Then he carefully pried the plastic case open, revealing the disk itself, a circular piece of mylar three and a half inches in diameter with a small circular metal piece in the center. He laid the disk on the counter, then ran upstairs and rooted through the pile of boxes and wrappings that had encased his last computer purchase. There. He picked up the anti-static bag that protected the delicate computer hardware from static charges that could corrupt or erase the memory.

Taking the bag downstairs, he carefully slipped the mylar disk into one corner of it, cut the bag to the size of the disk, then used clear tape to seal the edges of the bag. He pried out the plastic center that held the CD, and put the mylar disk behind it, taped to a square of paper which served the dual purpose of concealing it from view and keeping it from sliding around. Now the disk was invisible from the back, covered by the CD cover.  From the inside it was covered by the CD; when the CD was removed, the plastic holder and the piece of paper covered it. He clicked the case shut. It closed perfectly now; he opened and closed it several times, examining the inside to see if the disk was visible. It was not.  Unless a searcher received a direct revelation from God, he would not find the disk, and afterward he could pry open another disk case and replace the mylar disk when he needed to use it.

As he returned the CD with the hidden disk to the shelf with the others, he looked again at the front cover.  It was Verdi's opera *Un Ballo in Maschero, The Masked Ball*, whose story centered around a plot to assassinate the Swedish king. "A tale of deceit and intrigue" the cover announced.  Again, the smile.

*December 17, 1999: Day 15*

In the midst of their fourth meeting, Jerry pushed Annette's notes away with an exclamation of disappointment. "Still nothing."

"I don't know what else to do." Annette felt defensive. "He talks about himself. I've given you plenty of background information."

"Nothing that helps us, so far. I don't mean to be critical, Annette. It's just that our time is getting shorter.  Isn't there something you could do to make him feel closer to you?"

Annette realized what he meant.

"You'd like to me sleep with Volodya."

"Well, it is the time-honored method of extracting information." Jerry's voice was casual, but she saw tension in every line of body. He was as worried about the algorithm as they.  "But of course the Bureau would never ask anyone to do that.  If a person were willing, and did it on her own - well, that's different."

# Chapter 22

*December 18, 1999: Day 14*

At Midwest Bank, several people labored over the weekend. Janet Brock was not happy about spending the last Saturday before Christmas in the office; she wanted to go Christmas shopping. But she was conscientious, so she sat at her computer and reviewed test logs until her eyes ached. That was the trouble with suspicions. You couldn't just suspect the people you disliked. She'd known employees, otherwise pleasant, who'd embezzled from the bank, so she continued perusing her logs, suspecting everyone.

At two p.m. she switched her computer off, having found nothing. The stores were still open; she had time to finish her shopping after all. She would think about it while she was shopping; in fact, she would say a prayer and ask God to help her. She certainly wasn't coming up with anything on her own.

\*     \*     \*

In the bank's lower level, Leo and Tim and Harry shared a pizza at Tim's desk.

Conversation was desultory; nobody was finding anything that would implicate any of the programmers, and they had worked for two fruitless days.

"I've got to go,' said Harry at last. "Wife didn't want me here today anyway."

"I'll stay a little longer," Leo said.

"Then so will I," Tim said. He finished his slice of pizza and saluted as Harry lumbered out the door. "Although," he said to Leo, "I don't think we're close to finding anything. My bet is that this guy is too smart to have left us anything to find." He shook his head. "Maybe it wasn't an inside job. Hell, I don't know what to think any more."

With that cheering thought they went back to work.

*        *        *

Alex smiled at his daughter, who was dressed for a high school dance. She had called him at work, wondering what time he would be home. That in itself was unusual enough to bring him home early, and now he sat on Elizabeth's messy bed, trying not to think about the dinner he was so hungry for. Elizabeth, facing him, bent over to pick up something, and Alex winced at how clearly he could see down the front of her dress.

"You know sweetheart, you need to be careful when you bend over like that. Even around a nice boy like Andrew."

Elizabeth stared at him for a moment, then to Alex's alarm tears began sliding down her cheeks, faster and faster.

Alex drew his weeping daughter to sit down on the bed next to him. "What's the matter? Is it about the dress?"

Elizabeth looked at him. "It isn't the *dress*, Daddy. I mean, what does it matter what Andrew and I do if the world is going to end in a couple of weeks anyway?"

Alex stiffened, then willed himself to relax again.. "Elizabeth, what are you talking about, honey?" He smiled indulgently and extended an arm to embrace her.

She stood up, avoiding his arm. "Daddy, I know what you *say*. But I also know what I hear. I know you have nightmares. I've heard you screaming." Her voice was accusing. "And I heard you and Mom - *crying* the other night. You do think something horrible is going to happen and you just don't want to tell us!"

Alex couldn't speak for a moment.

"Elizabeth," he said softly. "We didn't want to frighten you. But those nightmares are something I can't control. I've spent the last ten years fighting to make sure that those nightmares won't come true."

"Why were you and Mom crying then?"

"Getting Sergei out of Russia was not as easy as it was supposed to be. I'm not supposed to tell you this, but I will, if it helps - I saw someone die trying to help him escape." Elizabeth stopped crying.

"It was awful, Elizabeth. I didn't even want to tell your mother, but she knew something was wrong. Talking about it made both of us cry." Alex drew a deep breath and looked into Elizabeth's eyes. "Y2k isn't the end of the world. We've been working hard to make sure of that."

Elizabeth gave a great sigh and collapsed against his chest. "I've been so worried. For months and months. I'd listen to you talk about it and be optimistic, and then you'd have another nightmare and I wouldn't know what to think."

"Poor baby." Alex held her gently. No wonder Elizabeth had been so difficult to deal with all these months.

She spoke with her mouth against his chest. "But what about Dr. Bob?"

"Dr. Bob? Sweetheart, Dr. Bob has been waiting for twenty-five years for the collapse of the U.S. government. Y2k is his latest hope."

"He *wants* the government to collapse?" Elizabeth sat up.

"For whatever reasons, yes. Anything he reads about y2k is a confirmation to him of what he already believes. One of the things that makes him so scary - and so believable to people who don't know his background - is that he's sincere."

"Maybe he's not so sincere, maybe he's just crazy."

"Honey," Alex smoothed his daughter's hair, "all crazy people are sincere."

He watched the inward struggle reflected on her face. "But Dad, nobody can really predict what will happen. Not even you."

To that he could only nod, and pull her closer.


*December 19, 1999: Day 13*

"Do you like some more wine?" Volodya asked her, and Annette pulled her straying thoughts back to the present.

"White, please. Chablis is fine." Annette glanced around the dining room of the Refectory, glad that she didn't see anyone she knew. "How is Mrs. Baranova?"

"She is well. And her cats." He made a face, then rested his blue eyes on her. "You are looking very beautiful tonight."

Annette was wearing a dark green, low-backed velvet dress, and her dark red hair was pulled up into a loose knot. She had dressed to catch his eye, and Volodya, whose broad shoulders admirably filled out his dark suit, had hardly stopped looking at her all evening. Feeling restive under that steady gaze, Annette made nervous conversation. Alex had come by the office that morning after church to pick up his laptop computer, and when he found her working in her office he had all but thrown her out.

"Annette, I want you to go home and rest," he ordered her. "You look exhausted, and you won't be any use to us if you burn yourself out before the end of the month."

She protested, but Alex was her boss, so she left reluctantly, drove home and fell asleep on the couch until four o'clock, when Volodya rang. Too sleepy to have her wits about her, she explained why she wasn't working, and Volodya swooped immediately.

"Then you will have dinner with me," he said. So here she sat while Volodya ate her up with his eyes, his after-dinner intentions absolutely transparent.

"Tell me about your college days," she said, seemingly at random.

Volodya shrugged. "I went to college early, at sixteen. I was prodigy like Leo. I studied three years, became one of youngest professors of mathematics. I teach for a while. Why do you want to know?" Did she imagine it, or was did the last question hold an edge of suspicion? And why should he be suspicious? It was an innocuous enough question.

"Just curious," she said. "Are the universities in Russia like the universities here?"

"They are far superior to universities here," he said. "My favorite professor was tops in world in his field. He was like mentor; I liked him very much. His name was Professor Kzhizhonovsky."

"K-zhi-zhon-off-ski," Annette repeated. She had an ear for languages. "An intriguing name."

"Is Polish name. His relatives came from there years ago." Volodya changed the subject. "Would you like to go now?"

"But did you know any dissidents in Moscow?" she asked. "I mean, I've always admired people who were willing to be jailed for their beliefs."

"Westerners are romantic that way." He swirled the wine in his glass. "I knew some, yes. For the most part they are stupid people, too stupid or too stubborn to work system. Why was there need to go to jail? Most of them want to be martyrs, to be admired by Western press."

"I don't believe that at all," she said. "Maybe they were tired of not being free to say exactly what they believed."

"Annette," he said. "None of us says exactly what we believe. Do we?" His voice was exasperated, but amused, and given that her entire evening with him was a lie, Annette could only drop her eyes, her arguments robbed of their moral force.

"Anyway," he continued, "you believe too much anti-Soviet propaganda. Our system was getting better until Gorbachev and Reagan screwed it up. The intelligentsia was revising system from inside. Stupid dissidents destabilized our plans for reform." He was silent for a moment, brooding. His words revealed a side of Volodya that she hadn't suspected.

"We go now, okay?" He was smiling, his attention again focused on her. As they left, Annette noticed how the eyes of all the women in the restaurant followed him across the room. In the lobby he slipped her coat on, then kept an arm around her shoulder as they walked to his car. Volodya unlocked the door, then wrapped his arms tightly around her and kissed her, hard, as though he couldn't wait until they were home.

"I could not resist any longer," he told her, and she thought that his handsome face looked more thoughtful than usual in the gleam of the parking lot lights. He cocked his head and studied her. "You should have fur hat and coat, like Russian women. You would look nice." He opened the car door and she slid in.

\*     \*     \*

Volodya was exultant. When Annette had agreed to go to dinner with him, he realized that tonight was the night, and surely she realized it, too, her hair pinned up seductively, her bare back gleaming in the candlelight. He savored the prospect as they ate, undressing her in his mind, unpinning her hair, carrying her to the bed.

She barely spoke on the ride home, but seemed unsurprised when he followed her into her apartment. He removed their coats and she casually invited him into the living room, seating herself on a nearby chair when he sat on the sofa. Perhaps she was nervous.

"Come and sit here," he invited her, patting the sofa cushions. "I have Christmas present for you."

"A Christmas present! But it isn't Christmas yet. And I don't have anything for you."

"It doesn't matter." He took the small box from his trouser pocket. "Come. Sit."

Obediently she sat next to him, taking the gold-wrapped box and holding it in her hand. "I will not be here for Christmas," he explained. "My friend Ilya is coming from Russia, and I arranged already to meet him in New York over Christmas holidays. I go to New York tomorrow evening and come back on day after Christmas." She sat looking at the box, but not opening it. Perhaps she was upset that he would be gone. "I am sorry to be away, but it was arranged some weeks ago. Didn't I tell you? Perhaps you could come with me."

"I'm staying at the Stauffers over Christmas," she said slowly. "But thank you for inviting me."

"Another time, then. Please, open box."

She busied herself with the wrappings, then snapped open the black velvet jeweler's box that was inside. Volodya watched her eyes open very wide; she gave a little gasp and drew the square cut emerald ring from the box. The gold setting was plain, but elegant, and the jewel caught the light and threw it back in little splinters.

"Volodya," she said finally, looking into his face, "it's beautiful, but I can't accept it. It looks terribly expensive."

Volodya had foreseen this difficulty. "I have friend who is jeweler in Russia. He can get me such things much more cheaply. This ring was bargain." It made him think of Annette's eyes,

"Please, put it on," he urged, then took the ring from her fingers and put it on her himself. "You have beautiful hands. Small and dainty with long fingers." He admired the ring for a moment, then turned her hand over and pressed his lips to her palm. She sat and looked at him with the same wide-eyed gaze she had leveled at the emerald.

"Volodya —"

"It made me think of your eyes." He placed his hand lightly on her bare back and moved it up and down the smoothness of her skin. He could feel the little rounded bumps of her spine with his fingertips. She shivered and he saw her shake her head again.

"Volodya —" He shushed her with a kiss, the softness of her mouth burning against his. Pulling her gently into his arms and across his lap, he began kissing her in earnest, one hand caressing her arm, up and down, the velvet of her sleeve soft and warm under his fingers, while his other hand tangled itself in her hair.

Her mouth opened under his and the room's temperature seemed to climb ten degrees. Pressed against her, he could feel her heartbeat, hear her sigh of pleasure. Volodya was so lost in his lovemaking that it took a moment for him for realize that Annette was trying to say something. He eased away a few inches, smiling at her.

"Now is not good time for conversation," he said, laying a finger on her flushed cheek.

"Volodya, I can't. Not the ring. I mean, I can't do this." Her voice sounded panicked, and he was taken aback by the fear in her eyes.

"What is wrong?" He still held her across his lap, her head resting on the arm of the couch.

"I have to tell you something. Please let me sit up." He pulled her to a sitting position. What could she have to tell him that was worth interrupting this moment?

Annette looked at her hands, clasped them together, then untwined her fingers and played with the emerald as she talked. Her voice was low; he had to strain to hear her.

"When I was eighteen I had an affair." She paused, and Volodya nodded encouragingly. "He was Irish. His name was Mick." This time the pause was longer. "He was in the IRA. I didn't know it." Her voice faltered, but went on. "Until he blew himself up accidentally. The police said that he was using me to get to my father." This time the silence grew and filled the room.

"Annette, I am not terrorist."

She put her hand on his arm. "Volodya, I should have told you before. I thought I would let you kiss me and see how I felt. I was afraid. You'll have to be patient with me."

She was serious, sitting just centimeters away from him, gorgeous and vulnerable, and telling him that he would have to be patient. Did any man have that much patience?

He rose abruptly. "I will call you, Annette."

"You're leaving?"  She looked as if she might cry.

"If I stay, I will make love to you. I will call you and we can talk. Now that you have told me, it will not be such a shock the next time." He managed a smile.  "I will never sleep tonight, Annette."

He left with her apologies ringing in his ears.

*       *       *

When Annette heard his car pull away, the tears slid down her cheeks. The ring - she didn't know what to make of it.  She knew he was a womanizer, if a charming one, and she had always assumed that he found her attractive and wanted to sleep with her, nothing more. Were his intentions serious after all?  How terrible if he were in love with her!

She found the aspirin on the sink - it was too much trouble to put it away, she always had a headache now - and gulped two down with a glass of water.  All she wanted was to go to bed and forget about all the things that were causing her headaches.  If he were innocent?  Annette rubbed her aching temples.  She would go upstairs, take a shower, and go to bed.

*December 20, 1999: Day 12*

"The FBI hasn't come up with anything new, Jerry tells me."  Alex was filling the team in on the latest, not particularly good, news.

A soft knock at the door, then a figure sidled in.  A Santa Claus suit hung slackly on his body, and his face was pleasant, if not jolly.

"Hello, everybody," the man said, smiling widely.

Alex was bewildered at this sudden apparition. He looked at the amused faces of the y2k team.  "Did somebody book this guy?" he asked.

"Homer Jones," Santa said.

Homer's eyebrows swooped upwards.  "I didn't book him."

"No, I'm looking for Homer Jones," the mock Santa explained. He surveyed the room.

"Uh - I'm Homer Jones," Homer said, poking his hand up in the air. Santa's face lit up.  "Homer!  Did you get my mail?"  He flung his arms wide as if to embrace him, and took a step closer.

"Homer, I'm y2k Ray."

*     *     *

"Y2k Ray came in the bank?" Katie said. "Dressed as Santa Claus?" Karen and the rest of the family were enthralled as they listened to the story at dinner.

"Alex, what a great story!" Karen said. " Is he the one then?"

Alex grimaced. "Hardly. The Santa suit was kind of a give-away, don't you think?"

"Well, who was he?" Ethan asked. They were all enjoying this; Alex hadn't brought any jokes home from work in a long time.

"As we figured in the beginning, he's just a goof. A y2k goof, as it turns out. I'm sure there's some irony there." Alex's voice was tired.

"Oh, sweetheart, I didn't mean to make fun," Karen said. "You never really took those notes seriously, did you?"

"I guess we're ready to grasp any straw," Alex said. "Anyway, y2k Ray really is named Ray. He told the FBI all about himself. He's been sending letters to everyone he does business with, warning them about y2k dangers. He has an account at Midwest, so he sent them e-mail. He sent e-mails to his dry-cleaner, the public library, the doctor's office, and so on. He's harmless enough, a kind of mainstreamed mental patient. And he writes everything as a poem, which is why we got poetry."

"Poor Alex." Karen sighed. "I'm sorry he wasn't the one."

"Well, the laugh is really on us," Alex said, grinning a little at last. "You know how he happens to be so y2k aware?" He paused a beat. "He's a member of our mail list."

*December 21, 1999: Day 11*

Leo sat slumped in his chair, depressed by the funereal atmosphere of the meeting. The only plus was that he might be able to salvage a few minutes afterward with Annette. He smiled at her across the conference table.

"Nothing." Tim shook his head at Alex's question. "We can keep looking, but we haven't found anything yet."

"Annette?" Alex turned to her.

"Perhaps there's nothing to find," she said with a shrug, avoiding his eyes. "Volodya didn't say anything incriminating to me."

The computer searches were proving fruitless, so far. Homer had told them earlier that the bank would certainly fold in the next two weeks if they could not find the bug.

Tired of the same bad news, Leo gazed at Annette again. She was toying with that silver pen she always used. That was one sparkly pen, he thought, then realized that it wasn't the pen, but a ring. A very sparkly green ring. An emerald? He'd never seen her wear it before. She glanced at Leo, then laid one hand casually over the other, covering the ring. He could tell from where he was sitting that her cheeks were pink. With a sick feeling he knew who must have given her the ring.

Leo listened to the rest of the meeting through a haze of misery. He waited outside the conference room afterward until he realized that Annette would not be coming, then trudged back to his office.

*     *     *

Annette came to Alex after the meeting.

"Alex, I feel like such a - " she seemed to search for the proper British term and then gave up. "Like a sleazebag."

Alex laughed at the incongruous word. "I don't see you in that role."

"It isn't funny." Annette let some of her frustration show. "Volodya seems to really like me."

"And how do you feel about him?"

"That is such an unfair question." She flicked her hair behind her ear with a quick, angry gesture. "It makes no difference how I feel about him. I would tell you if I knew anything. Maybe he doesn't tell me anything because there isn't anything to tell!"

The phone buzzed. Alex picked it up, listened, then nodded. "Okay, Tracy."

Annette rose to leave, but he motioned to her to sit down. "That was Jerry. You can talk to him about it."

Annette glared at him, then glared at Jerry when he entered, Homer trailing behind. "I've had enough of this. I don't want to see Volodya any more."

Jerry's eyebrows lifted and he sat down across the table from her.

"Annette, this isn't just another case of computer fraud. If Mr. Borodin is guilty, it threatens our banking system and our national security." His dark eyes did not leave Annette's face; Alex thought that he would not want to be interrogated by this man. "We are very serious about catching these people, and we need your help."

"Volodya may be innocent," Annette said.

"Annette, really, which is more important - shutting down this virus, or feeling unhappy about your relationship with Volodya for a few days? If he's innocent, fine. Help us find out."

Alex could see on Annette's face that some inward struggle was taking place. "Oh, all right." Annette surrendered, her unhappiness plain. "Of course I want to find the worm. But I'm afraid I won't see Volodya again until after Christmas. He's out of town."

"What?" Jerry looked askance at Alex, and all three men looked at Annette.

"He's in New York to visit a friend - well, Homer, don't look at me like I smuggled him out of town," she added sharply, seeing his expression. "I didn't find out until Sunday night, and naturally I assumed you knew. He must have put in for vacation time."

Homer groaned. "It didn't occur to me to check. What if he doesn't come back?"

"Oh, I think he's planning to come back all right," said Annette. She saw the way the agent was looking at her and blushed. "I mean, he stopped by my office yesterday evening to say good-bye, and - it was quite an enthusiastic good-bye. A kind of I'll-be-back goodbye." She was blushing furiously by now. "Alex!"

He saw her distress and intervened. "Jerry, couldn't you pick him up in New York if you needed to?"

Jerry nodded. "We could. But we never ask a suspect a question unless we already know the answer. I'd like to know a few more answers. And we really don't have anything solid yet, Alex. No links. No reason to question him." He stood up. "It's too bad the FSB didn't confide in Professor Krzyzanowski and tell him who they were sending the algorithm to."

"Who?" Annette's voice was sharp.

"Professor Krzyzanowski," Jerry repeated.

"But - you can't be pronouncing it properly." She appealed to Alex. "You said it was Professor Krizanowski or something like that."

Jerry flipped his notebook shut. "K-zhi-zhon-off-ski. You were fooled by the spelling. You pronounce the rz like a zh and the y like a short i. It's a Polish name, like mine, Stemkoski. I used to have a friend by the name of Stan Krzyzanowski, growing up in Cleveland. There's a big Polish population there. Krzyzanowski." He pronounced it again and grinned, but his watchful eyes stayed on Annette. "What is it?"

Annette was on her feet, her face very white and her eyes wide. "Oh, Alex, " she whispered, and he saw that there were tears in her eyes. "That's the name of Volodya's professor."

# Chapter 23

*December 22, 1999: Day 10*

After scribbling herself a note, Janet removed her glasses and rubbed her tired eyes. She didn't usually wear glasses, but all this staring at computer screens over the past month was doing her in. Ordinarily she would have been at home with the kids the week before Christmas; she always took her vacation then. As much as she hated missing her time with them, though, she knew that the banks had to do as much testing as possible before January 1st, and she was resigned to the long hours.

If only she could help Alex! Ever since he had asked her to check up on the Russians by looking at the test logs, she had been haunted by the feeling that she had missed something, and it had to do with Volodya. The knowledge hovered just at the edge of her consciousness, and when she tried to seize it, it dissolved. But still she felt it. She knew something, something that Alex needed, and being unable to remember it was driving her crazy.

She scribbled herself another note. Since her realization that she knew something, she had been writing down all the things that popped into her mind in the course of the day- pick up the dry-cleaning, mail the in-laws' gifts, buy something for the paperboy. Her theory was that if she emptied her brain of all the little tasks clamoring for her attention, she would clear out enough space to remember whatever it was that she needed to remember. So far it hadn't worked.

If it were any time but Christmas, she thought, when her mind was already preoccupied with the dozens of errands she needed to do, compounded by the demands of last minute y2k preparations. Think, Janet! She concentrated fiercely, frowning, but her efforts were useless.

She shook her head and returned to her test logs, wishing she could pitch the whole mess into the wastebasket and go home and bake Christmas cookies with her kids.

*      *      *

Annette slipped the emerald off her finger and into the envelope that Jerry was holding.

"I should have thought of it sooner," she said, apologizing. "You must think me naïve, but I was so shocked when I realized that Volodya used to be Sergei's pupil."

"No problem. You'll be surprised at how fast we can trace this. Maybe it's stolen." Jerry looked happy to have a piece of evidence that he could hold in his hand. "Once we find out where it came from, I'll give it back to you, so you can be wearing it when you see Mr. Borodin next. If we don't pick him up before that."

*December 23, 1999: Day 9*

The revelation that Volodya was a former pupil of Sergei Krzyzanowsky made Annette a heroine in the eyes of the y2k team. Annette was not interested in accolades.

"We could have asked Sergei long ago if he knew Volodya," she said, and now that they knew about the connection, they wondered why they hadn't. But the FBI had decided not to question Volodya until his return from New York. Jerry was hoping that the ring might lead them to something more incriminating.

The CIA, they knew, had questioned Sergei at length about his relationship with Volodya. Yes, he readily admitted that he knew Vladimir Borodin. Volodya was one of his prize pupils, perhaps the best he'd ever taught, a brilliant young man. He had encouraged him to remain in his field of study as a theoretical mathematician, but Volodya was more interested in computers. No, he had not kept in touch with Volodya, but understood that he had immigrated to the States. Yes, it was certainly possible that Volodya had been contacted by the FSB and asked to plant the code, but he insisted that he, Sergei, had had no knowledge of the code once it passed out of his hands, and he had had no contact with Volodya for years.

Leo listened to Alex reiterate what they knew at their meeting, and he watched Annette.

"This is our last meeting until Monday the 27th," Alex said. "I know that some of you don't understand why I'm giving you time off now, when we're so close to the rollover and we haven't yet collected any evidence against anyone."

"Yeah, you know we had our hearts set on working Christmas," said Eddie, drawing a laugh.

Alex grinned. "We're all brain-dead. Not that I think you've been doing anything less than an excellent job. As far as the algorithm goes, I think we're going to have to consider the possibility that it could be an outside job, unlikely as that seemed before. But let's give ourselves a few days' break and rest up. The toughest part is ahead of us. We don't know what the rollover will be like; we could be up for several days on end. We're all more valuable if we're rested. I don't want to have a bunch of zombies here making important decisions.

"So, we'll take off tomorrow, which is Christmas Eve, Christmas, and the day after Christmas, which is a Sunday. I encourage all of you who are so inclined to go to church and pray for God's mercy on us all. Then we report back on Monday. Thursday afternoon and evening, December thirtieth are off. Next day, the rollover starts in New Zealand at six a.m. and I want us all to be here." He set his hands on the desk. "Jerry told me that they still would like more information if they can get it, but they'll have to bring Volodya in for questioning some time next week. We've run out of time. Best scenario, forgive me Volodya, is that he confesses and we can get the bug out before Friday night, December 31st."

"What if he doesn't?" asked Harry.

Alex was silent. "I can't answer that," he said at last. "Annette, is he still calling you?"

"Yes, he's called me every day since he left."

"Good. Be sure to call me if you don't hear from him for a day." Annette nodded, and Leo felt helpless fury.

Tim, who had said little so far today, raised his hand. "I've been thinking," he said. "Why two algorithms?"

"I'll bite," Alex said. "Why?"

"Well, exactly," Tim said, nodding vigorously. "There's no reason for two. At first I thought that maybe two different programmers had placed the same bug. But that was a lapse of logic on my part - if the bug was the same, then Sergei's deactivation code would have deactivated it when it cleaned out all the others. And, if anyone puts the same algorithm back into the system now, the virus checkers will get it - that particular algorithm is useless now that we know how it works."

"So," he said, "it must be a different algorithm. Maybe just slightly different, different enough so that the virus checkers can't catch it with Sergei's deactivation codes, but something patterned after the original."

The group sat frowning, try to puzzle out what he meant.

"Don't you see? Sergei tells us that he designed the code for the FSB. Then the FSB gave it to some programmer to put into source code. Which that programmer did." He paused. "That programmer didn't profit. He was just following orders. But if he figured out what the worm would do, maybe he got the idea that he'd like a little of the action himself."

"Ah," Alex said. His eyes gleamed. "And that programmer decided to skim a little off the top by creating a parallel algorithm."

"Right." Tim rushed on, excited. "He could have put it into the system at the same time as the original, to cut down on the risk of being caught. That's what he must have done, in fact, because the money started disappearing again so quickly after the first worm was deactivated."

"Well done, Tim!" Annette said. "Now does this help us figure out who did it?"

Tim excited look vanished. "I don't know," he admitted. "Except that everything we figure out about this person and his motivation could put us closer to what we need."

The meeting adjourned quickly after that; they exchanged Christmas wishes and went their separate ways. Leo waited for Annette in her office; she looked unhappy and he said what he had wanted to say all afternoon.

"But he's guilty, Annette." He heard her sigh.

"We don't know that," she said. She glanced at him, as if trying to discern his thoughts. "You must know I don't feel like an honest person."

"Stop it, Annette," he said, fighting to be understanding, to encourage her. "You're not the bad guy here. And please don't tell me that we don't have any hard evidence against Volodya. We still have more reason to suspect him than we do anyone else."

She sighed again. "Will you come and see me on Christmas, at the Stauffers'?"

"Of course I will."

He tried to coax a smile. "I for one am looking forward to the new millennium. I intend to make up for lost time."

Annette smiled at that, but for Leo it was true. At least after January first, one way or another, this whole mess with Volodya would be behind them.

*December 24, 1999: Day 8*

Elizabeth was delighted to have Annette staying with them. She had arrived at lunchtime on Christmas Eve, laden with packages. At two o'clock Elizabeth was in the kitchen when an FBI agent stopped by to see Annette. She could hear them talking in the foyer, the agent's voice excited, Annette's voice too low to make out. "He bought it in Columbus" came through loud and clear, then "Six thousand dollars . . . Not on a programmer's salary."

Another moment and the front door slammed. Elizabeth backed away from the doorway, then smiled at Annette when she came in. Then her eyes widened.

"Wow, Annette, awesome ring," she said.

\*       \*       \*

Norman's corner of Building 6 was having its annual Christmas party; sans alcohol, but sedately festive nonetheless. Several conference tables had been swept clean and covered with red and green tablecloths and plates of Christmas cookies, many of them brought in by Helen Bergameyer, a stout grandmotherly payment clerk and superb cook whose specialties had been featured in the *Courier's* food section on several occasions. Feeling like a small, naughty boy, Norman parked himself next to Helen's tray of raisin tarts and ate them like peanuts, one after the other. Some people, he noted, were afraid of the name, raisin tarts, but these tasted very little like raisins and Norman could have eaten the whole tray by himself. Grudgingly he shared them with his fellow gourmets, rejoicing that most people there were too provincial to taste a tart that featured raisins for a filling.

"Leaving any for the rest of us, Norman?" Sylvia's sarcastic voice sounded right at his ear, and, startled, he nearly flung his raisin tart skyward. Turning around, he offered one to Sylvia.

"Merry Christmas, Sylvia! What are you doing over here?"

She shook her head, and Norman noticed that her eyes were heavily and unsuccessfully powdered in an attempt to hide a pink puffiness. From the look of it, Sylvia had been crying, and a good part of the day, too. Norman was at something of a loss. He considered asking her straight out what was wrong, but since her tears seemed close to the surface, that probably wouldn't be a good move. Still, she had approached him, so perhaps she felt like talking.

"Going home for Christmas?" The question was innocent enough, but to Norman's dismay, Sylvia began to sniffle, holding a Christmas napkin up to her pink nose.

Norman reconsidered. Sylvia was brash and unpleasant, but it was the season of brotherhood and good will and peace on earth, so he motioned for her to follow him, which to his surprise she did, leaving with a helpless backward glance at the party. Because his office was nearby and private, he took her there, and she stood eyeing him, clutching the napkin to her nose.

"You might as well tell me about it, Sylvia. What's wrong?"

Sylvia's brows knit together fiercely and she gave a sound between a sob and a snarl. "It's my damned boyfriend!" she wailed. "For months we've been planning to go to his friends' place in New York for Christmas. Now all of a sudden, for no good reason, he tells me he doesn't think we're right for each other. Never mind that I already have my plane ticket and my clothes and I've told my parents I won't be home for Christmas!" She glared, anger replacing sorrow. "He could have done the decent thing and stuck with me a few more weeks!"

"Sylvia, I'm sure your family would love to have you for Christmas, even on short notice," Norman said soothingly.

"When I think of the things I've done for that man!" Sylvia said.

"Things I'd never think of doing for anyone else! I thought it was for our future."

Norman listened patiently.

"Oh, Norman, I did something awful for him! Something really, really awful. I'll never forgive myself!"

What an odd thing to say. Sylvia caught his look and suddenly her tears dried. Closing her mouth decisively, she gave Norman a hostile glance, as though she feared she might have said too much, and suddenly Norman knew.

"What's this boyfriend's name?" he asked.

"Greg." At the sound of the name, Sylvia touched the front of her dress, where, judging by the tiny bulge under the red polyester, the enameled egg still nestled. The egg was Russian, Norman realized; he'd seen them before but hadn't made the connection.

"Greg."

Sylvia nodded, throwing surreptitious glances at the door. Ready to escape, thought Norman.

He indicated his desk chair. "You may as well sit down for a minute, until you feel better." Sylvia sat, and began fiddling with his tin of sharpened pencils. He watched as Sylvia chose a pencil and stirred it round and round in the canister, as if preparing some obscure soup that demanded her close attention.

"I had an interview with the FBI a few weeks ago," Norman remarked, and the canister of pencils shot out of Sylvia's hands and up into the air. Norman shielded his head from descending pencil points, then crawled around on the floor, helping Sylvia gather them up.

"Why?" she asked, when they were finished.

Norman chose his words carefully. "Well, I'm not allowed to tell you, but I'll bet you can guess what kind of thing the FBI would be investigating." Sylvia watched him narrowly through her thin blond bangs. "One of the things the agent told me was that the people who cooperate with them are always much, much better off than the people who don't. The people who come to them, the people who confess right away. George - that was his name - he said, 'The ones who get in the boat with us are the ones who make it. The others drown.'"

"Isn't that interesting?" Sylvia said. She fingered the candy cane earring attached to her left earlobe. "Was he trying to get you to confess to something?"

"Maybe," said Norman. "We were just talking, and I was thinking to myself that I wouldn't want to be sitting there answering his questions if I had actually done something wrong and was trying to hide it."

Sylvia stroked the matching candy cane pin on her dress, her eyes looking somewhere over Norman's left shoulder.

"And of course there's always revenge," he added. Sylvia's finger stopped tracing the candy cane; she raised her pale blue eyes to Norman's and looked directly at him.

"What do you mean?"

"I mean that in addition to getting better treatment from the FBI, some people cooperate to get revenge on their partners. When their partners double-cross them or something." Norman stood up; he wanted some more raisin tarts. "Let's go back to the party, Sylvia."

*     *     *

Leo set his violin carefully in its case, then sat down on the sofa, tapping the tip of the bow against the coffee table. The music wasn't helping him tonight, except to emphasize his need to confront the issues that were plaguing him.

The conversation with Annette a week ago still rankled. *I guess you would know.* That's what she'd said after he told her about e-mail hackers and why they couldn't be traced. *You would know.* And the sarcasm: she *guessed.* Lumping him into a category he suddenly wanted to disown.

And her assurances that she thought him innocent, which to Leo meant that for a time at least she must have had doubts. He deserved those doubts, had put himself in a position that made people doubt him. Alex, Tim, Homer. He wanted their good opinions back.

"Remember," his mother had told him, and he could see her thin, earnest face as if she were there, even recall the scent she always wore, "you're smarter than most other people, but being smarter doesn't confer some kind of moral superiority. Some people think it does. I don't want you to have that attitude. I don't want you to think that you can do something morally questionable just because you're smart. Understand?"

Evidently he hadn't.

At the time, Leo had not understood why his parents went on so about moral choices. They were good Catholics, they went to mass, they talked about right and wrong. Some of that had slipped away, Leo had to admit, now that he was on his own. He occasionally attended mass. He struggled to maintain his integrity in a world that didn't seem to value it much.

What else was it that his mother had said? Oh, yes. If your friends' behavior places you in a moral dilemma, then perhaps they're not the right friends.

*December 26, 1999: Day 6*

The Brock home wore that exhausted look that it always suffered from the day after Christmas. Decorations were askew, piles of un-wrapped Christmas presents dotted the living room floor, the tree seemed denuded without any packages underneath.

The children were cross from the excitement of the day before, and they groused about going to church this morning, but Janet insisted. Next Saturday was January first. Who knew what next Sunday would bring? Janet prayed fervently during the service for the safety of the world in the new millennium, and she added a codicil of her own. Please let me remember what it is I've forgotten about Volodya.

In the afternoon she fell asleep, and her husband Mitch made dinner, knowing how tired she always was from all the Christmas preparations. She was brooding in the easy chair while the kids set the table, and he came over and kissed her cheek. Mitch was not a demonstrative man, but he loved his wife and he knew she was worried. He caught her hand and looked into her eyes: "I'm sure you'll think of it, honey." For Mitch, this was a florid declaration of love.

For Janet, it was a revelation, for when Mitch held her hand and looked into her eyes, two things he rarely did, her memory suddenly flashed to that day in September in Volodya's office when she had interviewed him about his test log. Volodya had held her hand - longer than necessary, she had thought at the time - and looked into her eyes - she had blushed when he did it - and now she remembered what it was that Alex needed to know about him.

*       *       *

"I miss you, Annette." Volodya's voice was low and intimate, the usual undercurrent of mockery gone.

These phone calls were getting to be as tricky to handle as Volodya's presence. "I miss you, too," Annette said, because he expected it. She didn't care to explore the issue of whether she really missed him. "But you're leaving soon, aren't you, to drive back here?"

"I leave this evening," he said. "Are you wearing ring?"

"Of course I am." She watched it sparkle on her finger.

"Good. I am glad you like it." A pause. "We will go out for dinner tomorrow night."

"That would be lovely." Tomorrow night he would be in FBI custody.

*       *       *

Janet did now remember a problem with a file. She had gone to see a man named Volodya to ask him about it. Volodya had remembered her name, and Janet had been flattered.

"Let me get you a chair." Volodya pulled one over next to his and Janet sat down. "What can I do for you?"

"Well," said Janet, looking down at her notes, "I was looking through my personal y2k test logs and I discovered that this library was accessed last week. I was hoping you could tell me why."

"Your personal y2k test logs?" Volodya asked.

Janet nodded. "It's just my own little system. I have the compiler send me my own set of reports, direct to my desktop every time it compiles. The compiler vendors hate it," she confided, "because they have to add special code just for me. But the bank won't buy it unless they modify it like that; they know how much it helps me with my testing."

"Aren't you clever?" Volodya said.

Janet smiled modestly, but she was pleased. "Oh, it's just a little method I developed over the years. It helps me out from time to time."

"Can I see?" he asked, taking the clipboard from Janet's hand. What a handsome man he was, she thought. "Which library?"

"This one here." She pointed to the reference number and looked at him inquiringly. "You see, the main record shows no access of the library, and yet my report shows that you accessed it. And they both show changes in file size, which is also rather odd. I didn't notice that before."

"What day was that?"

"Just last Friday."

"Oh, file size change is just because of compiler upgrade," Volodya said, shrugging. "I remember that was day we first used it."

"Oh, of course!" Janet cried, pleased at having straightened out one problem. "Good thinking, Volodya." She wrote a comment next to the file.

"Probably it was just mistake, Janet," Volodya said. "I remember I was tired on that day; maybe I just hit wrong key."

He has the most gorgeous blue eyes, she thought.

"I really don't see how you could access that library accidentally," she said. "It's not even on your list to compile."

Volodya's face reddened, gorgeously, she thought. "I am embarrassed to admit, Janet," he said, "but sometimes I confuse Russian and English languages."

She waited.

"Look," he said, "you see x on compiler program. You hit key x for execute. Also in Russian, x is ha sound." He demonstrated the breathy syllable for her. "Sometimes I see x and I type h and sometimes I think *ha* and I type x, which is Russian letter, not English. You see?" He paused; Janet nodded uncertainly.

"So you see x hot key on compiler program is execute and h hot key is highlight?" he said again.

Hot keys were short cuts; strike a certain key once, execute a macro. Volodya continued at Janet's nod.

"Sometimes if I am thinking in Russian I hit h key to execute because h makes ha sound in English, but h is actually highlight, so then if I realize I have to unhighlight and hit x instead to execute." He caught her gaze and held it for a second, and again Janet noticed the blueness of his eyes before turning her mind back to the task at hand.

She tried to make sense of his ramblings. "Go on."

"So I am looking at compile list on computer to find right files to compile and I highlight wrong file accidentally. If I hit highlight two times, then file is unhighlighted. So I unhighlight file, but really I don't unhighlight file, I execute because I am hitting x key now instead of h, thinking of Russian sound, not English letter. And maybe I don't notice, or maybe even compiler has little bug and does not unhighlight properly." Volodya paused to draw breath.

Janet rubbed her forehead. "You're saying you got the highlight and execute hot keys mixed up. Because they have similar sounds. Depending on what language you're using. Is that what you're saying?"

Volodya nodded solemnly. "You are smart woman, Janet. I did not explain very well."

Janet smiled at him, oddly flattered. "Well, I guess it makes sense. And there may be a problem with the compiler upgrade, too. Okay, Volodya, thanks for taking the time to help me figure it out." She jotted some notes on her clipboard. "But why do you suppose that your name appears on my compile log and not on the mainframe?"

Volodya had a ready answer. "Oh, that would be bug in your little custom report program, I think. Probably unhighlight command is delayed and file is called and put on your log, then unhighlight command executes split second later and log is unhighlighted on mainframe. It must have never anticipated the keystroke sequence I used."

Janet pondered the scenario. "Yes, I guess that's possible," she said at last. "Actually, as long as I have the real story on how the library was accessed, and as long as the mainframe code passes all tests, I guess that's my bottom line." She stood up and awkwardly shook hands with him. "Sorry to take up your time, but I have to check these things out, you know."

"Oh, no problem, Janet," he assured her. He held her hand just a heartbeat longer than was necessary, and she felt her cheeks redden. "Are you sure that everything is OK now?"

"Oh, I think we're fine now," Janet said, still feeling a trifle flustered. "It's good to have such conscientious programmers on the team."

"Come and visit me again."

Janet had fled down the hall, wondering whether he had meant the harmless phrase to sound so suggestive, or whether it was her own over-stimulated imagination. And until her husband had held her hand just now, she had pushed the incident to the furthest corner of her mind and forgotten it.

\*       \*       \*

Leo was so anxious to see what Janet had found that he arrived half an hour early and was forced to wait in high anxiety in the car for fifteen minutes. Homer arrived with a bank key and passwords, and Tim, Janet and Alex pulled into the lot at the same time. Leo caught up with his boss at the front door and held out his hand.

"Thanks for letting me come, Alex," he said.

Alex hesitated only a moment before grasping Leo's hand. "It seemed only fair," he said. "Let's hope we come up with something this time."

"I can't promise anything," Janet warned them for the fourth time, as they reached her office, "but I did find it strange at the time."

After switching on her computer, she unlocked a desk drawer and rifled in it, then pulled out the notebooks in which she had first noted the library discrepancy.

"See there." She pointed to an entry dated September 28. "I was checking the mainframe compile log against my own desktop compile."

"You have a personal compile log?" Leo interrupted.

"Yes, that way if the mainframe is down, at least I have the most recent compiles. I don't have to wait until the end of the day for the whole day's run." Janet ran her finger down the list of entries, looking for Volodya's.

"Here it is. September 24th, the Friday before. My compile log shows Volodya accessing this library. The mainframe log doesn't show his name at all."

Alex raised an eyebrow. "And you found this unusual?"

"Yes! Two reasons, really. One, the two logs should have been the same. Both should have shown Volodya accessing the library. Two, that is an inactive library. There was no reason for him for access it." She waited for a moment while the three men thought, then asked eagerly, "Is that important? Is it a clue?"

"I'm not sure yet," said Tim. "I assume you approached Volodya for an explanation." She nodded. "What did he say?"

Janet put a hand in her frizzy hair and tried to think. "Well, first he said maybe it was a mistake because he was tired. But I didn't buy that because it seemed like he would have had to scroll to that library on purpose; it wasn't one that was on his list of libraries to compile. Then he gave me this really complex explanation about the difference between Russian and English sounds and alphabets. I can't tell you exactly, it was really hard to follow, but it sort of made sense."

"Volodya started studying English before he started elementary school," Leo said. He was growing more and more excited. "He told me he had a private tutor." He was wildly impatient to see the library; like a hound on the quarry, he thought, having scented blood.

Alex scratched his chin. "But if he accessed the library, and admitted doing so, then why wasn't his name on the mainframe log?"

Janet wrinkled her forehead. "He said that my desktop compile program might have a little bug because he had done an unanticipated keystroke sequence on the compiler." She shrugged. "Which is plausible."

"Or," said Leo, "he could have accessed the library and then deleted his I.D. But he wouldn't have known that he also needed to delete it on your private log."

Tim was studying Janet's notes. "Can we see the compile log on screen for September 28th?"

Janet keyed in the correct commands and waited a moment for the program to load. "There." She pointed as the screen came up. "That's the library." They studied it together.

"Okay, now let's look at the same thing for September 24th." Again Janet obliged.

"Look!" Tim cried. "The file size has changed. If all he did was access the library by accident and then exit, the file size would stay the same. Did you catch that before, Janet?"

To their disappointment, she nodded. "When I asked Volodya about it, he pointed out that the compiler upgrade, which was used for the first time that day, was probably the culprit. And that's plausible too," she added.

Alex turned away from the computer with an exclamation of disappointment. "Do you buy it, Tim?" he asked. "Seems like too many 'plausible' explanations to me. But you guys are the experts. Is there anything here?"

Tim nodded slowly and Leo felt his pulse quicken - he was willing to take the code apart bit by bit if Volodya were somewhere within it.

"The file size change is suspicious," said Tim. "Especially in the light of the two other problems. But if he planted the code in the library and Janet caught it - even though she didn't realize it at the time - then I'd expect him to go back in and remove the code at some point to make sure that nobody could find it if they checked that library."

"Then the library should show another access," Leo said, "and the file size should change again, sometime after Janet asked him about it." Leo wanted to wrench the keyboard away from Janet in his eagerness to do the search. "Janet, what day did you go to Volodya?"

Janet consulted her notebook again. "September 28th. Shall I pull the log back up?"

"Yes." Leo tapped his fingers impatiently on the desk. Her search took only microseconds, but today it seemed endless.

Finally the screen stopped scrolling and they all leaned toward it.

"There!" Janet, who was the most familiar with the code, saw it first. They all followed her pointing finger. "The library was accessed again that day. The same day I spoke to him." She clucked in distress. "I'll bet he did it right after I left."

"And look, his name is on the log - Vladimir Borodin." Alex chuckled with grim satisfaction. "I wonder how he'll explain that?"

"*And* the file size is changed." Leo spoke with quiet satisfaction, because this to him was the most damning evidence. Volodya had put the code in, been caught, and yanked the code back out.

# Chapter 24

*December 27, 1999: Day 5*

Norman looked out his window and marveled. Instead of his usual view of planes rising over Port Columbus, he saw planes on the ground, more planes than he'd ever seen before, not only at the airport itself, but also parked at DFAS, on the runways built when Rockwell owned the plant. As a precaution, virtually no one was flying over the New Year, so the planes were parked wherever room could be found. He'd heard that a number had been flown to the Arizona desert to wait until the all clear was given. Some countries, he had no doubt, would be unable to safely navigate planes in and out of their airports for months - mostly third-world countries, granted, but he wondered what the net economic effect would be. It was one of those incalculable equations.

A brisk knock interrupted his thoughts. It was only eight o'clock, and it was George; he knew that knock by now.

"Happy New Year, Norman!" George wrung Norman's hand with enthusiasm; this was the first time Norman had seen him in several weeks. Norman returned the greeting, waiting hungrily for news.

"And I should say, congratulations!" George was smiling broadly, now.

"You mean you caught them?"

"Thanks to you!" George made himself comfortable in Norman's only other chair. "Sylvia phoned me on Christmas Eve, and we picked up her friend Grigorii the day after Christmas."

"Did you arrest Sylvia?"

George shook his head. "She's out on bond until the trial. Grigorii's in jail. The DoD wants to keep a low profile on this, naturally, so you're sworn to secrecy for the time being."

"Will she go to jail?" Norman's light-heartedness at having cleared his own name was tempered by the thought of Sylvia.

"Well, hell, Norman, she's guilty! Confessed it herself. I hope she goes to jail. She'll probably get a lighter sentence since she came to us. Don't feel guilty. She told us that you figured out she'd planted the code and suggested she turn herself in. But if she goes unpunished, what deterrent is there for the next hacker?"

"I don't know."

"And we're going to have our work cut out for us after New Year's Eve!" continued George as if he hadn't spoken. "The year 2000 problem is a hacker's dream. All kinds of things are going to be blamed on y2k computer glitches, including problems caused by hackers, who have no doubt been waiting for the opportunity. Y2k is the ultimate scapegoat." George's long fingers played with the perfect knot in his tie.

"Well, Norman, thanks for your help. That was great detective work, maybe you should consider a career with the Bureau."

"Really?" Norman suspected that George was teasing him.

"I'll recommend you myself. Good luck in 2000! And Happy New Year!"

"You bet. You, too, George. Goodbye!"

After the agent left, Norman returned to his perusal of the planes. Special Agent Norman Krebbs. His wife Iris would have a fit, he suspected, and he really did like accounting. Still, it was nice for Captain Bean Counter to have a fallback career.

\*　　\*　　\*

Eleven o'clock already. Like everyone else, Annette was tense. The y2k team had met the two FBI agents earlier in the morning in the conference room. George and Jerry had answered a few questions and asked some of their own before sending them all back to their offices to wait until Volodya showed up. And he hadn't. Although Annette did not find this strange, given the time he must have come home last night, she was on edge like the rest of them.

"Annette!" She actually jumped out of her chair when Volodya came in; for some reason she had assumed he would go to his office first. She didn't know if she wanted to see him.

Volodya made it plain that he wanted to see her. He wrapped his arms around her and nuzzled her neck, then began kissing her with unconcealed passion. "Mmm, I have missed you." His breath was hot against her cheek. "We will go out for dinner tonight and then I will come over to your place. Yes?" Without waiting for an answer he kissed her again.

Annette fought for control. Guilty though he seemed to be, she was sickened by the knowledge that the FBI would come for him in a few minutes, that she knew about it and he didn't. So she didn't stop him from kissing her, even sought to return his kisses to the extent that she could. She felt she was providing the last meal of a condemned man.

His eyes were bright when he finally released her. "Maybe we should go to your place now. Or maybe I should just lock office door." His face was mischievous. And, she thought, still so rakishly hand-some, so smoothly self-confident.

"Volodya! I have to work." She smoothed her hair, smiling at him. "You can wait a few hours." Funny that she should feel like the crimi-nal.

\*        \*        \*

Volodya was smiling broadly as he entered his spartan room at the bank. The rest of his team was off work this week; little was left to do, and they were not needed there, so he was alone.

After only a few minutes of work, Volodya heard the click of the key card in the door. He turned questioningly to the two men who were coming in; he thought he saw Homer Jones in the hallway before the door closed, but he couldn't be sure.

"Are you Vladimir Borodin?" the tall, thin one asked. Both of the men wore suits. Volodya felt a sudden, faint premonition of danger.

"Yes."

"I'm special agent Jerry Stemkoski, and this is special agent George Mumford." The second man was black, not as tall as his colleague, slender and fit-looking. Both men were smiling as they held out their hands to Volodya to shake. He did so, hiding his instinctive recoil at having to shake hands with a black man.

"We're from the Federal Bureau of Investigation, and we hope that you can help us out by answering a few questions." Jerry was still smiling pleasantly as he showed Volodya his wallet identification.

"The FBI?" Volodya's mouth felt dry.

This time it was George who spoke. "We're investigating a case of bank fraud, and we thought you might be able to help us."

"Bank fraud?" He realized that he was echoing their words like a parrot. "What bank fraud?"

"Here at Midwest National," George said, as if that were an explanation. "Of course, answering our questions is purely voluntary on your part. We'd be grateful for your cooperation, but you don't have to talk to us."

"Of course," his partner added, "it's possible that we might have to serve you with a grand jury subpoena later, if you decide not to talk to us now."

"Would you like some coffee?" Volodya asked. The two men sauntered over to the coffee maker, making themselves at home while Volodya tried to decide what was going on. He manufactured a smile, then turned around with his coffee in his hand. "Sure, I will talk to you."

"Great! Makes our lives much easier." Jerry smiled at him warmly, but Volodya did not relax. These men were not here to be his friends.

"Sometimes we ask people to go downtown to our office to talk, but we can stay here, if you like, since this room is free." The more accommodating they were, the more nervous Volodya felt. No, he certainly didn't want to go downtown to their office.

"It would be more convenient to talk here," he said, aiming for the same casual politeness that they displayed.

"Great." Jerry moved a computer terminal off one of the desks and sat behind it. George sat in a chair nearby and motioned for Volodya to pull up a chair. Then Jerry opened his briefcase and removed a file, which he laid on the desk and opened.

"We'll just go through your information first to be sure we have it right, okay?"

Volodya nodded and took a mouthful of coffee.

"Let's see. Your name is Vladimir Vasilovitch Borodin, born 1967, Moscow, parents Vasily and Olga, no siblings. Showed promise of genius at an early age; admitted to special school of mathematics at the age of thirteen. Finished secondary school early, with honors, attended Moscow State, took advanced degrees in Mathematics and Computer Science. One of your professors was the renowned mathematician Sergei Krzyzanowski."

"Why do you have so much information in my file?" Volodya asked.

Jerry looked down at his papers again, as though looking for the answer. "That's hard to say, Mr. Borodin. You know, the Bureau has this huge computer bank, and once you have a file, sometimes information just seems to find its way in there." He shrugged apologetically. "You're a computer man; I'll bet you'd be interested in our computer center. We have an enormous amount of data stored there."

Volodya nodded politely.

"Sometimes erroneous information is entered into someone's file, which is why I'm going over these facts with you. Is that correct, that Sergei Krzyzanowsky was your professor? Because if not, I can delete it." Jerry waited, his face a question mark.

"It is correct."

"Okay, good." Jerry droned on through the resume of Volodya's life, his job in Germany, his emigration, his job in New York, his relationship with Viktor, his move to Columbus, his inheritance, his guardianship of Viktor's cousin, his company, his job at Midwest National. All the information was correct, and the file contained plenty of information. Jerry did not give him time to mull it over.

"Your turn, George," he announced, stretching. He took the chair that George had vacated, but George remained standing, urbane and intimidating.

"Okay. Volodya," he said, "explain to us what kind of bank access you have."

"Bank access? Same as other programmers. I access source code to compile it. I access EDI to remediate it."

"Do you ever access other people's e-mail?" George asked.

Volodya took a long drink of coffee, managing to keep his face impassive. His hacking was far too sophisticated to trace, and if someone had informed on him, it was only that person's word against his.

"No," he said, polite but emphatic. "Of course not."

"Volodya, we understand that you accessed Homer Jones' e-mail." George imparted this information with the same pleasant neutrality one gave to a comment on the weather.

"Who said so?" Volodya's indignation was unfeigned; only other programmers knew about the hacking, and to violate his secret was a breach of programming etiquette.

"We are not at liberty to tell you that," George said, no trace of apology in his voice.

"This is free country! How can I be accused by someone and you will not tell me who it is!"

"We can't tell you." George said again. "Do you have any idea who might have accused you of something like this, or why?"

That was a good question

"I cannot think of anyone." Let them give him the information.

"No one at all? A rival," George suggested, "or someone with a grudge against you?"

"Here? At bank? I have friends at bank." It must have been Leo, Volodya thought. "Leo Hermann," he said then. He would give them the right name, since they already knew.

"Well, I can't confirm or deny that. But why would this Leo Hermann say something like that if it's untrue?"

"Leo is my friend," said Volodya slowly. "I cannot believe he would do this." The agents looked expectantly at him. "Maybe," Volodya said at last, as though the words were dragged out of him reluctantly, "maybe it is because we are interested in same woman. Annette Ashby, who is y2k project head. Leo was in love with her; maybe he became jealous when he saw that she was interested in me."

"So that's your explanation?" George said. "That Leo made this accusation out of jealousy?"

Volodya shrugged. "That is my speculation. You must ask Leo why he did it." That put the ball neatly back in their court. He waited for the next volley.

George picked up another piece of paper. Volodya noticed that while one questioned, the other took notes.

"Harry Buehler was in charge of your security arrangements. Can you tell me how you felt about those arrangements?"

Was this still tied to the e-mail question? Volodya couldn't tell.

"I was not happy with arrangements. My team was given more restrictions than other employees." He allowed his voice to become sharp with resentment. As long as he could tell the truth, he would. It would make his lies more believable.

"Why do you think this was, Volodya?" George sounded sympathetic.

"He is bigot. He hates Russians. Not for good reason. He just hates us." Volodya looked pointedly at George. "You should understand such things."

George was impassive. "So what happened to the security arrangements as a result of your protest?"

"Restrictions were relaxed." Volodya did not bother to enumerate them; he was sure they knew exactly which rules were relaxed.

"Then in your opinion was it easier for the members of your team to practice computer fraud without these restrictions?" George had left his chair to perch on the desk; he sat relaxed and in control, his foot swinging.

"We were using dumb terminals. You understand term?" Both men nodded. "Was still not easier for us than for other bank employees. We could not take material in or out of this room."

Jerry wrote this down while George continued to question him. "So you don't think that anyone in this room could have used a dumb terminal to defraud the bank?"

"I did not spend my time thinking about it. I do not work at bank with intention of committing fraud."

The questions continued. Sometimes they asked him questions he had answered already. He answered them again, patiently and politely. In the morass of questions they asked, he could not always tell which ones were important. He wanted a break.

"It is lunchtime." Volodya said. "I am hungry."

"Oh, sorry, Volodya!"

"Maybe you could come back tomorrow to ask questions." Volodya saw the agents exchange glances.

"Well, Volodya, actually we do have a few more questions we'd like to ask you, and it would really help us out if we could get it all wrapped up today," Jerry said. "How about if we go in to the office for the afternoon? It's a little more comfortable there, and we can stop and pick up some fast food on the way. What do you say?"

Volodya ran a hand over his blonde hair and looked at the two agents, first George, then Jerry. He stood up.

"Should I call my attorney?"

George looked shocked. "Oh, no, Volodya, we're not filing charges against you. You don't really need a lawyer, although you're certainly welcome to one if it makes you more comfortable." George was looking very interested in his answer.

"No, lawyer is not necessary, then. I have never been questioned by FBI," Volodya added, making a joke of it, "so I don't know what to do."

They all laughed as if that were funny. Then Volodya accompanied the two agents to their car and took a ride downtown.

*        *        *

When they reached the tenth floor of the upscale twelve-story building that housed the FBI, Jerry stepped out and indicated the office on the right. "Right this way," he said, as though inviting him to some FBI social function. Ahead of them was a clear glass door with the FBI seal picked out in white. FBI, Columbus Residential Agency, Cincinnati Division. Just inside the door was a metal detector for Volodya to step through when he entered.

Volodya noted the TV camera that monitored their movements and the large FBI seal (this one in color) that graced the wall next to the receptionist's bulletproof window. His impression was of a well-funded federal agency that had the money to pursue a person relentlessly if it chose to.

"This way," said George. Volodya mastered an impulse to turn and run out of the office (where he would do what, wait for an elevator?) and followed George through the door.

"Here we are." George opened the door into a windowless room furnished with a desk and three chairs. The carpet was plush under his feet, and the furniture was new.

"Can I get you a soda?" asked George, ever courteous.

"Coffee, please." Volodya gathered his powers of concentration in the few minutes they took to settle themselves comfortably. Sipping his coffee, he waited for the first question. It was entirely unexpected.

Jerry handed him a small piece of paper. "Do you recognize this?"

"It is receipt for jewelry store." His voice sounded calm in his ears, but he took another quick sip of coffee.

"And that is your signature?"

"Yes, of course. It was Christmas gift for Annette," he added, anticipating their next question."

Jerry raised his eyebrows. "That's a pretty expensive gift."

"Yes." He sipped his coffee and waited. Jerry handed him several more receipts, which he quickly scanned. The FBI had been looking at him closely indeed.

"Mine also," Volodya said. "For purchase of computer equipment."

Jerry's expression was faintly incredulous. "You've spent a lot of money this month. Over eleven thousand dollars."

"All on credit cards," Volodya said. "Is not illegal to be in debt."

"Of course not," Jerry said. Volodya noticed that he made a habit of pulling on his left ear when he was thinking. "How were you thinking of paying off these debts?"

Volodya shrugged. "In usual way. Monthly payments. And I anticipate increased work for my company as result of year 2000 breakdowns in computers."

"I see." Jerry swirled the soda in his can, drank the rest, then set the can down on the desk with a click. "I suppose you could argue that you needed more computer equipment for your business. But what about the ring? Six thousand dollars is a lot of money. Is it an engagement ring?"

Volodya answered politely; he needed to stay in control. "It was impulse buy. I went into store to buy emerald earrings. I saw emerald ring, I had new credit card, I bought ring. It reminded me of her eyes," he added weakly. He smiled the rueful smile of a man in love.

"Okay, Volodya," said Jerry, "we really appreciate your cooperation so far. Everything works out much better when we cooperate." Volodya waited, said nothing. "Now, this may seem a little tedious, but we just want to go back over a few of the details we covered this morning. Go ahead, George."

Volodya drank more coffee. After an hour of covering the same ground they'd covered before, his concentration began to wane. Then he saw Jerry catch George's eye and nod. George pulled open the bottom drawer of the desk and dragged out a pile of computer printouts.

"We'd like you to take a look at these," said George, handing him the top inch or so of the pile. "Do you recognize them?"

Volodya's heart was pounding now, but he took the printouts and scanned them. "This looks like compile log."

"Actually, it's one of your compile logs from Midwest," George said.

Volodya looked at it more closely. "I don't recognize it. They all look alike." He sounded flippant. He noticed again the dryness of his mouth, and drank some more of their coffee. He watched George flip through the pile of printouts. Then he went back over to the desk and pulled out some more paper from the top drawer and handed it Volodya.

"How about this one?"

"More of my compile log?" he said, as if hazarding a guess.

"Look." George pointed to the library.

"Yes. Is library."

"And did you access it?"

"Yes, I think so," Volodya said. "If it is my compile log, then I must have accessed it. But this is old log" - he indicated the September 24 date-time stamp - "and I don't really remember it. I access many libraries."

They started in on him in earnest then, still polite, but less patient. Explain how you made the error. Explain it again, we don't understand what you mean. Why did the file size change, and then change again? What makes you think the compile upgrade has a bug? Isn't there a better explanation? Is it possible that someone put something into that library and then took it back out again? Whether you did it or not, wouldn't that be possible? Explain again how you could have made such a mistake.

For more than an hour they questioned him closely. Then at some prearranged signal, they stopped and asked him again if he'd like a soda, or if he needed to use the bathroom. In the bathroom he studied his face in the mirror; his expression did not reflect his tension.

He returned to the interrogation room and stood stretching his arms behind him for a moment. It was three o'clock.

"Can I get you anything?" George was as obsequious as a waiter at a fancy restaurant.

"Coffee, please." Volodya rubbed the heels of his palms against his burning eyes. He had driven from New York until four a.m. and slept until only ten because he had wanted to go to the bank and see Annette.

"Ready, Volodya?" asked Jerry, as if they were going out to play a round of golf, not resume an interrogation. Volodya nodded.

"Do you have any contacts with Brighton Beach?"

"Brighton Beach!" He had not thought of them since his meeting with Grigorii in July. "No! They are criminals. I want nothing to do with them."

"But you make frequent trips to New York?" Jerry's eyes never left Volodya.

"Yes, I visit friends there," Volodya said. "They do not live in Brighton Beach."

"Do you know Grigorii Popov?" Jerry asked. "Maybe he goes by Greg sometimes?"

"Grigorii? Sure, I know him."

"Grigorii claims that he approached you about working with Brighton Beach."

"And did Grigorii tell you what I said? Eh? I told him never to ask me again."

"Maybe he was trying to protect you," Jerry said.

"I do not think Grigorii cares what happens to me," Volodya said. "I said I know him, I did not say we are good friends."

"When did you find out he was working for Brighton Beach?"

"I do not know if that is what he is doing all the time, or if he does it only this once. He told me last summer, in July."

"Did you tell the police?"

Volodya lifted an eyebrow. "Tell them what? I had no proof of anything."

"What did Grigorii ask you to do?"

"I don't know." Volodya shrugged, shifting his weight on the hard chair. "He said it had to do with computers, and that was why he wanted to talk to me. I told him I was not interested."

They spent an hour on the topic of Brighton Beach, although he had nothing of interest to tell them. None of his close friends was connected with Brighton Beach for the good reason that Volodya avoided such friends. He wanted no connection with anyone who might one day decide to kill him, and he finally said as much to Jerry.

"Are you a U.S. citizen, Volodya?" George was taking a turn as questioner now.

Volodya took a drink of coffee. "No."

"Why did you state on your application to work at Midwest National that you were a citizen?" George, of course, had a copy of the offending document.

"You must have records," Volodya said, almost letting his irritation show. "My naturalization was delayed because INS lost file. I was due to become citizen in June or July."

"So you lied on your application?"

Volodya gritted his teeth, but remained polite. "My understanding was that I would have citizenship papers any day. I did not want to lose job because pay was high, and I thought date of citizenship was technical point."

"I see." George laid the application back on the desk. "So you are not actually a citizen of the U.S. at this moment."

"No."

"Okay," Jerry said. "I just thought we should be clear on that. If there is a question of a crime having been committed, we may have to put a hold on granting your citizenship. Deportation is certainly not out of the question."

The words brought a certain chill into the room, and Jerry smiled as if to reassure him.

"Volodya," he said gently, "we are investigating a case of computer fraud at Midwest National. We have reason to believe that you are involved. If you cooperate with us, your situation will be much easier."

"I haven't done anything!"

Jerry sighed, as if at a recalcitrant child. "Don't bother to pretend, Volodya. We can prove you were involved. We have your old professor, Sergei Krzyzanowsky, working on it for us now."

"Sergei Krzyzanowsky? He is here?"

"He's not here in Columbus," said Jerry, "but he's here in the States. And he identified you as one of his best and brightest pupils. He thinks he can crack your code. If I were you, I wouldn't gamble on it."

"The professor is here?" Volodya repeated.

"Yes, he's here." Jerry sounded a tad impatient. "Volodya, think about yourself, not about Sergei. Are you going to cooperate with us?"

"I have been cooperating with you all day. I cannot help you any more; I did not do anything to code." Volodya was still trying to work out how Sergei could be in the U.S. Sergei was an ardent Russophile, the most unlikely person to emigrate that Volodya could imagine.

A thought struck him.

"I would like to see Professor Krzyzanowski," he announced to the two astonished agents.

# Chapter 25

It was after seven when the two agents met the y2k team again in Alex's conference room. Jerry looked rumpled; George was as dapper as ever.

"What happened?" Homer asked anxiously.

"He denies it," Jerry said. His voice was resigned, his posture, slumped.

"But we did arrest the DFAS perpetrators," he added, brightening a bit, "the ones who put Sergei's algorithm into the DoD accounts. Arrested them the day after Christmas. Turns out that the same accountant who found the DoD problem also found out who did it. A woman who works in IT at DFAS - and she has a Russian boyfriend named Grigorii who supplied her with the algorithm."

"Where did he get it?" Alex asked.

"He got it from Brighton Beach - the Russian Mafia - and they got it from the FSB." Jerry shook his head. "I never heard of the FSB turning to organized crime for their targets. They had to pay the mob, who paid Grigorii, who co-opted his girlfriend. When he dumped her, she turned him in."

"Will she have to go to jail?" asked Annette.

George shrugged. "I don't know for sure. I would hope that she'd at least get reduced time. The funny thing about this is, Volodya knows Grigorii and admits it, but he furiously denied ever having anything to do with Brighton Beach. He even admitted that Grigorii asked him to do something for them, but claims he refused."

"He's lying," said Leo.

"It's too damned bad, because when Grigorii admitted he knew Volodya, I thought we had Volodya for sure. Unfortunately, their acquaintance seems to be just coincidental. And Volodya got quite indignant. Said he didn't want anything to do with Brighton Beach because they were criminals."

"What did you find on his computer?" Alex asked.

A look of disgust settled over Jerry's thin features. "Clean as a whistle," he said. "He must've wiped his hard drive recently, or maybe he was just too smart to keep anything on it. Our guys have been looking at it ever since they went over there with the search warrant this morning. They'll keep looking."

The agents would not share any other details of the questioning, although they did say that they had deposited Volodya at his car with instructions to go home and stay there until the next morning. Alex wondered why they would trust him that far, and asked them.

"Well, we have a couple of agents watching him, of course." Jerry seemed unconcerned. "But if he tries to run away, he looks suspicious. He doesn't want to do anything suspicious, because that contradicts his story that he's innocent. If we detain him overnight, he'll ask for a lawyer; once he gets a lawyer, we'll never get anything useful out of him. Also, he'll stay because he wants to see Sergei; we're going to fly Volodya to Walter Reed Army Hospital tomorrow morning."

That news raised a buzz around the conference room. Alex spoke for the others.

"Why are you doing that?"

"We talked to the CIA and we talked to Sergei. They all feel that Sergei may still have some influence over Volodya; Sergei thinks he might be able to persuade Volodya to fix the algorithm," Jerry said. "At this point, it's worth a try."

"How's Sergei coming on the algorithm?" Leo asked

"Sergei is not confident that he can solve the puzzle in time, which is one of the reasons he wants to talk to Volodya." George gave them something else to think about: "Volodya doesn't want to go to the East Coast alone; he says he doesn't trust the police. He wants someone from the bank to go with him." George paused and looked uncomfortable. "He asked for Annette."

This brought an outraged protest from Leo. Annette put her face in her hands; when the noise subsided she raised her head.

"I won't do it."

"Annette," Jerry said softly, "it might help us. He might say some-thing to you that he wouldn't to us, because he trusts you. If you went along he would let down his guard, be more relaxed."

"If I don't go along he'll be disappointed and nervous. I think he's more likely to make a mistake then." Annette shook her head again; her voice was firm. "I'm sorry, I don't have to do it and I won't. Find someone else to go with him."

"Maybe you're right," George said. "We'll save you for the last ditch effort, if he's still refusing to cooperate after he sees Sergei. Will you talk to him then?"

"Perhaps."

George seemed satisfied with that answer. "Why don't you write Volodya a note and ask him to go with us? Tell him you trust us."

Alex could see on her face that she did not want to do even that, but eventually she nodded. George found her a piece of paper and she scribbled something with the silver pen and handed the paper back to George, who read it aloud.

*Dear Volodya,*

*Alex does not want me to come with you. Please go with the agents; this is America, you can trust them not to do anything illegal. If you cooperate, things will go better for you. I will see you when you return.*

*Annette*

Jerry frowned. "Could you write, 'Love, Annette'?" He cut short her protest. "Just 'Annette' is a little cold. You can tell him how you really feel later." She took the paper, muttering, and wrote what he'd requested. "Great! Thanks, Annette." Jerry stood up. "You guys go home and get some rest. We'll call you if we need you."

After the two agents had gone, the y2k team sat in silence for a moment. Today was Monday, and time was slipping away. They had to eradicate the worm by Thursday, at the latest, because the world's banks would begin the millennium rollover at six a.m. on Friday, begin-ning with New Zealand. The year 2000 rollover could cause so many unpredictable glitches that removing the worm would become even more difficult, perhaps impossible. If Sergei were right about the replication, control of the worm might then pass out of their hands altogether, and its uncontrolled drain of the global financial systems would be followed by a slow sinking of the world into economic chaos.

## *December 28, 1999: Day 4*

Volodya lounged in the seat of the Gulfstream jet, ostensibly reading the *Courier* while Jerry and George chatted in the seat behind him. Flying made him nervous; he hated the loss of control inherent in the process. He felt in his coat pocket for Annette's note, which was so short that he had already memorized the contents. Perhaps she would have written more had she not known that the agents would read it before they gave it to him. A long love letter would have been a welcome distraction.

His eyes felt dry and scratchy; he had not slept well. When he had returned to his apartment last night, his computer was gone.

Their destination was a secret; he did not know how long they would be in the air, so he would try to sleep until they landed. Sergei was one of the most brilliant men he knew, and if Sergei were now on the side of the FBI, he would need to have his wits about him.

## *Washington, D.C.*

"Sergei, your visitor is here," said the nurse. Sergei struggled to sit up in the bed; he had been dozing. Before he could focus properly he was enveloped in a bear hug and kissed on both cheeks in the Russian way.

"Professor!" Volodya stepped back from the bed. He was taller than Sergei remembered, or perhaps it was just because Sergei was in bed. His hair was longer, he looked older, or at least very tired, but when he smiled Sergei saw again the brilliant twenty-year-old he had taught at university. He has tears in his eyes, Sergei noticed, thinking that he himself must look more ill than he realized. Unbidden came words from Dostoevsky: *The wicked are often sentimental.*

"Vladimir Vasilovitch," Sergei said. "How kind of you to visit me."

"Yes," Volodya said. "I had special escort." Sergei smiled at his pupil's familiar irony. He saw the two men standing behind him, one black, one white. They introduced themselves as FBI agents and shook Sergei's hand.

"You two have your talk. And keep it in English," said the one they called Jerry. "We'll be out here with your CIA friends." Sergei and Volodya were left alone in the hospital room.

"The room is wired?"

Sergei nodded. "One would assume so. Otherwise they would not leave." He sighed, pressing a hand over his abdomen, which some-times pained him since the surgery. "You see what we have come to, Volodya, since leaving our homeland. We cannot be trusted alone."

Volodya's face was impassive. "And how do you come to be here, Professor?"

Sergei waved a hand. "Oh, call me Seryozha, we are colleagues now. I think you must know why I am here." Volodya shook his head. Surprised, Sergei briefly recounted the events of his life since the FSB first contacted him about creating the worm. "And you?"

Volodya recited a biography that ended short of his arrival in Sergei's room.

"Yes, Volodya, but how do you come to be here in this room?" Sergei looked at his protégé kindly.

"My bank has worm like yours, and I am suspected of planting it. They mentioned that you were here in States, and I said that I would like to see you." His lips twisted with amusement. "They are very obliging."

"I see." Sergei shifted restlessly in his bed, and Volodya strode to the bed to help rearrange the pillows. "Thank you, that is better. So you do not admit that you planted the worms - yours or mine?"

"Is that what you believe?" Volodya asked, side-stepping the ques-tion.

"I purposely designed the worm to be difficult to plant. The more I thought about it, the more I feared what it would do. The FSB, of course, was not sophisticated enough to realize this. They would have been lucky to have sent it to you; you were the only one of my students who possessed the genius necessary to put the worm into source code." Sergei looked at Volodya expectantly. Volodya had pulled a chair near the bed, and his posture was relaxed.

"There was programmer who succeeded," said Volodya. "The worm also appeared in code of U.S. government institution, but they did not tell me which one. It must have been planted by second person because money disappeared there before it disappeared from bank."

"I had forgotten. Still, I appeal to you to deactivate your worm." His voice was beseeching. "I can break your code, Volodya, but I do not know if I can do it in time."

"In time for what?" Volodya made the polite response.

"In time to prevent the damage it will do. Volodya, you must know that I designed the worm to replicate itself in a different form if the virus checkers got close to it. It was a safety measure." He pointed to a pile of printouts on the hospital table. "Look at these." Volodya picked them up. "These are records from all the banks where the worm was found. For the amount of time the worm was activated, the number of replications is too great by a factor of five. A factor of five!" Sergei took a graph from the table and shoved it at Volodya. "Do you see the implications?"

Volodya gazed at Sergei. "Perhaps you will explain to me."

"The money disappears too fast," said Sergei, agitated. "The worm was designed to be self-limiting. After a certain amount of money was moved, the worm was to become inactive, perhaps for months at a time. What good was the money if we took too much? The economic system would collapse, and the money would have no value. I did not anticipate that the worm would be changed by another program. We were lucky that I was able to deactivate my worm when we did, because it was mutating. Yours will do the same, because it was modeled on mine. And if we do not get rid of it before the millennium, we cannot say what will happen, because systems will become unpredictable. Perhaps it will not even respond to a deactivation command." Sergei felt himself growing winded and he stopped for a moment.

"You must calm yourself, Sergei Ivanovitch," Volodya said, pulling his chair closer, concern written on his face. "If you are too excited, doctor will come in and end our little chat."

"Volodya, will you not do as I asked?"

Volodya sat back in his chair, studying his former mentor. "How do I know that you have not invented this apocalyptic data in order to frighten me into confession?"

Sergei was shocked. "Volodya, I give you my word -"

"Your word," Volodya interrupted him. "Come, Professor. It was you who planted worm for FSB, and you who betrayed your country."

"Do you think you can insult me more than I have insulted myself?" Sergei asked. "But you are wrong; I did not betray my country by coming here to deactivate worm. I betrayed my country by agreeing to work with FSB and create the virus. A dying man thinks about these things, Volodya. How much better that I should have said no to them."

"But then you would not have received new liver. You would be dead by now. How can that be better?"

"You would not be standing here if I had refused," said Sergei softly. "You would be working in Columbus, you would have committed no crime. I blame myself greatly for being the tool of your corruption."

Volodya's lips pulled back into a thin line. "Such scruples you have developed, Sergei Ivanovitch! Well, you may rest your fears, because I have not committed this crime. You are mistaken." Sergei saw Volodya's hands curl into fists.

"I expect you to lie about it, Volodya," Sergei said. "Do not expect me to believe your lies." Sergei's mouth was parched suddenly. "Please, can you pour me a glass of water?" Volodya obliged, solicitous again. "Thank you."

Sergei leaned back against his pillows, spent. How tiring was strong emotion!

"And have you married, Volodya? You are thirty now."

Volodya looked down at his hands. "No. There is woman - an American, but born in Europe - but we have no plans."

"Marriage is good," Sergei said. "Masha and I have been married now for thirty years. She is a great blessing to me." He hesitated for a moment. "What does your friend think of your present trouble?"

"I have not spoken to her since it began. She wrote me note, telling me that I should come to see you. I spoke to her about you before and said that I admired you." Volodya stopped speaking, clearly uncomfortable with the conversation. He rose suddenly, and thrust his hands deep into his pockets, then moved to the window, which looked out into a snowy courtyard. "We have no snow in Ohio," he remarked.

"Volodya, have you thought of your professional reputation?" Sergei asked, trying another tack. "If you are known to be the author of this

worm, your reputation will be gone. You will have no standing at all in
the community of mathematicians. You will never publish again. No
university will touch you."

Volodya appeared both amused and angry. "But, according to you,
I will be very rich."

Sergei became angry in turn. "You will be very poor! And so will
we all because the economic structure of the world will have collapsed!
Think of your selfishness, Volodya!" Sergei closed his eyes, suddenly
feeling dizzy. A nurse was standing over him when he opened his eyes.

"You must rest for a while, Mr. Kamenov," the nurse said. "Your
friend will be back sometime later."

Sergei nodded. These spells came upon him and all he could do
was succumb. He closed his eyes again and prayed for the soul of his
wayward pupil; if he could not reach him, perhaps God could. And if
He could not, then may He have mercy on them all.


*Columbus*


Alex sat at his computer at the Millennium Dynamics Office, absently using the drag and drop utilties to make his e-mail screens grow
larger and then shrink smaller again. Doodling with the mouse, Karen
called it.

He was ruminating on the end of the world. A post to the millennium mail list yesterday requested that he write a farewell letter of
sorts for this last week of December, giving them some idea of what he
thought was going to happen. If only he knew! Still, it was a fair
request, given that he had posted similar letters every six months for
nearly the entire five years of the mail list's existence.

With the question of Volodya still unsettled, Alex found it difficult to
concentrate on the business at hand. Homer was in the same state;
Alex had run into him several times since last night, and he had the look
of a lost soul. But he would not sit here and waste more precious time
with thoughts of Volodya when he had so much still to accomplish before the rollover. Concentrating on the computer screen, he thought
back over his years of y2k experience, about to come to a decisive
head, and slowly began to type.

*Dear Friends and Colleagues,*

*The last week of any year puts one in a reflective mood, the last week of the millennium, even more so, and this week of weeks, the culmination of years of work and the beginning of the year 2000 rollover - this week above all weeks moves us to examine what we've accomplished in the past years and what is to come in the next few days.*

*First, our accomplishments. None of us should doubt that that we have each been a player in our part of the y2k world. Each bit of code corrected, each person told, each letter written to a newspaper, each contingency plan laid, each speech to a Rotary club, each book given to a friend - each effort to correct, to mitigate, to make aware has made a difference. Without us, and I hope I say this modestly because no one of us could have done it alone, the world would be headed toward certain catastrophe come December 31st.*

*Have we accomplished all that we hoped? Sadly, no. Will we see disruptions that might have been avoided? Sadly, yes.*

*What will happen at midnight on December 31st? I can only tell you in the broadest of terms, but here is what I think:*

*1-We will see blackouts and brown-outs.*

*2-We will see y2k failures. Some small ones will ripple one into the other until they end in a large infrastructure failure.*

*3-At least one example of any predicted, reasonable y2k failure (no planes falling out of the sky, please!) will occur somewhere on the globe.*

*4-We will all be hugely inconvenienced by the rollover.*

*5-We will be amazed at the degree of interconnectivity we discover - x will influence y will influence z with results far beyond what we might have predicted.*

*6-We will see the majority of our population struggle through this difficult time with great good humor and courage.*

*7-Because people have prepared, we will not see the panic that so many feared.*

*8-Whatever happens here will happen more severely in other countries, especially those in Africa, Asia, and Eastern Europe.*

*9-Although we are accustomed to think of January first as D-day, we may find that the real problems will not be known for several weeks or months after the rollover. This is when the weaknesses in our supply and transportation systems will appear.*

*How long will the failures last? All I can say is, not as long as they would have if we hadn't worked so long and hard to get the word out. But overall, I am optimistic. I don't predict the end of the world. We will get through this trouble, however severe it turns out to be, and we will be stronger for having done it.*

*I know that all of you will stand fast, helping where you can, whether debugging a system or sharing food with a neighbor. God bless you all, and Godspeed to all of us in our millennial journey.*

*Best Wishes,*

*Alex Stauffer*
*Millennium Dynamics*

*Washington, D.C.*

Volodya speared a hunk of gray meatloaf smothered in sodium-rich gravy, and dipped it into the mound of instant mashed potatoes on his luncheon plate. If Sergei was existing on such fare, no wonder he was not recovering faster. Volodya was eating with the two FBI agents in an unoccupied room near Sergei's. George and Jerry made small talk for a while, but seemed disinclined to question him again. Perhaps their hopes were pinned on Sergei's influence over him.

He was still shocked at Sergei's appearance. True, he was a sick man, but he looked so old! He was old, of course, over fifty, but Volodya's memories were of a vital, dynamic man of forty, pacing up and down in the ancient mathematics lecture hall at Moscow State, lost in the excitement of sharing his mathematical discoveries with his pupils.

The weak and emaciated man in the hospital bed had looked nothing like that Sergei, although the old fire still had lit his eyes when he pleaded with Volodya to deactivate the algorithm.

*     *     *

After lunch and a nap, Sergei was looking better. He was even sitting in a chair this time when Volodya entered his room, dressed in shapeless gray sweats that were emblazoned across the front with *Go Army*! Volodya raised an eyebrow when he saw them, and Sergei shrugged. "Perhaps this is their little joke," he said. "Have you thought about our conversation?"

"May I look at your data again?" This time he studied it more carefully, although of course any kind of data could be faked. "Do you know why worm replicates itself too fast?"

"Since I created the original worm, there is a new virus checker in use at many banks, and it has that effect on the algorithm. I could not have predicted it. Still, it is a useful argument against this sort of tampering." He watched Volodya. "Do you know, Vladimir Vasilovitch, that when I received this liver transplant, the liver was denied to someone else?"

"I suppose that is logical assumption."

"It is even possible that someone will die because I received this liver and another liver will not be available in time. " Sergei handed Volodya a small pamphlet about organ donation. "Did you know that ten people die every day because of the shortage of organs for transplant? You should consider becoming a donor; you can add the information to your driver's license."

Volodya found the subject distasteful. "I do not like to think of my body being sliced up after I die."

"Russians are too sensitive about this subject," said Sergei. "But I bring it up to explain to you that I feel an obligation now to the people who saved my life. I must do my best to help them, even if it means that I must harm you."

He stood unexpectedly and caught Volodya's right hand in both of his, his grip still surprisingly strong.

"Volodya, you must deactivate the worm! There is no other way and the time is short. If you cooperate, it will go better for you. You know there is the possibility that I can find your worm in time; you were my pupil, I know how your mind works. Then what will happen to you?" Sergei's eyes burned into his.

"Professor, please sit down." Volodya helped him back to the chair. "I am afraid FBI exaggerates my abilities. I did not create worm. But I promise that I will think about what you said - about organ transplant, shortness of time - all of it."

"Thank you!" Sergei was fervent. "I trust you will make the right decision."

Volodya expected the FBI agents to end the interview now; he and Sergei had already said what was necessary. But they seemed to be in no hurry. In the end he stretched his long frame into one of the uncomfortable hospital chairs, Sergei ordered tea from the nurse, and they talked about old friends in Moscow. Masha joined them a while later; she was shy at first, but soon joined in the game of matching acquaintances, then the game of moaning about shortages and government stupidity. These were games all Russians played well. If they could have spoken in Russian, the time would have been perfect.

"We're leaving early tomorrow morning, Volodya." Jerry's voice interrupted his thoughts. "We've got an empty hospital room you can sleep in, but if you want to say goodbye to the professor, this is the time."

Their good-bye was brief. Sergei was emotional, embracing Volodya and asking God's blessings on him. "Good-bye, Volodya. Please forgive me." A tear glistened on his cheek.

"Of course," Volodya said.


*December 29, 1999: Day 3, Columbus*

Like the rest of the y2k team, Annette was taut with strain. They'd had no word since Monday evening, and the wait had been terrible. Now it was late Wednesday afternoon and when Alex sent word that the FBI agents were waiting in the conference room, she nearly ran the distance from her office. Had Volodya confessed?

"Annette!" Harry lumbered down the hall toward her like a great bear. "This is it, eh?"

"I suppose it is."

"Hey." Harry peered into her face. "Are you okay? You're white as a sheet."

"I'm okay, Harry." Annette squeezed his arm affectionately.

As they all seated themselves, Annette saw that the FBI agents were there already. Jerry looked tired, but jubilant. She glanced guiltily at the emerald sparkling on her finger.

Jerry spoke without preamble. "I think he's going to confess. He hardly spoke a word on the flight back. The things Sergei had to say seemed to have the desired effect." He smiled, then swung his gaze to Annette. She felt sick with dread.

"I don't want to talk to him," she said.

"Annette, he just needs a little nudge. You don't need to be with him for long. Just ask him to cooperate." Jerry turned to Alex, who was about to speak when Leo interrupted.

"Why should she have to talk to that sleazebag? You're the FBI agents, you make him confess! It's not her job!"

Alex motioned for him to sit down, but Annette had seen, had felt, Leo's concern for her, and she felt a rush of emotion when she looked at him.

"Please, Annette. You know we don't have any time to waste." Alex's tone was sympathetic, but firm.

She couldn't say no when so much depended on Volodya's cooperation. "It's all right, Leo." She rose.

Jerry led her down the hall to where George stood guard outside an office that was normally used as a small conference area. Volodya must be inside. As she opened the door, George smiled reassuringly at her. "I'll be right here," he said. "Don't worry."

Volodya was standing at the window, his back to her. He turned quickly, looked surprised to see her. Then he leaned against the windowsill and just looked at her. There was no humor in his face today; he looked proud and angry and tired.

"Did they send you in to beg me? Go ahead. I don't have anything to tell you; I didn't do anything."

"But, Volodya, they know. *I* know."

He shrugged. "You are only one, then. If they know, they would arrest me. They cannot prove anything."

"But they will - it's just a matter of time, Volodya. They know how you did it; they'll unravel it eventually."

"I did nothing." He crossed his arms and looked across the room. Annette was at a loss. What made the others think she had any influence with him? She moved closer so that he could not avoid looking at her.

"Volodya, please. If you deactivate your program now, you can make some kind of deal. If they have to figure it out without your help - they'll put you in jail, or deport you."

His face twisted a little. "They cannot do that."

"I think they can do what they want, especially if the world monetary systems crash!"

"Same as KGB," Volodya said scornfully. His eyes never left her face; it was disquieting. "You have on ring I gave you," he said, and she realized that she was still turning it nervously on her finger.

She twisted it off and held it out to him. "I brought it to give back to you." He made no move to take it.

"I thought you liked it."

"How can I like it any more, after what you did?" Annette cried.

To her utter amazement, he rose from the windowsill and put his arms gently around her. She trembled against him, outraged and touched, too surprised to move. She felt his lips against her hair.

"I am same person. Same person you liked when I gave you ring." Annette wrenched herself free and backed away from him; a shadow of distress flickered across his face.

"The person I thought you were wouldn't have done what you apparently did," she said quietly.

Volodya looked suddenly as vulnerable as a small boy, and Annette's anger fell away, leaving her with a deep sadness.

"I could never be with someone who acted the way you did. You were willing to hurt people to help yourself."

"Annette, if you were Russian living here, what would you do if FSB asked you to help them by putting algorithm in bank code?"

She stifled a gasp. "I would tell the FBI, or the CIA."

"Would you do that if your family was still in Russia and you are afraid for them?"

"That's a hard choice, I suppose. But I think I would trust the U.S.

government to help me."

"I trust the badness of my government more than the goodness of your government. How can you blame me?" His tone was low and persuasive. "How can you blame me? Either way, people can get hurt."

Even now, when she knew the truth, he could almost make her see it his way.

"Oh, Volodya," she said with a sigh. Misunderstanding, he took a step toward her. "Volodya, you didn't just put Sergei's code in. You wrote your own and put that in too. Nobody made you do it. Where's your philosophical justification for that? You were willing to steal from people for your own gain."

"I would never hurt you," Volodya insisted, rallying. He reached for her and Annette stepped back. His face settled into its old lines of pride and anger, and he turned his back to her, looking out the window again.

Annette sank into a nearby chair and dropped her pounding head into her hands. Leo and Tim and Alex - all the men, in fact - felt a deep, implacable anger toward Volodya. She was angry too, but underneath she felt pity. For all his brilliance and personality, Volodya had the moral sense of a child.

"Annette."

She raised her head from her hands to look at him; he was watching her intently. She saw his face soften.

"I am sorry to make you cry."

Annette realized that her cheeks were wet; she scrubbed away the tears with the backs of her hands.

"I do not admit anything, of course, but if I did plant code, and I agree to un-plant, what do you think about me then?" She heard the hope in his voice.

Annette felt panic. Volodya's tone was casual, but she understood the absolute seriousness of the question. What did he want her to say? That if he did as they asked, she would forgive him everything? She couldn't. And if she told him the truth, would he decide he had no reason to deactivate the code? Should she lie again and be like him? She was tired of lying. Her head whirled for a moment, then cleared.

"I would be happy that you did the right thing," she said, choosing each word, "but it wouldn't change anything between us."

Just for a moment, Volodya's expression faltered. His shoulders slumped, and Annette thought the game was over.

"You are hard woman, Annette," he said, smiling faintly. Then his shoulders went back, and the usual expression of amused arrogance wrote itself across his face.

"Okay," Volodya said briefly, businesslike. "I will do it. For you, Annette."

She stared at him, unable to speak. He laughed at her.

"Go tell them that I make deal. I want lawyer. No charges, no jail. No deportation. We work on details. Go." He waved his hand.

Annette stumbled to her feet and he caught her arm to keep her from falling. She opened her hand, remembering the ring she was clutching, and held it out to him. Volodya shook his head.

"That is condition of settlement." He closed her fingers gently around the ring again. "You must keep ring." His hand touched her cheek, smoothed back her hair. "To remember." He released her and Annette fled, feeling his eyes on her still.

She flew into the conference room and became the focus of all eyes.

"He'll do it," she announced, panting, to a chorus of relieved cheers, then collapsed sobbing on Leo's chest.

# Chapter 26

In the end, Leo took Annette to the Stauffers'. She was too upset even to talk to him coherently, but Karen seemed to understand.

"You go back to the office," Karen told him. "They need you there. Annette just needs to rest."

Annette didn't say anything to him when he kissed her good-bye, although she clung tightly to him for a moment. Then she pushed something into his hand. Karen sent him a reassuring smile and put her arm around Annette.

"I'll give her something to eat and put her to bed. She'll be fine."

Leo left reluctantly. After he climbed into the car he opened his hand. In the dim interior the emerald ring winked at him.

\*        \*        \*

By the time Leo had returned to the conference room at Midwest National, his colleagues were eating pizza while they waited impatiently for Volodya to conclude his negotiations. Leo had lost track of the number of agents coming in and out of the bank; Volodya's admission of guilt seemed to be too important for George and Jerry to handle alone.

"He did it," said Leo. "Can't they just make him take the worm out?"

The door opened suddenly; it was Jerry, his thin face pinched and frowning.

"Borodin's agreed to remove the worm," he said, dropping the polite form of address. "With the Bureau geeks and your geeks watching to see how he does it."

"Have you arrested him?" Alex asked.

"No arrest. At least not formally." Jerry nearly spat the words at them. "Because the worm is a national security risk, the President's top priority is to get the worm out, which Borodin agreed to do. But he won't do it if we prosecute or deport him. He's got an attorney in there, neatening up all the loose ends. The Attorney General is raising hell over the President's decision, and I don't blame her."

Jerry sounded more steamed by the second. "Now we drive him home to retrieve the deactivation code he hid. Hey, order some more pizza, would you? We can eat it when we get back."

An hour later they met at the bank's computer room. Volodya began reassembling a floppy disk, his expression unreadable, while FBI agents wolfed down pizzas and soda. No one offered any to Volodya.

One of the FBI agents seated George and Leo on either side of Volodya, while the rest stood and watched. The room became quiet suddenly; a taut, humming quiet. Twelve pairs of eyes cast glances of approbation at Volodya, who inserted the diskette into the port and began to explain what he was doing in the disinterested tones of a professor lecturing a rather slow class.

It was a monumental demonstration of skill. Leo listened and took notes, even asked an occasional question. With the surge of revulsion at Volodya's proximity, he felt a cooler admiration for his mathematical prowess. At one point he realized that he was gripping his pen so hard that his hand had cramped. Could Volodya really be unaware of the ill feeling being directed at him by every person present? Even Volodya's attorney, sitting at a nearby table, looked uncomfortable.

In an hour the ordeal was over. "I may go now?" Volodya said, as unruffled as when he had first sat down. Jerry nodded, and George, Volodya, and Leo stood up. Volodya walked toward his attorney, then turned back and spoke directly to Leo.

"Where is Annette?" he asked.

Leo swung cleanly, but George caught his arm before he connected. Volodya jumped back hastily, his face flushing, composure shaken at last. Leo heard a smattering of applause from the other agents, then a few chuckles. Volodya stalked from the room, trailed by his cringing attorney.

"I saw that one coming," George said. He was still holding Leo's arm. "You okay now?"

Leo nodded. The blood was pounding in his ears.

"I couldn't let you hit him in front of his attorney," George said.

*    *    *

"So the worm is out," said Karen.

"Out," Alex said, laying down his fork after a late dinner in the kitchen. He hadn't really had much appetite until he had seen for himself that Volodya had removed the worm. He changed the subject. "I was a little surprised by Annette's reaction earlier."

Karen rolled her eyes. "You ask her to use her emotional influence with Volodya, then you're surprised when she gets emotional."

"You're right," Alex said.

"I should think," Karen said. "Annette cooperates with the FBI and she gets hurt. Volodya commits a crime and he gets off scot-free. How fair is that?"

"I didn't say it was fair." Alex pushed his plate away. "You know, Karen, something has to change. Our society is held hostage to men like Volodya. This whole year 2000 fiasco is a variation on the same theme; we're dependent on a technology that we no longer control. And the people who do control it have no moral compass."

"You mean programmers?"

Alex nodded.

"Aren't you over-generalizing?" Karen asked. "Lots of programmers are good guys. Look at Leo and Tim and Harry and all the other people who have been sweating blood trying to get the systems fixed."

"Yeah, sure, there are a lot of good guys." Alex tried to articulate what had been bothering him for days. "But look at the temptation to be a bad guy. Like Leo was saying about his friends - the smart ones, the ones who break into computers to prove a point - it's okay for them, they think, because they're not malicious. But once you start thinking like that, how do you know when you've stepped over the line? How hard is it to do the right thing when you have an opportunity to do the wrong thing for personal gain? For God's sake, Karen, people *admire* hackers! Some teenage boy hacks into the Pentagon, gets his hand slapped, and then gets hired by some company in Silicon Valley because they can see he's got the right stuff!"

Karen looped her arms around his neck. "Well, never mind all that right now. We should let the kids know that the system is fixed; they've been so worried about it."

"Haven't we all?" Alex said. "And whether it's fixed remains to be seen. The big test is coming up. Two days and we roll over."

Karen shivered a little at the thought, then brushed her lips against his neck. "Well, before things go entirely bonkers around here, I think you should de-stress with some physical exercise."

"You're right, I haven't been to the Y in a while."

She punched him.

\*     \*     \*

Volodya stepped out of the bank and into the rain of the parking lot, waving jauntily at the security guard who had accompanied him. The guard declined to wave back. Volodya was famished; no one had offered him any dinner and he had been too proud to ask for it. He headed for a near-by Chinese restaurant, planning to pick up something and take it to one of his friends' houses to eat it.

He drove aimlessly for a few minutes, and found himself in Annette's parking lot. He could see that her apartment was dark. Her car had been in the bank parking lot when he left, but there had been no sign of Annette herself. Perhaps someone had taken her home early, and she was asleep inside.

Right now he could not think about Annette. He dialed Julie's number on the cell phone. Her inconsequential chatter would seem soothing tonight, and she was always happy to see him; making love would be a pleasant way to avoid thinking.

Julie answered on the first ring, but her greeting was cool. "Oh, Volodya. I was expecting a call from someone else."

"It has been very busy at work," he said.

"So busy that you couldn't call to tell me it was busy?"

"I am sorry. I missed you."

He heard a loud sigh at the other end of the phone. "Volodya, you haven't called in a month, and suddenly you miss me. What do you want?"

"I thought I could take you out somewhere, we could go dancing." Clearly she felt neglected. "Or if you are hungry we could go and get something to eat. We could catch up on things."

Julie laughed. "What you really want is to come over, isn't it Volodya?"

"You have read my mind." She was relenting, he thought.

"Volodya I'm seeing someone else. I'm waiting for him to call. He's working late tonight, but he did have the courtesy to call and tell me." Julie, the naïve, the doormat, sounded sarcastic.

Volodya sat surprised and silent.

"Well," Julie said, "at least I don't have to worry that you'll be too broken up about it. I'm sure you'll find someone else."

He heard a beep on the line. "That's probably him. Well, take care of yourself, Volodya. Good-bye." The line went dead and he automatically pushed the disconnect button.

So. Volodya slowly punched in Annette's number on his cell phone, then counted the rings before the message came on. He listened to Annette's voice, disconnected, and redialed. He listened to the message again. Halfway through his third call, a black security car with the name of Annette's apartment complex emblazoned on the side pulled up next to the BMW. A uniformed man stuck his head out the window, rain dripping steadily from the brim of his hat.

"You been here for a while, buddy. Something I can help you with?"

"No, I was waiting for my friend to come home," Volodya said.

"Maybe you should find someplace else to wait."

Volodya was too tired to argue.

"Okay, I am going. Goodnight, officer." The man waved dismissively and Volodya drove away from the apartments. He would go home and check his e-mail.

\*     \*     \*

The lighted clock dial proclaimed ten p.m. Annette slipped on Karen's bathrobe and padded to the top of the stairs, feeling disoriented. She'd been asleep for hours. What had happened at the bank?

"Annette." The first voice she heard was Karen's, but the first face she saw was Leo's. He stood at the foot of the stairs looking up at her, and at the look on his face she felt a slow shock of recognition, the first conscious realization of the feelings she'd been avoiding for months. Of course, she thought. I'm in love with Leo.

"I came to be sure that you were all right," he said, his eyes fastened on hers.

Karen swept them a shrewd glance. "Why don't you two go in my office?" she said.

The moment the door closed they were in each other's arms.

"Are you sure you're all right?" Leo asked, still holding her tightly. "What did that bastard say to you?"

Annette felt blissfully warm and safe snuggled next to Leo. "Never mind," she said. "We can talk about it later."

"I don't want you to stay at your apartment tonight, okay?" She heard the concern in his voice. "Volodya might try to see you." His hands chafed her shoulders gently. "You can stay with the Stauffers." A pause. "Or you could come home with me."

"But -" Her protest was automatic. He silenced her with a kiss, then looked into her face.

"You're the most conscientious person I've ever known," he said. He was smiling, but his dark eyes were serious. "But we're done working tonight, and tomorrow is December thirtieth - a holiday, remember? You can do this with a clear conscience. If you want to," he added, with less certainty.

"My agenda will be off by two days," she protested. She could see that he wasn't sure whether she was teasing him or not, but in her own mind she had abandoned her agenda, tossed it away forever at the look in his eyes when she had come down the stairs.

\*     \*     \*

If Karen and Alex were surprised by Annette's sudden departure with Leo, they were too gracious to say anything. Now Leo sat with her on the edge of his bed, a towel around his waist. Annette wore the bathrobe Karen had loaned her. She felt a bit shy.

Leo leaned over to kiss her, his hands playing with the bathrobe tie. "I wanted to ask you a few days ago, while Volodya was gone," he said, sliding the robe over her shoulders. "But you were so preoccupied and guilty."

"Then why tonight?" Annette asked. His hands roamed gently over her bare shoulders, pushing the robe lower.

"Because I love you to distraction. Because I'm tired of waiting.

Because I'm sick of Volodya." He untied the bathrobe tie and she shivered. "I don't want you to think about him any more." The robe fell away, and Leo looked at her with such evident pleasure that she smiled in delight and embarrassment. "I want you to spend tonight thinking about me. About us."

He kissed her again while his hands floated against her skin. Thinking about Leo was no problem at all, she found, as he moved against her. And even after rational thought had dissolved into sensation, it was Leo's name that she murmured, then cried out, then whispered against his skin before they finally slept.

*December 30, 1999: Day 2*

She felt safe and languorous, like she never wanted to move again. Leo smiled at her and she knew that she could come to no harm in his arms. But why didn't someone answer the door? The knocking grew louder, and suddenly the door flew open. Volodya stood in the doorway, his eyes mocking and dangerous.

Annette gasped and sat up. The room was still dark, though the clock said eight. She could hear the drum of rain outside.

"What's wrong?" Leo pulled her back down in the bed, nestled her against his chest, and tightened his arms around her.

"Nothing's wrong now," she said. "I just didn't know where I was for a second."

"You're safe with me," Leo said. So she was. She curled against him and went back to sleep.

# THE FINAL COUNTDOWN

# Chapter 27

*December 31, 1999:  The Last Day*

D-Day was not a single day, but a series of event horizons which would begin at six a.m Eastern Standard Time on December 31st, the moment when the clock struck midnight in the silent winter of Siberia and the bright summertime of New Zealand, fully eighteen hours before midnight on the east coast of the U.S.  Like a vast shadow the year 2000 would roll across the earth.  Two hours later, at eight a.m., the shadow would fall on Australia, and two hours after that, on Japan. Five hours later, on China.  When it was noon in the U.S., on Vietnam. At four o'clock the shadow would lengthen to touch the edge of the Middle East, and by five it would have crept to Eastern Europe and Africa, with Western Europe following at 6:00 p.m.  At ten in the evening, South America would enter the next millennium.

By the time ultimate midnight swept its way to the United States, the world would have an idea of what they might expect in the year 2000.  Watchers across the globe would follow the sweep of the midnight clock, looking for clues.  Would the telephones fail in Australia? Would the lights flicker and die in France?  More importantly, could the electric grid be brought back up again if it went down?  Credit card transactions of New Year's eve revelers in Auckland would take place in the year 2000, but the bank on which the card drew might be in another time zone, where the year was still 1999.  Monetary transactions would fall on both sides of the century for eighteen hours.

The turn of the clock at midnight was only the signal to begin a frantic scramble to bring the world's computers back online. Systems that ran twenty-four hours a day, seven days a week - the hospitals, the police, the fire departments, the banks - had no choice but to try to operate through the century change. Most companies would opt to take all their computers off line on December 31st, and power them up again after midnight. Assuming that the lights still burned (and using generators if they didn't), January first would not be a holiday, but a day of test scripts and data comparisons. If problems were uncovered, the testing and debugging might run for days, weeks, even months.

The unquantifiable variable in the equation was the behavior of the embedded systems with their microprocessors. Some would fail, but which ones was anybody's guess. Many were untested because time had run short to test the millions of tiny systems. Some systems were overlooked, and some ignored in the belief that they were not date-time sensitive. The truth was, the only known quantities were those that had been tested and okayed or replaced. Some of the others would fail, and they could so little predict which ones that the failures would seem random.

In fact, even in best case, with the infrastructure of the world still in place and most computers online again, the year 2000 was rife with dates that must still be checked. Check January third, the first working day after the turn. Check January seventh, the first weekly pay day. January thirty-first, the first month-end day. February twenty-ninth, a leap year day. March first, the first day of the last month of the first quarter. The list continued through the year 2000 and into 2001.

The greatest danger was not even a computer's crash. Programmers could find and fix the obvious bug, but the system that made error after silent error, compiling corrupt data and passing it to other systems, was the nightmare that every y2k project manager strove to avoid. For that reason the year 2000 would be a year of testing and retesting, a year of constant vigilance against the many bugs that would have crept into the world's computer systems simply as a result of having fixed the original problem.

1999 had been a dress rehearsal. Computer professionals around the world had watched and cursed as their remediated systems behaved exactly as remediated systems are wont to do, when every line of code corrected has the potential to introduce a new error. Systems thought to be debugged failed when they reached an event horizon, often one that involved scheduling or projections into the next century. Systems that tested perfectly by themselves became schizophrenic when tested together. Systems that tested well within a company crashed and burned when asked to interface with systems from outside.

If 1999 was the dress rehearsal, then the New Year's Eve rollover was the curtain raiser for the real thing. The greatest number of computer failures would cluster around the January first date, and no one denied that failures were inevitable. The question became: how many simultaneous systems failures does it take to send a computer-dependent society over the edge? Soon, they would learn.

*5:45 a.m., December 31, 1999*

Couldn't be worse, thought Karen. The first one in the household awake, she was watching Channel 4's rotund, pleasant weather anchor predicting freezing rain and snow for the last day of 1999. They would be spending most of the day and night at the bank, of course, but the snow would really slow down emergency vehicles that might need to answer y2k calls.

Alex clattered down the stairs and hurried in to join her. "How close are we to New Zealand's rollover?"

"Five minutes." Karen flipped the station back to CNN. "This is already nerve-racking. I'll be a mess by the end of the day."

CNN's studio was transformed for the millennium with an enormous lighted map of the world in the background. Major cities were indicated by red lights that would turn green when they reached midnight. Around the perimeter of the map was a series of clocks that indicated the time in the U.S. when various regions would enter the twenty-first century. Right now the camera was trained on the clock which read *0600 New Zealand*.

The news anchor in Auckland was chatting about this and that, a bit nervously, Karen thought, as the cameras showed New Year's Eve revelers partying on Waikanae Beach in Gisborne. When the countdown began, the station switched to festivities at the Auckland Hilton.

"Ten. Nine. Eight. Seven. Six. Five. Four. Three. Two. One. Happy New Year!" Partygoers shrieked and blew horns while the news anchor blathered along in the background, evidently relieved that nothing much had happened. Then the TV screen went blank.

Karen clutched Alex's arm. After a moment the CNN studio re-appeared and the camera panned to a grave-looking American reporter.

"We appear to have temporarily lost contact with our sister station in Auckland," he said. "Could this be the result of a year 2000 power outage? We don't know yet, of course - wait a moment."

The reporter put a hand to his ear and appeared to be listening intently to his headphones. His gaze returned to the audience. "I'm told that the news crew has a generator for the TV cameras that they hope to have set up in a few minutes. Until then, we'll be standing by here." As he launched into a layman's description of the Year 2000 computer problem, Alex shook his head.

"How could anyone not know by now?"

They ate breakfast silently. New Zealand had spent nearly the last two years working on her electrical utilities after the breakdown of two of her four main power cables in Auckland had left the downtown without power for more than two weeks in 1998. With systems that were so new, and with the memory of the difficulties of an extended outage to spur them on, most on the y2k mail list had not expected to see problems in New Zealand, and both Karen and Alex felt some shock at the news.

"Look, Alex," said Karen. The original newsperson was back, still standing in the hotel ballroom, eerily dark except for the lights set up by the camera crew. The partygoers appeared to have sobered up pretty fast.

"Well, we're back with you live, having hooked ourselves up to a generator," the reporter said. "As you can see, the power has gone out here. The hotel staff tells us that the hotel does have a generator, and the power should be returning any time now." As he spoke, the lights flickered and came on, illuminating the relieved faces of the hotel guests, who cheered and whooped.

"Well, we have power. Let's see what the rest of the city looks like." The camera followed him through the hotel and out the front door to a main thoroughfare.

What light there was came from car headlights and buildings with their lights still on; evidently a number had purchased generators, either as a result of the last big outage or in anticipation of the year 2000 problem. The street lamps were dark. The camera panned across the city skyline, which was not utterly dark, but dotted with islands of light.

"Good morning." Karen's father joined them in staring at the screen. Both Alex's parents and Karen's parents were staying over New Year's as a precaution. Alex had been adamant. "If things are bad, I want you here where we have a generator and enough food. I don't want us to have to worry about your safety." The grandparents would stay in the house that night; the Stauffers planned to stay at the bank.

"Good morning, Dad. I'm afraid that's New Zealand." The rest of the adults straggled downstairs to eat their breakfasts in front of the TV. The news anchor reported that outages were spotty; Wellington and Christchurch were maintaining power, as were many small towns. Telephone service was unreliable within the country and foreign calls were only wishful thinking. Because most large manufacturing plants were shut down no one could say yet what other problems might develop, but so far, the announcer said, New Zealanders seemed to be bearing up well.

Karen's father snorted. "Bearing up well? They've only been without power for an hour!"

Alex would go to Midwest this morning; Karen and the children were to follow in the afternoon. Alex grabbed his ski parka and gloves. "Don't forget to bring the cell phone," he cautioned Karen as he got ready to leave. "And please drive carefully. Happy New Year to the rest of you!" He exchanged kisses and hugs with his parents and in-laws and they listened patiently as Alex explained yet again how to start the generator. When he headed to the garage, the rest looked out the front door, exclaiming at the downpour.

*6:45 a.m., December 31, 1999*

Leo and Annette had not left his apartment yesterday. Today they watched the rollover at Annette's while she collected a change of clothes, then they took separate cars to work. When she pulled into her parking space at the bank, Leo was already waiting for her, holding an umbrella.

"Thanks," she said, scurrying underneath. "Darn, Leo, I forgot my boots and they're predicting snow."

"Distracted, were you?" he asked, kissing her.

"Mmm." She kissed him back. "You can distract me any time. Except today."

As soon as Alex strode through the bank doors he reminded them that they were meeting. In a few minutes the y2k team was assembled in the bank conference room.

Alex stood with his arms crossed, surveying them. "Hard to believe the day is finally here," he said. "I assume you all watched the New Zealand rollover?" They nodded. "Well, it wasn't too bad, although of course it's too early to tell for sure. I was surprised that Auckland would have problems."

His eyes ran over them, and he laughed a little. "You know, I don't really have anything to tell you at this point. I'm sure that we're as prepared as we're ever going to be, and you all know what you're to do today, and in the next few days. I'm also going to be on call to the city's E-Op - that's emergency operations - Center for y2k for the next couple of days. The location is downtown, and the mayor wants y2k people there in case they have problems, which I think is a prudent decision on his part. I'll plan to stay here at the bank until after midnight; then, if they need me, I'll go to the Center. I'm sure you can handle things without me. Karen and the kids may stay here for a while after I leave, depending on the extent of the disruptions." He spread his hands.

"Annette, will you come up here?" She joined him, her eyes questioning, and he put an arm around her shoulder. "We've all worked hard, but I'd like to specially recognize our y2k project manager, who spurred us all on with her unsparing efforts, not only at the bank, but all over town." Everyone applauded, grinning at Annette's blushes. "Would you like to say anything, Annette?"

"Well," she looked at them all fondly, "I know it was terribly hard work for everyone, but I don't know when I've enjoyed a job more. The sense of shared purpose, the feeling that we were all pitching in for a common goal more important than just a paycheck - well, it was just wonderful." Her mouth quivered and she sniffled and tried to laugh. "Look what you've done, Alex, made me all sentimental." She sat down, dabbing at her eyes.

Alex patted her shoulder.

"We also have word from Sergei," he said. "The hospital tells us that he's doing very well, and he is highly relieved to think that his worm is finally expurgated in all its forms."

"Okay, that's it, then. Let's go see what happens in Australia." Alex led the way out, and Leo hung back to be with Annette, who was gathering her file and papers.

"Hey." He came around the table and took her folder away from her, putting it down on the desk, then gathered her in his arms and kissed her. "Happy New Year."

She stood on tiptoe and looked into his brown eyes. "Happy New Year yourself," she said, kissing him back. "I suppose that was for the New Year in Australia?"

"That was for New Zealand." He admired her dimples, her flushed cheeks. "This is for Australia." He bent his head to hers, savoring the taste of her warm mouth. When he finally released her, she sighed and snuggled against him.

"Mmm. How many time zones do we have left?"

Leo laughed. "Don't you think the others will notice if we disappear every hour on the hour for the rest of the day?"

Australia did well. Again, they saw spotty power outages, but they seemed less widespread than in New Zealand, where, the news anchor reported, the utilities and the telecoms were working feverishly to restore power and communications.

Homer stopped by to report soon after. "No problems upstairs," he said, jubilant. "We're low on cash reserves, and a lot of people are asking for print-outs of their accounts, but then, we prepared for that. We sure haven't had a run on the bank. Just keep the system up and running and I'll be a happy man."

Nobody wanted to rain on Homer's parade, but they were all waiting nervously for the next series of rollovers. Asia was known to be well behind in its y2k efforts.


*8:00 a.m., December 31, 1999*


Jim Frazier arrived at the E-Op Center promptly at eight, as requested, cursing the rain and stifling a yawn. The mayor had been reluctant to have a reporter at the E-Op, and Jim suspected that the early call to duty was the mayor's retaliation at having been pressured by Jonas Driver, the paper's influential owner.

Jim felt a tad guilty for bundling his wife off to her sister's on this momentous New Year's Eve, but he was thrilled to have this story. This was The Big Story and a plum assignment. A colleague would be working in the Public Information Center, which was being manned in the building next door, but Jim would have first access to what was happening y2k-wise

Jim's guide, a young, energetic guy named Pete, showed him the E-Op. "You could call it the War Room," Pete said. "The command center. The city has a lot to oversee. The emergency services - hospitals, 9ll, police, fire, hazardous materials, for instance. Water and sewage. Energy. Traffic. Municipal buildings and offices. The schools. Taxes. The bus system. Plus we're coordinating with the county. You get the picture."

Pete also showed him the central database that would track and monitor year 2000 failure in other parts of the globe. "When a failure occurs in a particular piece of equipment," he told Jim, " it will be logged on to the central data base. If the same failure is likely to occur in one of our agencies, we'll notify the agency to watch it, and in some cases, to shut it down, before the rollover. Same for business and industry. And if we find out that something isn't going to work, we can develop contingency plans."

"So what's your assessment? Off the record?"

Pete spread his hands eloquently, and crossed one khaki-clad leg over the other.

"I don't know what to tell you. We've prepared, but I don't know what will happen. Could be huge, could be a yawn."

Jim gave a shout of laughter at Pete's last statement. "Pete, you have the makings of a politician."


*Noon, December 31, 1999*


"Who ordered Chinese? Is this a joke?"

Annette smiled weakly at Harry's jest, but most of the y2k team gathered around the lunch table were too worried to find it funny. Asia had, for the most part, gone black.

Japan began the debacle at ten a.m. Tokyo managed to pull up the power several times, but they couldn't keep it on. At eleven a.m. Beijing and Hong Kong blinked off, followed by Malaysia, Thailand, and Vietnam at noon - in fact, the whole of the rest of Asia except for Singapore, which remained the only shining star in the blacked-out continent.

"Any joy with the Internet, Leo?" Alex had assigned him the task of checking web sites and sending e-mail to test the integrity of the Web.

Leo munched an egg roll. "It's really slow. I can still get some sites in Asia, but it takes a long time. The e-mail is pretty goofy, too. I've sent some off, but I haven't had any replies yet. Seems to work fine here so far."

"Heard anything from the E-Op yet, Alex?" asked Tim, drumming his fingers on the table.

"No, but it's only noon. I have a feeling that things will start humming soon." And then he wondered if that was a good thing or a bad thing.


*12:30 p.m., December 31, 1999*


Pete had been right about one thing, Jim thought, and that was that the pace in the E-op would pick up at noon. At least fifty people packed the center; Jim recognized many of them from his work as a reporter. He saw Mary Lowery, from the Safety Department, and there was Ben Nichols, head of the Traffic Department. He greeted the people he knew and stayed in the background, observing. Occasionally Pete would appear at his elbow to fill him in on something.

"The mayor wants to be sure you get it right."

"So do I."

Shortly before one p.m. Pete reported to Jim. "Thought you'd be interested to know that Japan's power is back on, for the most part. That's the good news."

"And the bad news?"

"Their automated train signals are down, at least in Tokyo. They're also reporting problems with their automated gas pumps."

Jim scribbled busily in his notebook. "Does that mean we'll have problems with our pumps?"

"Unless it's some new bug that nobody caught, I wouldn't think so. We have a fuel truck standing by for use by city vehicles. And some pumps have been altered so that they can be pumped manually, although that's very slow, of course.

"Here's one from Australia. A medical device that measures and monitors dosages of medicine. It failed, but continued to operate on the assumption that 00 meant 1900. A pediatric case was assigned the dosage that would have been given to a hundred year old man. The baby almost died before they caught it."

### 3:15 p.m., December 31, 1999

Leo was schizophrenic. He was sober and vigilant, dedicated to his y2k job, and more than a little concerned about the rollovers he'd seen so far. He was also euphoric. Annette had declared her love, and no mere global catastrophe could flatten him.

He was fixing himself a coffee when Annette appeared at his elbow, carrying her coat.

"Where are you going?"

"I just need to run home and pack a few more clothes," she said. "And get my boots. We don't know how long we'll be here, do we?"

"I'll walk you to the door." Leo abandoned his coffee, a small sacrifice for the chance of a few seconds alone with Annette in the elevator. There they marked the turning of the New Year for all the countries of Asia and emerged breathless. Leo looked around; the bank lobby was empty now, and dimly lit; he steered Annette into a corner and planted a lingering kiss on her cheek.

"Happy New Year in Iran," he murmured, moving to her other cheek. "And Iraq." Her chin. "And Turkey and Armenia." Each eyelid. "And Saudi Arabia." His lips brushed hers softly. "And Pakistan." She moved closer as his kisses became more insistent. A door slammed far away downstairs, and Leo sighed. Reluctantly he stepped away from her, and Annette opened her eyes.

"Have you run out of countries already?" she asked, her voice shaky.

Leo traced the line of her nose with his finger. "And I thought that having you mad at me was bad for my concentration." Taking her hand, he pulled her back to the lobby. "You'd better go. I don't want you to get stuck out there somewhere if it starts to snow."

"I'll be ever so quick, Leo." Annette shook her head as if to clear it; her straight shiny hair swished around her face. "I have my cell phone; I can call you if I get in trouble."

"See that you don't get in trouble." The security guard unlocked the door for them and Leo watched Annette run to her car, its yellow color the only cheerful note in the dark, drizzly afternoon. Turning to go back downstairs, he found it difficult to maintain the sober outlook that the day called for. Systems might be crashing elsewhere, but in his little corner of the world things were copasetic.

*3:30 p.m., December 31, 1999*

Driving back to the apartment, Annette noticed that the rain no longer splatted on the windshield of her sports car; now it stuck, then slid, still liquid but with a definite crystalline form. Sleet. The roads would be icing up next. She slowed the car, not wanting to risk a skid. By the time she pelted from her car to her apartment door, the sleet had turned to a wet, wet snow.

Annette found her boots and grabbed another change of clothes. When she passed the telephone in the hall on her way out, the phone shrilled beside her. Startled, she automatically answered it.

"Hello?"

"Annette! I am so glad you are there! I have been trying to reach you." Volodya's accented English pounded into her ear.

"Volodya. I can't talk now, I was just leaving to go back to the bank. They need me there."

"It's Gospodina Baranova, old woman with cats. She is ill and asking for you." Volodya was panting.

"Why would she ask for me?" said Annette. "What do you mean? How ill is she?"

"I don't know. She has fever; maybe she is delirious. I think she grows worse. I could not reach 911 number; I do not know why she asks for you. She remembers you, she likes you, she is old and ill." Volodya's voice was pleading. "Annette, please come to her apartment. Maybe she will calm down if she sees you. I do not know what to do."

"Volodya, I can't do that!" Annette was angry that he expected it. "Just put her in the car and take her to the emergency room if she's ill.

They'll know what to do."

"Annette, please! She is very old. What if she is dying? Just stop
for a moment. Please."

Annette was about to refuse when her memory flashed to the
wrinkled old woman smiling at her, ankle-deep in cats, clasping her
hand as they left the apartment. Poor woman, all alone except for
Volodya and her cats, maybe dying.

"Oh, all right. But I'm not staying, and I'm not going to the hospital
with you. I'll be there in twenty minutes." She hung up on Volodya's
fervent thank you's, cursing her soft heart and softer head.


*4:30 p.m., December 31, 1999*

The clock on Leo's computer screen declared that it was after
four-thirty. Leo's stomach was ricocheting as it used to do before his
turn in a violin recital. He pushed his chair away from the terminal and
ran upstairs to stare out the window at the snow swirling under the
lights in the parking lot. Already several inches had accumulated; the
wind scoured the snow off one side of the asphalt and blew it into drifts
on the other.

"Leo." He swung around to see Alex. "I followed you up. What's
the matter? You've been jumping up and down for the last hour."

Leo turned back to the window and studied the snow. "It's Annette.
She's not back yet, and she left at three-fifteen."

"Look at the weather, Leo. She's in that little car of hers; I'm sure
she can't drive it very fast in the snow. She'll be here soon."

Alex's voice was meant to be reassuring, but Leo heard an undercurrent of concern. "Maybe I should go out and look for her. I can't
reach her. She hasn't called and she has her cell phone. She may be in
a ditch somewhere." His stomach twisted as he said it

"C'mon Leo!" Alex joined him at the window. "What good does it
do to have two of you out there in a blizzard? She may have taken a
different route because of the storm, or maybe she's held up because
of an accident."

Leo stared at the snow. The blizzard was so fierce, and Annette's
car so small. "I should have gone with her. It wasn't snowing when
she left. I just didn't think."

Alex put a hand on Leo's shoulder and turned him back toward the stairs. "We're going to be eating in another half hour," he said. "If she hasn't called by five-thirty, we'll talk about it again. We can call the highway patrol, maybe; they can retrace her route. You come and do your job now, take your mind off it."

Leo stumbled down the stairs behind Alex, unable to shake the black feeling that shadowed him.

*4:30 p.m., December 31, 1999*

The car door opened so violently that she nearly tumbled into the snow of the parking lot. "Annette!" Volodya half-pulled her from the car's interior. "I was so worried. It has been hour since I spoke to you, I was sure that you had accident." He was pulling her out of the wind and into the apartment lobby as he spoke, and once inside he bent to kiss her wind-stung mouth and cheeks before she could stop him.

"Volodya!" Annette twisted away, furious. "I agreed to come over to see Mrs. Baranova, and I could have been killed doing it. The roads are awful. I didn't come to see you."

"You came when I asked." He was looking at her in the old way.

"You are hopeless," she said. "Just take me up to see her."

When he opened the apartment door a wave of sweet, sickly air flowed out to meet them. Volodya wrinkled his nose, but took Annette's arm and marched her inside, where they were overwhelmed by a flood of cats, hungry and and vocal.

"She is in bedroom." He pulled her through a door off the living room.

The old woman looked small and sunken in the bed, as though some-one had deflated her round figure slightly. Several cats lounged at the end of the bed and Volodya began brushing them off roughly, then gave an exclamation of pain when one of the cats fought back.

At the commotion, Mrs. Baranova opened her eyes and riveted them on Annette, then thrust out a surprisingly strong hand to clasp her fingers. Annette held the hot dry hand in her own and tried to smile at the old woman, touched and surprised she had recognized her.

"She's burning with fever, Volodya. You must get her to a doctor."

Volodya nursed his injured hand. "Phones are not working. Maybe solar flares again. Or maybe storm. I think ice could take wires down."

"But it wasn't icy when you first called - before I got here. Try again. Please."

Volodya shrugged and obliged. "Static. Same as before."

Annette noticed that the old woman's eyes were closed again, and she tried to ease her fingers from Mrs. Baranova's grasp. She awoke at once.

"Annette," she said in her heavy Slavic accent. She fumbled for Annette's hand, took it in a death grip, then closed her eyes again.

Volodya watched with detached amusement. "I told you she would be calmer if you were here."

"What are we going to do?" Annette asked. "I can't stay here all night and hold her hand. And she needs a doctor."

"Ah!" he said. "I will try my cell phone. Network is different." He dialed.

"Yes!" he cried. "I have old woman here who is ill - can you send ambulance?" He swore suddenly, then dialed again. "Line is impossible. Very difficult to hear through static." Again the hospital answered, and this time Volodya was able to give their address. "They will come, but we must wait."

"I talked to my friends in Russia today," he added.

"I thought that telecommunications were down."

"Friends were at Moscow State University Computer Center," he said. "They have different network there. They say situation is much worse than they predicted. They all want to emigrate."

"They'd be better to stay put and help get the country back on its feet!" Annette spoke sharply; she was beginning to feel that she was trapped, unable to go where she wanted to go and needed to be. Why hadn't Volodya just climbed in his car with Mrs. Baranova and driven her to the hospital hours ago? She hated to think what the answer might be. A smile tugged at her lips. Even Volodya would not be so crass as to try to seduce her here.

Encouraged by the faint smile, Volodya continued. "If my friends emigrate, I can give them jobs, grow my company. Maybe we could move to East Coast where there is more work."

"I thought you had to stay in Columbus with. . ." Annette looked at the old woman, then accusingly at Volodya. Was he seeing her as a corpse already?

"I did not mean that. But she is old woman; she cannot live for-ever." His blue eyes surveyed their patient as he placed a dispassion-ate hand on her forehead. "She is still very hot."

Annette watched him from the other side of the bed, observing the curve of his mouth, the arrogant tilt of his head. He was so handsome, so passionate, so totally lacking in some vital quality. If they were in a lifeboat, Annette thought, he would be the first to calculate the food supply and decide whom to jettison.

"I would like to go somewhere warm. With you." Without waiting for a response he stationed himself behind her chair and she felt the weight of his hands on her shoulders as he began kneading them. She stiffened.

"Stop it. I didn't come here for that."

His strong fingers dug into her flesh for another moment, then he moved away.

"That is good question, then," he said. "Why did you come?"

"I came because of Mrs. Baranova." Annette could tell he didn't believe her; he still thought that her coming was the result of some feeling for him. "I didn't like to think of her being old and ill and prac-tically alone except for you and her cats. You said she asked for me."

"You come here for old woman you meet one time?"

"Yes," she said. "I think we need to phone the hospital again."

He retrieved the cell phone. This time he spoke to them in the other room, and she could hear his voice rise in frustration.

"They will not come." His voice was clipped and angry. "They say roads are too bad."

Annette made herself stand up, even though Mrs. Baranova pro-tested strongly in Ukrainian when she released her hand. "Then we'll have to take her there ourselves."

Volodya stared at her. "Annette, roads are terrible. We will never make it."

"You have a big car," Annette challenged him. "There won't be much traffic. I'm not going to sit here and watch her die. You can take her to the hospital, and I'll drive my car back to the bank."

"Gospodina Baranova will be calmer if you come with me to take care of her," said Volodya. "You come with us to hospital."

"Can I use your phone?" Annette asked, ignoring his black look. She dialed the bank number, praying that the connection would hold.

Leo answered on the first ring.

"My God, Annette, are you all right?" The concern in his voice made her want to weep.

"Don't be angry, Leo. I've gotten myself into a mess." She told him what had happened while Volodya looked on, arms crossed, expression stormy.

"Annette, don't drive your car," Leo said. "The roads are much worse than when you left, and that little sports car is just too dangerous. I'll meet you at the hospital. And be careful. We can keep in touch on the cell phone. I love you."

"I love you too, Leo," Annette murmured, but she didn't know if Leo had heard or not.

Volodya moved a cat with the toe of his shoe, none too gently. "You do not love Leo," he said.

"We need to go now," she said. "I think it would be best just to wrap Mrs. Baranova in the blankets from the bed. If you turn the car heater on and let the car warm up, she should be all right." As she turned to go back into the bedroom, he caught her wrist.

"I am the one you want, Annette. You keep my ring, you come here in blizzard when I call. We are alike, both Europeans. We are not narrow, like Americans; we understand life and its pleasures. We belong together." His grip on her wrist tightened fractionally.

"Let go of me." She refused to meet his gaze. "You don't know what I feel. And I don't have your ring anymore."

He gave a soft chuckle and she jerked her head up to glare at him. "You don't know how you feel. I know how you feel; you show me by your actions." His blue gaze bored into her. "You think you should choose Leo. But you still want me." His tone was low, underlain by a thread of purpose that made her shiver. She tried to jerk her wrist away, but he still held her.

His hand slid from her wrist to her elbow, pulling her closer. "You are afraid of what you feel for me," he said, nearly in her face. "But you still feel it." He released her so unexpectedly that she almost fell. "I will go and start car."

# Chapter 28

*5:00 p.m., December 31, 1999*

At five o'clock most of the E-Op Center personnel trained their attention on the television mounted prominently on the wall in the War Room. In contrast to the New Year's celebrations featured so far, the cameras were watching Israel's rollover from the Wailing Wall in Jerusalem, which was surrounded by a solid mass of bodies, many in prayer. Jews and Muslims prayed next to the pious Roman Catholic, Eastern Orthodox, and Protestant believers who had come in simple celebration of the two thousandth anniversary of the Incarnation. Fundamentalist Jews were there to await the coming of the Messiah, along with Christian sects awaiting the second coming of the Messiah, and thousands of other pilgrims awaiting salvation, destruction, or God knew what else.

Midnight struck. Faces looked skyward. No thunder, no lightning, no parting of the firmament. Evidently the Messiah was on a different timetable. Expectant faces still gazed at the sky when the television station, less patient, cut to a picture of reveling Muscovites in Red Square.

No nuclear missiles had been launched, thought Jim. Missiles were said to default to a shutdown mode, but the U.S. still feared that a y2k glitch might cause Russia to think that they were under attack. To avoid any possibility of miscommunication, the two nations had agreed to do an exchange of nuclear command center personnel. Right now, Jim assumed, one or two Americans sat somewhere in a bunker in Moscow, ready to reassure the Russians that the U.S. was not launching missiles. And somewhere in Washington D.C., their Russian counterpart sat at the American command with the same assignment.

Jim surveyed his notes, with the growing list of y2k failures. Most ominous was the report of a toxic waste release in Indonesia, but no one had any details yet. Some communications had already been affected by the rollover; a plan was afoot to patch the E-Op center to an Australian satellite to bypass problems here.

People were trying their damnedest, Jim had to give them credit. If only all these computer fixes hadn't been started so late in the game, but that seemed to be human nature. Jim found that people usually fulfilled his low expectations of them, but he was willing to be surprised. Hoping to be surprised. Hell, Jim thought, given the alternative, he was praying to be surprised.


*5:14 p.m., December 31, 1999*


Leo drove slowly onto the road. His headlights disappeared into the snow just a few feet in front of him and the light from the street lamps did not seem to even make it as far as the street. God, it would take hours at this rate!

He had borrowed Tim's Blazer, dumping the contents of his own car trunk in the back of the vehicle. He hadn't grown up in Minnesota for nothing, he told Alex, he knew how to drive in snow, and he'd be damned if he'd leave Annette with Volodya.

Cell phone in hand, Leo pushed the speed-dial button; he had programmed Annette's number so that he could concentrate on the road. She answered at once.

"Leo!" He could hear the relief in her voice.

"Annette, it's going to be a while before I get there, and I'm afraid the batteries may run down if I phone too often."

"Never mind, then. We haven't left yet. Mrs. Baranova isn't being very cooperative. We couldn't dress her, and I spent half an hour convincing her to take her medicine." Annette's voice was tight and discouraged. "She'll have to go in the car in her bedclothes. Call me as soon as you can."

Her drive would be even worse than his, with a sick old woman in the car. And Volodya at the wheel. He would not think too much about Volodya, because anger would cloud his judgment, and he needed to have a clear head.

"Be brave," Leo said.

"Righty-o." Her Britishism was an effort to make him smile.

"I love you."

"And I you." He heard her faint sigh before she hung up.

*5:32 p.m., December 31, 1999*

The BMW was a big, heavy vehicle, and it took every ounce of steel to keep the car on the slippery road. Driving slowly was torture for the Russian, who always drove fast; visibility was cut to a few feet, and Volodya's eyes soon ached with the effort of sighting through the snow that danced like a dervish across the windshield.

Volodya braked carefully and the BMW crept on to Riverside Drive, parallel to the Scioto River. He saw little evidence that the road had been plowed, but at least traffic was minimal.

"At ten miles per hour, we will arrive at hospital in one hour," he announced. The snow seemed to be falling as fast as ever; the flakes swarmed like gnats in his headlights. "I think I will be blind by the time I get there."

He was looking for sympathy, but Annette made no response at all.

*5:45 p.m., December 31, 1999*

Leo was playing a frantic game of catch-up. He had left Midwest fully half an hour before Annette and Volodya, and his four-wheel drive vehicle gave him the advantage in speed, but they were still far ahead of him. The drive south on 315 was treacherous; on both sides of the road he saw cars abandoned in the ditch, snow drifting over them already. The snowplows were busy, though, and his progress was not as slow as he feared it might be

*5:55 p.m., December 31, 1999*

Mrs. Baranova slumped against Annette, her breathing rasping audibly in and out, but with little other sign of life. Oh, Lord, let us not be too late, Annette thought, tightening her grip on the old lady's hand.

Volodya was not making life any easier. Several times since their treacherous drive began, he had asked her if she would like to go away with him "somewhere warm" when their ordeal was over and the planes were flying again. Annette was by now feeling so claustrophobic, shut into the car, cocooned by snowflakes, that she felt she never wanted to be in a confined space again. Certainly not one that was also occupied by Volodya.

To forestall any other conversation, Annette decided to put a CD in the player. She chose one at random from a box on the back floor of the car. Holding it toward the front seat, she could just make out its title in the glow of the dashboard. Oh, this was perfect.

"Look, Volodya, Vivaldi's Four Seasons. Maybe we could play the Winter theme."

Volodya turned violently in his seat and his arm shot out, snatching the CD and its case from Annette. Unable to stuff it into his overcoat pocket because of the seatbelt across his lap, he unbuckled the belt and jammed the CD into his pocket. Annette watched in astonishment. Was that fear she had seen on his face during the second he was turned toward her, or something more calculating?

It was on Annette's lips to ask what he was doing when she heard a rumble, muffled by the snow and growing nearer, then saw the snow-plow before them in the glow of the headlights. The BMW had moved left of center when Volodya turned around, and, she saw with horror, was drifting gently toward the approaching vehicle.

"Volodya, look out!" she screamed, and he gave the steering wheel a savage jerk. The car shuddered, but continued its inexorable slide across the ice. Then the snowplow was upon them.

# Chapter 29

*5:55 p.m., December 31, 1999*

Leo jabbed at the speed-dial button again, waited with growing fear as it rang five, six, seven times. It was his third call in as many minutes and Annette still had not answered. Trying to control the racing of his heart, Leo skidded on to Riverside Drive at last. He dialed again. Still no answer. In disgust he tossed the phone on the front seat and clutched the steering wheel with both hands, white-knuckled.

He ignored the twist of dread in his stomach. If Annette were not answering because they'd been in an accident, he would see their car because they were still on Riverside. Clenching his teeth, he forced himself to drive slowly enough to scan the sides of the road. He would not panic, would not accelerate, because Annette was depending on him to find her and he would not let her down.

The car's headlights probed weakly through the snow as he drove on.

*5:55 p.m., December 31, 1999*

The snowplow rammed them with a sickening whomp of metal scraping metal. It was a glancing blow, and for a moment the two left front bumpers were locked as the vehicles began a dizzy, circling dance. Annette was flung backward, then sideways, and Gospodina Baranova thumped to the floor. Volodya's door popped open on impact; Annette saw him clinging to the steering wheel, and then, as the car slid faster, he simply disappeared.

Another quarter turn and the vehicles separated, both careening off the road on a diagonal to the right. Time slowed. Annette saw a low stone wall, a stand of trees. She could hear her own voice, screaming. With a tremendous thud the BMW slammed into the corner of the wall and through it, and at the same time the driver's door slammed viciously shut, walloped by a passing tree. Behind them she heard the ferocious scrape of metal on stone as the snowplow ground sideways into the wall. Before her in the headlights she saw the faint gleam of water as the car arced through the air and plunged with a splash and a roar into the Scioto River.

The BMW shuddered violently, floated for an instant, and began immediately to fill with water. The shock of the icy water on her feet brought Annette to life. Feeling around on the floor, she found the heap of blankets that was Mrs. Baranova.

"Please, please," Annette pleaded. Then she tried to open the door. It would not budge, nor would the other back door. She scrambled into the front seat; Volodya's door was dented in from the impact with the tree, and the passenger side was battered by the wall. Neither moved.

The windows, then. She pushed frantically on the buttons, but the windows were electric, and they remained closed. The car was floating in the water; it rocked like a boat every time Annette shifted her weight. When the water quickly rose to the bottom of the back seat, Annette clambered into the back again to be sure that Mrs. Baranova's face was above the water; she was such a short woman. Annette felt a whimper of fear at the back of her throat, but she tried to ignore it. She hadn't much time.

Leaning back on her forearms, Annette lifted both booted feet together, and attempted to kick out the back window. The kick jolted through her spine, once, twice, then again, but the window held.

She'd have to find something to break the window then. Blindly she plunged her hands into the icy water on the floor of the car, and hauled out the first object her hands grasped, a heavy flashlight. Taking it in both hands she swung it with all her might against the window while Mrs. Baranova keened in terror. The glass shivered and cracked, and Annette swung again, hampered by the small space and the rising water. Again! The window suddenly collapsed inward under the pressure of the water outside, and the black water poured in.

## 5:59 p.m., December 31, 1999

When Leo saw the wrecked snowplow, he slowed, stopped, leapt from the car. A man huddled next to the snowplow. Volodya stood staring at the river, holding his head with both hands. Annette was nowhere to be seen. My God, he thought, and began running.

"Where's Annette?" he cried, grabbing the Russian by the front of his coat.

"I do not know. Car is there." He pointed.

Leo stripped off his coat and boots and was in the water. The frigid water took his breath away for a moment, but he would not let it dull his concentration. "Annette!" The snowplow's headlights reflected on the water near the shore, but further downstream he could see nothing. Had she been carried that far? He could feel the tug of the current; he let it carry him downstream a little, holding on to the tree trunks at the edge of the water. "Annette!" He dove beneath the water, frantically flailing around with his arms; he could see nothing in the blackness. He surfaced. "Annette!" It was half a sob, he was growing frantic.

"Leo?" He could barely make her out; she was caught in some branches just a few feet away, somehow holding Mrs. Baranova in her arms. "Leo, you woke me up."

"You drive," Leo said tersely to Volodya. Mrs. Baranova was in the front seat, covered with blankets from the trunk. He climbed into the back seat and levered Annette into a sitting position, where she huddled, eyes closed, as Volodya pulled the Blazer out onto the road. Leo was choked with fear; Annette was not shivering, which was a dangerous sign. Shivering helped people get warm again. "Annette, you musn't go to sleep," he said, shaking her none too gently. She opened her eyes, frowning. "I'm going to take your wet clothes off and put some dry ones on you, okay?" Her eyes widened, but she nodded obediently. As he removed the sodden sweater and fumbled with the hook on her bra, her eyes never left his face.

"Leo," she whispered, still drowsy, "this isn't the way I imagined it."

# Chapter 30

*6:00 p.m., December 31, 1999*

At six o'clock most of Western Europe had rolled over, and at seven, the U.K. The electric grid there was stable, but reports about the National Health program were grim. Under-financed from the beginning, the y2k remediation effort had been disorganized and spotty. The result: entire data banks had gone down, and people's medical records disappeared. Already one person had died while in the hospital; staff blamed a y2k problem with some piece of medical equipment.

The faulty equipment was duly registered in the E-Op database, as were Sweden's problems with traffic signals, Italy's computer-aided dispatch problems, and Greece's shipping communications problems. Ominously, they had heard nothing from Eastern Europe beyond the rumor of a vast and devastating release of toxic gas in Ukraine; Jim suspected that they were so poorly prepared that the avalanche of failures was overwhelming. Jim took notes and prayed. At least so far, most of the problems were not life threatening.

*10:30 p.m., December 31, 1999*

Although Annette was blissfully warm and cozy, and so comfortable that any movement seemed unthinkable, some unfinished business forced open her eyes and set her brain in motion. She could think again, she noticed; that frightening numbness of mind and body was gone.

She sat up.

"Leo!" He was dozing in a chair pulled up right next to her bed, and he was immediately awake at the sound of her voice. He picked up her hand and held it against his face, saying nothing for a long moment.

"You're so much warmer," he said. "You were like an ice maiden after you came out of the river. I was afraid you'd never warm up."

Dear Leo. "You saved my life," she murmured.

"That was easy." He moved to the bed and pulled her into his arms. "Thank God you're all right," he whispered. "I was scared to death."

"I see your wife is feeling better." A nurse came in, all smiles at having surprised them. "Open up." She stuck a thermometer into Annette's mouth. "Ninety-eight point four. That's remarkable. You're almost up to normal again."

"Could I have something hot to eat, please?" Annette was famished suddenly.

"Of course." The nurse vanished.

Leo was still sitting on the bed. "You told them I was your wife?" Annette asked.

"I was afraid they wouldn't let me stay with you otherwise," said Leo, unrepentant. "And I couldn't leave you." He paused a second. "You could be, you know. My wife, I mean."

Annette laid her hand on his face. "I love you," she said, kissing him gently.

"What am I going to wear?" she wondered aloud. "My boots floated away in the river and my other clothes are in my car, which is still in Mrs. Baranova's parking lot -" She stopped her search suddenly. "I wonder how she is?"

"You're not going anywhere," said Leo.

"Leo, please, we have to be at the bank for the rollover." Surely Leo realized how important this was to her. "I'm all right. You heard the nurse. No frostbite. We'll drive slowly. Anyway, there aren't any rivers on the way to the bank."

Leo changed the subject. "Why did Volodya's car go off the road, anyway? I asked him, and he said he didn't remember."

Annette snorted. "Well, I remember! He steered the car right into

the path of that snowplow!" She paused, frowning. "He turned around
in his seat to say something to me, and the car went left of center. He
was apologizing for grabbing a CD out of my hands."

"What?"

"I picked up a CD and asked to play it, and he went berserk."
Annette paused, playing it back in her mind. "Grabbed it out of my
hands, unbuckled his seatbelt, and stuffed it in his coat pocket. It was
very odd. What's wrong, Leo?"

"It could be hours before anyone from the FBI can make it out here
in this storm. Volodya could be gone." He gave her hand a quick
squeeze. "We'll have to get the algorithm ourselves."

"What algorithm?"


*11:30 p.m., December 31, 1999*


Annette clutched Leo's hand nervously as they walked to the in-
tensive care waiting area. Volodya was the last person she wanted to
see, ever again. But Leo was unlikely to be able to retrieve the CD on
his own, and she was the obvious decoy. She could see Volodya now,
his long legs stretched in front of him, slumped in a vinyl chair with his
eyes closed. He held an ice bag to his forehead, which was creased in
pain; he must have bumped his head in the accident.

When they were standing in front of him, his eyes opened. Startled,
he jumped up as if to embrace Annette, then drew back at the look on
Leo's face.

"Annette wanted to see how Mrs. Baranova was doing." Leo
spoke for both of them; his arm supported her and she could hardly
bring herself to meet Volodya's eyes.

He led them to the old woman's room; they could not go in, so they
stared for a moment through the glass of the door. "I do not think she is
doing well," Volodya ventured. Annette's lip quivered and she sniffled
despite herself. Volodya spoke again when they returned to the waiting
room.

"Annette, I am glad you are feeling better!"

"I *am* feeling better, thanks, Volodya." Annette's voice was as
cool as the Scioto. "Nice of you to say so." She raked him with an
angry gaze, her green eyes judgmental.

"Annette!" Volodya appeared shocked. "You know that it was accident." Leo had moved closer to the TV to hear the rollover news, and Volodya took advantage of his absence to move closer to her.

"It was accident," she mimicked. She watched him flinch at the scorn in her voice. "You fooled me for such a long time, Volodya." She could almost see Volodya's mind working, trying to think of some way to charm her, when Leo reappeared and put his arm around her.

"I've got it," he said.

She sagged against him in relief, then turned to Volodya.

"You were a fool to hide the algorithm in the car." Her voice was low. "Why didn't you give it to them? Why couldn't you just let it go?"

"He couldn't do that, Annette." Leo could not hide the triumph in his voice. "He always had to show everybody that he was smarter than they were. And now he's outsmarted himself."

Annette turned back to watch as she and Leo waited together for the elevator. Volodya looked stunned. She saw him fumble for his overcoat, paw at the pockets, search through one, then the other, then both again. Then he took a frantic step down the hall toward them. When the elevator door opened, Leo and Annette stepped in together, then turned hand in hand to face Volodya. They had the algorithm. Volodya knew it, and they knew that he knew.

*11:50 p.m., December 31, 1999*

All eyes swung to the millennial clock which had been ticking away the minutes till 2000 for more than a year now. Eleven-fifty. Ten minutes more of ordinary life.

On TV, the drill was routine by now. Choose a capital city and find a party, then count down to New Year's and wait a suspenseful instant to see if the electricity went down. In New York, the city of choice for most TV stations, an enormous outdoor crowd boogied the century away.

"I really thought that seeing all the power outages in other countries would keep people out of Times Square tonight." Alex marveled at the size of the crowd; it appeared as large as it was every year.

"Never underestimate the power of denial." Tim had just returned from a quick, pointless check of the mainframes.

"The crowd below seems unconcerned that the lights might go out," said the CNN reporter. Alex noticed that CNN did not have a reporter stationed in the crowd this year. "Our TV cameras are running on a generator now, so if the worst happens, our broadcast will continue uninterrupted."

"It's just that nobody else will have the electricity to watch it," someone at the bank muttered.

Alex noticed that the families represented in the bank moved together as midnight approached. Tim was holding his wife's hand, and similar family groups clustered around the TV. Katie had already climbed into Alex's lap. Ethan draped his long arm protectively around his mother, and Elizabeth was sitting on the floor, leaning against his legs. Alex took Karen's hand in his and squeezed it.

"This is it, everybody," he said as the ball in Times Square began its descent. "God bless us, every one."

# Chapter 31

*Midnight, December 31, 1999*

"Happy New Year." The wishes were subdued, everyone staring about them, eyes wide, ears pricked, senses alert for disaster. The lights flickered, off and back on, briefly illuminating the faces of everyone in the room. Then the room went black.

Tim at once flicked on the flashlight he was holding. "Hang on, everybody. The generator should kick in in a minute." Several other flashlights came on as he trotted out of the room to check on the mainframes.

The lights flooded the room again and the TV flickered to life. A harried-looking CNN commentator was gesturing at the cheering crowd behind him. "As you can see, New York still has electricity. However, we've learned that the major ice and snowstorm that is now harrowing the Midwest has taken an unexpected turn. Forecasters now predict that New York will see the same weather in another six to eight hours, and the mayor is urging all those who came here to see the millennium in to return to their homes in an orderly fashion as soon as they can.

"The word here is that only a portion of the East Coast electric grid has failed, at least so far. The South looks good as well, but we are seeing a number of failures in the Midwest. We'll be bringing you the latest updates as we have them."

Alex spoke tersely. "Turn on a local station."

Two of the four channels were not broadcasting. On Channel 4 a lone woman reporter was standing in the swirling snow outside a darkened Statehouse. "This is an eerie feeling, standing at Broad and High Streets, the busiest intersection in the city, and not a street light shining." The reporter waved a hand at the Vern Riffe Building. "As you can see, a few buildings do have generators, and the lights are shining in those buildings. Fortunately, the city decided to cancel this year's First Night celebration, so many people are staying home this year who otherwise would be stuck downtown in the blackout. Representatives from OhioPower tell us that they are hard at work getting the electricity back on, but of course their work is hampered by the weather. We'll be bringing you a report from their headquarters later. The mayor urges citizens to stay home tonight because of the snow. If your home is electrically heated and you are without heat, and have neighbors with a stove or fireplace or gas heat, take shelter there. Neighborhood shelters in school buildings will not be opened until road crews have cleared city streets so that people may travel safely to the shelters. Repeat, take shelter with a neighbor if you are without heat."

The reporter continued to give emergency directives while Karen sat stupefied. This was it then, the worst of the worst. No electricity while a blizzard raged. They were all right, of course, but what about other people? She thought of her parents and in-laws, and hurried to pull the cell phone from her purse. After five minutes of frustrated dialing, she still had not gotten through.

*12:15 a.m., January 1, 2000*

When Alex came into the mainframe room, Tim and Harry were studying printouts. Janet Brock would be in Sunday morning; they had decided to spare her the rollover vigil.

"How does it look?"

"Our y2k compliance was brief and glorious," said Tim, gesturing toward the printout he held. "The batches ran for fifteen minutes in the year 2000, then - BOOM! Abend, abend, abend." Abend meant abnormal ending, an indication that the computer had not been able to do the requested processing. A program abend was annoying, but an operating system abend, like this one, was serious.

"And what do you think?"

Tim again bent his grizzled head over the printouts. "Ask me in twelve hours."


*12:16 a.m., January 1, 2000*

The detour to recover the algorithm had taken too long; Leo and Annette would miss the rollover at the bank. They decided to watch it on TV at the hospital, and then go to the bank immediately after. They were sitting on the hospital bed in Annette's room, watching the TV, when the power went out, a disheartening but not entirely unexpected occurrence. After an enthusiastic New Year's kiss (they were, after all, alive and in love), they waited with confidence for the lights to come back on; of course the hospital had an emergency generator. Hospitals always had them. After ten minutes without lights, Leo spoke.

"I think we've got trouble in River City."

"You mean the generator's broken."

"Something like that." He felt his way cautiously to the window and opened the drapes. The room lightened imperceptibly. "On a clear night, with a full moon, that might do some good. In this storm—"

He groped his way back to the bed and felt for Annette's hand. "Ordinarily I'd be thrilled to be sitting in the dark with you. On a bed." He thought for a second.

"We can't do much - wait, I've got a flashlight." A little fumbling located the coat and the flashlight; Leo clicked it on and swept the beam around the room. "Not much, but better than nothing."

"Where's the CD?" Annette asked.

"It's in my coat pocket," Leo said. "No pockets in my sweat pants. Listen, I'm going to use the bathroom. The plumbing isn't electric. You keep the flashlight."

"No, you take it. I'm just sitting here; I'll be fine. I don't want you to trip over something in the dark."

Leo took the flashlight, crossed to the bathroom, and closed the door. Annette sat alone in the dark, her eyes wide, listening to the muffled chaos in the corridor outside.

\*       \*       \*

The door flew open and a light shone directly into her eyes, blinding her.

"I'm all right," she volunteered, thinking it was a hospital staff person. The flashlight came nearer and suddenly a heavy hand went across her mouth, pushing her down into the mattress. For a moment she was too surprised to struggle.

"Where is CD?" Volodya's voice hissed in her ear and she could make out his face now in the dimness behind the flashlight; his expression intent, his eyes cold. Not an expression that she had seen on his face before, not for her. Furious and frightened, she pushed his hand away from her mouth.

"Let me up! Leo!" she tried to scream. Volodya's hand was across her mouth at once, hot and relentless, pressing her back down on the bed. She was too breathless for a real scream; Leo couldn't have heard her.

"Where is CD?" She shook her head under his hand, indicating that she wouldn't tell him, but involuntarily her eyes flicked to the coat on her lap. She saw him smile. His hand moved from her face to the coat, and she clutched at the heavy fabric, seeking to wrestle it away from him. Volodya's face was a mask of frustration as he tried unsuccessfully to twist the coat free of her fingers. He was much stronger, but he still held the flashlight in one hand and both her hands were free. If only she could hold him off for a moment -

The bathroom door opened and they heard Leo's shout. Volodya looked from her to Leo, hesitated for an instant, turned an anguished face back to Annette. His face set and he raised the flashlight and brought it down with a crack across her exposed knuckles. The blow tingled from her fingers to her elbow; she gave a scream of pain, released the coat. Volodya grabbed it and fled into the hallway without a backward glance.

"Leo, the CD," Annette panted. He spotted the stairwell door and sprinted toward it, Annette behind him.

They confronted the stairwell together; the beam of the small flashlight hardly penetrating the blackness. They were thirteen stories up. Below them on the stairs they could hear the clatter of Volodya's pounding feet.

"You take the flashlight." Leo pressed it into Annette's hand; he could run faster without it, and after the first flight of stairs he could count them as he ran, so he would know when he came to a landing. When he got closer to Volodya, he could use the light of his flashlight.

He put his hand on the coldness of the metal stair rail and plunged into the darkness. In moments he was flying downward so fast that the banister burned under his fingers. He saw the gleam of Volodya's flashlight and redoubled his efforts, taking the steps as fast he dared; he had to be close enough to know where Volodya went when he left the stairwell.

Closer, closer - then his feet skidded on something soft. He plunged headlong down the stairs, his fingers clawing frantically at air.

\*     \*     \*

Annette stopped dead at the sound of the fall, then pushed herself faster down the stairwell, panicked. Was it Leo or Volodya? She heard groans, but they came from several flights beneath her. She stopped to shine her flashlight over the rail, down into the darkness. A figure slipped from the dim patch of light and continued down the stairs. She ran on, and a moment later the beam of her flashlight picked out Leo's coat on the steps where Volodya must have flung it. God, it must have been Leo who fell.

Heedlessly she flung herself after him.

\*     \*     \*

Leo had banged against the stair rail as he fell, and a desperate grab at the rail broke his fall. Although his arms were wrenched and his whole body felt bruised, he had saved himself from disaster, and now he hurtled downward in pursuit of Volodya as fast as before. Maybe faster. His rage propelled him.

The stairwell exploded into light. Volodya was crouched at the bottom of the stairs, and he lifted a surprised face to Leo's. The cover of darkness gone, Volodya sprang for the door, but Leo launched himself into the air and brought Volodya down so hard that both men lay still and breathless for an instant. Then Leo grabbed hard for the CD in Volodya's hand, bending his fingers back unmercifully. Volodya answered with a knee in Leo's stomach, and flung the CD down the stairs; they could hear it ricochet off the wall and skitter down the steps to the next landing.

Leo scrambled for the stair and the CD, but Volodya flung himself after, knocking him off balance and down the steps. Leo staggered to his feet and swung, feeling a wet slipperiness on his fist when it connected with Volodya's jaw. Volodya tackled him, they skidded across the landing and on to the next flight of stairs. By the time they reached the CD, Volodya was gasping. With a desperate lunge he managed to tip the CD over the edge of the steps on to the next landing. For several minutes the dance went on like this, in grunts and groans, blows glancing or landed, knuckles scraped, bodies propelled from one side of the stairwell to the other, now clutching, now gouging, now trying to escape and reach the algorithm.

They were too evenly matched, Leo thought, dizzy from the last blow. Then he managed somehow to squirm away from Volodya and bolt down the two flights of stairs to where the CD lay. He picked it up, gulping air, uncertain of his next move. Annette was somewhere up there.

Then he heard her scream.

Leo raced up the stairs. Volodya had her. She was white-faced, tears rolling down her cheeks, standing on tip-toe; Volodya held her, one arm twisted behind her back. When Leo put his foot on the stair, the Russian began screaming at him.

"Stop!" Volodya bellowed. "Give me CD or I will break arm!" Leo stared from the landing below them, the CD in his hand.

"Stay where you are! Throw CD up on landing." The blood on Volodya's mouth gave him a fierce, vulpine look.

Leo still stared. Surely this was a bluff. Volodya didn't have a knife or a gun. If Leo gave him back the CD now, Volodya could destroy the algorithm and the evidence against him would be gone.

"I will break her arm," Volodya repeated. Before Leo could move, Volodya gave Annette's arm a quick, upward jerk. She cried out and stopped struggling, her eyes fixed beseechingly on Leo's face.

Helpless, furious, Leo tossed the CD up the steps. It clattered on the landing and slid to Volodya across the linoleum. Leo winced as Volodya raised his foot and brought his heel down heavily on the case.

Crack! He heard the plastic splinter.

Then Volodya flung Annette to one side to concentrate on the CD case. Leo darted up the stairs. If Volodya came down hard and ground his heel on the disk, that would do it. The disk would be rendered unreadable, the algorithm destroyed. Leo knew as he raced up the stairs that he would be too late to save the algorithm. Halfway to his goal, he saw Volodya raise his foot again.

Annette threw herself at Volodya's knees and knocked him headlong down the stairs. His body bounced against the steps with a sickening thud. Grunting with pain, he slid in a heap to the landing below and lay motionless.

# Chapter 32

*January 17, 2000*

Alex rose from his desk and moved briskly around his office in an effort to speed his circulation and warm up a little. With the thermostat perpetually set at sixty degrees, at the request of the electric company, he never felt very warm, and like most other CEO's, he had shed his business suit for long underwear, jeans, and a turtleneck sweater.

This morning was even colder, because the office was not scheduled for electricity until the one to seven shift. He had come into the office an hour early with his laptop, which was battery-run; his window provided sufficient light to work by.

The rationing of electricity was a good idea, it was just damned inconvenient, as was most of life these days. After the initial wave of blackouts, aggravated by downed power lines from the ice storm, had nearly taken out the entire Eastern electric grid on New Year's Eve, the electric utlities had declared emergency rationing. Rationing would stay in effect until all storm-related damage was repaired, and power plants with unsolved y2k problems (mostly the municipals and the small rural electric co-ops) were stabilized.

Alex heard a click and then a hum as the electricity came on and the gas furnace kicked in. Thank goodness! As he strode down the hall to the conference room, Tim materialized at his shoulder.

"Hi, Boss."

"You working at a garage now?" In his one-piece overalls, Tim looked ready to slide under a truck on a dolly.

"Hey, it may not be elegant, but it's warm!"

The conference room filled up quickly. Karen was there in honor of the team's last y2k meeting. Harry lumbered in wearing his usual clothes, a long-sleeved shirt his only concession to the cold. Just looking at him made most people shiver, but Harry was complacent. "One of the perks of obesity."

Annette and Leo came in together. On the fourth finger of her left hand Annette wore a new ring; an opal surround by diamonds

The last arrivals, Eddie and Homer, set off a wave of hysterical laughter when they arrived together wearing identical sets of scarlet and gray sweats bearing the Ohio State insignia.

"Okay," said Alex as the laughter died, "this is the farewell meeting of the Midwest Bank Consortium y2k team. It's a little sad, but it shows we did our job. Tim, what's your assessment?"

Homer stood up, interrupting them, an imposing figure in his scarlet sweats. "We're going to miss you," he said simply. "As far as I'm concerned, you saved the banks in the Consortium. Twice in fact - once from y2k, and once from Volodya." He sat down again.

"Any news of Volodya?" Tim asked.

"Well," said Eddie, standing, "Jerry told me they'll probably charge him and try him here in the U.S. They're afraid that if they deport him, he'll end up doing the same things for the FSB over there that he was doing for them over here. Mrs. Baranova, the old woman whom Annette rescued, died a few days ago."

Harry made his announcement from his chair. "I'm going back to retirement and the grandkids."

The group assured him that he would be missed. Alex then posed a question.

"We've survived the rollover," he said. "Any predictions for the future?"

"I predict a wedding," Karen said, prompting a smile from Leo and the predictable blush from Annette.

"That's too easy," Alex said. "I meant y2k predictions."

"Well, I see a recession," Tim said. "Looks to me like a lot of small businesses that weren't ready are going under. That causes a ripple effect across the economy."

"Globally, too." Annette was visibly more relaxed these days now that the combined pressures of love and the new millennium had been resolved. "Look at all the Third World countries whose airports are still closed, and likely to remain so for months. No tourism. No exports. No money."

"And did you read the paper this morning?" Alex asked. "Oil rigs in the Middle East - they mentioned Qatar and Kuwait - are having a real problem supplying oil due to embedded systems failures in the rigs. The U.S. has a three-month oil storage capacity, but it seems inevitable that gas and oil prices will go up. We could see rationing."

"Well," Harry said, shifting his bulk more comfortably in his chair, "you're a gloomy bunch. I'm pretty happy about my prediction." He looked around the room, grinning. "The IRS screwed up their y2k remediation, like they screw up everything else. I predict that the IRS will be abolished and a flat tax instituted. Otherwise the government won't collect a penny's worth of taxes this year. By damn, I've been campaigning for a flat tax for fifty years!"

Amid the general laughter, Karen agreed with Harry. "It's not all gloomy, you're right," she said. "Look how this crisis has brought people together. Community. Y2k has really built local community. That's a good thing."

"The legal profession's happy, too," Eddie said, to a chorus of groans. "With all the suits that are being brought against companies and boards of directors, y2k is becoming a whole new career path for some of my colleagues."

"With that happy thought -" Alex said, rising to adjourn the meeting. "Don't forget, y2k team party at my house tonight. Bring your own bottled water."

After the last team member had left, Alex and Karen drifted upstairs. Passing Annette's office, they found the door ajar, Annette and Leo embracing in silhouette against the window. Karen and Alex grinned at each other and backed away silently.

"There's more than one way to keep warm, I guess." In his own office, Alex took Karen in his arms and kissed her. "I'll call Annette's office in a few minutes and invite them for dinner. We're going to brainstorm and see what they might do if they stay with Millennium Dynamics."

"I'll miss Harry."

"Me, too. But life marches on. After ten years of y2k it'll be a treat to do something new, even though I'm not sure yet what it will be."

A new millennium. It was a clean slate of sorts, waiting for the marks that society would write on it. Maybe this time, he thought. Maybe this time we can learn from what happened, and write a better story.

Alex slipped an arm around his wife, and Karen laid her head on his shoulder as they stood together at the window, contemplating the gray January day. Alex felt at once content to be where he was, and eager for what lay ahead. God willing, they would do better. God willing.

*To arrange an interview with the author, please contact:*
*Mary Beth Zacks, 1-614-231-0721*

# Order Form

| | | |
|---|---|---|
| ☝ | Order via the **Internet** at: | **www.chaosprotocol.com** |
| ☎ | Order by **Telephone** at: | **1-800-889-6909** (use for quickest delivery) |
| ⊠ | Order by **E-mail** at: | **orders@chaosprotocol.com** |
| 🖷 | Order by **Fax** at: | **1-614-864-7922 (Fax the Order Form below)** |
| ⌨ | Order by **Mail** at: | **Mail the Order Form below** |

NOTE: When ordering by **E-mail**, please include the information requested on the Order Form below. If you do not wish to use a credit card, send a check or money order to the address below. When ordering by **Mail**, please send a check or money order (no cash or C.O.D. orders) to:

**Malmesbury Books**
Post Office Box 292609
Columbus, Ohio 43229 USA

| | | | |
|---|---|---|---|
| **A** | Number of Copies Wanted | | If ordering more than 5 copies or for re-sale, discounts are available. |
| **B** | Price per Copy | **$ 19.95 U.S**<br>**$ 28.95 Canada** | Outside the U.S. & Canada, convert the U.S. Price |
| **C** | Order Sub Total | | Multiply **A** by **B** |
| **E** | Ohio Sales Tax | **5.75%** | For Ohio residents ONLY |
| **F** | Total Ohio Sales Tax | | Multiply **C** by **E** (Enter "O" if you are NOT an Ohio resident.) |
| **G** | Shipping Cost per Copy | **$ 0.95** | U.S. |
| **H** | Total Shipping Cost | | Multiply **G** by **A** |
| **I** | Handling Charge per Order | **$ 3.95** | |
| **J** | **TOTAL ORDER AMOUNT** | | Add **C, F, H** and **I** |

| | |
|---|---|
| Your Name | |
| Address | |
| City, State, Zip / Postal Code | |
| Country | |
| Telephone | |
| Credit Card (check one) | ☐ Visa ☐ MasterCard ☐ AMEX ☐ Discover |
| Credit Card Number | |
| Credit Card Expiration Date | |
| Your Signature | |
| Where did you first hear of *The Chaos Protocol*? | |